Praise for
STARFIST I: FIRST TO FIGHT

"CAUTION! Any book written by Dan Cragg and David Sherman is bound to be addictive, and this is the first in what promises to be a great adventure series. *First to Fight* is rousing, rugged, and just plain fun. The authors have a deep firsthand knowledge of warfare, an enthralling vision of the future, and the skill of veteran writers. Fans of military fiction, science fiction, and suspense will all get their money's worth, and the novel is so well done it will appeal to general readers as well. It's fast, realistic, moral, and a general hoot. *First to Fight* is also vivid, convincing—and hard to put down. Sherman and Cragg are a great team! I can't wait for the next one!"

—RALPH PETERS
New York Times bestselling
author of *Red Army*

By David Sherman and Dan Cragg

Starfist
FIRST TO FIGHT
SCHOOL OF FIRE
STEEL GAUNTLET
BLOOD CONTACT
TECHNOKILL
HANGFIRE*

By David Sherman

Fiction
The Night Fighters
KNIVES IN THE NIGHT
MAIN FORCE ASSAULT
OUT OF THE FIRE
A ROCK AND A HARD PLACE
A NGHU NIGHT FALLS
CHARLIE DON'T LIVE HERE ANYMORE

THERE I WAS: THE WAR OF CORPORAL
    HENRY J. MORRIS, USMC
THE SQUAD

By Dan Cragg

Fiction
THE SOLDIER'S PRIZE

Nonfiction
A DICTIONARY OF SOLDIER TALK
GENERALS IN MUDDY BOOTS
INSIDE THE VC AND THE NVA (with Michael Lee Lanning)
TOP SERGEANT (with William G. Bainbridge)

*forthcoming

TECHNOKILL

Starfist
Book Five

David Sherman
and
Dan Cragg

A Del Rey® Book

BALLANTINE BOOKS • NEW YORK

A Del Rey® Book
Published by The Ballantine Publishing Group
Copyright © 2000 by David Sherman and Dan Cragg

www.randomhouse.com/delrey/

Library of Congress Catalog Card Number: 00-103287

ISBN 0-345-43591-5

Manufactured in the United States of America

First Edition: August 2000

10 9 8 7 6 5 4 3 2 1

PROLOGUE

Graakaak, High Chief of the Cheereek, cocked his head this way and that as he looked past his circle of guards to study the vista that swept beyond the roof of his High Tree. Under his eyes, Cheereek darted to and fro about their daily business, their cries a cacophony of caws, hoots, and warbles. High Chief Graakaak saw the small clusters of sharp-eyed guards spotted around the perimeter of the sprawling rookery, watching all possible approaches. The landscape was properly barren from the guards to the horizon.

Graakaak dipped one hand to his perch, richly studded with yellow, orange, and purple stones, and plucked one. He held the stone before his critical eyes, decided it was worthy, and popped it into his mouth. Instantly he swallowed and the stone rippled down the length of his throat. He refocused his eyes and looked at his guards, resplendent with iridescent sashes sparkling beneath their pectorals of shinies. But that wasn't what caused him to break out in gleeful reaction. No matter how often he looked upon it, the sight of his guards all holding the Clumsy Ones' weapons swelled his chest with a power and pride that demanded to burst out and be announced to the world. Rising from his squat, he stretched out his neck, leaned forward, splayed the skin-fringes on his bowed arms, spread his tail fringe, and crowed. Beyond the high tent, Cheereek paused in their chores and looked up at their High Chief. Many returned his jubilant cry. Pleased, Graakaak ruffled his neck and shoulders. His breastplate of shinies, far larger than the pectorals of his guards, sparkled

1

and jangled with the movement. He lowered himself back to a squat, plucked at the iridescent sash that crossed his chest under the glittering breastplate, then lowered his head to nestle restfully at the top of his chest.

Someday soon, he thought, enough of my warriors will have Clumsy Ones' weapons for me to attack. Then the wide world will tremble at the name of Graakaak.

After a time, naked slaves brought bowls of shredded meat mixed with seeds and berries and other peckings, and held them before three of the guards. Graakaak cocked his head and carefully watched the guards as they held the bowls close to their faces with one hand and pecked the food into their mouths with the other. When the guards stopped pecking and handed the bowls back to the slaves, Graakaak continued to watch them while the slaves, heads held as high as their necks allowed, faces pointed at the ceiling, brought the bowls to him. When enough time had passed, and none of the guards showed any sign of distress, Graakaak pecked his fill from the dishes, knowing the food was safe to eat.

The High Chief had barely finished when his eyes spotted a mounted scout galumphing toward the rookery. He watched the dull-dressed scout all the way into the huge encampment. Cocking his head and observing through the gaps in the floor of the High Tree, Graakaak saw the scout jerk his eeookk into a skidding, wing-milling stop, then bound to the lattice-branches and scrabble up the High Tree toward him. Under the roof, the scout stopped less than two paces in front of the central guards, standing fully erect, neck stretched up, face pointed to the roof. The scout waited to be commanded to speak.

"Tell me," Graakaak commanded.

"Clumsy Ones come, High Chief," the scout announced. "I followed their tracks until they disappeared on the Frying Rocks. There I waited long enough to miss two meals. The Clumsy Ones finally appeared in the middle of the Frying Rocks, riding their Clumsy Ones' steed in this direction. I waited until I was certain they were headed this way, then I galumphed with all speed, taking a course their steed could not follow so I could reach you before they did."

Graakaak looked out beyond the roof of the High Tree and saw a cloud of dust rising on the horizon. Deep within the cloud he saw the shimmery speck of the Clumsy Ones' steed. He stood and crowed. Yes, soon he would have enough weapons to arm all of his warriors.

"You missed two meals and you brought me timely news of the Clumsy Ones' coming," Graakaak said to the scout. "You have done well. You may lower your face."

When the scout complied, Graakaak pecked a stone from his perch and tossed it to him. The scout snagged it out of the air with his mouth and swallowed. The stone rippled down the length of his throat.

"Take him away and feed him."

A slave approached the scout, stretched her neck up, then chirped and gestured as she scampered down the lattice-branches. He followed.

"That artificial tree with the tent on top of it," Dr. Spencer Herbloc said to the landcar's driver, "that's where we'll find him."

"Then you've been to this camp before?" Jum Bolion asked. "I thought they were nomads." He remembered Herbloc's earlier instructions and adjusted the air-cushion pressure to raise the landcar and increase its speed.

"No. That's just the way they are, the big mugwump always has the highest place." He chuckled softly. "When they say 'top of the ladder,' they mean it literally."

The landcar whooshed over the hard, rippled dirt of the ancient lake bed, its air cushion kicking up a huge rooster tail of dust and pebbles. It sluiced into the hollow of an ancient, dry cove, becoming invisible from the encampment save for the wake it had stirred.

"I thought they're supposed to be fighters," Bolion said as he looked around at the size of the broad dip. "Someone could hide an army down here and get awful close before those Cheereek know they were here."

Herbloc chuckled again. "After you've been here a few times you'll be able to spot the sentries. I can see three watch-posts from here. There's probably more."

Bolion couldn't spot anything that looked like a watchpost. He glanced at Herbloc to see if the man was joking, but Herbloc was taking a nip from his flask. Bolion tried to hide a wince. If he'd known how much Herbloc drank when he was planetside, he might not have volunteered to be the driver on this two-man parlay. Even though he'd never been on Avionia before, during the voyage he'd read everything about the planet the *Marquis de Rien* carried. The people—if "people" were the right word—were apt to fight over any slight, real or imagined. The two of them wouldn't stand a chance if Herbloc got drunk and said something he shouldn't, even though they were illegally armed with Confederation military hand-blasters.

Herbloc saw the half-hidden wince out of the corner of his eye. "Don't worry about it, boy-o," he said, and took another nip. "They need us. Their mugwump wants to conquer his neighbors, but they're bigger than he is. He can't do it without our weapons." He took another nip before tucking the flask back into a pocket.

They reached the far side of the dip and skittered up its bank. The encampment spread before them when they topped the rise. Hundreds of sideless tent roofs were scattered randomly. Some hunched over low-walled hollows scraped from the ground, others hung over low mounds. A few were mounted above stilt-legged towers. The highest tower held the largest tent, and it was at this that Bolion pointed the speeding landcar.

"Don't dodge them," Herbloc reminded the driver. "Just plow straight through. They'll get out of the way. And if they don't . . ." He shrugged. "We're showing power. They respect power."

Moving with a speed that startled Bolion, the Cheereek

scattered out of the path of the landcar, shrieking and chirping their fear and indignity—but none made any threatening move.

Again remembering his instructions, Bolion didn't brake until the last possible moment. The landcar bucked to an abrupt stop that caused a huge cloud of dirt to bellow as high as the tent roof above them. They waited for the dust to settle before breaking open hatches and dismounting.

"We're supposed to climb that?" Bolion asked incredulously as he looked at the helter-skelter assemblage of wood spars from which the artificial tree was constructed.

"It's stronger than it looks, boy-o. And we've got to climb if we want to see the mugwump." Herbloc reached for a spar above his head and began to climb.

Guard Captain Cheerpt paused in his inspection of the perimeter sentries to eye the two Clumsy Ones. His hands twisted on the Clumsy Ones' weapon he held and his head bobbed in resonance, causing the triple string of shinies hanging on his chest to tinkle.

He eyed the pouches at the waists of the Clumsy Ones as they awkwardly lumbered up the High Tree, and knew they held weapons, though the Clumsy Ones never withdrew anything from them. He was certain those weapons were more powerful than the weapons the Clumsy Ones dealt to the Cheereek. If he had one of those weapons, he would challenge Graakaak, and the Cheereek would have a new High Chief.

Graakaak watched with amused interest as the Clumsy Ones labored up the High Tree, and marveled again that a people so ungainly could make the wonderful weapons they did. The Clumsy Ones paused under the eaves, gathering breath in their puny chests, then approached his perch.

The two Clumsy Ones walked with delicate balance, fully upright on their legs instead of easily balanced between them, as were the Cheereek and all other people Graakaak had ever

seen or heard of. When the Clumsy Ones were three body
lengths from his guards, with one sudden movement Graakaak
rose from his squat. He thrust his torso forward horizontally,
arm fringes splayed at his sides, tail fringe fully opened,
stretched out his neck and shouted his battle cry.

The Clumsy Ones stopped in place. Much less swiftly than
Graakaak had, they dropped their torsos to horizontal, legs
bent to compensate for lack of a counterbalancing tail-nub,
stuck out their short necks, splayed their fringeless arms to
the sides, and shouted their battle cries back at the High
Chief.

The High Chief and the two Clumsy Ones held their threat
postures for a long moment as their battle cries changed to
prolonged hisses.

So fast the Clumsy Ones' weak eyes couldn't follow the
motion, Graakaak stood erect, arms down, neck stretched upward. He did not point his face up, as propriety required. He
had no desire to indicate to the Clumsy Ones that they were
powerful enough for that obsequiousness.

The Clumsy Ones, too, now stood erect, their movements
slower than any but the feeblest of the Cheereek. They
dropped their arms to their sides and stretched their necks as
far as their short length allowed. But despite the formality of
this submissive posture, exposing their soft parts to demonstrate acceptance of the other's dominance, they did not hold
their faces up, but instead arrogantly returned Graakaak's
stare.

After a long moment, Graakaak abruptly squatted again on
his perch. The High Chief watched with disinterest as slaves
brought out the odd perches the Clumsy Ones preferred to
squat on, perches on which they rested their upper legs. At an
almost imperceptible gesture from the High Chief, the guards
who stood between him and the Clumsy Ones moved to take
new positions behind the visitors, denying them retreat.

"What have you brought me this time, Clumsy Ones?"
Graakaak demanded in the trading language used by all peoples
of the steppes. Of course, the Clumsy Ones had difficulty in
speaking even that simple language.

"Have I got a deal for you," said the Clumsy One called Heerk-kloock, and twisted his obscenely soft mouth parts in what he understood was an expression of friendship.

CHAPTER ONE

"Move, move-move!" Sergeant Bladon's radioed shout reverberated through Lance Corporal Rock Claypoole's helmet.

"Blow that hinge, Rock!" Corporal Kerr shouted, adding his demand.

"I'm trying, I'm trying," Claypoole shouted back.

"Want some help?" PFC Wolfman MacIlargie asked. "Let me in there, I'll get it." He had already blown his hinge.

"Stay away," Claypoole snarled, and tried again to clamp the blower onto the upper lever, where it hinged into the airlock hatch. MacIlargie squirted closer and bumped him. For a vertiginous moment Claypoole spun slowly away from the spaceship in orbit around Thorsfinni's World. His tether jerked him to a yawing stop a few meters away. "Back off, Wolfman," he snapped, and hauled himself back to the hatch that second squad's second fire team was trying to breach. In his ungainly armored vacuum suit, Claypoole struggled to lock his boot magnets to the hull and hatch on either side of the hinge. He managed to seat the cup of the blower over the hinge. He reached one thickly gloved hand to the crimper and pulled on it. The cup closed securely onto the end of the arm.

Claypoole looked down the length of the meter long tool and decided it was perpendicular to the hull and his feet were widespread enough. He gave the top end of the blower a quarter twist, bent it down to a ninety degree angle to expose the trigger, stuck a gloved finger through the trigger guard and pulled.

The shaped charge inside the blower jetted its force into the metal, abruptly raising its temperature from near zero

Kelvin to more than a thousand degrees centigrade. The rapid temperature change shattered the hinge, buckled the metal around it, and sent shock waves thrumming through the surrounding hull and hatch. One of Claypoole's feet was knocked loose, but the magnets on the other boot held.

"Move, move-move!" Bladon shouted again.

Claypoole shifted one foot so both were on the hull and removed the blower. The tool drifted at the end of its tether.

Kerr clomped carefully to his side and slapped the end of the puller he held against the hatch. He gave the handle the twist that shot its mollies into the metal, then raised a hand in signal.

"Do it," Corporal Linsman said, and Lance Corporal Watson slapped the Go button on the winch. The cable that ran from the tripod to the puller tautened and the hatch slowly lifted. The Marines readied their weapons. As soon as the hatch was clear of the hull, Watson slapped another button on the winch to move the hatch to the side.

When the gap was wide enough, Kerr demagnetized his boots and stepped over the lip of the hatchway. He fired a quick puff from his suit's top jet and plummeted down into the airlock, where he twisted around so the inner hatch was in front instead of below him. He reactivated his boot magnets to hold his feet to the deck. Claypoole and MacIlargie followed.

"Hey, watch it," Claypoole snarled at MacIlargie, who bumped into him as he tried to mimic Kerr's maneuver.

"Sorry," MacIlargie replied, and used handholds to pull himself away from Claypoole. "Kind of cramped in here." Their boots clunked to the decking as they activated the magnets.

The airlock was big enough to hold four vacuum-suited deckhands along with the equipment they'd need to work on the hull, but three combat-armed Marines in armored vacuum suits filled it almost to overflowing. The inner hatch was barely wide enough to admit them one at a time.

"Quiet," Kerr ordered, and bent his attention to opening the inner-hatch access panel. He freed three corners of the small plate and swiveled it aside on its remaining corner screw. He briefly examined the boards and crystals inside the control box while he fished an override from a cargo pocket on his thigh, then stuck the override onto the right crystal. "All secure?" he asked.

Claypoole and MacIlargie made sure they each had a grip on a handhold and a tether clipped onto another. "Secure," they replied, and pointed their blasters toward the inner hatch.

Kerr checked his own tether then tightened his free-hand grip. He made a quick visual check of his men to affirm that the two of them gripped handholds and held their blasters pointed at the inner hatch, then pushed the activate bar on the override. The inner hatch began sliding to the side.

Ship's atmosphere explosively evacuated through the widening opening, slamming into the three Marines as it gushed into the vacuum. They twisted to keep their blasters pointed at the opening, strained to avoid being pulled loose and thrown out, and managed to ignore the pings and thumps of the small, unsecured objects that bombarded them in the atmospheric blast.

The hatch stopped halfway open with a grinding they could feel though the soles of their boots and the gloves that gripped handholds. Kerr punched the override again. The hatch ground again, but didn't open any farther.

"Damn, it's jammed!" Kerr let go of his blaster, grabbed the lip of the hatch and gave it a jerk. It didn't budge. Rushing air continued to pummel the three Marines. "Hold me."

Claypoole extended his left leg and planted it as firmly as he could behind Kerr's right leg. MacIlargie, behind Kerr, leaned forward and pushed against his back.

Kerr let go of his handhold and gripped the edge of the hatch with both hands. He strained against it, and it opened a few more centimeters before again grinding to a stop.

Spots of red light suddenly speckled the three Marines from inside the spaceship and sirens went off in their ears.

"All right, Three-two-two—" Gunny Thatcher's voice was booming even before the sirens stopped. "—you're dead. Get out of there."

The inner hatch, which had so strongly resisted opening, gently eased shut and cut off the evacuating atmosphere.

It took a couple of minutes for the three Marines in ungainly armored vacuum suits to exit the airlock and stand on
the hull of the spaceship. Sergeant Bladon stood looking at
them from next to the winch. The bulkiness of his suit and the
near opaque facemask made it impossible to tell, but it
seemed to all three of them that he was shaking his head.

As one of his primary functions in garrison, Gunnery
Sergeant Thatcher was responsible for the daily training
regimen of Company L, 34th Fleet Initial Strike Team. He
didn't officially pick the training exercises—that was the
province of Captain Conorado, the company commander—
but the Skipper usually followed his advice on what training
the Marines needed. He was also the man in charge of making
sure the company's Marines had everything they needed to
conduct battalion- and FIST-level training exercises. Thirty-
fourth FIST hadn't trained in ship-boarding tactics during the
time Thatcher had been the company gunny—and he himself
hadn't participated in one since he'd been a squad leader many
years before. The only null-g work most members of the company had done since Boot Camp was the routine boarding and
disembarking of navy vessels during deployments—few of
them had even worn an armored vacuum suit since Boot
Camp. The equipment the Confederation Marine Corps had
available for hostile boarding of a ship in vacuum was cumbersome, not very efficient, and probably outdated as well,
though nobody had anything better. Still, at Camp Ellis,
Thatcher had done his best to orient everyone on the use of
the breaching equipment, though equipment didn't perform
the same in null-g vacuum as it did in the bottom of a gravity
well with atmosphere. Moreover, years had passed since a
FIST had had to board a hostile ship in planetary space. So
nobody could blame him if the Marines of Company L failed
so miserably in the training evolution.

But Gunnery Sergeant Thatcher took his responsibilities very
seriously, and he was very unhappy. When Gunny Thatcher was
unhappy with the men, they were unhappy as well. He made
sure of that.

"COMP-nee! 'Ten-HUT!" Thatcher bellowed as he hauled himself into the troop hold in the amphibious landing ferry, CNSS *Sergeant Charles McMahon*.

The hold filled with clattering and clanging as the hundred-plus Marines swung from their hammocks, propelled themselves from the head, or otherwise moved from whatever position they'd been in to vertical, in relation to the hold's deck, and gripped handholds to stay that way. Amphibious landing ferries didn't bother with artificial gravity.

Thatcher grasped a handhold and pulled himself out of the way of the company's platoon commanders who followed him. The Gunny didn't often glower at the men—he usually left that to First Sergeant Myer, who was so much better at it. But Thatcher glowered at them, and his most ferocious expression was aimed at the platoon commanders as they joined their men. He gave them a moment of silence to let the tension build.

"Never, in my thirty-two years in this man's Marine Corps, have I seen as egregious a display of sheer ineptitude as you put on out there today," he said in a soft voice that carried clearly throughout the hold. Then he shrieked, "You were a disgrace!" He paused as his words reverberated through the hold, and gave a satisfied jerk of his head when he saw how everyone, including the officers, flinched.

"Out of thirty fire teams, gun teams, and assault teams in this company," he continued after the echoes ebbed away, "only four managed to successfully enter the objective. Of those four, only one was fast enough to keep from getting wiped out by the ship's defenses." He looked down and shook his head.

"You may be thinking that just because the *McMahon* and the training hulk are only going to be in orbit around Thorsfinni's World long enough for every infantry unit to have one training evolution that you're done with this abortion. Well, you're wrong. From now until we deploy again, you're going to be training with the breaching equipment whenever you aren't doing other training. You're going to train in hostile-boarding tactics until you can do them in your sleep." He gave a last, red-faced glower that seemed to be directed at each Marine in the hold, then spun about and arrowed out.

The Marines of Company L cast cautious glances at each other, but no one spoke for a long moment. Then a lone voice broke the silence.

"Hey," MacIlargie said, "is it our fault they gave us equipment that doesn't work?"

"Hit him for me, Corporal Kerr," Sergeant Bladon said. "The equipment works. We just don't know how to use it properly."

Kerr cuffed MacIlargie on the back of the head. But not hard. Privately, he agreed with the junior man.

CHAPTER
TWO

Val Carney's anger mounted with every kilometer of the suborbital flight from Fargo to the Republic of Liliuokalani. While the flight was short and pleasant, that did not mollify the congressman's anger at Oncho Tweed for demanding a personal visit before he would agree to accept the wonderfully lucrative deal that Carney offered. The sonofabitch! he thought. I've made the bastard rich, and now that I've got the one deal that'll really matter, he demands I come to him halfway across the goddamned Pacific!

Carney's anger began to boil over when they reached Honolulu. Instead of Tweed meeting him there as he had expected, to discuss business in one of the island capital's plush resort hotels, another jet was waiting to fly the congressman the three hundred kilometers to Tweed's corporate headquarters in Puuwai, on Niihau Island. He was almost speechless with rage as an attendant ushered him into the waiting aircraft. He had half a mind to turn back right there, but too much was riding on the deal.

The Republic of Liliuokalani, formerly the state of Hawaii, had seceded from the federal union near the end of the Second American Civil War. Named after the last queen of the Hawaiians, the new republic had prospered as an independent nation. To encourage business development in the islands, the government of Liliuokalani had removed almost all restrictions on taxing and licensing of every kind of enterprise, from gambling to research and development. Both a gambler and a researcher, Oncho Tweed found the republic a most hospitable place to do business.

The citizens of the Republic of Liliuokalani derived their major revenue from tourism, as had their ancestors for hundreds of years. Unfortunately, Val Carney was whisked about so quickly he had no time to take in the sights. Once on the ground in Puuwai, he was unceremoniously but politely loaded into a Bomarc Executive Starship and whisked straightaway to the island of Siargao on the other side of the Pacific, just north of Mindanao in the Philippines. More than once in the hour-long flight from Liliuokalani to Siargao, Carney wondered why Tweed hadn't just sent the Bomarc straight to Fargo.

As he sat alone in the Bomarc's passenger compartment, his anger slowly cooled to a dull throb behind his right eyeball. A few minutes into the flight, he lit up a Clinton. The alcohol and the fine cigar soon calmed him down. He wondered just what Tweed had in mind for him when the Bomarc at last gracefully touched down at Tweed Submersible Recovery Operations' field testing facility in the Philippines.

"Valley! Valley, my good friend," Oncho Tweed rasped as he extended one hamlike paw toward the little politician. Carney hated people calling him "Valley." Among his close acquaintances, only Petunia got away with it.

Carney shook Tweed's hand perfunctorily.

One massive arm around Carney's shoulders, Tweed propelled the little man toward a hydrofoil bobbing alongside the nearby wharf. Carney was always aware of Tweed's huge size and strength. He could kill me right here, he told himself. He put the thought out of his mind, but it was not the first time it had occurred to him. He looked longingly at the low concrete laboratory buildings that made up the test facility. At least they would have full climate control. Where they were, in the open, it was hot and damp. Already Carney was perspiring. Tweed, however, looked comfortable.

"How was your flight, my dear partner?"

"Smooth." Carney caught himself as the anger welled up in him again. "Goddamnit, Oncho, why in hell have you gotten me all the way across the world like this just to talk business? Next goddamned time, you come to Fargo!"

Tweed rumbled sympathetically. With his free hand he stroked his thick black beard, but the other steered Carney relentlessly toward the waiting hydrofoil. "My dear friend, too much is riding on this deal. I feel safe discussing the particulars only somewhere secure from the big ears that festoon the sanctified halls of the Confederation Congress. Forgive me, Valley. I'll have the Bomarc fly you directly back when we're done. A mere two-hour flight and you'll be back in your office. I apologize again for the inconvenience, my dear friend."

"Oh, stop this phony bonhomie, Tweed! You despise me." He sniffed, straightening his clothes diffidently as he spoke.

"I don't despise you, my dear boy!" Tweed protested as the two men took their seats. "Our relationship has been very cordial and profitable and I owe you for that." He reached over and patted Carney lightly on the knee. Carney sighed.

The hydrofoil sped away, due west, into the Philippine Sea. Two hours later, 150 kilometers west of Mindanao, it heaved to alongside Tweed's deep-sea research vessel, the *Tammany*. To his credit, Carney had not gotten seasick. He was queasy, but not seasick. He had sat glumly throughout the voyage, watching the waves as Tweed gorged himself on a tasty lunch and tried to make small talk.

The *Tammany* was one hundred meters from stem to stern and displaced more than 5,300 metric tons. She had a crew of ninety-five, was equipped with a 500-horsepower heavy stern winch that could handle 9.5 kilometers of cables for dredging, coring, and other deep-sea industrial operations. She was also equipped with two fifty-horsepower hydrographic winches that could be used for serial temperature measurements, lowering light instruments such as small coring apparatuses, and taking water samples. But the *Tammany*'s main purpose was to support the Gotham, Tweed's undersea lab.

Once on the deck of the *Tammany*, Carney stumbled and would have fallen if Tweed, laughing, hadn't caught him by the elbow at the last minute. "You'll soon get your sea legs, m'lad," he promised. Several crewmen stood about, smirking at the landlubber. Carney noted with rising horror that the queasiness in his stomach was beginning to turn violent. He forced himself to hold down his breakfast. He would not give these roustabouts the satisfaction of seeing him get sick.

"Captain!" Tweed shouted to a Filipino on the bridge, "Ready the *Boss*!"

"Aye aye, sir!" the officer responded.

A flurry of activity erupted about the *Tammany*'s stern as winches swung a small submersible out of its berth and lowered it gently into the swells. It bobbed there merrily as technicians swarmed aboard to ready it for submersion.

"What . . . ?" Carney asked.

"Valley, my friend, that is the *Boss*! I use it to visit Gotham, my pride and my joy and the heart of the operation that's going to make both of us richer!" He slapped Carney hard on the back.

Carney coughed and staggered under the blow. Then a disturbing thought occurred to him. "In that?" he gasped suddenly.

"You bet!" Tweed answered enthusiastically.

"Wha . . . ? H-How far is the Gotham from here?"

"Four thousand meters, Valley, not far at all."

"F-Four thou-thousand meters . . . ?" Carney pointed at the deck.

"Straight down, m'lad, straight down!" Tweed roared.

Val Carney doubled over and threw up on the deck.

Gotham was actually a small city built on the ocean floor. It was staffed by nearly a hundred technicians and engineers who field tested the many devices Tweed Submersible manufactured to support a variety of operations to explore and exploit the oceans on every habitable world in Human Space. Tweed's great-grandfather, Onan Tweed, had founded the company, which was then run by his son, and then Oncho's father, Otho. In the fifty years since Otho Tweed's death, Oncho had run the vast enterprise with skill and cunning. He had been especially successful at getting lucrative government contracts, those let by the governments of individual worlds and ones the Confederation required. Most were obtained legitimately. Others he got through a web of contacts painstakingly developed over the years, people who could influence decisions at the highest levels in the government acquisition process. It cost him in kickbacks, but Tweed Submersible Recovery could afford them.

And one of the key people in fixing contracts was Val Carney. Not only was Carney the senior member of the Ministry of Justice Oversight Committee, he was also Chairman of the Acquisition and Development Committee, where he was able to exercise great influence over the Confederation government's contracting process. His position on the Justice Oversight Committee also gave him access to confidential investigative reports, so Carney knew in advance which companies were under surveillance. Generous bribes to lawyers on the Justice Ministry's staff had more than once quashed investigations implicating Tweed Submersible and other companies Carney had sweetheart deals with. Finally, by cutting funding to the Ministry of Justice's Bureau of Fraud, Waste, and Abuse Investigations, he had been able to ensure it had neither the staff nor the money to perform its duties effectively.

It was inevitable Tweed and Carney would strike big deals. The Tweed Hull Breacher would be one of the biggest for both of them. Carney was counting on their arrangement to help him swing another deal, truly the biggest one of his life, so he had to treat Tweed with utmost care.

The Confederation Navy needed a hull-breaching device that would permit boarding parties to enter hostile warships without degrading the vessel's life support systems. Navy warships could breach the hull of any known vessel and had done so numerous times in combat. Breaches were usually attained by devices that tore open airlocks, triggering ships' integrity systems, which were designed to instantly seal ship compartments and prevent loss of proper life support environment. That meant boarders had to enter a breached ship prepared to operate in a vacuum, then break through airtight hatches in passageways and into compartments until the airlock could be brought back on line. Then the boarding party had to blast its way into the rest of the ship to face a crew fully alert and ready to fight back.

Salvage and emergency rescue operations in space were another matter, one the navy handled very competently, but they required techniques that were laborious and time-consuming. In combat, every second was vital. So most navy commanders facing a hostile situation preferred to blast a ship into submission rather than launch a laborious and dangerous boarding operation. That worked well in combat, but a hostage situation was a different matter.

Not long before, political dissidents had hijacked a passenger vessel, and the navy commander on the scene used his ship's Marines in a combat-boarding operation. Unfortunately, hostages were being held in the very loading compartment the breached airlock opened into. The loss of life when the dissidents began executing the remaining passengers was terrible. To make matters worse, the ambush the dissidents set for the boarding party nearly wiped it out. As a result, the navy decided that a better and less predictable technique was needed to get inside a spaceship's hull quickly and safely.

The specification written for the hull-breaching contract required that a successful prototype would: (1) Be fully transportable on board the smallest navy line vessel. (2) Be able to operate independently of a mother ship and capable of maneuvering extensively over a considerable distance for up to six hours. (3) Hold up to a ten-man squad of combat-loaded Marines. (4) Be able to breach any known hull construction in less than thirty seconds. (5) Be easy to operate, so infantrymen could employ the device without technical expertise.

The contract also stipulated that once the bid was awarded, the successful bidder would deliver a prototype within six months of the award and provide all necessary training in the maintenance and operation of the device. Before the device was put into service, the manufacturer would guarantee a stock of spare parts to keep a small fleet of them fully operational. The manufacturer retained the right to license other companies to make spare parts, and the navy agreed to buy them from only the manufacturer or its licensees at prices to be agreed upon. Finally, the navy would pay for periodic overhauls to be performed by the manufacturer, who also agreed to keep technical representatives on call for emergencies.

Only three companies bid on the contract. The first two, Tweed's competitors, submitted sealed bids far in advance of the closing date of the announcement. Carney managed to get Tweed copies of those bids, which he underbid when submitting his own proposals. Some contracting officers in the navy were dubious about giving the award to Tweed since projects that Tweed Submersible Recovery had previously done had raised questions about overbilling, cost overruns, and the workmanship itself. Carney had the objections quashed.

This one contract alone would keep a company solvent for years.

"It's a beauty," Tweed sighed. He never grew tired of operating undersea vehicles, and was an expert at it. Of all the submersibles he'd had designed and built over the years, the *Boss* was his favorite.

"Yes," Carney agreed, thinking he meant the deal they'd brokered for the hull breacher. His initial panic at the *Boss*'s steep descent had diminished as Tweed expertly guided the craft toward the ocean floor. At two thousand meters Tweed stopped their descent and set the onboard navigation system to maintain their position.

"We won't be visiting Gotham on this trip, Valley. We'll just hang suspended here, have our little discussion, and then bob back to the surface and get you on your way home."

That was fine with Carney, who had no desire to be anywhere near the bottom of the ocean. He wondered how much pressure there was on the hull of the *Boss* at their depth and swallowed nervously.

Tweed leaned back in his captain's chair and put his hands behind his head. "I think we can talk securely now, Valley. We are the only two people on board the *Boss*. I have all my facilities swept periodically to keep electronic eavesdroppers out anyway, but now we have only our own ears to worry about."

"You got me all the way out here and into this, this . . ." Carney gestured at the bulkheads. "I mean, we've done business before without going to these—these extremes."

"Yes," Tweed agreed. "Security is not the main reason I wanted to talk to you under these circumstances. No. I wanted you to come out here so you could see for yourself what it is I represent." He paused. When Carney said nothing, he added, "I want you to know that I am a man who actually works for a living. I make things. I make things that really work. This submersible is an example of that. I spare no expense when it comes to constructing things—machines, prototypes, or plans—that affect me personally, Valley."

Carney nodded. Of course Tweed would not stint on the quality of materials or workmanship if he had to trust *his* life to the outcome. Carney, however, caught the implication of the word "plans" in Tweed's statement.

"I cover my back, Valley."

Carney saw where things were headed. "Oncho, my dear friend!" he protested. "You can count on me! You always can count on me. All I want from this project is what you will make on the bogus cost overruns. And possibly the loan of some of your equipment."

"You mentioned the use of my Bomarc and possibly one of the interstellar cargo vessels I keep in my fleet. Why? What will you do with them?" Tweed grinned.

"I am not at liberty to say, Oncho," Carney replied stiffly. "My, um, gems—er, I mean my associates, do not want me discussing their business with someone else."

"Who are these associates, Valley? Maybe I want in on this deal."

"I am afraid not, Oncho," Carney said with unaccustomed firmness. It would be very bad to offend Oncho Tweed, but it would be infinitely worse to betray the confidence of Madam Piggott Thigpen. Infinitely worse. The fear of that made him bold. "You shall get the vessels back and a very tidy profit from this contract. That was our deal, and you should be satisfied with it. Haven't I played straight with you in the past, Oncho? I've gone a long way toward making your enterprises solvent. A very long way," he concluded.

"You have profited too, Valley. And this hull breacher—the kickback I'm giving you for your help will finance your re-election campaign, maybe more."

"Well . . ."

"Valley, there have been . . . inquiries."

"Who?" Carney was alarmed.

Tweed shrugged. "The usual snooping the Bureau of Investigation carries on."

Carney made a dismissive gesture with one hand. "The BOI are useless. I have had them neutralized. If necessary, I'll speak to the Attorney General herself. She listens to me more carefully than to the President." He could not resist the boast. What he did not mention was that when the time was right, he would carefully leak enough information to the Bureau of Investigation to put Tweed in jail for the rest of his life. But the time was not yet right.

Back in Puuwai, Tweed considered his future. Why did that little rat Carney want to borrow starships from his fleet, and who were his mysterious partners? Carney was being paid well enough to cooperate, and indeed would come through for him. But something really big was afoot, and he was not to be a part of it.

Gems. Carney had mentioned gems. He tried to cover it up as a slip of the tongue, but he'd actually said "gems." Tweed pondered that. What the hell could he and those partners of his be planning that included gems of any kind? What was going down in the gem market? Well, his old friend Sly Henderson would know. Sly knew the market better than anyone.

But the real problem was that he could not trust Carney. Carney knew too much and was in a position to use that knowledge to destroy him. If some stupendous deal really was going down, Carney would want to cover his tracks, and that, Tweed knew, meant that Carney would have to neutralize him. It was time to sever relations with Carney, and he knew just how to do that.

What was that investigator's name? He'd been snooping around asking for interviews. No subpoenas for his business records, just an informal inquiry. Tweed had talked to him briefly before refusing to cooperate, but the man had impressed him with his quick intelligence and acumen. He could be dangerous. Nast, that was his name, Nast. Well, it was time Oncho Tweed gave Special Agent Nast a bone. It was high time someone took a large bite out of Val Carney's skinny little ass.

CHAPTER
THREE

PFC Jorge Hayes took his time returning from morning chow. Not because he was enjoying a casual saunter on a nice morning; there was nothing about the fishy drizzle that he found enjoyable. A short distance ahead of Hayes, PFC Longfellow was walking just as slowly, head down, shoulders hunched against the drizzle. When Hayes left the mess hall, PFC Gimbel had been lingering over a last cup of coffee and ignoring the dirty looks the messmen were giving him for delaying their break. If Gimbel didn't start moving soon, he'd be late for morning formation, and Gunny Thatcher would give him more than a dirty look.

Hayes, Longfellow, and Gimble were new men in third platoon, Company L, 34th FIST. New men, especially men on their first duty assignments, were almost always hard chargers, doing their best to impress everyone with their eagerness to do anything and be the first to do it. But not these three. They wished they were somewhere else. Hayes glanced back when he reached the barracks. He saw someone following through the gloom and rain and thought it was Gimble.

Inside, he climbed the stairs to the second floor and turned toward the small room he shared with Corporal Dornhofer and Lance Corporal Schultz, the other two men in his fire team. The low voices coming from the room stopped as soon as he reached the doorway. Dornhofer glanced at him.

"Better hurry," the fire team leader said, "or you'll be late."

Schultz didn't look up from his preparations for morning

formation. He didn't even grunt to acknowledge Hayes's presence.

Hayes repressed a shiver. He'd heard about the clannishness of Marine infantry units, how they excluded outsiders. But he'd never heard of the Marines in an infantry unit treating their own new men so coldly. Well, sometimes, maybe. If a new man was replacing someone who'd been with them for a long time, someone who'd been well liked. But the Marine he replaced, Dobervich, had been killed before anyone had really gotten to know him. It was a bit different with Longfellow. He'd been brought in to replace Lance Corporal Nolet, who had been with Company L for so long he was on the short list to rotate to a unit on another world. Nolet had been well liked. The same applied to PFC Clarke, a Marine who'd been with the gun squad for nearly two years, and was replaced by Gimbel. Neither Nolet nor Clarke was dead, just badly enough injured to need replacement. Hell, they might even return to the platoon when their injuries healed and their physical therapy completed.

But none of that explained to Hayes why the three new men were treated the way they were. Everything could be going all right for a little while, then someone would say something about "Waygone," or "skink," and conversation would stop, which left the new men feeling purposely excluded.

In fact, before the new men arrived, third platoon had been dispatched to a planet designated Society 437 to find out why a scientific mission had missed making two scheduled reports. The official story was that a native microorganism decided it liked human hosts and wiped out the mission. Supposedly, that microorganism had also killed Dobervich and sickened Nolet and Clarke, who were sent to the Center for Extraterrestrial Disease Control in Fargo on Earth for study. A day or two before third platoon returned to Thorsfinni's World, a high-ranking emissary arrived from Headquarters, Marine Corps, with a verbal message from the Commandant himself about their involvement on Society 437: "What happened is classified as Ultra Secret, Special Access." Dire but unspecified

consequences were threatened for anyone who divulged any
information.

Though 34th FIST's entire command structure was out-
raged, there wasn't a thing it could do about it.

"Third platoon, formation!" a voice boomed in the passageway. Hayes recognized it as Staff Sergeant Hyakowa, the
platoon sergeant.

"Formation! Formation! Formation!" the voices of the squad
leaders echoed.

"You ready?" Corporal Dornhofer asked Hayes as he
grabbed his blaster and stood up.

On his way out of the room, Schultz brushed past the new
man as though he wasn't there.

"I guess," Hayes said, and picked up his weapon. He didn't
know if he was ready or not. Frankly, he didn't care.

In moments Company L was standing in formation behind
the barracks. In the rain.

Everybody in the Company knew they had to stand formation in the rain instead of inside because the command unit
was so unhappy about the secrecy surrounding third platoon.
Everybody knew that after Captain Conorado finished giving
his morning briefing, Gunny Thatcher would conduct an inspection. They also knew that the men of third platoon would
be the only ones to flunk the inspection, and since the rest of
the company resented the silent treatment they'd gotten from
third platoon, standing formation in the rain was marginally
bearable for them.

It was fifth day. At sixteen hours liberty call sounded, they
were off until morning formation on first day. Two whole days
of freedom to drink and chase the local women and participate
in the fights the men—and some women—of Bronnoysund—
the town located just outside the main gate of Camp Major
Pete Ellis—gleefully had at the slightest provocation, or at no
provocation at all.

Liberty call. Except for third platoon. Third platoon had to
spend extra time cleaning weapons and fixing garrison uni-

forms because they had, to a man, flunked that morning's inspection.

At 1715 hours Staff Sergeant Hyakowa called for the men to assemble in the company classroom. They quickly reassembled their weapons and ran. Maybe Gunny Thatcher would let them pass the inspection this time and they could take off on liberty.

Gunny Thatcher wasn't there. Gunnery Sergeant Charlie Bass, their platoon commander, was. His face bore an unreadable, stony expression.

"Shut up and sit down," Bass said as his men boiled in and tried to arrange themselves into a formation in the limited open space between the chairs and the front of the classroom. The lean, tallish veteran stood with arms akimbo, watching his men as they took seats in the front rows. Hyakowa stood next to the door and closed it as soon as the last man was inside.

When everyone was seated, Bass said, "Hammer, front and center."

Lance Corporal Schultz jumped to his feet and stood at attention in front of Bass.

"Inspection, arms," Bass said softly.

Schultz sharply brought his blaster up to the port arms position, held diagonally across his body, and jacked open the battery port to show it was unloaded. Using sharp, parade ground movements, Bass slapped the blaster out of Schultz's hands and twirled it around. He glanced at the open battery port and at the muzzle, then held it out for Schultz to retake.

"Third platoon has passed this inspection," Bass announced. "Lance Corporal Schultz, resume your place."

"Aye aye, sir," Schultz replied, executed an about-face and briskly stepped back to his chair.

Bass visibly relaxed. "I had a talk with Gunny Thatcher," he said. "Also with Top Myer and the Skipper."

Hyakowa cut off a snicker. He'd been at the "talk" Bass had with the company's command unit. Read them the riot act was more like it.

"The Mickey Mouse is over. Nobody likes the fact that we can't talk about what happened on Society 437." He glanced at the three new men and sadly shook his head. "Not even to you. I'm sorry, but that's the way it is. Nobody likes it, but I convinced the Skipper, the Top, and the Gunny that it's neither fair to anyone in the company nor proper Marine behavior to treat third platoon the way they've been treating us. Liberty call will be sounded for third platoon when we're through here. When you return from liberty, things should be back to normal with the company.

"As for you," he indicated the new men, "I know you've been through a rough time. We found something . . . most remarkable on Society 437. The powers that decide these things determined that no one who wasn't there should know about it. That has put a considerable strain on everyone in the platoon. I have to apologize to you for the cold shoulder you've been given. It's nothing personal. Normally we greet newcomers quite warmly." He shot a glance at a few of the veterans who snorted at that. "Really. We're a team. We have to work closely together if we're all going to survive when we go in harm's way. It's the stress we've been under that has had everybody—including, I'm sorry to say, me—closing you out."

He looked at the entire platoon. "That will cease as of now. These men are members of third platoon, they are to be treated as such."

He looked at the time. Nearly 1730 hours. "I've held you up long enough. Liberty call is sounded. Now get out of my barracks. I don't want to see any of your ugly faces until morning formation two days from now."

The men of third platoon jumped to their feet. Their headlong rush toward the exit stopped abruptly when Sergeant Ratliff, the senior squad leader, called out, "Toon! A-ten-HUT!"

Everyone stopped in place and snapped to attention.

Ratliff faced Bass and said in a loud, clear voice, "Gunnery Sergeant, the men of third platoon thank you, sir. Three cheers!"

The Marines all turned to face Bass and roared out, "OOURAAHHH! OOURAAHHH! OOURAAHHH!" The cheers rattled the windows.

Bass looked down for a moment and swallowed. When he looked up, his face was stern. "I thought I told you to get out of my barracks."

Ratliff grinned at him. "And we'll take good care of our new men too." He reached out and gave Hayes's shoulder a squeeze.

"Better get out of here," Hyakowa said, "before he decides you like the barracks so much you want some additional duty."

They scrambled.

"How did HQMC find out about it so fast?" Lance Corporal Joe Dean asked.

"Damned if I know," replied Lance Corporal Rachman Claypoole. He didn't bother asking either of the other men who sat with them on the gravel bank of the fjord. It was the afternoon of the next day, and they'd finally managed to break away from the welcoming party third platoon's squad leaders had decided they needed to throw for the new men they'd been neglecting so badly. The party was still going strong an hour earlier when they snuck away. They suspected it would still be going whenever they decided to return to it. Probably everyone in the platoon would pay quiet visits to the company's corpsmen to get something to sober up before the next morning formation.

"Must have happened when we were on New Cobh," PFC Wolfman MacIlargie opined. "The skipper of the *Fairfax County*, what was his name, Tuit? He probably sent a drone to Earth."

Dean shook his head. "Not enough time." Interstellar communications was slow; the only way to send a message and have it arrive during the lifetime of the recipient was to send it on a starship. It would have taken four months for a message to get from New Cobh to Headquarters, Marine Corps, on

Earth, for HQMC to come to a decision, dispatch a messenger, and have that messenger intercept the *Fairfax* before it reached Thorsfinni's World. The HQMC messenger, a major general, was waiting for the *Fairfax* at its last jump point, little more than one month after they left their unscheduled liberty call at New Cobh.

"I think Captain Tuit sent a drone as soon as he found out what we were up against on Waygone," said PFC Izzy Godenov. "That's the only way there could have been enough time."

MacIlargie snorted. "How would HQMC have known when we'd be at that jump point? How would they even know we'd survive to get there?"

"We're Marines," Godenov said softly. "Some Marines always survive."

"That major general couldn't have known when we'd get there," Dean said after mulling it over for a moment. "He must have been sent as soon as they got the message. I wonder how long he had to wait for us?"

MacIlargie thought about it, then his face lit up. "Wow! A major general had to hurry up and wait for us! Think of that." He laughed. "Makes me feel damn important."

"The only thing you're important for is cannon fodder," Corporal Kerr said as he joined the four. "Been wondering where my problem children disappeared to." He found a flat rock that wasn't too wet and sat down. "Shadow, Izzy." He nodded at Dean and Godenov. "You sure you want to hang around with these two? They set a bad example, you know."

"I know," Dean said solemnly. "That's why Izzy and I are here, making sure they keep out of trouble."

Claypoole punched at Dean. Godenov grinned. MacIlargie put on his best innocent look.

"Maybe waiting so long was why that major general acted the way he did," Kerr said. "Ever think of that?"

MacIlargie shrugged. "He's a major general. That's the way flag officers act."

Kerr slowly shook his head. He'd never had much to do

with generals, but he'd met more of them than MacIlargie had. He looked at the frigid water gently lapping against the gravel of the fjord's beach and remembered.

The CNSS *Fairfax County* had come out of Beamspace relatively near where the astrogator had aimed. It took little time for the astrogator to determine the ship's exact location, and hardly more time to plot the next jump, which would bring them into planetary space near Thorsfinni's World. What took the most time, several hours, was for the Beam drive to wind down following a jump and wind back up to make the next. During those hours the ship's comm shack had come to life on receipt of an unexpected radio message. It was rare for a navy ship to receive a message while in transit from one world to another, but it was sometimes necessary, which was why ships always had one or two predesignated jump points they were required to hit during a cruise. This last jump point before Thorsfinni's World was one of the required points.

"Gunnery Sergeant Bass reporting as ordered, sir," Bass had said when he arrived on the bridge in response to a call from Captain Tuit, commander of the CNSS *Fairfax County*.

"Gunny." Tuit nodded at him. "We're going to be here for a while and I thought you should know why."

Bass looked impassively at the ship's captain.

"We've got company," the captain said.

That was a surprise. "Sir?"

Tuit nodded. "The fast frigate CNSS *HM3 Gordon* is waiting for us. It has a special courier on board who needs to transship and have a little chat with us."

Bass raised an eyebrow. " 'Us,' sir?"

"Ship's crew and Marine passengers, that was the message." Tuit looked at the wall of viewscreens that showed the space forward of the *Fairfax County*. "The message didn't say, but it managed to convey the impression that this courier carries a lot of rank and is delivering a message from someone with a lot more rank. I thought you'd like to know so you could get your men ready."

Bass nodded. "I hope nobody minds that we didn't bring our scarlets with us, sir."

Tuit laughed. "Just don't wear your chameleons; he'll want to know you're actually present for the briefing." The captain returned to his duties. Bass was dismissed.

Bass headed for third platoon's troop compartment to pass on the message.

"The *Gordon*?" Claypoole asked. "Isn't that the frigate we sailed on a couple of years ago?"

Kerr slapped him lightly on the back of the head. "Fast frigate," he said. Company L had sailed to Elneal on the fast frigate *HM3 Gordon*. Kerr had nearly died on that operation. His injuries were bad enough that he'd only returned to the company shortly before the mount out to Waygone. "If you live long enough to get some salt on you, you'll sail on a lot of ships more than once."

It took more than three days standard for the two ships to rendezvous. When the courier was piped aboard, the biggest surprise was that he was a Marine Corps major general; most of them had expected a navy captain or an admiral. Major General Mowooglhi first met privately with Captain Tuit, before having him call in the ship's officers and Gunnery Sergeant Bass. Then he met with the crew of the ship. Finally, resplendent in his officer's scarlets—bloodred, stock-collared tunic over gold trousers—and an impressive array of decorations and medals on his left chest, he entered the troop compartment to meet with the men of third platoon.

"Attention on deck!" Staff Sergeant Hyakowa shouted as the general ducked through the hatch.

The Marines, already lined up in compartment formation, snapped to attention.

Major General Mowooglhi took a step inside the compartment so Bass could follow without bumping into him. His glowering eyes swept across the men, none of whom met his eyes—they were all looking properly straight ahead.

The general clasped his hands behind his back and slowly walked through the compartment, along the ranks of Marines, looking each of them in the eye. Now and again he asked, "What's your name, Marine?" or, "Where are you from, Marine?" or some other routine question. It was just like a brigadier's inspection in garrison. When he was finished, he returned to stand just inside the hatch. He nodded at Bass, who shut and dogged the hatch. The glower never left his face.

"All right," he said after a moment's silence. "What happened on Society 437?"

There was another moment's silence while the Marines wondered what to say and who wanted to be the first to speak up to a general officer. Mowooghli spoke before any of them did.

"You found a mission that was wiped out by an alien microorganism," he said. "That's all. There were no aliens; there were no pirates; there was no acid. Just microorganisms. It happens, everybody knows that. If anybody asks, that's all you have to tell them. Otherwise, what happened is classified Ultra Secret, Special Access. Everybody who needs to know what really happened already knows. No one else needs to know. Any questions?"

"Sir?" a nervous voice said.

"What's your name."

"Corporal Goudanis, sir."

"Speak, Corporal."

"Sir, we lost three men to the skinks, one dead, two who might not be able to return. What do we tell people when they ask about that?"

"I say again. When people ask you what happened on Society 437, there was an epidemic. Three of your men caught it. One man died, the other two survived but are very ill. They've been taken back to Earth for treatment and study. Any other questions?"

"Sir." Another voice, not quite as nervous.

"Your name?"

"Lance Corporal Chan, sir."

"Speak, Lance Corporal."

"Sir, begging the general's pardon, sir, but that's not what happened on Waygone. Even without meaning to, it's likely that sometime, someplace, someone will inadvertently say something that will tell people what we found."

Major General Mowooglhi considered for a moment, then said, "Does the name 'Darkside' mean anything to you?" He continued without waiting for a reply. "Anyone who says anything about what happened on Society 437 will suddenly and summarily find himself on Darkside. I hope that's clear. Are there any other questions?"

When no one spoke, Mowooghli said, "That is all. A microorganism wiped out the mission on Society 437." He nodded at Bass, who undogged the hatch and opened it for the general.

After the general left, Bass snarled, "Gather around. Sit." The Marines crowded close and sat on the deck in front of him. "Major General Mowooglhi," he said when the rustling they made getting in place was done, "is Deputy Chief of Staff, Intelligence, at HQMC. The orders he just delivered came from someone even higher than the Commandant." He paused to let that sink in—who was higher than the Commandant? "Let me repeat that order. When somebody, anybody, asks what happened on Waygone, we tell them it was a bug. That's it. A bug. Nothing more. We change the subject. If they persist, we tell them we don't want to talk about it. If they still persist, we are to report their asses. We cannot tell anyone what really happened. Not your best buddy in the next platoon, not Captain Conorado, not Brigadier Sturgeon, not your wife, girlfriend, mother, or brother. No one."

He shook his head. "With what happened on Waygone classified the way it is, we're lucky we aren't on our way to Darkside right now." He paused to let that sink in. "Some of you may remember from your European History studies a place called Devil's Island. Darkside is like that, but less well known, and harder to escape from. Now think about that. Think about it real hard before you come up with any more questions. And remember, nothing out of the ordinary happened on Waygone. It was a bug."

There was a moment of silence as the Marines digested what had just happened, then a voice piped up.

"Gunny, Mr. Baccacio and what's her name, that woman. We already let them loose on New Cobh. Aren't they a threat to tell?"

Bass looked at Claypoole and considered the question and how to answer it. Then he knew and shook his head. "I don't think they're any threat at all. They know that if they say anything to anybody about aliens, they'll have to explain about pirates and how they know. Then they'd find themselves tried as pirates facing a long prison sentence, maybe even execution. They won't talk; it's too dangerous for them."

Abruptly, Charlie Bass spun about and opened the hatch. He left.

They were quiet for a long time before they stood and drifted off in twos and threes to murmur among themselves. Hyakowa followed Bass. As platoon sergeant, the only person he could talk to about the situation was the platoon commander, and he badly needed to talk to someone.

Kerr shook himself. He had accumulated two things that were almost impossible to live with. First was the fear he carried after nearly being killed on Elneal. Then there was the absolute prohibition against saying anything about one of the most significant things to happen to humanity since the invention of fire. He was strong and he was experienced, yet the two things were very difficult, almost impossible, for him to carry. He wondered how the junior men, Marines with neither his strength nor experience, would manage to keep silent about Waygone for their entire lives. He wondered if they would all eventually find themselves on Darkside.

He stood. "Let's get back to the party. Wouldn't want the entire platoon out looking for us." He looked at the others. "Unless someone knows where there are five women who'd just love our company for the rest of the weekend."

"I know where there's two," MacIlargie said.

"Not enough. Let's go back to the party."

For a long time, Kerr thought, the platoon has to stick together. None of us can go off on our own. We need one another's support so no one slips and finds himself on Darkside.

CHAPTER FOUR

The Philosopher

Waakakaa the Philosopher squatted on his high perch, idly pecking lice from beneath his shawl. He cocked his head, studying the eyestretcher mounted in front of the low perch. It was a wondrous thing, the eyestretcher, for a philosopher who desired to understand the nature and meaning of the glitterers that adorned the night sky. Those glitterers meant nothing to most people because few were still awake when they appeared in the darkening sky, or yet awake before they vanished in the sky of dawn. The moon, so far as most people knew or cared, was but a ghost that sometimes was visible in the morning or evening sky. Yet, through the ages, a few people were awake during the long hours when Aaaah made his way unseen from the west to the east to make the sky bright once more. The few were mostly those charged with protecting the sleepers from the night-hunters that sometimes preyed on them. A very few were Philosophers. Philosophers wondered about everything, but there were not many of them, and most Philosophers wondered little about Aaaah-lit matters. Only a few among them ever remained awake during the dark to observe and wonder about the glitterers.

Over the ages, the few Philosophers who did wonder had mapped the glitterers of the dark, seen patterns in their scattering, and given the patterns names. Six stickles written by ancient Philosophers formed the core of the library of Waakakaa the Philosopher. He had spent many years studying those stickles, as well as the few more he had access to in the university library when he was a student, and he knew how thinking about the glitterers had changed over the ages. From the stickles and his own observations, he knew that the glitterers were constant in number and position—save for the few wanderers whose odd paths were well mapped— even though different Philosophers grouped the glitterers into different patterns with different names. There were other glitterers, of course. Almost every dark, glitterers came from nowhere to streak across the dark and die. Then there were the infrequent strange, tailed glitterers that moved across the dark over a period of months, growing then shrinking, and then were gone.

Many Philosophers guessed about the nature of the glitterers, but rarely did any two Philosophers agree. The glitterers remained then as they had always—a mystery to those few who saw them and wondered.

There was one exception to the constancy of number, position, and type—the New Glitterer. When Waakakaa was but a fledgling and not yet concerned with the glitterers, a new one was seen. Then, in his youth, Waakakaa didn't have a stickle of his own that told of the coming of the New Glitterer, but he had journeyed to the University at Rhaachtown to study its library's stickles, which told of it. At first it was the smallest speck in the dark, visible only to the sharpest-eyed Philosophers. It grew over a period of darks until it was visible as one of the brightest glitterers. During its time of growth it had a tail. Then it stopped growing and its tail died. It settled itself in the pattern of the High Tree, near the split in the bole, and remained there.

There were several oddities about the New Glitterer. It was the first glitterer that jittered slowly in position, from time to time drifting slightly and then abruptly moving back into place. When it suddenly returned to its place, it seemed to grow slightly until it resettled. Infrequently, once or twice a year, small, tailed glitterers came to it, vanished for a period of nights, then left it.

Altogether, the New Glitterer was very strange. So recently, when Waakakaa heard of another Philosopher who had invented a machine to see at a distance, he journeyed to far Zheekeech to visit him and learn of his invention.

Kcoock the Philosopher had his tree constructed at the top of a cliff overlooking a great sea. Waakakaa the Philosopher briefly wondered at the gray, pounding waves that shattered against the foot of the cliff and sometimes sprayed foam all the way to Kcoock's tree. But Waakakaa's wondering interest was about the darkness glitterers, so he left the wondering about the gray sea to Kcoock.

Kcoock the Philosopher believed that the world was round, like a ball, and had spent his life in an attempt to learn the size of that ball. His library contained stickles from all the known world, ranging from the southernmost principalities to exploratory journeys to the far North, as well as the farthest East. The stickles told Kcoock the length of time Aaaah took to traverse the sky. During the winter months, Aaaah sped briefly across the sky, as though hurrying to get in out of the cold. During the summer months, he traveled more sedately, and made a longer day. In far Zheekeech, where winters were longer and colder, Aaaah sped more rapidly across the winter sky, and lingered longer during the summer. Also, the stickles that told of the farthest South said that Aaaah traveled across the northern sky rather than the southern. All of this held sublime meaning for Kcoock the Philosopher. So did the fact that wild fliers seemed to sink into the sea at its farthest edge, even though their manner of movement was that of flying or gliding, rather than landing.

For many years Kcoock had taken measurements of the wild fliers and determined from those measurements how far away the edge of the sea was. Using all of his knowledge, he constructed a marvelous ball on which he plotted all the lands of the world that were known to him. Most of the globe was devoid of lands. Kcoock believed his measurements were wrong, that the earth could not be mostly void of land. So he desired to refine his measurements. But he was aging and his eyes grew weak, so he could no longer see the wild fliers as they dropped into the edge of the sea. Thus, Kcoock constructed a device that allowed his weakened eyes to see to the edge of the sea, so he might continue his measurements.

Waakakaa knew as soon as he looked through the eyestretcher that it would be of immeasurable aid to him in studying the night glitterers. Indeed, he spent several nights gazing through it while Kcoock slept. At length he knew he must return to his own tree and construct his own eyestretcher. Kcoock instructed him on how to refine crystal shards and a length of reedtree trunk to build an eyestretcher.

Back at his own tree, constructing the eyestretcher took far longer than Waakakaa had expected. The refinement and placement of the crystals was far more precise than he had imagined from what Kcoock the Philosopher had told him. Also, experiment taught him that eyestretching during the day was different from eyestretching during the dark. He experimented again and again before he finally managed to construct an eyestretcher that let him see the glitterers of the dark as well as Kcoock's eyestretcher had.

The view gradually came to disappoint him.

The glitterers were all points of light the same as he had seen them without the eyestretcher. To be sure, he saw far more of them than he ever had before, but they were still mere points that told him nothing about their nature or purpose. During the darks when the moon shined so bright as to blot out many of the glitterers, he gazed on it. He saw what could only be mountain ranges, plains, and seas, even though they were all white and gray and black instead of green and brown and blue. But the moon wasn't what interested him; he wondered about the glitterers.

He continued to experiment with eyestretchers, determined to construct one that would tell him more about the glitterers in the dark. Even though he made eyestretchers that showed him smaller and smaller mountains on the moon and revealed its rivers to him, the glitterers remained mere points of colored light. Until tonight.

Tonight he turned his eyestretcher on the New Glitterer. What he saw made him wonder more than he had ever wondered before. Unlike the other glitterers in the dark, the New Glitterer wasn't a mere point of light, it showed a disk.

The disk was small, far smaller than the moon seen with the naked eye, and featureless. But Waakakaa saw something on it that no one had seen before, and he wondered what it meant. He knew it had to mean something; perhaps it held the knowledge of all the other glitterers.

It happened that he had looked upon the New Glitterer during the time it grew brighter and moved from its drift back to its place near the split in the bole of the pattern of the High Tree. Waakakaa saw, then, that the reason the New Glitterer was brighter during its time of movement was small flames that jetted from the side of it opposite its direction of drift. What did this mean?

He hopped off the high perch and returned to the low perch. He bent his neck to hold his eye against the cupped crystal at the bottom end of the reedtree section. Perhaps like Kcoock the Philosopher, who had spent his life measuring wild fliers when they dropped into the edge of the sea, and in constructing his marvelous globe, he too would spend the rest of his life studying the New Glitterer before he came to an answer. If he ever found an answer.

Waakakaa the Philosopher studied the New Glitterer for several years before he published his preliminary findings in a stickle so small it was hardly noticed by other Philosophers. But after a time the small stickle came to the attention of the Dean of the School of Philosophy at the University at Rhaachtown. Dean Ouoop read the stickle with growing interest, then called in his school's chief accountant and instructed him to find money in the budget to accommodate a

Visiting Philosopher, including all of his travel expenses, lodging, food, and a healthy honorarium. The chief accountant grumbled over the expenditure, as is the nature of chief accountants, and went about shifting budget numbers to locate the necessary funds. Dean Ouoop then dispatched a messenger to Waakakaa.

The Nomads

Graakaak, High Chief of the Cheereek, perched in a council of war. Lined up before him on a lower perch were Chief of Staff Oouhoouh, Captain of the Guards Cheerpt, Chief Councilor Tschaah, and Head of Scouts Kkaacgh.

"Say again what you found, Head of Scouts," Graakaak said.

Kkaacgh resisted an urge to preen. It wasn't often someone of his perching was called upon to brief the likes of the Chief of Staff and the Chief Councilor. And to think he was to speak to them before even the Captain of the Guards! Kkaacgh puffed his chest and stretched his neck up to its full length and spoke toward the ceiling.

"High Chief, three foraging rides to the west, my scouts found an encampment of Aawk-vermin hunters numbering about fifty. They seemed to be unaware or uncaring that they encroached upon Cheereek hunting lands."

"How do you know it is a hunting party and not a war party?" demanded Oouhoouh, exposing his throat and other soft parts to Graakaak.

"Honored Chief of Staff, they carried bows and stickers. They carried shields, but did not wear armor or war helmets."

"Why do you believe they were wandering hunters and not forerunners for a camp?" Tschaah didn't bother to expose his vulnerability to the High Chief when he spoke. He had been Chief Councilor to Graakaak's father and was too old to be any physical threat.

"Honored Chief Councilor, they had no females among them to build nests for. They raised only one tree, a covering over a shallow pit for their leader."

Cheerpt snaked his head close enough to Kkaacgh's

throat that a twitch would draw blood, before he stretched his own upward. "How do you know your scouts reported true?"

"Because I went there myself and saw it with my own eyes, Honored Captain of the Guards. I report what I know to be truth, not what my scouts wish me to believe."

Graakaak crowed out a laugh. Kkaacgh was not acting like the most junior member of this council, he was handling himself quite well. He plucked a pebble from his perch without looking and tossed it to the Head of Scouts. Kkaacgh snagged it and held it admiringly before his eyes before popping it into his mouth to let it ripple down the length of his throat.

Graakaak made his decision. "Oouhoouh," he commanded, "arm a hundred warriors, twenty of the Guards and eighty others, with Clumsy Ones' weapons. Cheerpt, you will lead the raid. Bring me fifty tail-nubs. Kkaacgh, you will personally scout for the raiders. Do it."

The Chief of Staff, Captain of the Guards, and Head of the Scouts hopped off the perch and bounded out of the high tent.

Chief Councilor Tschaah lowered his head and cocked it, the better to look at the High Chief. "Graakaak," he said in a voice pitched low enough so it wouldn't carry to the guards arrayed around the perimeter of the High Tree, "is that a wise thing to do at this time? The Aawk-vermin may not be armed as well as we are, but there are many times more of them in their rookeries than there are of us in our one rookery. I know that warrior by warrior they are no match for the Cheereek, but they could overwhelm us by sheer numbers."

Graakaak flashed a look of anger at the old councilor, then crowed out in joy once more. "Kkaacgh did not say all he knew. The Aawk-vermin have more than one hunting party out. After we kill this one, we will kill the next and the next and the next, one at a time. By the time the Aawk-vermin realize they are under attack, they will have lost hundreds of warriors. They will not then have the numbers to overwhelm us. Soon, the entire world will tremble at the name of Graakaak!

"Leave me now. Have my eeookk prepared. I wish to watch my warriors kill with the Clumsy Ones' weapons."

Kkaacgh sat proudly on his eeookk as it galumphed through the rivulets, rifts, and dry gullies of the steppe. For Graakaak to pick him to personally scout for this raid was a singular honor. It clearly demonstrated that he was Head of Scouts of the Cheereek because of ability, not because his father was clutchmate of the High Chief. And he knew the honor was deserved. This was *his* land. He'd lived in it his entire life, and prowled its contours ever since he grew large enough to slip out of his parents' nest and roam on his own. He chuckled at the memory. He wasn't even fully fledged when he made his first foray onto the ground. Oh, how his clutchmates had hammered at him when he clambered back into the nest, trying to keep him out so more of the food their parents brought back would be shoved down their greedy gullets. But he was proud even then, and strong—though he wasn't the largest in the clutch. He had tweed mightily and pecked and pecked and driven his clutchmates back from the edge of the nest to make space for him. When a parent returned soon after with food, Kkaacgh's was the first gullet to be filled.

Now he galumphed a short distance ahead of the hundred warriors sent to kill the Aawk-vermin hunters who dared encroach on the lands of the Cheereek. The Aawk-vermin did not know this land. They would look across it and see it flat as far as their eyes could see. But Kkaacgh knew the land, every ripple and irregularity of it. He knew he could lead the war party unseen and so close to the Aawk-vermin hunting camp that they could not miss when they shot their Clumsy Ones' weapons into the camp. He looked back over his shoulder and saw the way Cheerpt sat his eeookk at the head of the vee of warriors, and knew the Captain of the Guards would not be content to kill the Aawk-vermin from ambuscade, but would attack in proper manner. Kkaacgh crowed out a cry of ecstasy.

When the Cheereek warriors attacked, he would also attack, even though he didn't have a Clumsy Ones' weapon. There was no prohibition against the Head of Scouts also being a warrior.

Aaaah had been halfway up the skyroad when Graakaak gave his orders, and nearly at the top by the time the war party set out. Aaaah was getting close to the bottom of the other side of the skyroad when Kkaacgh reined his eeookk and waited for Cheerpt to join him. In the near distance he could hear the cries and gobbles the Aawk-vermin made as they ate and prepared their night-roost. He stretched his neck up when Cheerpt reached him but didn't lift his head; that obesience was reserved for the High Chief. He nodded toward the cries of the Aawk-vermin.

Cheerpt listened for a moment, then asked, "Over the rise?"

"Around that bend, then over the rise." Kkaacgh pointed to where the gully they followed turned to the left.

Cheerpt twisted around on his eeookk and made a series of signals with his arm and neck. The war party would proceed quietly around the bend. When all were in place, they would attack over it. Kkaacgh held back a crow of pleasure; the plan seemed perfect.

"Lead on," Cheerpt ordered.

Kkaacgh kneed his eeookk and the animal trotted forward. Cheerpt and the warriors followed. In moments the hundred-Cheereek war party was around the bend in the gully, facing the rise beyond which lay the hunting camp of the Aawk-vermin.

Cheerpt craned his neck to both sides and, satisfied that all were ready, held his Clumsy Ones' weapon above his head for a few seconds, then swept it forward.

As one, the hundred Cheereek warriors shrieked their war cries and heeled their mounts into a headlong charge up the side of the gully, holding their Clumsy Ones' weapons one-handed, pointed ahead of them. The eeookks' claws dug gouts from the hard dirt, screeched against rock. Their excited brays added to the cacophony. Kkaacgh shrieked his cry with them and joined the charge, wielding his stabbing-spear the way the warriors did their Clumsy Ones' weapons.

The Aawk-vermin hunters were caught by surprise, even the half-dozen warriors traveling with the party as guards were away from their posts getting ready for night-roost. The ragged line of Cheereek galumphed through the encampment, their Clumsy Ones' weapons cracking thunder, belching fire and smoke. The Aawk-vermin screamed in panic and ran about seeking safety. Some of them staggered and fell under the impact of the randomly flying bullets from the rifles, some collided with one another or tripped over carelessly placed camp gear, to be trampled and rent under the feet and claws of the charging eeookks. One eeookk screamed in shocked pain when its rider sent it through a still-smoldering cookfire and flung about the glowing coals.

Kkaacgh leaned low over the shoulder of his eeookk and thrust his stabbing-spear at the back of a fleeing Aawk-vermin hunter. He threw his head high and crowed in victory when the point of his weapon slammed through its target. He jerked the spear free and held it high for all to see the blood and gore that dripped down it. Then he lowered his head and looked for another target.

Past the encampment, Cheerpt jerked hard on his eeookk's reins, causing the animal to flail its stubby wings as it skidded and spun around. He crowed with glee at the sight that met his eyes. Most of the Aawk-vermin were down. Some of the downed still shivered with life, but most lay twitching in new death. A very few remained on their feet. He lifted his Clumsy Ones' weapon to his shoulder and looked along its barrel, the way the Clumsy Ones had taught him. When the barrel was lined up with a running Aawk-vermin, he squeezed the trigger. He crowed when the fleeing hunter pitched forward and lay spasming as death took him. Cheerpt looked around. His warriors were running down the last of the Aawk-vermin. In another moment it was over, and the Cheereek warriors shrieked victory cries.

* * *

On a slight rise in the middle distance, Graakaak sat tall on his eeookk and watched the brief and one-sided fight. When the last of the Aawk-vermin fell, he heeled his eeookk into full galumph toward the encampment.

The warriors stopped gathering the meat cured by the hunters when Graakaak, accompanied by Chief of Staff Oouhoouh and a party of guards, reached the encampment. They gathered in a semicircle in front of the High Chief, separated from him by the line of guards.

"Cheerpt," Graakaak said, "did the Clumsy Ones' weapons perform satisfactorily?"

"They did, High Chief," Cheerpt replied, neck stretched full up, face pointed at the heavens.

"I watched. You all did well." Graakaak swung his head in an arc to look at each warrior. The warriors met his gaze then pointed their heads high.

"Kkaacgh, find another Aawk-vermin hunting party for us to kill tomorrow."

"High Chief, I know where there is another. If we go now we can reach a roosting place close enough to it to attack before the hunters leave in the morning."

"Lead us to this roosting place, Captain of Scouts."

Kkaacgh jerked at the title Graakaak used. *Captain of Scouts!* His chest swelled with this most singular honor.

"I saw you in the fight," Graakaak said. "I have never seen a Head of Scouts join in a fight except in defense. When we return to the High Tree you will begin training in use of the Clumsy Ones' weapons. Now lead us to roost."

Chest swollen almost to bursting, faint with dizziness at the praise and honors heaped on him, Kkaacgh bounded onto his eeookk and began trotting in the direction his scouts told him another Aawk-vermin hunting camp lay.

In three more days the Cheereek war party, led personally by High Chief Graakaak, attacked and wiped out six more Aawk-vermin hunting camps. They lost three warriors, one guard, and two eeookks. Graakaak crowed mightily. It was time to gather his full army and attack the Aawk-vermin High Tree.

CHAPTER FIVE

Madam Piggott Thigpen groaned with pleasure, not so much from the action Val Carney was happily performing at her feet, but from the effect of the dazzling gem that hung around her neck.

"Gorgeous, gorgeous," she muttered, slowly twirling the priceless beauty a few inches from her sweaty face.

Thinking she was complimenting him on his technique, Val Carney straightened up and wiped saliva from his lips. His heart raced as he gazed upon her enormous thighs. Then his spirits plunged when he realized that it was the gem, not himself, that captivated his lover's attention. He ran his hand across his lips once more.

"Mmmm," Piggott Thigpen murmured. Her eyes, normally hardly visible in the moon of fat that was her face, were now reduced to mere slits. "Ahhh," she whispered. Her eyes blinked open suddenly. She seemed surprised to see Carney kneeling naked beside her.

"I was about to start on your ankles, Petunia," Val Carney said apologetically. Only he dared call her that, or so he believed, and only because he'd earned the right by performing the service at which he'd just been interrupted. "Put that bauble away, my dearest, my mound of ecstasy, I was just warming up!"

Piggott Thigpen only grunted. Clearly, the mood was broken. Val Carney arose and began gathering up his clothes. She lay on her couch, totally naked, one enormous breast slopping over nearly to the floor.

"What is it you see when you stare at that thing?" Carney asked, miffed that he'd been upstaged by a mere piece of what he considered costume jewelry. He nodded his head at the gem hanging from a necklace gleaming greasily around Piggott Thigpen's neck.

"Money," she grunted. But she saw far more than that in the iridescent gem, although she could not explain just what visions it conjured. "Do you know how much this cost me?"

"Yes, my love, exactly." He smiled. He also knew that ten percent of the profits that might flow from the evening's meeting would more than finance his reelection campaign and possibly secure for him the seat of the Confederation presidency.

"It cost a fortune, Valley, my sweet-lipped little dynamo. Sit me up!" she commanded the microcomputer that controlled her orthosofa. Obedient to her spoken command, groaning mightily all the while, the sofa rotated her into a standing position and then gently lowered her feet to the floor so she could stand without assistance. "And that is why our guests will be meeting us here within the hour," she added, shuffling ponderously across the floor toward her dressing room. Carney, minus his trousers, rushed forward to assist her. Standing, she loomed over the thin little man. "Thank you, my succulent little boy," she grunted wetly, and with one huge hand carefully massaged him for a few delightful moments. When he began groaning with pleasure she turned abruptly with a laugh and waddled into her dressing room. The door hissed shut behind her.

Val Carney, elected representative from Katishaw to the Congress of the Confederation of Worlds, senior member on the Justice Oversight Committee, glared longingly after Madam Piggott Thigpen.

Clad in resplendent robes of the finest quality, Madam Piggott Thigpen, representative from Carhart's World to the Confederation of Worlds, welcomed her guests. Fully dressed, she was an imposing figure. Her apartment was large and very luxuriously appointed, but she dominated it with the force of her personality and the sheer volume of her physical presence.

Val Carney was the only other person who ever stayed very long in Piggott Thigpen's quarters, and never longer than overnight. When she entertained, she placed ordinary furniture about the apartment for the use of her guests. Only she was allowed to occupy one of the several New Brooklyn Orthosofas strategically located throughout the suite. The most sophisticated and modern servomechanisms attended to all her needs. That way her business remained private. Besides, she could not tolerate the presence of another person for very long in her living space. The closest thing she had to a pet was the gem hanging about her neck.

The first guest to arrive was Senator Henri Morgan. With his trademark smile, the one that showed perfect white teeth offset by his florid complexion, he gently kissed the back of Piggot Thigpen's hand. "Madam," he murmured. His flowing mane of pure-white hair swished around his shoulders. He was the perfect image of a legislative solon—and he knew it. He gave Val Carney the tips of his fingers for a perfunctory shake.

A servobot glided soundlessly up to the trio and asked Senator Morgan what he was drinking. "Katzenwasser 'thirty-six," he answered. "What's the stock market quote on Consolidated Dolomide today?" Morgan asked the servo. Obligingly it rotated a vidscreen to an angle where the senator could easily read it, and the latest market quotes flashed before his eyes. The senator grinned. "A small investment, friends," he muttered, nodding at Val Carney. "I highly recommend it." As the servo poured the wine, the senator continued watching the screen. "Show me the prospectus for AVI, Limited," he said. He laughed outright and slapped his thigh loudly when the prospectus flashed onto the screen. "Will he come?" Morgan asked Piggott Thigpen over his shoulder.

She shrugged. "He said he would. Who can predict what Sam'll do? But there's big money to be made tonight, Henri.

Sam'll be here." She waddled to her orthosofa and sank heavily into its cushions. Gently the sofa rotated into a comfortable position.

Val Carney sat in an ordinary chair beside his mistress. He frowned distrustfully at the orthosofa. He'd heard once that one of them had malfunctioned and crushed its occupant to jelly in a death grip. Maybe it was just getting even for something. He'd never be caught in one of the damned things.

For the better part of an hour the trio sat discussing the fourth guest as they waited for him to arrive. Piggott Thigpen clearly showed her frustration at being kept waiting. She had no choice but to wait, patiently or otherwise, because the fourth member of the party was the only man who could bring off the coup she and Morgan had been plotting.

"Madam," a servo announced politely from the doorway, "a gentleman calling himself Sam Patch is here to see you."

Sam Patch was dressed in a dirty jumpsuit. Except for the web of scars that crisscrossed his right cheek, his face was handsome. He kept them because he thought they enhanced the menace of his appearance.

"My ship was late," he said to no one in particular. He spoke without inflection in a flat tenor voice. "Reindeer Ale," he demanded of the servo as it rolled up to him. He snatched the glass from the servo and plopped into the nearest sofa with a sigh. As it began to adjust itself to his bulk, he said, "Stop fucking with me." Obediently, the device assumed the configuration of a normal chair.

Patch offered no greeting to any of the others. Reaching into a breast pocket, he took out a cigar stub and lighted it. "Nice digs," he said almost to himself.

"Sam, I'd rather you didn't smoke in here. The air scrubbers—" Piggot Thigpen began.

"I'll leave, then," Patch responded, getting to his feet in one lithe motion that belied enormous physical strength and control. "Send your proposals to me in care of the Hotel Milner, downtown."

"Oh no, Sam! It's fine! It's okay!" Piggott Thigpen called

after him. Halfway to the door he hesitated and then walked back to his seat. Val Carney, who enjoyed a good cigar as much as anyone, sniffed diffidently. The thing Patch had stuck into his mouth smelled like burning excrement.

Sam Patch was a man who had lived all his life on both sides of the law, usually the wrong one. But he was very smart and very quick and those qualities had made him rich—and kept him out of jail.

"Sam, do you know these gentlemen?" Piggot Thigpen asked after an embarrassed silence.

"I know Senator Morgan by reputation. Who're you?" he asked Val Carney. Carney introduced himself briefly. "He in on this too?" Patch turned to Thigpen, disbelief heavy in his voice.

"Yes," she replied.

"What's your angle?" Patch asked Carney directly, jabbing his cigar at the congressman.

"He has connections at the Ministry of Justice," Thigpen answered quickly. "And he knows someone who can provide the equipment you will need." Carney, whose eyes were beginning to water from the foul cigar smoke, glowered at the latecomer, but it was pure bravado. His instincts told him Sam Patch was no man to cross.

Patch only snorted. Then he said, "Well, I don't know what you're up to, but the fewer who know, the better, I always say. Now why don't you tell me why you asked me to come here."

The other two looked to Piggott Thigpen. She held out the gem from her neck. "Do you know what this is, Sam?"

"Yeah, one of those artificial gemstones created by AVI, Limited. One slightly larger than yours sold at auction recently for six figures."

Piggott Thigpen smiled. "You certainly keep up on things, Sam."

Patch gulped his ale. "I was thinkin' of stealing one, if you must know." The others laughed at the remark, but Patch had meant it seriously.

Swaying from its chain, the roughly raindrop-shaped stone

shimmered brightly. It was about seventy-five millimeters long by forty wide and weighed 100.13 grams. As light reflected off the stone's highly polished surface, the gem appeared to coalesce and turn almost transparent. Staring at it closely, one could almost imagine he was looking through a tiny window into a world composed of slowly shifting and changing clouds of many brilliant colors. But in the hand, the stone took on a life of its own, generating a sensation of warmth and security that, combined with its radiant, coalescing colors, could virtually hypnotize a receptive owner. That was why some people found the stones absolutely fascinating and would pay a fortune to own one.

All Sam Patch saw—and Val Carney too—was a highly polished stone worth a lot of money.

"What do you know about AVI, Limited?" Morgan asked.

Patch shrugged. "Avionics, Limited. They make airframes for atmospheric fliers. They figured out how to make these things ten, fifteen years ago and since then they've been selling them in small quantities on the rare gems market." He shrugged again, as if to say, What's so special?

Morgan and Thigpen exchanged smirks.

"Mr. Patch," Morgan began in his most mellifluous senatorial tones, "AVI, Limited is owned by the Confederation's Ministry of Science. The gems it supposedly manufactures in its 'labs' are actually produced through a natural process on a world called Avionia. The ministry began importing the gems for sale to help cover the expense of, um, monitoring events on Avionia."

Patch raised an eyebrow but remained silent, sipping at his glass of ale.

"It gets better, Sam," Piggott Thigpen continued. "Avionia is inhabited by an alien sentience—"

Patch abruptly stood. "Piggy, you've fed me a lot of lines over the years," he said angrily. "I've never believed any of them and I'm not starting now." He headed toward the exit.

"Sam, Sam!" Thigpen squealed. "Don't go. This is true! Really."

Patch glanced over his shoulder but didn't stop. "Then why haven't I heard about them?"

"Because their existence is a state secret, goddamn you!"

Patch turned back to the representative of Carhart's World. "How the hell does anybody expect to keep an alien sentience a secret? What's to keep them from dropping in on any world in Human Space?"

Madam Piggott Thigpen gave the control panel of her sofa an agitated slap and it raised her to an erect sitting position. Her jowls jiggled as she shook her head. "They won't. They can't. The Avionians aren't space-faring—they don't have the technology. They're pretty much like our Middle Ages."

"Fifteenth century, actually," Senator Morgan said.

"With everything that implies," Carney hastily added.

Patch slowly looked from one to the other of the politicians. *Maybe,* he thought, and returned to his seat. "Tell me about them."

"They're descended from something analogous to the birds of Earth." She nodded so forcefully that ripples washed up and down her body as she spoke. "Like many birds and reptiles, the Avionians require assistance in digesting their food, so they swallow a certain type of stone. Eventually, the stones are passed—"

"Then these 'gems' are—are—" Carney laughed.

"One man's shit is another man's bauble," Patch commented dryly, still not sure whether to believe them.

"Well, I wouldn't put it quite that way," Piggott Thigpen said, "they are more correctly gastroliths. But yes, the stones pass through the digestive tracts of the Avionians. By the time they are, er, passed, some internal chemical process in the locals has given them their unique qualities. Or maybe the digestive process enhances qualities already existing in the stones. Nobody quite understands it yet."

"How intelligent are these birdmen?" Patch asked.

"Very," Morgan answered. "As I said, the most technologically advanced society on the planet is about a thousand years behind us. When the world was first discovered about thirty years ago, it was decided the Avionians should be left alone, to develop naturally, without human assistance. The Ministry of Science felt that introducing twenty-fifth century technology to a fifteenth century world would destroy them. The ministry has been monitoring the place ever since."

Thigpen leaned forward on her sofa. "Avionia's existence was a very closely held secret until some idiot in the Ministry of Science got the brilliant idea that they could defray the cost of the monitoring operation by selling small quantities of the gastroliths in Human Space. AVI Limited was created as a front to handle the tax and licensing requirements. The scheme has worked quite well."

"But as government representatives, you got on to it," Patch said.

"Yes." Morgan took a long sip of his wine. "Avionia is just beyond the fringes of Human Space, so there have been no visitors except for government observers. The ministry keeps a space station in orbit around the place to monitor the Avionians, warn away potential interlopers, and to snatch a few stones occasionally. So far nobody's connected the gems with the existence of a quarantined world. And nobody has seriously questioned why the planet is under quarantine when they're told it has diseases deadly to humankind."

"And you want me to put together a crew, go to this place, defy the ban, and bring back a load of the gems." It was a statement, not a question.

"Yes," Thigpen and Morgan answered together.

"The split?" Patch asked, leaning forward in his chair. He was beginning to believe them. Unless the whole thing was a setup. But it couldn't be a setup; he had too much on Thigpen and she knew it.

"We finance the operation," Thigpen replied. "Henri and I split fifty percent of the profits. Val here gets ten percent. You get what's left."

"Agreed," Patch said without hesitating. He began to count off his requirements on his fingers. "I'll need two starships, a Bomarc executive-class vessel for my own use, and the smallest commercial ship available, one capable of landing on a planetary surface. I'll need that one for crew and equipment. I'll transport the gems in the Bomarc." He finished his ale and demanded a refill from the servo. As it poured the powerful amber fluid for him, he continued, "I'll need navigation charts and complete background information on this place, which I presume are highly classified. I need to know about the aliens that live on this world: how they communicate; if they are dangerous; will they interfere with my operations; what they might want to deal with me. I need to know the tracking capabilities of the space station if I'm going to reach planetside without being detected. That means I'll need pretty sophisticated electronic countermeasures and stealth suites. That'll cost a lot. I can put together a crew, no problem there, but you pay for them. I'll need money for my own expenses too. You got that kind of cash?"

Piggott Thigpen only smiled. "All the information you need is on this crystal." She handed a tiny chip to Carney, who tossed it to Patch. "There is also the name of the man who can help you with the aliens on there. His name is Herbloc."

"Tell me about him."

"He used to be with the Ministry of Science," Morgan explained. "He was 'retired.'"

"Why?"

"Greed. He collected several gems for himself and got caught. Since the entire Avionian operation is a secret, he was pensioned off and sworn to secrecy; criminal prosecution would've blown the ministry's cover. But he's avaricious. He has valuable knowledge about Avionia and contacts with one of the native groups. He'll be useful to you."

"Hmmm. Anything else I should know about this guy?"

"Dr. Spencer Herbloc is a drunkard," Thigpen said. "That was the official reason for his early retirement. One more thing, Sam. In order for this plan to succeed, we cannot flood the market with stones. You must leave their disposal entirely in our hands. We have contacts who can fence them slowly and surreptitiously at the best prices. If we flood the market for quick profits, the Confederation will get on to us, but worse, we'll be left with a collection of pretty baubles not worth what it'll cost us to get them. Do you understand?"

Patch nodded. He pocketed the crystal and stood up. "I'll study what's on here and get back to you within twenty-four hours. If I accept your offer, I will deal only with Madam." He nodded at Piggott Thigpen. With that he walked out of the room.

"Whew!" Morgan exclaimed and laughed as soon as Patch was gone. "Where did you meet him?" he asked Thigpen.

She smiled mysteriously. "We had some business long ago, Henri. He is a very useful man."

"And very dangerous, Madam," Carney warned. At Thigpen's request he had run a background check on Patch through a contact at the Ministry of Justice.

"Tweed will cooperate, Valley?" Morgan asked the little man.

"Entirely. He is too deep in my debt not to."

Morgan turned to Thigpen. "Can we trust Patch?"

"Of course not," she answered with a wet laugh that seemed to work its way out from deep within her mounds of flesh. "But he will recover the stones. Of course he will skim off a good many of them for himself, and, if I know Sam Patch, he'll keep at it until he's flooded the market with them. He'll try to beat us into the markets to make a vast fortune for himself and leave us with stones worth only a fraction of today's value. So I will have him removed after the first or second shipment . . . depending on the quality of the stones he gets for us. Trust me." She made that gurgling rumble of a laugh again. "Franklin!" she commanded the servo, "refill our drinks! We have cause to celebrate!"

"And scrub the stink of his presidential from the air," Morgan added sourly.

Sam Patch could have stayed at the finest hotel in town if he'd wanted, but a cautious man, he never drew attention to himself. So he got a room at the Hotel Milner on the outskirts of the capital's sprawling spaceport. A relic of the days before the Confederation moved its government to Earth, the Milner lacked the polish of the better hotels, but it was private. Spacemen looking for outward bound ships, crews waiting for consignments, and prostitutes and devious characters of all types stayed there. Patch fit right in.

Alone in his room, he popped the crystal Thigpen had given him into a reader. He was impressed that his new "partners" seemed to have thought of everything. He gave a low whistle when he discovered how much money they'd put into a private account for him at a local bank. The contractor, Tweed, was supposed to outfit him with ships. He read the reports on the Avionians carefully all through the night, making notes as he went along. He would talk to Dr. Herbloc about the aliens, but by the time he was done reading he already knew what it was he'd give them, the "Cheereek," for their help. He chuckled and made a note to require Tweed to equip the larger of the starships with a machine shop.

He considered a short list of men he wanted for the job. He had no intention of sharing all the gems with his sponsors. So he'd need Sly Henderson to work the market for him. Sly could handle operations planetside, reducing the personal risk to him as much as possible. Sly could pick the rest of the crew. And he'd need Art Gunsel. Given the tools, Art could make anything. And he would have them. Fortunately, Gunsel and Herbloc were both residents in Fargo. In the morning he'd contact them and set up interviews.

But he would have to protect his back. He needed someone to keep an eye on Thigpen and her friends. He'd known the fat woman nearly thirty years, and they'd done business before, quite successfully too. But she was not to be trusted, and when she figured out how he'd cheat her, she would turn vicious. Morgan and Carney were political hacks. They'd run at the first sign of trouble. But Thigpen would never be satisfied until she'd had her revenge on him. Patch remembered another man who'd cheated her. She had supervised the traumatic removal of his testicles and personally performed other indignities on the unfortunate gent. He would have to kill her to be entirely safe. He would arrange for that to be done.

Until then someone would have to keep an eye on the fat bitch. It would be easy enough to have someone bug her offices and monitor things there for him, but getting into her apartment would be a different matter entirely. He thought for a moment. The orthosofa! The company's chief maintenance rep, an old friend, lived right there in the capital. The complicated devices required frequent maintenance and software updates. He'd make it well worth his friend's time to personally service Thigpen's sofas.

He leaned back happily and drew on his presidential. Who'd ever have thought a pile of bird droppings could be worth so much?

Patch disliked Spencer Herbloc the moment he saw the disheveled scientist. Herbloc had stipulated the penthouse bar in one of Fargo's most expensive hotels for their meeting, and as soon as he found Patch's booth, he ordered a huge mimosa. The servo poured and mixed the concoction to Herbloc's precise instructions then rolled off immediately to attend another customer. As soon as the privacy shields were up again, Herbloc said, "Cheers, old boy," then gulped half the drink in one swallow. He sighed, belched loudly, and inserted his glass into the service console mounted in one wall of the private booth. Since the servo had already programmed his drink, it was immediately refilled. The console blinked once and added the refill to the tab. Without asking, Herbloc punched the keypad for "one bill." He smiled tightly at Patch, who sat nursing a glass of Biere 33 Export. "You called me, old boy; your nickel." He belched.

"You were on Avionia Station, Doctor. You stole gems. You were fired," Patch said.

His drink halfway to his lips, Herbloc paused, a look of alarm on his face. "I've spoken to no one about that," Herbloc stuttered.

"Unless you talk in your sleep," Patch answered. "You don't talk in your sleep, do you, Doctor?"

"Listen, boy-o," Herbloc replied, his face flushing, "I—"

"No, you listen, you fat sot." Patch leaned forward menacingly across the table as he spoke. "You can talk to those things. I need you to do that for me. You'll be very well paid. We got a deal?"

Herbloc leaned back, a self-satisfied smirk on his face. "Who told you I can communicate with the Avionians?"

"I know you can, after a fashion," was all Patch offered.

" 'After a fashion.' " Herbloc sneered. " 'After a fashion,' eh? Listen to me, boy-o. I could not only 'talk' to them, I could 'converse' with the ugly buggers! I did it through studying Avionian physiology and building computer models of their squeaks and squawks that I recorded in the field. And I learned to communicate with them like a native, me boy-o! That bitch who runs the station, Hoxey, and her stuck-up 'colleagues,' they all thought I was a useless drunkard. Well, I showed the bastards! It was me, Spencer Herbloc, who really got inside the Avionian head. Now it's all right here." He tapped his head with a forefinger. "They fired me; they can figure it out for themselves."

Herbloc's flushed face and rambling speech told Patch the man had been drinking long before their meeting and was well into a binge. He did not like that. Drunks were unreliable. But he had no choice. "Good." Patch grinned. "I'm putting together a team to go back there. I'll need you to go along with us."

"Well, boy-o, I don't come cheap!" Herbloc chortled.

Patch leaned quickly across the table and grabbed Herbloc's bulbous nose with his left hand. With his right he placed the blade of a razor-sharp boot knife under his chin. He pulled Herbloc out of his seat and forward over the table. "You have just been recruited, you bag of guts," Patch whispered. "There's no backing out now, no negotiating. You work for me until I don't need you anymore. You'll get what I think you're worth, 'Doctor.' Otherwise, consider yourself lucky to live long enough to go to Darkside. But you mess with me, forget about a one-way trip to Darkside, I'll fillet you like a fish.

Now you get your sorry ass home, pack a bag and meet me at Port Fargo at six hours tomorrow morning. Be sober or I'll remove one of your body parts with this knife." He let Herbloc go.

The scientist slumped back into his seat, breathing heavily. Quickly, as a man slaking his thirst at a desert water hole, he finished his drink. Half the liquid spilled onto his shirtfront but he ignored it and wiped his mouth with the back of one badly shaking hand. Eyeing Patch warily, Herbloc drew himself up with as much dignity as his ruined ego and inebriated state could permit. "I, sir, am your man," he said, and scurried out of the booth.

"I need a shoulder-fired, small-caliber, semiautomatic weapon that weighs less than a kilo and has little or no recoil. It should be equipped with a detachable magazine that carries no more than five rounds. I need a hundred of them. You go along with us to effect repairs and train the Avionians in how to use them. But I don't want them armed with weapons that would pose a serious threat to us, should things go sour. Can you do it for me, Art?"

Art Gunsel regarded Sam Patch carefully as they sat opposite each other at a small table in Patch's room at the Milner. The two had worked together before and they respected each other. He had shown no reaction at all when Patch told him the startling news about the existence of an alien sentience. "When do you leave?" is all he asked.

"I leave at six hours tomorrow. Give me a list of everything you need by tonight and I'll have the freighter equipped with the necessary raw materials and gunsmithing equipment. I'm going to sequester this Herbloc guy with me at Luna Station until everything's ready. I'll let you know when to join us."

Gunsel stood up. "See you tonight" was all he said before leaving. He had not once asked about pay; Gunsel was a craftsman, not a crook. He worked for those who could present him with an interesting challenge, one that would put all his skills to the test. He did not care how his employers made their money. He knew that Patch was generous with those who did good work for him.

At the Fargo Main Library he found an unoccupied carrel and slipped inside. "Good morning," a pleasant male voice announced from the research console as soon as the door was closed. "I am Jeremy Postlewait, your library assistant for this session." Postlewait's face appeared on the computer screen. He looked to be in his sixties with a close-cut beard and mustache shot through with gray. His expression was one of boredom. Occasionally he sniffed or coughed gently into a hand. "I must excuse myself. Allergies. My colleague next door has them too. When we both get to hacking away we say we are playing 'dueling catarrhs.' How may I help you?"

"Antique firearms. Exploded views, please. I will need all the information gathered from this session supplied to me on a crystal when I am done." Gunsel wondered if the image on the screen was a real librarian or a computer-generated personality. He guessed the latter, since Postlewait was so obsequiously polite, but he had to chuckle at the ingenuity of the programmer to invent such an oddball personality.

"May I have an account number to which this service can be billed?" Postlewait asked.

Art Gunsel started. "Since when did you start charging for your services?"

"Forever," Postlewait replied. "This is not a free library."

Gunsel shrugged and gave him the information needed. A menu flashed onto the screen.

For the next several hours Gunsel lost himself in the library's exhaustive firearms catalog. The technical detail he found there fascinated him. Occasionally he transferred something to a crystal. He would master the science of ballistics and the art of gunsmithing on the long trip to Avionia. What he needed was the data to permit him to do that. Eventually he found what he wanted in the pages of an obscure magazine published monthly during the latter half of the twentieth century: the Schumer .22 caliber survival rifle. "Thank you, National Rifle Association, whatever you were," he whispered.

The Schumer was ultralightweight, manufactured from aluminum and plastic. Gunsel would have to make every screw, every part for this rifle, from scratch. Should it have a collapsible stock? He would make one and see which model the Avionians preferred. Either way, the stock would have to be made out of durable high impact plastic with an aluminum buffer and recoil spring.

In another publication he found instructions on how to make an efficient sound suppressor. But would the Avionian primitives want a noisy weapon, to intimidate their foes? He would make one anyway and, like the collapsible stocks, see how the Avionians reacted to the device. Perhaps he would design a "deluxe" model with collapsible stock and sound suppressor exclusively for the use of the—Cheereek, did they call themselves?—leaders, to distinguish them from the warriors.

Next he turned his attention to gunsmithing tools. He would need an array of instruments so he could fix the rifles in the field.

He studied ballistics, bullet, and cartridge specifications. He decided on a .22 caliber long-rifle standard velocity rim-fire brass cartridge for his rifle. The cartridges would require extractor grooves since his rifle would be semiautomatic. He would use a smokeless double-base propellant charge, nitrocellulose supplemented by nitroglycerine in a ratio of ten-to-forty percent—he would determine the exact mix once he was en route to Avionia and had time to experiment. He found that smokeless power is produced by colloiding nitrocellulose with special solvents followed by a drying process and that the nitroglycerine bonded with the nitrocellulose and would not separate in storage. That would be an excellent feature for ammunition to be used and stored by the warriors of a fifteenth century culture.

Because the reference articles were, almost literally, ancient history, all the tables were in yards and inches and feet per second, so he had to make the conversions in his head. He decided on a forty-grain bullet fired from a barrel ninety calibers, or eighteen inches long, which was the optimum barrel length to develop the highest muzzle velocity, 1,150 feet per second, with a maximum range at sea level of about 4,800 feet. At a hundred yards that velocity would have dropped to 976 feet per second and hit with eighty-five foot pounds of energy, more than enough to wound or kill a man at that range. From what little he understood of Avionian physiology, that would be enough to kill them.

He would have to design and construct the equipment needed to make bullets and cartridges and load them. He would have to learn how to manufacture the high-quality double-base gunpowder needed to propel the bullets and then make a machine to load the shells. He would have to craft several hundred magazines, all from scratch. That should be simple, he realized. All he needed was a light hollow metal box, a base plate on one end, a spring and a follower on the loading end, the whole thing big enough for five tiny brass cartridges. He decided to make three for each rifle. That way each warrior could ride into battle with fifteen rounds. If that proved insufficient, he could make more magazines and Patch could sell them to the Cheereek for exorbitant sums.

He'd also need an indoor test range on board the ship, to test-fire the weapons as they came off his production line. The manufacturing process was complicated but everything he needed to know was somewhere in the data bases at the Fargo Main Library. And best of all, the starship would be equipped with a miniaturized, fully automated Dillon precision-tool factory suite.

"Information is where you find it," Librarian Postlewait said as Gunsel placed his final order. "May I ask you, sir, why you are interested in these old firearms?"

"Certainly. I'm an antique firearms enthusiast. I build them to original specifications and then with a few friends I run about in the woods, pretending to be a twentieth century American Libertarian. It's great fun."

"Goodness," Postlewait exclaimed, "thank heavens those days are long gone! Well, sir, do play safely."

"Oh, I will, Librarian Postlewait, I certainly will." On his way out of the library, Gunsel concluded that Postlewait had to be a real person; no computer programmer would ever create anything so hopelessly naive.

CHAPTER
SIX

Dr. Spencer Herbloc, distinguished graduate of several prestigious universities, sat groggily on the edge of his bed. His head throbbed and his stomach churned dangerously. He ran a shaking hand through the thinning hair on his bulbous head then sighed. He grimaced at the odor on his breath, foul with the fumes of the rotgut alcohol he'd consumed the night before. Apparently he'd fallen into his bed fully clothed. His shirt and trousers were crusted with dried vomit. "God, it must have been drunk out last night," he muttered. He groaned. Speaking made his head ache.

Carefully working on his balance, he got painfully to his feet and staggered to the bathroom console set into the far wall of his tiny cubicle. The effort made his head spin; his stomach lurched sickeningly. He leaned with both arms on the basin, breathing heavily. The short trip across the room had exhausted him. "Water, cold," he croaked, wincing at the pain that shot through his head. Dutifully the lavatory system spewed cold water into the basin. Cupping his hands, he gulped mouthful after mouthful of the ice cold liquid. That doused the fire in the pit of his stomach but left him feeling bloated. He splashed water onto his face and over his head; he put his head under the tap and let the water run over him for a full minute. Finally, soaking wet, he staggered back to his bed and collapsed.

He tried to remember the events of the evening. Up to midnight everything was still clear in his mind, the alcohol-induced euphoria, the admiring barflies, the beautiful prostitute named . . . named? He couldn't remember her goddamned name! He'd picked her up in the Fifth Reich Bierstube on Luna Station's fifth level. Dressed in second-skin stranglex pants and legionnaire boots, she'd been stunning, as her kind usually were to men who've had enough to drink. She'd prodded him playfully in sensitive places with her riding crop. Her costume had left her breasts bare, and they hung before his hungry eyes all night, as gloriously enticing as ripe melons. Throughout the evening Herbloc had tried unsuccessfully to get his lips on her enormous red nipples but she'd had no trouble fending off his increasingly drunken advances. She'd promised him a night of sensuous pleasure but he couldn't even remember leaving the bar with her.

But, clearly he had left the bar. He groaned and reached for his wallet. It was empty! He'd had a thousand on him last night, what was left of the advance Patch had given him for expense money while they waited at Luna Station for Tweed's ships to be readied. Some of the money had gone to buy round after round of drinks for the barflies he'd attracted. But Whatshername had gotten the rest. He'd been rolled. It wasn't the first time. God protected drunks, not their wallets. He could feel no new bumps or bruises on his body so he hadn't been assaulted. She must've picked his pocket when he passed out somewhere. At least that was something. One night a whore in New Carnavon had cracked his skull wide open to get at his money.

"Time?" he asked the clock by his bedside.

"It is now six hours," a melodious voice answered. He sighed and tried to relax. He vowed, for the umpteenth time, never to touch alcohol again. But Herbloc knew from experience that with the aid of hangover drugs he would be halfway human again by noon and ready once more to break that solemn vow. Why, he wondered, with a universe of harmless euphoria drugs available, did he have to be an alcoholic?

The buzzing of his door flashed through Herbloc's skull

like a lightning bolt and jolted him almost upright. "Wh-Who is it?" he croaked.

"Patch."

Oh my God! What the hell was he doing there at this hour? Herbloc rolled painfully off his bed and threw a robe over his stained clothing. He shuffled to the basin and turned the water on. "Come in," he said around the toothbrush he crammed into his mouth.

Sam Patch took two paces into the room and stopped. He wrinkled his nose.

"I'm fine, sir, just fine," Herbloc mumbled over the running water.

"Listen, you miserable gutsack, the ship will be ready by noon. Be on board, Herbloc, all your shit packed. If you aren't there I'll have my men come and get you, and once we're on our way, I'll have Sly teach you sobriety. The next drink you take on my payroll will have to be fed to you through your asshole. Now get yourself together, Doctor."

Herbloc's insides churned horribly. He knew Patch would not kill him—not until the job was over. But Spencer Herbloc had no doubt that Sam Patch would maim him very painfully if that's what Patch thought was needed to keep him in line. He turned his head and gave Patch what he hoped was a smile of confidence and poise. But Patch saw only an idiot's leering grin, one with toothpaste dripping from the corners of the mouth, when Herbloc said, "Not to worry, old man! I've never missed a day's work in my life because of drink."

Without warning, an enormous fountain of tap water and bile gushed up from Herbloc's stomach and cascaded out onto the floor, some of it splashing Sam Patch's shoes.

Art Gunsel had never been happier than on the long flight to Avionia. The Dillon fully automated tool and die suite Tweed had installed on the small freighter *Marquis de Rien* was just what he needed. With the detailed drawings and hundreds of screens of text produced by his research, he had not been seriously challenged in his effort to reproduce the Schumer rifle or manufacture its cartridges.

"Boy-o," Herbloc had said one day, picking up one of the tiny shell casings and examining it, "the Cheereek will be ecstatic over these things! They love shiny stuff."

"As much as you love booze?" Gunsel answered, hunched over his workbench.

"Humpf. Boy-o, a small toddy for the body is just what a man of advancing years requires to inure him to— to—" Herbloc gestured at the bulkheads. Somehow he had managed to smuggle a supply of whiskey on board the *Marquis de Rien*, but mindful of Patch's threats, he had gone easy on his drinking for several weeks. Patch's deputy, Sly Henderson, knew Herbloc occasionally took a nip from his supply, but so long as the scientist remained in control of himself, Henderson did not interfere with his drinking.

"You just better watch out you don't piss Sam off, Doctor," Gunsel said.

"Boy-o, we will see very little of the estimable Sam Patch on this voyage. He is leaving planetside operations to Mr. Henderson and keeping to the *Lady Tee*." The *Lady Tee* was the Bomarc executive-class starship Patch was using for himself. He did not plan to spend much time on the surface of Avionia. He certainly was not going to be there if anything went wrong.

"We, my dear Artie," Herbloc continued, "are under the command of the indefatigable Sly Henderson, a man in my estimation who—"

At that very moment Sly Henderson stepped into the machine shop. "Who what, Doctor?" Henderson asked.

"Ahem." Herbloc coughed politely, his face reddening. "I was just saying to our estimable craftsman here how much we admire your management and leadership skills." He bowed slightly at the waist.

"Shouldn't you be off somewhere, studying your Cheereek

lexicon or something? Brushing up on your chirps and cheeps?"

"Ah, no need to, my dear sir," Herbloc answered. "It's all right here, boy-o, all up here." He tapped his head with a tobacco-stained forefinger.

"Doctor," Henderson said, nodding toward the companion-way, indicating that Herbloc should leave them alone, "that's an interesting aftershave lotion you're wearing. Is that a hint of vodka? Or is it gin?"

Herbloc's face twitched in an embarrassed smile and he excused himself.

Henderson shook his head and smiled. Heavyset, about sixty-five years old, when Henderson spoke he was clear and to the point. He had little tolerance for men who would not follow orders, and he was well known around the Confederation underworld as a man who could follow orders himself. Even if those orders were to kill someone.

"Sly, why did you stick me with that overeducated winesack?" Art Gunsel glared up at Henderson from his workbench.

"Without him we have no operation, Art. He's going to have to talk to the Cheereek for us. And since he's the only one who can, you'll need him when it comes time to train them on how to use the rifles. How many do you have now?"

"Fifty-five. The sweetest little babies you ever saw. I'll have the rest by the time we make planetfall."

Henderson stepped to the bench and picked up one of the completed rifles Gunsel was polishing. He hefted it and sighted along the barrel as Gunsel had told him how to aim it. He set it down and examined a full magazine. "These little things can kill a man?" he asked.

Gunsel nodded. "Yeah, if you hit him in a vital spot. These little pellets, these 'bullets,' will leave this thing traveling at nearly four hundred meters a second. Herbloc says they'll go right through the Cheereek. But I made them out of soft lead, see, so they hit a bone and they'll flatten out to three times their size. Make a big exit hole. Also, you shoot them from far enough away and they'll start to tumble end over end. Make a big mess when they hit. Sly, I've been thinking. What if those Avionians decide to turn these things on us? Herbloc says these Cheereek are fighters."

Henderson smiled. The *Marquis de Rien* had been equipped with an array of the most modern—and illegal—weapons. It carried Confederation military infantry weapons for Henderson and the people who had direct contact with the Avionians, and the ship itself had weapons that could easily beat off even the most determined assault by the Avionians. But Patch had been very clear that Henderson was to avoid any contact with the scientists from the station. To be successful, the operation had to be totally clandestine. "Don't worry about that, Art. We have them outgunned." He smiled again, more broadly this time. "How're you going to train the Cheereek to use these things?" he asked.

Gunsel shrugged. "Well, guess we'll pick a few of the smartest and teach them and then they can teach the others. I'll hang around to advise, and if there're any malfunctions, fix them, of course. Sam said he expected we'd be out on this job a couple of years? Plenty of time to train the Cheereek."

Henderson nodded his satisfaction. "Art, when it comes to training the Cheereek how to use the rifles, you are in charge. Herbloc will be your interpreter. But when it comes to trading with the Cheereek, Herbloc's the man. That's just the way it's got to be."

Art Gunsel made a wry face. "Can't we just get along with sign language, Sly?"

Henderson smiled. "We just might have to, if that old boozehead gives me any more of those 'my dear fellows' and 'boy-os.' "

Because Tweed had installed a full array of stealth gear on both of Patch's ships, the captain of the *Marquis de Rien* was able to guide them to an undetected landing a reasonable distance from where the nomadic Cheereek lived during what Herbloc jokingly called "their brooding season." Once the base camp was established, the *Marquis de Rien* would remain on Avionia until the operation was completed. Patch, in the *Lady Tee*, would ferry the gems back to civilization. Under anyone else, that arrangement might not have been acceptable, but the men Henderson had recruited all knew Patch personally or by reputation, and they feared him.

Henderson had recruited twenty-five men, including the five-man crew he needed to navigate and maintain the *Marquis de Rien*. They brought with them a variety of skills and talents. Some would process the gems in a lab on board the ship so they would be immediately marketable once Patch got them back to civilization. There was even a small dispensary staffed by a doctor and his assistant, who were trained and equipped to perform the most delicate medical procedures. And finally there were men to provide security.

Since Herbloc was the only member of Henderson's team who had ever set foot on Avionia, the closer the *Marquis de Rien* came to making planetfall, the more important the scientist became to the whole operation. He briefed the crew on what to expect on the surface of Avionia. He proved to be a very good teacher—except for the fact that he was arrogant and peremptory, openly sneering at some of the questions the crew members asked. His superior attitude did nothing to endear himself to the hardened criminals, and it got worse the closer they came to disembarking.

"We are stuck with each other, like Damon and Pythias, boy-o," Herbloc confided to Art Gunsel just before landing. "Yes, yes, me boy-o, like Achilles and Patroclus, that's us." He laid a flabby arm boozily across Gunsel's shoulders. Gunsel shook him off angrily. "Oh my," Herbloc exclaimed in mock surprise, "Hephaestus, artificer to the gods, is a moody little chap, isn't he?" But he removed his arm.

"I'm busy," Gunsel replied testily. "Besides, I don't want to get drunk from your breath." When reasonably sober, Herbloc could be very funny and entertaining, but the more the scientist drank, the more maudlin he became. Herbloc's boozy bonhomie made Gunsel very nervous, and he couldn't stand being around Herbloc when the man had been drinking.

"Oh me, oh my, we *are* in a bad mood today, aren't we?" Herbloc laughed.

The land of the Cheereek lay in a southern hemisphere just below the planet's equator. Their continent was as yet undiscovered by the more advanced races in the northern realms. The nomadic tribes that inhabited the deserts and steppes were constantly at war with their neighbors. War was a way of life with them, so Patch and his sponsors knew that once the Cheereek realized the vast potential in gunpowder, a brisk and profitable trade in gems could be established.

Neither Patch nor anyone else involved in the human side of the venture considered what might happen on Avionia if the Cheereek, with their newfound firepower, ever figured out how to cross the ocean that separated them from the civilized tribes. In fact, they didn't care.

The *Marquis de Rien* landed in a narrow valley between two buttresslike ridges that flowed from the flank of a long, steep mountain range. A vast dry lake bed separated the great massif from the Cheereek country, about forty kilometers south. Henderson immediately established his base there. Except for the security detail, however, most of the crew preferred to stay inside the ship, since the weather was very hot just then. The air was also full of nasty flying things, insect analogs that were attracted in swarms by the movement of large animals.

Despite those discomforts, the crew was ecstatic to be on Avionia at last. Each man had been promised a percentage of the profits according to his importance to the mission. The crew of the *Marquis de Rien* was being paid the standard union wage for such a voyage and would receive a hundred percent bonus when the operation was over; Art Gunsel and Spencer Herbloc would each receive five percent of the profits. And five percent of what Patch expected to make would be enough to set any man up for the rest of his life.

* * *

"What the . . . ?" Art Gunsel exclaimed as he walked in on Herbloc and heard him making strange, birdlike noises.

"Oh, just practicing my maiden speech in the trade language of the Avionian nomad tribes. Loosely translated, I was telling them, 'Friends, Romans, countrymen! Lend me your ears.' Very important, Art, I get it right, or our first meeting with the Cheereek mugwumps might just go awry.

"Have a nip?" Herbloc offered Gunsel his flask. Gunsel shook his head. "Boy-o, you should not look down your nose at the nectar. As Scotland's poet laureate wrote, 'Well oiled by thee, the wheels of life gae skreekin' downhill with rattlin' glee.' What is it, boy-o, what is it?"

"I just came to tell you the landcar is ready." Art Gunsel's heart raced. Only he and Herbloc were to make the first contact. "You really do speak that crazy lingo, eh, Doc?"

"To perfection, boy-o, to perfection!"

"Doc, what's it like to go into one of their camps? You know, what are they like?"

"In the wild, Artie?"

Gunsel hesitated, not understanding the question. "Yeah. Where they live and all that. What're they like?"

"Oh, 'fraid I can't say." He shrugged, taking a nip from the flask. "You see, I've never talked to one in the 'wild,' as you might say."

Gunsel stared at Herbloc in disbelief. "Wha— You— You've never been in one of their camps, Doc?"

"Well, contact with the natives is against the rules, you see. I was only allowed to study them from concealment and from a distance," he answered lightly. "But not to worry. We took several specimens and I was able to interrogate them extensively on the station. None from the Cheereek tribe, unfortunately, but in our situation, mastery of the trade language is what counts, boy-o."

"But—But what about the rituals these Cheereek follow? I mean we can't go in shaking feathers if they greet each other by scraping their coxcombs!"

"Tut tut tut," Herbloc said. "We shall manage. Leave it to me, boy-o."

"Oh God!" Gunsel groaned and put his head into his hands.

"Artie, boy-o, calm must now prevail! Worry not! When we encounter these Cheereek, we shall, ah, um, well, ha ha, we shall simply 'wing it,' no pun intended."

CHAPTER SEVEN

Eventually, almost everyone got off third platoon's back over what really happened on Society 437, but Gunny Thatcher still had a wild one up his nether end over the mess the company had made of their hull-breaching training. True to his word on the *McMahon*, he had them spend every free minute training on the hull-breaching equipment.

"This doesn't make a damn bit of sense," Claypoole grumbled.

"Right," MacIlargie agreed. He hefted the blower he was supposed to be clamping onto a scrap of metal that simulated an airlock hinge. "This sucker's heavy; it isn't heavy in null-g."

"It still has mass in null-g," Corporal Kerr said with more patience than he felt. "Think of the weight as mass."

"You turn something in null-g, it turns you." Claypoole wasn't about to give up on complaining.

"Learn the basic moves. Then you can replicate them in null-g. Now shut up and do it." Kerr's patience was wearing thin.

MacIlargie got the blower clamped onto the simulated hinge and gave its handle the right twists. He pulled the trigger. The shaped charge went off with a loud bang and slammed its force into the "hinge." The metal glowed briefly and let off a series of pops. He lifted the blower and looked at what it had done. A small hole had been bored through the hinge, but was barely cracked. He handed the blower to Kerr and accepted another with a fresh charge. He clamped it to the hinge and fired. The metal broke!

Shaking his head and muttering under his breath, Claypoole clomped high-footed onto the plate of metal simulating a hatch.

"Step it up, Rock!" Kerr snapped.

"I'm simulating walking with magnetic shoes in null-g," Claypoole snarled. He clonked the end of the puller onto the middle of the metal plate and twisted its handle. The mollies slammed through the plate and locked in place. Claypoole lifted his arm to signal the winch team that the puller was in place, then clomped off the "hatch."

Lance Corporal Chan, in charge of the winch, clapped PFC Rowe's shoulder and said, "Lift it."

The winch screamed in protest and might have overbalanced if Chan and PFC Longfellow hadn't stood on its rear steps to counterbalance the metal plate. The slender boom bent under the weight it lifted.

Claypoole watched the winch. "See? That's what I mean," he said. "None of this stuff works right in the bottom of a gravity well. The metal's not cold enough for one hit with the blower to break it. The winch has to deal with weight as well as mass."

"And we aren't doing this in the right gear either," MacIlargie added.

They had the blowers, the pullers, and the winches, all designed to be used in null-g by men wearing armored vacuum suits, and they were using them in the bottom of a gravity well while wearing their normal garrison utility uniforms. It was a wonder the equipment worked at all and that nobody got injured using it. But Gunny Thatcher was determined, so as often as he and Sergeant Souavi could cobble together scrap metal to simulate an airlock hatch, the company worked with the breaching equipment.

Around the time they were having difficulty finding usable scrap, Captain Conorado made a surprise announcement at morning formation.

"A new suite of equipment just arrived at FIST," the captain said. "You'll begin training with it sometime in the next few weeks. I'm sure you'll do well enough with the new equipment to make Gunny Thatcher happy."

A pace to Conorado's left and rear, Thatcher's glower didn't look like he was anywhere near becoming happy.

"Someone high enough that mere company commanders aren't told how high," Conorado continued, "has come to the conclusion that the existing Fleet ship-breaching equipment is inadequate for the job. A new hull breaching system has been designed and is being distributed to every amphibious ship and ships of the line in the Fleet that carry Marine complements. A ground-training dummy has just been delivered to 34th FIST. An amphibious ship and a training hulk are due to arrive next week. Commander Van Winkle has selected Kilo Company as the first company in the FIST to train on it. They'll begin their training with the ground dummy tomorrow."

Gunny Thatcher's glower grew fierce. He thought Company L should be the first to train on the new breacher. Captain Conorado understood that his commander had selected a different company for the first training evolution because of Gunny Thatcher's almost fanatical attitude toward training with the existing equipment. Conorado was glad Van Winkle had picked a different company because he'd hate to see Thatcher's reaction if everything didn't work exactly right the first time some Marines from Company L used it.

"I'll tell you everything I know about it. The Tweed Hull Breacher"—Conorado didn't bother to consult the specs he carried on his clipboard—"is a self-contained, semiautomated unit designed to cut an opening through the hull of a ship without going through airlocks. It forms its own airlock, which will hold a full squad of Marines in armored vacuum suits ready to enter a ship as soon as an entry has been achieved." He smiled lightly. "No more blowers, pullers, and winches. That's all I know about it. That's also all the announcements I have this morning."

He turned toward Thatcher. "Company Gunnery Sergeant!"

Thatcher made a right face and raised his hand to salute Conorado. "Yessir!" he barked.

Conorado returned the salute. "The company is yours."

"Sir, the company is mine. Aye aye, sir."

Conorado cut his salute. A beat later Thatcher cut his. The Gunny turned to face the company.

"COMP-ny, ten-HUT!"

The hundred plus Marines of Company L snapped to. Conorado about-faced and headed back to the barracks. The platoon commanders broke ranks and followed their company commander.

Gunny Thatcher waited until the company's officers were inside, then clasped his hands behind his back and began pacing in front of the company. After a moment he stopped and faced them. "You heard the Skipper," he said with slightly less volume than a bellow. "We don't get to be the first to train with the new hull breacher. But I'll tell you this: we *will* be the best at its use. There will be no company in the Fleet more competent in the use of the Tweed Hull Breacher than Company L, 34th FIST. And I don't care how hard I have to bust your asses to get you that competent." He came to attention and looked the company over from one end to the other, then said, "Platoon sergeants, you have your assignments. Your platoons are yours." Glowering, he executed an about-face and marched to the barracks.

Gunnery Sergeant Charlie Bass, third platoon commander, had experience with new equipment. A few years earlier, on Fiesta de Santiago, he was the gunnery sergeant of a company that was assigned to give a new field computer its first true field test. Unfortunately, they were chasing real guerrillas at the time, and the guerrillas were armed with modern Confederation weapons and wearing Marine chameleon uniforms. The Universal Positionator Up-Downlink, Mark I, failed just before his reinforced platoon ran into two companies of guerrillas. Most of the Marines in that reinforced platoon were killed before Bass was able to establish alternate communications and get help. Unlike Gunny Thatcher, he wasn't at all unhappy about Company L not being the first unit in 34th FIST to use the Tweed Hull Breacher. He was downright suspicious of new military technology.

"Skipper, who tested this thing?" Bass asked as soon as the officers and senior NCOs reached the company office.

Conorado stopped at the entrance to his office and slowly turned around. He knew about the incident on Fiesta de Santiago. And he was aware of how the UPUD, Mark II, had failed on Elneal when 34th FIST was there; it was his company—and Charlie Bass's platoon—that tested it.

"I don't know, Charlie," he said softly. "That wasn't in the briefing material."

"Then who made it?" Throughout history some companies made superior military equipment and some could be counted on to make inferior products. Matters hadn't improved in the twenty-fifth century.

Conorado slowly shook his head, concern visible in his eyes. "I guess it was designed by someone named Tweed. Probably his company made it. Other than that, I really don't know anything."

There was nothing else Bass could ask that the captain could answer, so he simply nodded and said, "Thank you, sir."

When Conorado entered his office and walked around his desk, Bass turned to Thatcher. Thatcher was glaring at him. Bass ignored the look and dipped his head to the side, wordlessly indicating that Thatcher join him in the passageway outside the office.

"Gunny, can you find out?" Bass asked when they were outside. Thatcher had contacts that Bass didn't; he was able to find out a lot of things.

"If it was someone named Tweed and his company, what's that going to tell us? They don't have a record with military equipment." He looked like he wanted to punch Bass.

"If it's Tweed and his company, it'll tell us what their business is. Then we can find out how good they are."

"It was designed and built by Tweed Submersible Recovery Operations," Top Myer said, the company first sergeant joining them. "I had the same questions you did, so I checked it out during formation."

"Submersible Recovery Operations?"

Myer nodded. "They design and manufacture equipment to allow people to live and work in the deep oceans."

"What does that have to do with space operations?" Bass asked.

Myer shrugged. "They're both environments that'll kill an improperly protected man in seconds."

"There's a universe of difference between deep sea and vacuum."

Myer spread his hands then pointed a finger up. The decision to use the new equipment was out of his control.

"Any idea about how thoroughly it was tested?" Bass asked.

"I'm sorry, Charlie. I wasn't able to find out anything about the testing."

"Well, thanks, Top. I guess we'll just hope Kilo Company comes out of it all right."

"Let's," Myer rumbled deep in his chest. He turned and headed back into the office.

Bass looked at Thatcher. The Gunny still looked angry, but his expression also had a trace of doubt.

Under the command of a petty officer first class, navy ratings maneuvered the bulky Tweed Hull Breacher into position against the skin of the training hulk that hung in orbit over Thorsfinni's World, then applied a sealant to form an airtight lock where the breacher met the hulk's hull. Two squads of armed Marines in armored vacuum suits were already in position on the hull facing outward, forming a defensive circle around the unit. As soon as the first-class seaman was assured that the sealant was holding the large box in place, he signaled his sailors to jet back to the amphibious landing ship. When he saw that all his men were on their way, he jetted to the hatch in the outboard side of the breacher and signaled the squad of Marines who had trailed it from the ship to enter the breacher. Ten Marines tapped the jets on their suits and aimed for the lock. The first-class seaman caught each man as he reached the hatch and gave him a nudge to redirect him through it.

"All right, people, you've been through this planetside," Sergeant Sianfrani, first squad leader of K Company's first platoon, said into his suit's radio. "You know what to do. Move carefully and take your places."

Inside, the Tweed Hull Breacher was an almost empty room three meters high, six meters wide, and five meters deep. The side attached to the hull of the training hulk held the two halves of hatch that could join together to form the inner door of an airlock. With the hatch halves open, the cutter mechanism was visible, a rectangle bearing the gas nozzles that pointed at the hull. A sailor stood to the side of the opening, in front of one of the hatch halves. The controls for the hatch and the cutters were on a panel in front of him.

The Marines activated their magnetic soles as soon as they entered the hull breacher and took their places. One stood a meter in front of the blank wall that would soon be an opening into the interior of the ship. Three abreast behind him, the others stood back to belly, their blasters held at port arms. The compartment barely had space to hold them all.

When the last Marine was inside, the first-class seaman shut and dogged the hatch from the outside, plugged into the communications jack next to the hatch, and said, "Ready, Quincy. Run it."

The sailor inside the breacher pressurized the compartment then fired up the torches. Unfortunately, the hull-cutting torches had been designed by engineers accustomed to working deep in the ocean, in the high heat-absorption medium of water. The gasses, compressed appropriately for use at the bottom of a gravity well and under many atmospheres of pressure, shot from the nozzles at a far higher temperature and pressure than the breacher's nozzles were rated for. Tiny globules of molten hull metal began to spray about. The rest of the gases, far too great a volume to be consumed in the self-destruction of the nozzles, recoiled backward and ignited the atmosphere inside the chamber. In seconds overheated gas canisters exploded and the hull of the breaching unit burst open, propelling charred, dented Marines into space.

The two squads of Marines forming the protective ring

around the breaching unit were jarred loose from their magnetized holds on the hull and tumbled away. The first-class seaman in charge of the breaching unit was hit in the chest by a jagged chunk of metal torn from the bulkhead in front of him. The vapor that sprayed from his vacuum suit was tinted red with blood.

In seconds rescuers from the CNSS *PFC Thomas Parrish*, some in maneuver suits and others in equipment haulers and escape pods, raced out to snare the scattering Marines. By then many of the Marines had stopped tumbling, but only a few were drifting back. The Marines' armored vacuum suits had small attitude controls, but very little in the way of propulsion; they were designed for movement on a surface, but not for travel between surfaces more than fifty meters apart.

It took the sailors more than twenty minutes to get all the Marines back to the *Parrish*. Long enough that most of the men whose suits had been breached died before they reached an atmosphere.

CHAPTER
EIGHT

Dr. Omer Abraham, Chief Scientist at Avionia Station, leaned closer to examine the print in the mud. He swatted at a buzzing insect steadily circling his head.

"It's human," Bernie Korytsa said. Bernie was one of the ground crew assigned to monitor the movements of the local Avionian tribe.

"Well, maybe one of us came through here recently. Are you sure we didn't leave the print here last visit?"

"Doc," Bernie said patiently, "it's fresh. It's been made within the last couple of days. More than one too. I've been through this whole area. Quite a few people have been here, and so have the natives. Means only one thing, Doc: somebody's been trading with them for the stones." Korytsa admired Abraham, but sometimes the scientist got so absorbed in his research he failed to see the obvious. "And look at these." Korytsa handed Abraham three tiny brass capsules.

Abraham examined the tiny capsules. They were very bright, about twenty-five millimeters long, ten millimeters in diameter, and capped with a soft gray metal, perhaps lead, at one end. "What the . . . ?" He looked up.

Korytsa shrugged. "Trade goods?"

Abraham rolled the capsules in his palm. "They're shiny. You know how the Avionians like shiny things. Yeah. Trade goods. Well, the Avionians didn't make these things, that's for sure." He slipped the capsules into a pocket, straightened up, and wiped perspiration from the side of his face. "Shit," he said. "I knew we should never have gotten into retailing the gastroliths. I knew that would blow the whole operation."

"We make one orbit per day." Korytsa chuckled. "All they had to do was come in from the opposite direction—and we never look outward unless we're expecting visitors. Gutsy bastards."

"Goddamned criminals," Abraham snorted. "But you know what, Bernie?"

"They're gonna get rich, Doc?"

"No," he answered carefully. "Well, yes, if they get away with poaching. Yes, they'll get very rich, Bernie. But something else: they know what's going on here. They know there's no incurable plague infesting Avionia."

Korytsa shrugged. "So they took a chance?"

"Maybe." Abraham was silent for a moment. "But I bet they knew the plague story was only a cover. And if they knew, Bernie, that can only mean someone talked. One of us."

Korytsa said nothing for a moment. "I don't think so, Doc." Bernie Korytsa was not an academic; he was a man with vast practical knowledge and experience, and Dr. Abraham had come to respect his judgment. "We all sign the confidentiality and security oaths, and you know what happened to the last guy who blabbed. But, Doc, there are people high up in government who are cleared to know what we're doing here. And they don't sign any damn agreement to keep quiet."

Abraham was silent for a long time. "Well," he said at last, "let's get the team together and return to the station. Dr. Hoxey's got to know about this."

Looking ahead to the time when the Avionians would have full contact with the humans of the Confederation, finding out more about the birdlike inhabitants of Avionia was the major focus of activity at the station.

Descended from evolutionary analogs to the birds of Old Earth, but without ever having developed flight, Avionian physiology was strangely familiar to xenobiologists like Omer Abraham. This was because the Avionians also possessed features reminiscent of mammalian development. The Avionian brain, for instance, was fissured, much as it is in mammals, but with large optic lobes, as in birds. But most fascinating of all to Abraham was that the superficial cerebral cortex in the Avionian brain was thick and fissured, unlike that of birds. On the other hand, the corpus striatum, very important in avian brains because it received and integrated sensory perceptions, also appeared to play a significant role in Avionian brain function.

Likewise, both the cerebellum and cerebrum of the Avionian brain appeared to be of equal importance in its function. As a result, the locals possessed the motor functions of birds, such as excellent balance and the learning and reasoning ability of the higher mammals. How those apparently contradictory features interrelated so well was a major question scientists like Abraham were devoted to solving.

The station itself was actually a McCormick-class commercial space station converted for scientific research. It belonged to the Confederation's Ministry of Science, Bureau of Human Habitability Exploration and Investigation. It required a crew of twenty, and could accommodate fifty-five scientists and technicians. There were a total of three hundred scientists, technicians, and crew in the Avionian Program. The normal tour at the station was five years, so station complements—a total of three, with a fourth on standby from which replacements could be drawn—rotated at five-year intervals. Each complement was known as a shift, and was identified by a letter, A through D. Dr. Hoxey was the head of C shift.

Each person in the program had signed a contract with the BHHEI to complete at least two full tours at the station, which guaranteed a pool of experienced and knowledgeable personnel to conduct necessary observations and experiments, and limited the number of people who had direct knowledge of the project to a relatively small group. Good incentives—long-term, very lucrative employment—encouraged them to keep quiet about the place while performing other jobs between tours. The most binding, however, was that the contracts stipulated if an employee broke the vow of silence about Avionia, swift criminal prosecution would follow:

talkers were summarily consigned to a penal world, their sentences to run for life or until secrecy about Avionia was no longer required.

Until recently, it seemed to have been working.

At intervals it was necessary to adjust the orbit of Avionia Station, and it was assumed that the rocket burn had been observed by the more advanced Avionians, but since Confederation policy strictly limited contact to only the most primitive inhabitants, the effect of the firings in the night skies was unknown.

Officially, the station was in place to quarantine the world because a strain of bacteria deadly to human life had been discovered on its surface. Ostensibly, Confederation scientists were working to find a cure, to prevent its spread to other worlds. They could not do that safely on an inhabited world, hence the necessity for keeping a space station in orbit around Avionia. That story worked to keep most intruders away.

Strapped into the imaging machine, the creature, one of several recently abducted from a remote region of the planet, emitted a high-pitched shriek.

"For Christ's sake, Thelma, if you can't stop the goddamned procedure, at least turn the sound off!" Dr. Abraham shouted. He had just come into the laboratory, the mud of Avionia still fresh on his boots.

"It is essential."

"Everything's 'essential' with you, Thelma," Abraham grunted disgustedly. In fact, "essential" was one of Dr. Thelma Hoxey's favorite words. "Thelma, I've got some very important news—"

"It is essential," she continued, "that we discover how the creatures' brains function." Hoxey had been Chief of Avionia Station for two and a half years. She had been picked from the replacement pool after her predecessor died when his entry vehicle burned up on a landing. Her first edict after taking over had been that Chief of Station would no longer make any landings on Avionia.

"Thelma, three of them have died in that thing so far. They're ultrasensitive to the X rays."

"All right, Omer," Hoxey sighed. She signed to a technician to stop the imaging process.

"Thank you," Abraham said, relieved. He hated it when Thelma went stubborn on him.

"You are certainly welcome, Doctor." Hoxey bowed slightly. Dr. Thelma Hoxey was by-the-book and formal in all her professional relations. Her eyes connected with Abraham's. He couldn't help but feel a twinge of affection for her, but damnit, this was business and he wasn't going to back down.

The obvious pain experienced by the Avionians during the probes greatly disturbed Abraham. In his opinion, the creatures should be treated like human beings, not experimental animals. Hoxey, however, had already convinced the bureaucrats in the Ministry of Science that the experiments were essential to gathering a complete understanding of how the Avionians functioned. But just then Abraham had other bones to pick with his boss.

"Thelma, we've had visitors." He held out the three brass capsules they'd just found. She looked up at him inquisitively. "These, whatever they are, were left behind on the surface just recently. I believe someone's been trading with one of the tribes for stones."

Hoxey held out her hand and examined the capsules. Abraham told her about the evidence they'd just found indicating other humans had been on Avionia. Briefly he outlined his reasons for concluding they were poachers.

"Why didn't you look harder for them, Omer?"

"I think they'd already departed. Besides, Thelma, anyone who'd take a chance on life in a penal colony to come here wouldn't balk at killing a bunch of interfering scientists, would they? We're unarmed."

"Good God, Omer," she gasped. "What do we do if these poachers decide to come here?"

Bernie Korytsa, who'd been standing silently nearby during the exchange, stepped up to the two scientists. "Be ready to leave orbit at a moment's notice, and send a drone back home right now. Call in the Marines."

" 'Call in the Marines,' " Hoxey mimicked. She'd had plenty of time to recover her composure, and now she considered Korytsa's recommendation irresponsibly hasty.

Omer Abraham, lying beside her in the semidarkness of her room, reached for his cigarettes. "Smoke?" She took one and they lighted up. He drew deeply and exhaled. "Bernie— and I too, Thelma—think other humans have visited Avionia, poachers, people after the gastroliths, undoubtedly. We need to report this at once."

"But honestly, Omer, the Marines?"

"It's just an expression, Thelma. BHHEI will decide how best to handle the situation." For all her education and experience, he sometimes found Thelma incredibly naive and literal. "But we have to report this, love. Jesus! Poachers on Avionia? Why, they will not only ruin everything we've been working to preserve, they'll destroy the native cultures of the planet. We can't let that happen."

Hoxey only grunted and blew smoke through her nostrils. She was perfectly aware of the threat the poachers represented. But what bothered her more than their danger to the Avionian environment was that an investigation would require the presence on her station of people she could not control. Dr. Thelma Hoxey was very jealous of her authority as a shift leader. She could handle the constant disagreements among her scientific staff, especially over the practice of experimentation on live Avionians, but if some kind of police contingent were sent to Avionia Station to apprehend the poachers, it would not operate under her orders and would probably be able to override her decisions if there was a conflict of any sort.

"I don't see any reason to get too concerned without more information, Omer."

Abraham, about to draw on his cigarette, stopped in midbreath. "You don't?"

"Well, don't we need to know more about who might be

down there, darling? And if they've already got what they wanted and left, well, asking for the Marines might be over-reacting, don't you think?"

"Thelma, those men are probably still down there some-where, in violation of laws that carry the harshest penalties. They undoubtedly are armed. We are not. If we go interfering with what they're doing, they will not hesitate to kill us."

"Well, I don't want to do anything too hasty, Omer."

"God's balls in a basket!" Abraham shouted. "I swear, Thelma, there are times when I just don't understand you at all!" Angrily, he mashed out his cigarette. "This is serious, Thelma. We can't afford to delay sending a drone for help."

"It is essential we think this thing through, Omer. I want to discuss this with the staff tomorrow."

"Damnit, Thelma!" Abraham sighed. He knew how stub-born Thelma could be. He lit another cigarette. They lay silently together, smoking.

"Omer?"

"Yes?" He didn't feel like talking to Thelma any more that night. When he finished his cigarette, he was going to return to his own quarters.

"Let's get married."

Abraham started. She had to be joking. "We may as well be married, the way we argue all the time, Thelma," he replied. They had been lovers for years. Given the lengthy assign-ments, marriages and liaisons were a common fact among the scientists and technicians who staffed Avionia Station. No one considered it remarkable at all that C shift's chief scientist and its leader had paired up. They were mature professionals and able to keep separate their personal relationship from their official duties. But marriage?

Abraham thought about the proposal. Thelma Hoxey was a brilliant woman, if a bit stuffy at times, and still in her prime. She did not spend much time or effort on her personal appear-ance, but there was plenty of fire under that dowdy exterior. Despite their often bitter professional disagreements, the two got along well together.

"Well—okay," Abraham said. "We can have the administrator draw up the papers tomorrow and then—ye gods!" he exclaimed as Thelma rolled over and grabbed him. Omer Abraham forgot about going back to his own room.

"My my, don't we look a bit haggard this morning?" Dr. B. P. Gurselfanks remarked as Abraham took his place at the conference table.

"Ahem. Bad night, Chief?" Bernie Korytsa asked, winking broadly at Gurselfanks. The other two members of the staff present at the emergency meeting—Dannul Gragg, the station administrator and "Sparky" Markoney, C shift's communications expert—exchanged amused glances.

"Where's Thelma?" Bernie asked, kicking Gragg under the table.

"She'll be right along," Abraham muttered. He couldn't help smiling. The night before was the best night's sleep he'd ever lost.

Thelma breezed in, full of energy and smiling broadly. "Well well, let's begin!" she said cheerily, taking her place beside Abraham. "We have a decision to make, gentlemen. You know what it involves."

"Here are the options," Abraham said. He laid them out plainly: send a drone immediately to ask for assistance, or wait until they could find out on their own if the poachers were still down on Avionia and what their strength was.

"We particularly need to know what contacts they've had with the inhabitants," Gurselfanks responded. If the poachers had established relations with the Avionians, it might mean he could too, and thus learn more of their language, *in situ*. He chafed at the no-contact restrictions BHHEI had put on them. "I say let's wait until we know more."

"Dan?" Hoxey asked.

"Well, I dunno," the station administrator said carefully, stroking his beard. He never liked to commit himself until he was sure his decision would be justified by higher authority. Frankly, he wanted to know what the others thought before he volunteered an opinion.

"Sparky?"

"Thelma, you're the boss." Markoney smiled.

"We know where you stand, Omer," Hoxey said. "You too, Bernie," she added. "Looks like it's four to two. We wait."

"Just a minute, Thelma," Korytsa said. "Those tracks we discovered yesterday, they were still fresh. The poachers are not gone. But look at these." He picked several shiny cylinders from fifteen or so in a specimen bin. All but one were open at one end. "Smell them." He handed them around.

"Ugh," Gragg exclaimed. "What are these things? They have a burned smell about them."

"Look at the flanged bottom parts," Korytsa said. "Look at this one. See how it's crimped around the lead tip? I did some research last night. I think I know what these things are."

Hoxey raised her eyebrows. "What are they, then, Bernie?"

"Well, I think the ones with open ends are expended cartridges from a projectile weapon operated by the action of exploding gases."

"You mean *gunpowder*?" Gurselfanks asked, turning one of the little brass tubes in his fingers. "Why, nobody's used gunpowder in—"

"Hundreds of years," Abraham finished.

"Nevertheless, that's what I think these things are. Gunpowder cartridges. If that's so, then these poachers are supplying the Avionians with weapons."

Gragg looked nervously at Thelma Hoxey. "Thelma, if Bernie's right, why, these poachers, they'd—they'd—"

"If Bernie's right, Dan, these men will stop at nothing," Omer said. "And you can be sure they brought modern weapons with them. There is so much potential for money here that they would not hesitate to add murder to their other crimes."

"Good God," Gurselfanks whispered. "Thelma, maybe it would be wiser if we did call for assistance?"

"Maybe Omer's right," Gragg muttered. He handed the cartridge back to Korytsa as if it were still hot.

"Hey," Markoney interjected, "these guys, these poachers, they've got to have a ship of their own. They could come up here, Thelma, any time they want to. I didn't sign on to become a target for criminals. Let's call for help. Damn straight!"

"Have you spoken to anyone else about this?" Abraham asked Korytsa, nodding at the expended cartridges. Korytsa shook his head. "Good. Don't. We don't need to panic the others. Thelma?"

"Sparky, send a drone," she said, resigned but not convinced.

Abraham held up a forefinger. "One more thing, Thelma. Until help does arrive, we'd better not send anyone from here planetside."

"Omer! We can't stop sending observers. Observation is a prime directive!"

"Thelma, I don't know how many times I've got to tell you this, but those men down there mean business. They are—"

"Very well, Omer, you don't have to shout. I'll cancel all planetside operations until help arrives."

"What are you going to tell the staff, Thelma?" Korytsa asked, then regretted he'd asked the question.

Hoxey's face turned red with anger and frustration. "I'll tell them what I damn well please, Bernie. I am the goddamned shift leader up here! Sparky, send the drone. Call in the Marines."

CHAPTER
NINE

When Brigadier Sturgeon got the order, five months after Avionia Station decided to ask for Marines, it didn't take him any time at all to decide to deploy Company L. He thought if he rid himself of the immediacy of the mystery surrounding third platoon, he might be able to think more clearly about what they'd actually found on Society 437. He knew good and well it wasn't any goddamn microorganism.

Three days later Company L, mounted on Dragons, boarded Essays and were lifted into orbit to rendezvous with the CNSS *Khe Sanh* for transshipment to Avionia. Of course, all anybody knew at the time was that they were going after poachers on some godforsaken, uninhabited, quarantined world somewhere out on the dismal rim of Human Space.

"Why us? Why do we have to go way the hell out there?" Godenov wailed when they got the orders.

"Mother Corps sends, we go," Schultz rumbled.

Godenov cast a wary eye at Schultz and decided not to press the issue.

Fifteen days into the nineteen-day voyage, they assembled in the ship's physical recreation compartment for a briefing by Captain Conorado. The men sat on two banks of benches laid out facing a lecturn. Top Myer paced, hands clasped behind his back, scowling out at the men while they waited for the company commander to arrive. The platoon sergeants stood watchfully behind them.

When Top Myer spotted the company commander outside the entrance to the compartment, he stopped pacing, snapped to attention, and bellowed out, "COMP-nee, A-ten-HUT!" The Marines jumped to their feet and stood at rigid attention.

Conorado wasn't the first officer to enter the compartment. He was followed by a navy captain none of them had seen before. The captain went directly to the lectern. Conorado stood next to him and looked at his Marines. He appeared distinctly shaken.

After a moment he said, "Sit," and there was a brief ruckus as the Marines of Company L resumed their seats. If any of them had turned to look, he would have seen the platoon commanders join the platoon sergeants in the back row of benches, and that all of them except Charlie Bass looked even more shaken than Conorado. Bass had a look of barely controlled fury.

The seated Marines were concerned. Captain Conorado was normally unflappable. If he was shaken, it seemed they would be going into a situation far more dire than they imagined. And who was the squid? Few if any of them had ever seen a navy officer give the final briefing before deploying Marines reached their objective.

"This is Captain Natal," Conorado said when the noise died down, "from the New Science Division, Office of the Chief of Naval Operations. He just briefed me and the company officers on what we're going to find where we are going. Now he's going to brief you." He looked at the navy officer and said, "Captain," then stepped aside.

"Thank you, Captain," Captain Natal said. He glanced at the navy rating who, under the supervision of a petty officer third class, had begun setting up a holoprojector next to the lectern while Conorado spoke. "Thank you," he said, and accepted the control from the third class. "You may leave." The two sailors left the compartment as fast as dignity allowed. Gunny Thatcher closed and dogged the hatch so no sailors would accidentally wander into the briefing.

Captain Natal stood erect behind the lectern and studied the Marines in front of him for a couple of seconds before saying in a crisp voice, "What I am about to tell you is classified Ultra Secret, Special Access. That means there are very few people who are authorized to know it. Therefore, you are not to talk about this to anybody. Everyone on this ship who is authorized to know is present in this compartment right now. No one in the ship's crew, from Commander Spitzhaven to the lowest seaman in the black gang, is authorized to know. The penalties for divulging to unauthorized personnel what I am about to tell you are very severe." He paused and looked at them sternly for a long moment before he folded his arms on the lectern and leaned forward.

"We are not alone," he began in a low, earnest voice. "You are about to learn something that is classified at the highest levels. Only a few hundred people in all of Human Space know anything about this."

He pushed a button on the control and an image of a bipedal figure that wasn't very manlike at all appeared and began rotating above the holographic projector. It was large in the chest. Massive thighs swelled above spindly lower legs. Its neck, both in length and curvature, was swanlike. A crest of something similar to feathers topped its head, and a webbing that also resembled feathers connected its chest and upper arms. Its buttocks were conically protuberant. In place of lips, a rim of horny tissue surrounded its mouth.

"If any of you studied the history of science, you might recognize my opening sentence as the title of a mid-twentieth-century book on the search for extraterrestrial life. For a couple of centuries, encompassing both the twentieth and twenty-first centuries, there were numerous serious and not so serious searches for extraterrestrial life. There was a great deal of speculation about what it might be like.

"All along, there were those who said sentience was so improbable an evolutionary development that we were likely the only one around. It wasn't until decades after the discovery of the Beam Drive, which allowed men to explore the wide Universe beyond the home solar system, that those who said we are alone won out and the search ended. Well, they were wrong. We are *not* alone. There's a world we have named Avionia which has a native sentience. Avionia is quarantined, but not because of danger it represents to humans. It is quarantined to protect the sentient species that populates it."

An interested buzz arose in the Marines. But Captain Natal noticed that one block of Marines looked appalled rather than excited by the news. He wondered why.

He casually lifted a hand to quell the questions and exclamations. "In due time I will take questions. Right now, just sit and listen." The navy rank of captain is the same as a Marine colonel. When someone with that much rank tells enlisted Marines to shut up and listen, they do. Even if the man with the rank is only a squid.

"The Avionians are at a level of development similar to our own fifteenth century. If you remember your history, you'll realize that means they have a broad range of cultures, ranging from neolithic hunter-gatherers to something similar to the city states of Renaissance Italy. Think about it for a moment. The highest culture on this world is centuries away from such basics as electricity, efficient mass transit, and anything we would recognize as basic public sanitation. They don't have microscopes or telescopes. They think disease is caused by bad air or by devils. In most parts of Avionia, the locals believe they're all there is; they have no idea that the rest of their own world exists.

"Now think of the impact on them of contact with us, a twenty-fifth-century culture that spans more than two hundred worlds and can travel between the stars, which they think are lights hung on the celestial ceiling by whatever gods they believe in. Contact with us could be devastating to them. It might even kill them, literally.

"The Confederation has a choice. We can leave them alone, let them develop on their own, or we can contact them and quite possibly destroy the first alien sentience we have encountered in three centuries of interstellar travel. We, that is, the Confederation, decided to leave them alone until they reach for the stars on their own. Avionia is quarantined for the protection of its indigenous life.

"Unfortunately, the secret got out—at least to a few people. Avionia has a unique source of wealth, and no, I'm not going to tell you what it is." He barked a short laugh and shook his head. "That's all anybody needs, a company of Marines who find out how they can become fabulously rich almost overnight. You'd be unstoppable." He rubbed a hand across the short burr of hair on his head, then continued. "As I was saying, someone found out. A small band of smugglers has been trading with a relatively insignificant band of nomads in a fairly isolated part of Avionia."

He pushed a button on the projector control and the Avionian disappeared, replaced by a rotating globe that showed oceans, continents, mountain ranges, large forests, and major rivers. A small red circle glowed in the vastness of an almost featureless area on a large landmass splayed across the equator. "We might think the items the smugglers are using as trade goods are incredibly primitive, but they are advanced far beyond anything the Avionians have developed themselves. Imagine the impact on the Avionians if knowledge of aliens coming and dealing with them gets out. Imagine the impact on their development if this relatively insignificant nomadic tribe becomes powerful and manages wide conquest by virtue of having advanced technology." He shook his head. "I don't want to think about the implications, and I don't want the guilt on my soul.

"Your job is to put an end to the smuggling. You are to capture—kill if you can't capture, but try to capture—the smugglers, and destroy their base of operations. If possible— and quite frankly, I don't have any idea how it would be possible short of going to war—you are to retrieve everything of advanced technology that has been given to the Avionians.

"Now, are there any questions?"

"Sir!" Someone from first platoon jumped to his feet. "What *are* the advanced trade goods?"

Captain Natal pushed another button. The rotating globe was replaced by a primitive rifle.

"Twenty-two-caliber repeating projectile rifles. The most advanced firearms the Avionians have developed on their own are similar to Earth's arquebus, which was a matchlock." He noted the confusion on the faces of some Marines. "You probably know what a flintlock was. A matchlock is even more primitive. These .22 caliber repeaters are centuries beyond the matchlock, and with them one insignificant tribe is well on its way to becoming the most powerful military force on its world. Any other questions?"

A big, fierce-looking Marine in the block of men who looked appalled stood up. Anger blazed from his eyes and his chest heaved with the effort to keep himself under control. "Sir, with all due respect, I don't want to protect the aliens. Aliens are dangerous. We need to call for more Marines before we go down there and kill them."

"Or stay in orbit and nuke them," someone else in the same block said.

Natal blinked in surprise. The reaction of the two Marines shocked him. He expected surprise and excitement, not fury and blood lust. Before he could speak, a Marine in the back row stood up and shouted.

"Belay that, Hammer," Charlie Bass shouted. "You too, Wolfman. Both of you, sit down and shut up."

Schultz spun around to face his platoon commander. "Gunny, this is bullshit and you know it. Protect aliens? After what—"

"Hammer, I said shut up!" Bass's voice overrode Schultz. "You stop right now. Don't you say another word."

Schultz gave Bass a glare that would have made a lesser man back off in fear for his life.

But Charlie Bass wasn't any man, he was Schultz's commander, and one of the few men alive willing to go face-to-face with him when the big man was in a killing fury.

Schultz's fists clenched and unclenched at his sides. Veins swelled on his temples and throat. Nearby Marines began to edge away.

"Lance Corporal Schultz, sit down and be quiet," Bass said in a low, menacing voice. "That's an order."

There was absolute silence in the compartment, all eyes fixed on Schultz to see what he'd do. Slowly, rigidly, as though a wrong move would shatter him into a million pieces, Schultz turned toward the front of the room and sat.

Captain Natal avoided looking directly at Schultz as he scanned the company. Nobody else looked eager to ask a question after Schultz's outburst, so he turned to Captain Conorado. He had to clear his throat before he could speak. "Captain Conorado, that's the end of my briefing. It's your turn." He stepped away from the dais and headed for the hatch. Gunny Thatcher undogged and opened it for him then closed and redogged behind him.

Conorado approached the dais slowly, obviously thinking. When he reached it, he looked directly at Schultz, who resembled a volcano frozen in the process of erupting. "I suspect you were on the verge of saying something you aren't supposed to say." He quickly held up a hand. "Don't say it now either. We'll all be in deep shit if you do. I can forgive and overlook your upset, but I can't and won't forgive you if you get us all in trouble."

Schultz looked away and said nothing.

The Marines in the other platoons looked at one another and cast glances at third platoon. Suddenly everyone knew what third platoon had encountered on Society 437. It wasn't microorganisms.

"All right," Conorado said softly. "We know what our mission is. We are going to be seeing something virtually nobody has ever seen before. We'll get all the necessary details when we reach Avionia Station. We have a mission, and we are going to accomplish it. That is the beginning of it, that is the end of it. I hope everybody understands." His eyes didn't leave Schultz. "Now I'll turn you over to Top Myer, who doesn't know a damn thing more about this than I do."

"COMP-nee, A-ten-HUT!" Myer bellowed, and everybody snapped to, even Schultz. Myer waited until Thatcher dogged the hatch behind Conorado and the other officers, then began pacing. He hadn't had time to think about what to say because he wasn't at the briefing Captain Natal had given the officers and this was the first he'd heard of the aliens. Finally he stopped pacing and stood in front of the lectern facing the company, arms akimbo.

He looked directly at Schultz and said firmly, "Lance Corporal Schultz, the Skipper said he can forgive and forget your upset, so I have to go along with that. But if you get out of line like that again, I swear you'll find out you aren't the toughest man in this company. And I don't care how many of us it takes to convince you of that. Do you understand?"

Schultz returned Myer's glare, then nodded. "I understand, Top." He slumped, resting his arms on his knees.

"See to it that you do." Then the first sergeant started pacing again and began the unofficial briefing that he always gave the company shortly before planetfall on a new operation.

"The Skipper said I don't know any more about the situation we're going into than he does. Well, in the sense of what these ali . . . the Avionians are like, or who the smugglers are, or how the trading is taking place, he's right. Without more information, I can't tell you a damn thing about what's happening planetside or what we're going to do about it." He paused in his pacing to look over the company. "But I can put the situation into historical perspective for you. Captain Natal—" He rolled his eyes when he said the name of the navy officer, nodded when many of the Marines chuckled in response, then resumed pacing. "—said this is for the protection of the Avionians. There are a couple of instances in human history that clearly demonstrate the dangers involved when a relatively backward culture encounters a vastly more advanced culture.

"A millennium ago, at the time of the Renaissance, Europeans discovered that they could cross the Atlantic Ocean. On the other side of the Atlantic they discovered a whole new world, two complete continents that nobody had seen before. Well, no Europeans other than some wandering Norsemen who didn't stick around very long had seen them. Except, the two continents were already populated.

"In many ways the Europeans were the most technologically advanced people the world had ever seen. They were on the threshold of discovering the basic principles of physics. They were making major breakthroughs in agriculture, animal husbandry, optics, and machining. They had firearms, armor, and the horse. The people who inhabited the Americas were far from that advanced and ran a broad gamut of development. Some of them were so primitive they might have been paleolithic. Others were neolithic hunter-gatherers or agriculturalists. The most developed cultures were the equivalent of ancient Egypt's Old Kingdom, though maybe none were as advanced as the Babylonia of Hammurabi." He looked over the Marines again. "If that wasn't enough, few of them had writing, not many of them had metalurgy, and the little they had was gold ornamentation. And none of them had the horse or had even figured out how to use the wheel.

"You want to talk about disparity?" He shook his head. "The thing that saved the native populations at first, most of them, was the difficulty the Europeans had in crossing the ocean. It took time for enough Europeans to get into the Americas and do more than enslave a few small populations, or upset balances of power in selected locales. Eventually that changed as transportation became easier and more affordable and more European nations began sending colonists to the 'New World,' as they called it, and reaping its resources for their own benefit.

"That's when all hell broke loose. Over the next two or three centuries the European colonists effectively destroyed the native populations of the Americas. Many populations were completely wiped out. Sometimes it was accidental, sometimes the result of miscommunication, often the result of sheer malice. Ultimately, the uncontrolled contact between Europeans and the aboriginal Americans reduced the native population by as much as ninety percent. Many of the survivors, these descendants of neolithic hunter-gatherers and horseless and wheelless neo-Babylonians, devolved to a form of mysticism in which they claimed their ancestors had talked to trees, animals, and the wind, and lived in full harmony with nature—despite massive evidence that they had depopulated broad areas of their food animals, deforested large tracts, and collapsed water tables. It took another couple of centuries for these remnants of the native American populations to get over it and join with the larger human population for the common good.

"That was an example of contact with an advanced culture destroying a relatively backward one. It's also possible for it to work in the other direction, and the Japanese present a case that nicely illustrates the point.

"Incidentally, for the later reference, during the Rennaissance, the nations of the West, that is Europe and later the Americas, began a period of technologic development unparalleled in human history.

"The ancient Japanese were a warrior people, though isolated on their islands the way they were they fought mainly among themselves, and with great vigor. Nearly the entire history of Japan is one of overlapping wars. When they weren't fighting among themselves, the Japanese had ambitions of foreign conquest. They conquered Korea on more than one occasion, and at various times held portions of China. Then came an event on the other side of the world, in a place the Japanese had no idea existed—once more, it was the European Rennaissance.

"The Europeans didn't stop with the discovery and conquest of the Americas. Hell, that was an accident. The Europeans knew about China and its wealth and wanted direct trade. So they didn't only go west across the Atlantic, they went around Africa and headed east as well. By another accident, they found Japan. Japanese development at that time was roughly analogous to the European Age of Chivalry. It didn't take the Japanese long to realize that European might was a threat to their way of life, and they managed to rid themselves of Europeans and close themselves off before Europeans had a strong enough hold to prevent the closure.

"A couple of centuries later, the young United States of America decided it needed to open trade with Japan. To that end, the United States sent a navy flotilla to the remote island nation. The ships were larger and more powerful than anything the Japanese had. And," he smiled and nodded at the men, "the flotilla was accompanied by a company of Marines.

"Japanese culture was still at a level roughly analogous to the Age of Chivalry, where the United States flotilla and

Marines were far more powerful than the Europeans had been a couple of centuries earlier—armored knights swinging swords don't fare very well against cannons and minnie balls. Through a combination of cajolery, bribery, and threats, they got Japan to agree to open itself to the outside world and the United States got the desired trade agreements.

"The Japanese were shaken to their core. But they weren't about to give up on being fighters. They studied Western methods and technologies and duplicated them so that by the beginning of the Twentieth Century, barely half a century after coming out of their equivalent of the Age of Chivalry, they had become a world power. Neither had they forgotten their ambitions of conquest. As the Twentieth Century wore on they took a large part of Siberia, all of Korea, much of China, Indochina, Indonesia, and most of the islands of the central and western Pacific Ocean."

He stopped talking for a moment, simply paced back and forth, looking at the deck before his feet, thinking. Then he looked up and resumed. "The Twentieth Century was an interesting time. I'm sure you all know what sociopaths and psychopaths are. During the Twentieth Century several nation-states, major and minor, were headed by psychopathic sociopaths. Most notable among these were Hitler, Stalin, Mao, Pol Pot, and Milosevic. They were responsible for the deaths of eighty to a hundred million people.

"Japan didn't have a psychopathic sociopath as its head of state. During their conquest of eastern Asia and the Pacific islands they murdered untold millions of people. In one Chinese city alone, they slaughtered upward of three hundred thousand people. It was a hint the rest of the world ignored: that the entire population might consist of psychopathic sociopaths." He shrugged. "Were they? Nobody knows, nobody ever asked the question. All I have is my own suspicions based on their deeds.

"Anyway, during their time of great conquest, the Japanese made a major mistake. They launched an attack against the United States so they could take the Philippines, and convince the West not to interfere with their 'Greater Asian Co-prosperity

Sphere.' The attack didn't work. The war that resulted lasted nearly four years and culminated with the first use of nuclear weapons.

"Shaken to the core again, the Japanese proved their resilience. They rebuilt—with American assistance. Again they set about their campaign of conquest, but they didn't do it by force of arms this time. Instead, they used trade and economic manipulation. In a generation they were second only to the United States in wealth and economic power. That's when things got really tough.

"The United States and the European nations had, over several centuries of commerce, developed mechanisms for fair trade that benefited all of them." He held up a hand to forestall protests from anyone who had studied history. "I'm not saying their trade was fully equitable. It was relatively fair among themselves, because they had laws that ensured fairness. When they dealt with others, they could be, and often were, quite rapacious.

"The Japanese felt no such restraint. They were engaged in a war of conquest. One thing to bear in mind here. Among the European and American countries, government and business were separate. Government might regulate business, but it didn't run it. Japan was the opposite.

"I said earlier that at the time Japan opened to the west, Japanese culture was roughly analogous to Europe's Age of Chivalry. It's a very rough analogy. They had a knightly class, the Samurai, who fought and owned property. But there was a major difference. In Europe, the concept of *noblesse oblige* had developed, which was codified in the Code of Chivalry. What it meant was that the strong had an obligation to care for and protect the weak. Many of them didn't live up to it, but they did have the concept. Under the Code of Chivalry a knight had loyalty to his lord, his king, his god, his peers. He had obligations not only to all of them, but to those under him as well. Japan had the Code of Bushido. Under the Code of Bushido, a Samurai was required to have loyalty to the Emperor and to his lord. That is also where his obligations lay. Nowhere else. The Japanese were historically a brutal people."

He aimed an apologetic half shrug at Staff Sergeant Hyakowa. "Anyone weaker than you was to be stepped on. Any Samurai had the right at virtually any time, in any place, for any provocation, to kill a commoner."

He stopped pacing and looked at the spellbound Marines. "Lance Corporal Claypoole!"

Claypoole jumped to his feet and looked anxiously at the first sergeant. He hadn't been sleeping or talking, so he wondered why the Top was calling him out.

"Lance Corporal Claypoole, Brigadier Sturgeon is your lord. What would your reaction be if he told you to go to the barracks, get out your combat knife, and cut your belly open so that you died from the wound?"

"Top?" The question baffled him.

Myer shook his head. "You heard me, Marine. What would you do if Brigadier Sturgeon told you to kill yourself?"

Claypoole blinked a few times, then shook his head and said with some hesitancy, "Top, I think I'd have to say, 'With all due respect, Sir, go fuck yourself,' and then take my chances with a court-martial."

Myer nodded sharply. "Right. That's the reaction I'd expect from any of you. That's the reaction you'd expect from just about anybody who's ever lived. That's not the way it was with the Samurai. A Samurai's loyalty and obligation demanded that if his lord ordered him to go home and murder his wife or his children, he had to do it. More than that, if his lord ordered him to go home and commit suicide, he was bound to do that. And they considered it an honor!

"The late Twentieth Century Japanese applied a variant of the Code of Bushido to international commerce. They still had the Emperor, and the lords had become high government officials and business leaders. They worked hand in hand.

"The earlier Japanese saw nothing wrong in lying to anyone to whom they did not owe loyalty. The late Twentieth Century Japanese had no loyalty to anyone else in the world. Time and again they promised that they would obey the basic laws of international commerce, and then they conducted business in violation of most of those laws. Unfortunately, they didn't have the centuries of experience in international commerce the West did. They still believed the only way to prosper was to take over other countries. They became so influential in the economy of other nation-states that when their lack of experience in international commerce finally caught up with them, it caused the collapse of the economies of half of east Asia, and damaged the economies of most of the rest of the world.

"That's an example of a relatively primitive people causing massive damage when encountering a more advanced culture."

Top Myer stopped pacing and stood facing the Marines, hands clasped behind his back. "That's why the Confederation has decided to keep the Avionians quarantined. Nobody knows what will happen if we open contact with an alien sentience. The contact could kill them—or it could turn them into the most virulent enemy humanity has ever faced." He shot a warning glare at Schultz, who looked like he was about to say something. Schultz withdrew.

"I don't think there's room for any questions until you've digested what I said. Platoon sergeants, take your platoons." Top Myer walked down the aisle between the rows of benches and left the compartment.

In the small wardroom given over to their use during the journey, Captain Conorado and his officers were joined by Captain Natal. Conorado had earlier made arrangements with the captain of the *Khe Sanh* for audio to be piped from the physical recreation compartment to the Marine officers' wardroom. Company L's leaders were going to eavesdrop on Top Myer's briefing.

The first thing they heard was his dissertation on the state of development in Renaissance Europe. Captain Natal listened quizzically, his expression changing from minor confusion to consternation. He had the grace not to say anything to interrupt the Marines who were listening with great interest and occasionally shaking their heads.

When the briefing ended, Natal looked at Conorado and said, "Can you explain that, Captain?"

"Yessir, I can," Conorado replied calmly. "The first sergeant wants to tune the men up before an operation, get them focused on the mission so they don't make as many mistakes as they might. He sometimes gives history lessons. His details may be off, and his conclusions occasionally leave something to be desired, but he's often dead on. He wants to save Marines' lives. In this case, he also wants to impress on them the importance of a mission they might not understand." He smiled.

Natal nodded thoughtfully. He looked around the room at the Marines. "Thirty years ago I was about to enlist in the Marines. But a navy recruiter convinced me that life aboard ship was more desirable than a life spent slogging through alien mud while getting shot at. The first sergeant's briefing has convinced me I made the right decision." He ruefully shook his head. "I don't think I would have advanced farther than lieutenant commander if I had to spend my career matching wits with men like your first sergeant."

Gunnery Sergeant Bass, the only noncommissioned officer in the room, laughed. "No problem, sir; if you'd joined the Marines, you would have started off as a private and learned to coexist with first sergeants from the ground up."

CHAPTER
TEN

Jum Bolion hit the landcar's fans hard crossing the ancient lake bed. He wanted to raise the biggest possible dust cloud, before the Cheereek camp came into sight. After three visits planetside, he was learning to spot the guard posts by the presence of tall animals that vaguely resembled extinct, giant, flightless birds from Earth called, he thought, orstriks—something like that anyway. In the local language the animals were called something close to a warbled *eek*. He shook his head; he had trouble with the local language; it seemed to be mostly vowels with a bunch of slurs and a very few, very hard consonants thrown in seemingly at random. The Cheereek warriors used the eek the way humans used horses, as riding animals. The warriors rode them, that is. Females, young or old, walked. But the warriors rode everyplace they could—he'd seen a warrior step out of his nest, hop on his eek, ride ten meters, then hop off and step into another nest.

An eek that stood in place instead of running from the landcar had to be domesticated, and that had to mean a Cheereek was hidden very nearby. Up ahead, just off his starboard bow, a lone eek was calmly ignoring the roar and dust cloud of the landcar. On his right side two stood placidly together. Two more stood off to the left and paid the landcar no more attention than the others. That meant at least five guards were nearby—except they were too well hidden for him to spot. The Cheereek were warriors, they liked to fight. Bolion wanted to impress them with the power of the landcar; that would help keep them from attacking him and Herbloc. So he hit the fans hard.

Spencer Herbloc, in the passenger seat, chuckled and took a nip from his ever-present flask. He knew why Bolion hit the fans. He also knew which guard stations his driver thought he knew about, the three with the eeookks. He himself saw four others, but there was no need to upset the driver by telling him they were surrounded by more potentially hostile aliens than he realized. Herbloc wasn't concerned, however, about the potential hostility. He knew how badly the Cheereek wanted his trade goods. He thought of those fools up there in the space station and snorted.

A drunkard, was he? Hah! If a taste for the juice was just cause for termination, he knew scores of other scientists who should be sacked. No, it wasn't his drinking that had cost him his position, it was jealousy, pure and simple. He was sure that bitch Hoxey was behind it. She was "studying" the Avionians by vivisecting captives. Sure, she learned things about Avionian neurology and brain-control functions that couldn't be learned by other means, but he was making faster progress in deciphering their language and discovering their responses to various stimuli through limited, carefully controlled contact with select Avionians in their own environment. He conducted standardized psychological tests and applied basic anthropological parameters. So what if almost all direct contact between humans and the indigenes was forbidden? His research was more direct and was proving more immediately fruitful. It was putting Hoxey's "studies" in jeopardy. So they'd conspired to entrap him for stealing the stones. He snorted again. He wasn't the only one who picked up a few of the gems for personal use. Everyone who went planetside did. And everyone who went planetside gave a few stones to the mugwumps who stayed in the station and never ventured to Avionia's surface.

He gritted his teeth when he remembered how they had threatened him with that semilegendary horror called Darkside. He didn't have hard proof that others were taking stones for themselves—and he had no legally admissible record of the gems he gave the mugwumps—it would have been his word against theirs. If he'd had the proof, he would have threatened to blow the lid off the entire operation. But he didn't have that proof! So when faced with the choice of dismissal for incapacitating alcholism or disappearance onto Darkside, he accepted dismissal and reinitialed that absurd agreement not to divulge anything to anyone. He grinned, recalling that he hadn't had to divulge anything. Someone came to him and hired him to do what someone else had told them he could do. So there he was, dealing with the Cheereek again, getting richer than he would have ever imagined. He took another nip.

Bolion cast a quick, concerned look at Herbloc. Sometimes the man worried him even more than the Cheereek warriors did. He believed Herbloc was mentally unstable, the kind of man who could do something that would get them all killed.

The landcar reached the far side of the lake bed, and Bolion brought it up to full power so it seemed to fly up the ancient embankment. They roared into the Cheereek camp, sending females, young ones, and oldsters scattering out of their way. He no longer needed to be told where to go—the high latticework of scrap that looked so flimsy was his destination. When he pulled the landcar up in front of the High Tree, Bolion held the machine on hover for several seconds to raise a huge cloud of dust.

Herbloc laughed delightedly. "That's the way to impress these birdmen, boy-o! Let them eat more dust than an entire herd of their eeookks can raise." He chortled and looked at the ceiling of the landcar's control cabin as though he could see through it. "We're going to have to wade through a thick layer of dust when we get up there. They'll probably still be choking and coughing when we walk in." He took another nip and eased back in the seat to wait for the dust to settle.

"Do you have them?" Graakaak demanded as soon as the ritual challenges and obeisances were completed. A sharp glance stopped the slaves who were bringing out the Clumsy Ones' perch. The humans weren't going to squat comfortably on that visit. After the way they fouled his nest with the dust of their arrival, the only reason he didn't have them held for lengthy, painful death was his overwhelming desire for more of their weapons. Even though their defeat of the Aawk-vermin made the Cheereek far more powerful than they had been, there were still more powerful tribes to conquer, and he didn't yet have sufficient strength. If he killed these two, he was afraid the others would deal with his enemies.

So, instead of allowing them to rest their thighs on that odd perch they favored, he left the Clumsy Ones standing in their precarious balance and spoke to them in insulting tones.

"We have fifty rifles and two thousand rounds with us, High Chief," the one called Heerk-kloock replied. Like Graakaak, he spoke in the simple trading language used by the steppe people.

"Only fifty?" Graakaak stood and held his arms bowed out to the side, his neck stretched threateningly forward. "You promised me a hundred!"

"We have a hundred, and four thousand shooting-stones, just as promised," Herbloc said, and twisted his soft mouth-parts in that obscene manner the Clumsy Ones insisted was an expression of friendship. "We put the rest elsewhere. Once we have what we came for, we will lead you to them."

Graakaak hissed, and his guards became even more alert than they already were. Several leveled their weapons at the humans.

"You do not trust me to keep my end of the bargain?" Graakaak's eyes glittered with menace.

Bolion blanched and swallowed, his fingertips tatting on the holster of his hand-blaster.

Herbloc didn't seem fazed by Graakaak's overt hostility. "High Chief, a failure to trust is not part of the equation," he said in English. If the trading language could express that concept, he didn't know the words.

Graakaak hissed threateningly.

Herbloc leaned forward and splayed his own arms. "I am following the business practices of my people," he said, switching back to the trading language. "We pay half down and half on delivery when we buy something of value."

Graakaak held his attack posture. "Your mount has a hard shell, hard enough to stop the shooting-stones from our weapons. It is faster than our eeookks. How do I know you will not run and not pay us the other half?"

Herbloc pulled back from the threat posture. "You will know because I will ride with you on an eeookk."

Bolion forgot about the guards and gaped at Herbloc. "H-How . . . ?"

"Don't worry about it, boy-o. I know what I'm doing."

Graakaak slowly drew back from his threat posture. Yes, if Heerk-kloock rode an eeookk, he could not run from the Cheereek. "Let it be so," he said, and resumed his perch. "You may collect your goods. A slave will show you the way."

Both sides were impatient for their trade goods. Previously, the humans had only given the Cheereek a dozen rifles and a couple of hundred rounds on each trip planetside. This trip would garner enough gems for them to take a trip back into the civilized parts of Human Space, and a chance for some well-earned R&R on Carhart's World, or wherever Sam Patch decided to take them.

A naked Cheereek with its crest clipped off tottered into the room, carefully balanced on legs held straight and neck stretched up. It went to the tent's entrance and clambered to the ground. Herbloc and Bolion followed. At a nod from Graakaak, Chief of Staff Oouhoouh went with them.

Guard Captain Cheerpt and Scout Captain Kkaacgh stood in positions of honor behind the High Chief, ostensibly guarding his back. Kkaacgh watched the two Clumsy Ones and wondered whether they could be trusted at all. He suspected the pouch the quiet one tapped with his fingers contained a weapon that was more powerful than even the weapons the Clumsy Ones traded to the Cheereek. He wondered if he should say something about it to the High Chief—visitors should not be allowed to come armed into the High Tent. Cheerpt wondered if he could somehow follow the Clumsy Ones after the transfer and find their roost, find where they kept their cache of weapons. He knew if he could capture that cache, nothing could stand between him and becoming

High Chief. Especially if he could also capture a cache of the even more powerful weapons he was certain the Clumsy Ones carried in the pouches at their hips.

"We're close," Herbloc said as they neared the eastern fringe of the Cheereek camp. "You smell it?"

Bolion grunted. Of course he smelled it. He felt it in his eyes and the back of his throat as well.

"They must be the work party." Herbloc gestured toward a group of eight or ten crestless Cheereek that stood waiting.

Herbloc and Bolion put on the gas masks they'd picked up when they stopped at the landcar to hand the rifles and ammunition they'd brought with them over to Oouhoouh. They had also changed into disposable overalls and picked up their sifting equipment. In another twenty-five paces they reached the drop-off the crestless slaves stood next to. The slaves exposed their soft parts to the humans and waited for orders. The six warriors Oouhoouh sent with them to guard Cheereek interests and make sure the Clumsy Ones didn't take more than permitted readied the collection bags.

Before them a pit six feet deep stretched more than a hundred meters from side to side and half that across. A trelliswork was erected over the pit. Cheereek squatted here and there on the trellis, dropping black-speckled white globs from beneath their tail-nubs.

"Guano," Herbloc said, his voice hollow-sounding through the gas mask.

"What?"

"Guano. There are places on Earth where birds shit. If enough of them shit in one place it builds up to pretty considerable depths. It used to be mined for use as fertilizer."

Bolion looked at him, his horrified expression hidden behind his mask. "People did that? The mining, I mean?"

Herbloc nodded. "They didn't use gas masks either."

"Did it smell like this?"

Herbloc nodded again and grimaced behind his mask. He should have taken a nip before he put the mask on, but he wasn't about to take it off there. The odor emitted from the "lavatory" not only gave off an incredibly acrid stench, it burned the eyes and nasal passages. He suspected it would kill a man who was exposed to it for too long. He didn't even want to think of what might happen to a human who fell into the pit.

"No point in standing around when we've got slaves waiting for orders." Using a combination of words and gestures, Herbloc told the slaves what he wanted them to do. The slaves jumped into the pit, went out about fifteen meters, and began scooping out the black-speckled goop. They carried the goop to the pit side and began making a pile of it. The goop was soft, too unstable to make a very high mound.

Bolion shook his head and tried to ease his suddenly queasy stomach. "How can they stand to do that?"

"Your own farts never smell as bad as other people's. Besides, they're slaves, they don't have any choice."

Using small shovels, the two humans scooped the droppings into the sifter. When it was full enough, Herbloc aimed the disposer tube toward a vacant area of the pit and turned on the power. A whirring sounded inside the sifter, then a cone of white jetted out of the disposer tube and spatted down about thirty feet away. Very little of it got onto the trelliswork.

"Wish I knew how this thing worked," Bolion muttered.

"What?"

"I wish I knew how the sifter worked," Bolion said more loudly.

"Why?" Herbloc watched the indicator that showed the volume still remaining in the hopper.

"What do we do if it breaks while we're here? Do you know how to fix it?"

Herbloc shook his head. "I'm a psychologist and anthropologist, not an engineer or a mechanic. I know how to work it, not how it works." The indicator showed the hopper was empty. He flipped off the power and opened the hopper. He made a displeased noise when he saw it was empty. "More." He began scooping more of the goop into the hopper. Bolion joined him.

"So what happens if it breaks? Are we supposed to root

through this shit with our hands? If I knew how it worked, I could fix it if it breaks."

Herbloc laughed. "The engineers who designed and built this sifter were paid very well to make sure it didn't break down." The hopper was filled again. He closed the lid and turned the power back on. He checked the direction of the spray while he continued, "And it was made very clear to them what would happen if it did break."

Bolion swallowed behind his gas mask. He'd never met the people behind the operation and didn't even know their names, but he'd heard rumors about how they operated. They were vicious, and wouldn't hesitate to kill anyone who crossed them. If it wasn't for the fantastic amount of money he was making, he'd quit—if he had a way to leave and go home. But he didn't, so he did his job and made more money than he ever imagined.

The indicator showed empty again. Herbloc powered down, opened the hopper, and exclaimed in glee. He dipped a gloved hand into the hopper and withdrew a tiny stone. The irregularly shaped, finely polished stone was covered with a grayish film. Even through the film, they could see its iridescent glow. "There's two years' rich living for a working stiff's family in this little pebble." He handed the stone to a guard who dropped it into one of the collection bags.

They refilled the hopper. Six hours later the four collection bags the guards had were full of the stones.

"Time to go, boy-o. The mugwump won't like it if we try to take more." He briefly looked out over the pit. "We need to get access to the mugwump's privy," he murmured. "He uses better stones."

Bolion grunted. His back was hurting a bit from bending to fill the hopper and his legs were tired from standing for so long. Just then he didn't care about stone quality. They stopped fifteen meters from the pit and stripped off their overalls, then headed toward the landcar which waited in front of the High Tree. Behind them two slaves scooped up the discarded, contaminated overalls and gloves. To the slaves the garments were wealth, which was why they didn't mind doing the filthiest job any slave had ever had to perform.

Graakaak waited next to the landcar and watched carefully when Bolion opened a small storage bay on the vehicle's side and his guards dumped the contents of the four collection bags into it. Then he looked at Herbloc and said in the trading language, "Your mount is there." He pointed at one of two eeookks that stood riderless in a cluster of mounted animals. The mounted Cheereek included Cheerpt and Kkaacgh.

Herbloc looked at the animal. It was smaller than the others that stood around it and looked feebler. He shook his head. "No. I'm too heavy, that one can't carry me." He knew that for all their upper body mass and the size of their thighs, the Avionians were much lighter than humans. Even though the Cheereek warriors were taller than he, he outweighed them.

Graakaak looked down at the puny Clumsy One and hissed. "You ride that one," he insisted.

Herbloc shrugged expressively. "If you insist." He walked to the animal and put a hand on its throat the way he'd seen Cheereek warriors do it. Now to find out if the training I've been doing on the pommel horse pays off, he thought, and bounded up to throw a leg over the eeookk's back. His mount would have been perfect if his weight hadn't staggered it. As it was, he barely kept from falling off the other side. The eeookk squawked a protest and braced itself against the unaccustomed weight.

Herbloc lifted a palm. "See, I told you I'm too heavy for this one."

"You did that with your clumsy mount," Graakaak snapped. "We go now." He gracefully bounded onto his own eeookk.

Herbloc made a face. "Lead on," he told Bolion.

"You want a full dust cloud?"

"Just remember I'll be following you. Don't get me too dirty."

Bolion shrugged, then boarded the landcar and started it

with a roar. He didn't raise as large a dust cloud as on the way to the camp.

Five kilometers beyond where the Cheereek guard posts could see the dust cloud from a landcar, Bolion stopped in the shade of an outcropping of igneous rock and dismounted. Even though he'd driven slowly, he had to wait several minutes for Herbloc and the Cheereek to catch up. When they arrived, the reason they hadn't kept up was obvious—Herbloc's eeookk looked like it was about to collapse underneath him.

Herbloc stretched and twisted from side to side to loosen his back. The pommel horse excercises might have helped him get onto an eeookk, but they didn't do a thing to help him ride. He ached in too many places to catalog.

"Show them," he said to Bolion before Graakaak could express the impatience that was visibly growing in him.

Bolion grabbed a prybar from the landcar and went to the outcropping. He used the bar to lever a small boulder away from the foot of the rock to reveal a cavity. He pulled one of several wooden cases from the cavity and pried it open to expose the rifles it held.

Graakaak gestured and two warriors dismounted and shouldered Bolion away from the cavity. They pulled more cases out, then groped for more.

"That's all of it," Herbloc said when six cases were exposed.

Bolion pried all the cases open. Five cases each held ten rifles, the other had two ammunition canisters of five hundred rounds each.

Graakaak preened at the sight of all those weapons. "Go away, Heerk-kloock. Come back when you have more weapons for me."

Herbloc nodded. "I'll come back when you have more shit for me." He signaled Bolion. The two humans got in the landcar and took off.

Herbloc took a deep swig from his flask as soon as they were moving. "This time it truly is medicinal," he said. "Riding that damn thing was a lot more uncomfortable than I imagined." He arched his back and kneaded it in the small, then gingerly repositioned himself on the seat in an attempt to avoid aggravating the chafed area.

Behind them Graakaak momentarily considered the exhausted eeookk Herbloc had ridden. "When we get back to camp, feed it to the slaves," he said.

Kkaacgh looked after the speeding landcar. It was going too fast for him to follow, but he knew more of its route than he had before. Perhaps the next time it came he could wait for it beyond the Frying Rocks and follow it to its roost.

CHAPTER ELEVEN

"What did he say?" Gunsel asked. One of the five Cheereek warriors Graakaak had picked to be trainers for the rest of his tribe, squatting before Gunsel, apparently had asked a question.

"Translating very loosely, he asked if this new weapon is magic or science," Herbloc responded. "I told him, of course, that it was magic." Herbloc laughed then took a nip from his ever-present flask.

Gunsel was gaining new respect for the birdmen. The day before, he'd given Graakaak a private session at a makeshift range on the outskirts of the Cheereek village. In front of his warriors, the great chief himself could never stoop to take lessons from anyone, much less humans, so Gunsel went one-on-one. The chief had been a quick study. After several near misses at fifty meters, he had actually put five rounds into the target.

"Aw, you didn't tell him *that*, did you, Doc?" That the warrior knew the difference between science and magic had impressed the artificer. Gunsel was a craftsman and he enjoyed sharing his skill with others, even if they were smelly Avionians who didn't know a hawk from a handsaw.

"No, no, boy-o," Herbloc answered, raising the flask to his lips again. "One must give credit where credit is due, and you are due much. I told him it was science and you are the chief practitioner. Please, Guns, get on with it, would you? Christ on a conveyor, it's *hot* out here."

Gunsel had manufactured a mock-up of the Schumer Survival Rifle with larger-than-life-size movable parts. He intended to use it to demonstrate the functioning of the weapon.

He wanted to start with a description of the parts and then explain how they worked when the weapon was fired. Herbloc was there to translate. The day before, training Graakaak, Gunsel had not gone into the nomenclature, assuming that all the chief needed to know was how to load, aim, and fire the weapon. But with the would-be instructors he wanted to go into more detail. In addition to basic maintenance, he was hoping to teach the five warriors how to quickly clear jams and other malfunctions. The rifles were self-lubricating so all a shooter had to do was swab the bore occasionally and keep as much dirt out of the receiver as possible, but he wanted them to be able to field-strip the weapon, identify the components, and be able to replace defective parts. The five warriors personally selected by Graakaak himself needed to know such things if they were to teach others how to use the rifles.

"All right," he told the attentive warriors, "this here is the 'operating rod handle.' You pull it to the rearward to charge the weapon, like so." He pulled the mock rifle's operating rod lever to the rear, exposing the dummy round loaded into the magazine.

"Hold on, boy-o." Herbloc held up a hand. "There is no word for 'operating rod handle' in their language. The best I can do is 'pull work thing back to work.' Remember, the Cheereek are not a technologically advanced tribe, so keep this technical stuff very simple, Guns. I have neither the time nor the patience to translate human jargon into the Cheereek language."

Herbloc translated. The warriors squatting in a tight semicircle about Gunsel's mock-up were silent for a moment and then broke into a series of high-pitched cherps and warbles. They began flapping their arms wildly and rocking back and forth on their feet.

"What the . . . ?" Gunsel put a hand over his nose. The warriors' wild flapping stirred up the ever-present aroma of excrement which clung stubbornly to every Cheereek.

"Ah, um . . ." Herbloc looked confused. "That's how they laugh. I must have mistranslated something." He pulled out the handheld microcomputer and whispered into it. He held it to his ear and nodded. "Well," he announced confidently, "the phrase I used for 'pull back' actually means to part the fringe covering the female cloaca and—"

"Fuck!" It was an expletive, not a comment.

"Ah, precisely," Herbloc answered brightly. "Precisely!" He took a long drink from his flask.

"Don't that thing ever run dry?" Gunsel asked disgustedly.

"Never, boy-o. And thank your stars for alcohol, because otherwise I could never survive five minutes in this goddamned heat in front of these goddamned stinking bags of birdshit. Shall we proceed with our didactic operation?"

Herbloc had tried to explain the Avionian language to Gunsel on the long drive from the *Marquis de Rien*. Very few nouns in their language stood alone. But the Cheereek language abounded in verbs, adverbs, and adjectives. Adding a suffix, which literally translated into English as "thing," to a verb identified nouns. So, in literal translation, *trigger* became "squeezing thing"; *cartridge,* "death thing" or "noising thing"; *bullet,* "shooting-stone-thing," and so on with all inanimate objects. It was the same with living things, although the Cheereek only recognized one form of intelligent life and that was themselves. *Cheereek* in fact meant "people" in their language. The other Avionian tribes, and human beings, were considered little more than animal life. The distinction between inanimate objects and Avionians not of the Cheereek tribe was indicated by modifying the word "thing" with the word "living." Thus Herbloc became known among the Cheereek as "talking living thing," while Gunsel was dubbed "making" or "teaching living thing," though when talking to the humans they made an attempt to pronounce their actual names.

From his studies at Avionia Station, Herbloc knew that the tribes living near the Cheereek used the same linguistic conventions. It was assumed that the so-called civilized Avionians of the northern continent might have a more highly developed language, but nobody knew for sure because the research protocols forbade contact with them.

"But boy-o," Herbloc had said in his worst professorial

manner, "do not think the languages of the Avionians are just 'make work thing' and such babytalk. No, no, no! Oh, that's all those fools on Avionia Station know. But *I* know the Avionian languages are rich with expression and the nuances of meaning. I fully expect the civilized nation-states to the north could easily discuss with an educated human the concepts of Kant and Schopenhauer, that's how highly developed their thought processes and verbal skills are. Oh, the words and phrases I've taught you are literal translations, and the literal translation of almost any word lacks true meaning, can in fact be misleading." He'd taken a long swig from his flask at that point and gestured expansively with one arm. "Life experience, culture, emotion, all influence the learning and development of language. These Cheereek, for instance, primitive savages that they may be, are actually very fond of oratory and speech-making. They have a highly developed oral tradition, in fact."

"Doc, how the hell do you know all this when you were only on the station for a couple of years, and all those other brains up there couldn't figure it out, not according to you, anyway?"

Herbloc leaned back in his seat and regarded Gunsel through half-closed eyelids for a moment. He raised his flask again and drank before replying. "My dear Guns, as I have often told you, to the derisory gibes of lesser intellects, I am, simply put, a genius."

And Gunsel was forced to admit that he was right.

Under the vicious Avionian sun, the day wore on tediously. Gunsel could not tell if the warriors were paying any attention to him or if Herbloc was translating his words correctly. At least there were no further outbursts of Cheereek laughter.

Gunsel called a break when the sun was at its zenith and the two men retreated into their landcar, where they could enjoy the vehicle's climate-control system. Herbloc immediately stretched out in the passenger seat and within seconds was snoring loudly. After a while Gunsel dozed off too. Neither awoke until the late hours of the afternoon. Alarmed, Gunsel rushed outside to find the five Cheereek right where they'd left them at noon time, dozing quietly on their haunches.

What was left of the afternoon, and well into the evening, was spent in the handling of real weapons, which included dry-firing and sighting. Gunsel realized the Cheereek really had paid very close attention to his demonstration. Apparently, Herbloc's translations had been excellent.

The actual range firing was disappointing. One major difficulty was that each shooter became highly distracted by the expended brass cartridges when they were ejected after firing. The Cheereek had an alarming tendency to throw the rifles down and go chasing after the shiny brass cartridges. And only when one of them sustained a minor wound—a bullet hole and the burn caused by a muzzle blast in his arm fringe— did they begin to settle down and practice better weapon safety.

Once the warriors realized the rifles could hurt, Gunsel stepped to a nearby bush and plucked a seedpod from a low-lying branch. He mounted it on one of the targets and returned to the firing line. Using the standing offhand position, he emptied a magazine into the pod, demolishing it in four seconds. The Cheereek rushed forward to inspect the damage. Gunsel did not need Herbloc to tell him the warriors were impressed with his shooting. They were beginning to get a picture of what the rifles could do to one of their kind. What neither man could know was that the five warriors thought them crazy to trade such wonderful weapons for a handful of their gut stones.

They broke for the night and practiced live-fire with the rifles through all the next day. At the end of that time Gunsel was convinced the Cheereek fully understood the principle of how gunpowder worked and how the rifles functioned, but of more than a thousand rounds each warrior had fired at a large target only fifty meters from the firing line, few scored a bull's-eye. Gunsel decided it was satisfactory if they just hit the target at that range. At twenty-five meters they were much better shots. Gunsel sighed. He could not teach the Cheereek proper trigger control, breathing, and proper firing posture;

the standard firearms training he'd gotten from old books just would not work with them. He couldn't tell whether it was because their anatomy and physiology were so different from those of humans or they simply didn't have the necessary focus to keep from being distracted when the spent cartridges were ejected.

But after a week Gunsel pronounced the five warriors certified firearms instructors.

Equipped with a large bag of gizzard stones—their "pay" for teaching the five warriors how to shoot—the two men eagerly headed back to the *Marquis de Rien*.

"Boy-o, you did a capital job! Capital!" Herbloc saluted Gunsel with his flask and drank.

"Goddamnit, Doc, after a week with you in the hot sun, isn't it time you shared that rotgut with me?"

Herbloc handed the flask over. Gunsel drank and coughed. "Allah on an asteroid, Doc, that stuff is *strong*!" He coughed again and pounded his chest as the whiskey burned its way down into his stomach where it finally came to rest, a comfortable warm ball of liquid joy. "Whew!" Gunsel preferred beer, and he occasionally drank liquor, but he'd never had anything like that before. He drank again and handed the flask back. "What do you call this stuff, Doc?"

"Whiskey, my dear boy. All the better drinking establishments have it. When we get back to civilization I shall introduce you to a few such places."

"Not if it turns me into a drunk like you, you won't," Gunsel replied in an offhand manner. The artificer had decided soon into the long flight from Luna Station that he would not let Herbloc intimidate him with his superior education. He understood few of the literary allusions the scientist was fond of making, but he knew that when Herbloc quoted Shakespeare, he meant it as a putdown on someone. The other men on the *Marquis de Rien* knew that too and they hated Herbloc for it, but after a time Gunsel began to enjoy sparring with the scientist. And it did not take Herbloc long to discover that Gunsel was quick on the verbal draw. Grudgingly but respectfully, Herbloc became wary of the craftsman's devastating tongue. In time he actually came to enjoy the repartee.

"But Doc," Gunsel added, the whiskey making him expansive, "I've got to hand it to you. If whiskey makes you so damned good at what you do, Patch should find out what brand you like and give it to some of those other guys."

CHAPTER
TWELVE

As a young man Major General Alistair Cazombi had performed an act of such desperate heroism he had never been the same since.

During the Katusan Insurrection of 2425, as part of the disastrous retreat of Confederation forces from the high plateau country, his platoon had been surrounded on a rugged ridgeline above the Weejongboo River in Lagoda's southern province on St. Katusa. The Katusans had surprised the understrength Confederation task force sent to restore order and driven it back on the Weejongboo, where its commanders established a tenuous defensive perimeter.

Cazombi's company had been decimated in the fighting, and by the time they found themselves isolated on the ridge, they were down to thirty men who could fight. The Katusans, realizing Cazombi's position was vulnerable, seized the opportunity to break the Confederation defensive line at that point and repeatedly attacked him over the course of two days. On the morning of the second day a shell fragment had shattered Cazombi's spine, paralyzing him from the chest down. Lying behind cover, he continued to direct the defense of his position, killing several of the enemy with his personal weapon. That night, he ordered the survivors to abandon the position. Realizing it would be too difficult for them to carry him down the steep ridge without alerting the enemy, he ordered them to leave him behind. He requested that someone give him a fully charged weapon.

He had to threaten the company first sergeant to get him to obey the order to move out. Finally, as the handful of surviving soldiers stood about in the deepening darkness, reluctant to leave their commander, he grabbed the first sergeant's sleeve and pulled him close. "You try carrying me down that ridge, Top," he whispered, "and you'll make so much noise the bastards'll know you're leaving. Stay with me, and tomorrow at dawn they'll crack the line here and we're all dead. You get out quietly tonight, reach Battalion, let them know we've got a hole up here, and maybe they can plug it. Otherwise the brigade is going to get knocked out of this war."

The old first sergeant made as if to protest again. Then, swallowing hard, he nodded and repeated the order quietly to the rest of the men. They gathered up their weapons and slipped silently down the ridge. As each man passed the spot where the captain lay, they reached down and squeezed his hand. In seconds Cazombi was completely alone.

The freezing night dragged on forever. Several times Cazombi thought he'd passed out or dozed off. The pain from his wounds had subsided but he was completely immobile from the chest down and very weak from loss of blood. He had been left positioned so he could see down the slope to the river below. Toward morning a dense fog developed in the river bottom and crept up the ravines, giving the enemy excellent cover almost to the top of the ridge where Cazombi lay. He was able to repulse the initial probes until the sun was well over the horizon, but once the Katusan commanders realized only one position was firing on their men, they ordered a massive charge. Hundreds of screaming Katusan soldiers swarmed up the ridge.

Cazombi fired until his blaster's power pack was expended. He was fumbling for another when someone laid a hand on his shoulder. He turned his head slowly, apprehensively, expecting almost to see an angel ready to bear him off to paradise. What he saw was even better: his old first sergeant with what remained of the second battalion, only a hundred-odd men, but they were enough.

Two months later Cazombi was back on his feet. Not firmly, his mending back still weak, but standing nonetheless. He had been given a new company command. That was when the malcontents within the company began to call him "Cazombi the Zombie." It stuck. Those two nights on that ridge had done something to Alistair Cazombi. As the years passed and he rose in rank, he built a reputation as a cool, totally unflappable officer who thought things through quickly and then unerringly made the right decision. Commanders admired him because no job was too difficult for Cazombi and he never complained about even the most odious assignments, carrying them out with quiet efficiency. As a commander, his men loved him. He never applied more discipline than required and never asked anyone to do anything he wouldn't do or hadn't done himself.

Beyond an occasional shrug or a slightly raised eyebrow, Alistair Cazombi never showed emotion of any kind. Those who knew him well could judge his moods by those two gestures. "The Old Man gave a three-quarter eyebrow, so watch out! He's really pissed!" subordinates would joke. That is not to say he never felt emotion; he just never allowed it to surface. Asked how he remained so calm always, never demonstrating anger or passion, he replied evenly, "That all ran out of me a long time ago." He did have a sense of humor, though it was very dry. When making difficult decisions, ones that if wrong could get him into a lot of trouble, he would only shrug at warnings and say, "What're they going to do, ship me back to Katusa?"

Alistair Cazombi only wore two ribbons on his duty uniform. One was midnight-blue with silver diamonds, the Army Heroism Medal, the highest decoration for bravery the Confederation could bestow. That one was for his action on the windswept ridge above the Weejongboo River. The other was the Army Good Conduct Medal, earned as an enlisted man before he was accepted into Officer Candidate School. He would often remark of his enlisted service, "Kitchen police builds men. I know what it's like to clean out the mess hall grease trap. Did that in basic training on Arsenault. Didn't like it much."

*   *   *

Major General Alistair Cazombi raised his right eyebrow slightly but otherwise had no obvious reaction to the momentous information Admiral Hastings Sudbury, Chairman of the Combined Chiefs, Confederation Armed Forces, had just given him.

The information about the existence of Avionia had come as a big surprise, but a mild one, compared to what the admiral told him next. "These Marines of the, um, 34th FIST, er, Lima Company, third—maybe fourth, I don't remember—platoon, General, we're sending them because they have encountered an alien species before." He explained what had happened on Society 437.

General Cazombi only nodded. "Marines. Yes. Well, sir, Marines are excellent fighters. Very disciplined men. I can handle this job, sir." He had just moments ago been informed that the Combined Chiefs were sending him along on the Avionian mission. His role would be to represent the Combined Chiefs, ensure the Marines of the 34th FIST adhered to the strict rules of engagement that would apply on Avionia, and to make sure the Marines kept quiet about the whole thing.

Admiral Sudbury leaned back in his chair. "You know, Alistair, I've only been Chairman for six months, and we haven't really had much opportunity to talk."

"That is correct, sir."

"I mean, your periodic briefings are so—so—" He shrugged. "—so complete, I never have a chance to ask you any questions." He laughed.

General Cazombi said nothing. For two years he had been the C-1, the personnel officer for the Combined Chiefs. Only Admiral Sudbury, his deputy, a four-star army general, his intelligence officer, known as the C-2, and the Judge Advocate knew about Avionia and what was going on there. Quietly they had reviewed the records of several officers whom they might send along to monitor things, and all had agreed Cazombi was the man.

"One more thing," Admiral Sudbury said. "Someone else will accompany you. A cop."

* * *

Special Agent Thom Nast sat in the Attorney General's office studying the file she had just handed him. The wattles on the AG's neck turned a bright red as she watched him, remembering the meeting that had just concluded with the Confederation President. That goddamned half-breed bitch, Chang-Sturdevant, had virtually ordered her to dispatch an agent to the Avionian station to deal with the poaching. The AG had promised Val Carney her office would not interfere with the operation there, and it wouldn't. Nast couldn't trace his way to the men's room, much less any leads he might develop on those behind the poaching.

"You're going along with an army general, Whatshisname. It's in the file," she croaked. "He's going along to keep the Marines in check. They catch any of these guys," she continued, "you escort them directly to Darkside."

"No trial?" Nast asked as he read his instructions.

"Of course not!" the AG replied as if talking to an idiot. "We go with a public trial for these guys and it'll blow the whole Avionia operation. Even the President agrees the Confederation Constitution is suspended in this case." She pronounced the word "President" disdainfully.

Nast nodded. He was a meticulous investigator who always went by the book. He was cautious and thorough and often his superiors had criticized him as being slow and indecisive. But the thought of putting anyone in jail without due process, especially on a place like Darkside, where only prisoners serving life sentences were confined, troubled Special Agent Nast. And besides, poaching—criminal trespass under the Confederation Criminal Code—was a Class 6 felony that carried a maximum penalty of five years' confinement, not life, which is what the poachers would face if taken.

"Clean your desk out, Nast," the AG cackled, "you're going to be gone a long time on this one!"

"Special Agent Nast, thank you for coming on such short notice," Madam Chang-Sturdevant said, walking out from behind her desk and offering Nast her hand.

Nast had been shocked to receive a peremptory summons to meet with the Confederation President. He'd been packing his bags to depart for Avionia Station when the call came through.

"Let's sit down over here," Chang-Sturdevant said, gesturing to a low table and some comfortable chairs in one corner of her office. "Would you like some refreshment?"

"Thank you, ma'am, thank you very much. Perhaps a glass of effervescent tonic?" Nast carefully seated himself on the edge of one of the chairs, his knees primly together, hands in his lap.

"Relax." Chang-Sturdevant laughed. Nast leaned back in his chair and crossed his legs with an embarrassed smile.

A servo immaculately attired as a waiter rolled soundlessly across the room. "Might I ask the gentleman his pleasure, sir?" Nast was openly surprised by the servo's basso profundo voice.

Madam Chang-Sturdevant smiled and nodded at the servo. "That's Larry. I like a deep male voice," she said, "it gets me, right here." She patted her abdomen and laughed.

"Uh, Larry, could I have a Schwepp's tonic, please?"

"Very good, sir. Madam?"

"Same for me, Larry."

The servo began pouring the drinks. "Sir," it addressed Nast. "I thought I should inform you that the front of your trousers is slightly open."

Nast fumbled with his fly. "I came out in a hurry," he explained, his face turning red.

"I am sorry, sir," Larry said as it served Nast with his drink, "but I thought it best to advise you."

"Uh, thanks, Larry." Nast toasted the servo with his drink. He was beginning to think of Larry as a real person. The face actually looked human and its lips were perfectly synchronized with its words. The tuxedo-clad torso mounted on the serving cart was remarkably lifelike in its movements.

"Will there be anything else, Madam?" The servo inclined its head respectfully in Madam Chang-Sturdevant's direction.

"Not for the present, Larry."

"I shall be available if you need anything," the servo said. It rolled silently into a niche in a far corner.

The two sipped their drinks for a moment. "You know where you are going and what you are to do when you get there?" Chang-Sturdevant asked abruptly.

"Yes, ma'am."

"Good. Now get this: you work directly for me from now on. I've had my personnel director reassign you from the Ministry of Justice to my personal security staff. You will have police powers extraordinary for the duration of this assignment. From now on your reports will be filed with me and you will receive your directions from me. You no longer work for the Attorney General. Is that clear?"

The news took a moment to sink in, and then Nast smiled slowly. "Yes, ma'am," he said. "Police powers extraordinary?"

"Yes. You will have the authority to arrest anyone, and if you deem such action appropriate, the authority to drop the case or any of the charges. Few law enforcement officers are ever granted such power—or responsibility. And, as you will be working for the President, directly, neither the AG nor any of her crooked cronies in the Congress will be able to interfere with your investigation.

"Don't worry about your career in the Ministry of Justice, Thom. The current AG is suffering from ill health. She's resigning soon." Chang-Sturdevant smiled. "When this operation is over and you return to the Ministry of Justice, I'm sure you'll find the atmosphere over there greatly changed. She thinks you're an idiot. I don't. Her replacement won't either, I guarantee you that."

Nast nodded but said nothing. He already knew what his superiors thought of him, but long ago he'd made up his mind not to compromise his methods to win praise.

It was that quality Chang-Sturdevant recognized in Nast from almost the moment she had opened his file. Quite by accident the Attorney General had picked the wrong man for the assignment. She smiled to herself, imagining the rage the old bitch would fly into when word came to her that the Confederation President had assigned her "bumbling fool" to her personal staff. The Attorney General would spend her last few days in office wondering if the idiot would accidentally stumble onto something incriminating.

"Thom, this poaching goes far, far beyond the men who are on Avionia collecting the gems. I want that whole operation canceled and I want everyone involved removed from the confines of polite society, no matter how high their money or connections may place them. *Everyone*. Is that clear?"

Nast smiled more broadly. "Yes, ma'am," he replied enthusiastically. "That is very clear!"

Well, well, well, Nast thought as he drove back to his apartment. Old Tweed might be onto something after all. Tweed had contacted him the week before with somewhat vague information about a gem-smuggling operation involving Val Carney and his associates. Now it was coming together. That was what the President had meant when she'd said the poaching involved high-ranking individuals. Now how did she know that? And what did the Attorney General know that the President did not—for reasons that were quickly becoming clear—want to share with him, her man in the field?

Nast had two days before he was to meet with General Cazombi and depart for Avionia Station. He would employ them fruitfully. Mentally, he rubbed his hands. It would be an interesting two days. Special Agent Thom Nast was beginning to enjoy himself again.

"After you, General, it might be mined." Nast laughed as he, Captain Conorado, and General Cazombi prepared to enter the gangway from their ship to Avionia Station.

"Been there, done that," Cazombi answered as he stepped into the device. He could never get used to the things. The gangway device was entirely trustworthy but it swayed just slightly under a person's weight, giving the impression it was very fragile protection from the vacuum surrounding it.

Inside the station, Dr. Hoxey and her staff waited to greet the new arrivals. Their first impression of Dr. Hoxey was not a favorable one; she was not very tidy, and her stringy gray hair and short, squat body did not project an aura of confidence. But it was evident she was relieved to see them.

"When will the Marines land?" she asked as soon as the introductions had been made.

"When I give them the word, ma'am, and when Captain Conorado here says he's ready," General Cazombi replied. "First, we need a complete brief on what's going on down there. On our way here, we read the reports you've filed. We understand everything you reported on the poaching. What we need to know is more about the Avionians. Too damned much scientific jargon in those reports. Can someone tell us in plain English what makes them tick?"

Very quickly Omer Abraham was lecturing them on what he knew of Avionian brain functions and physiology. At length; like most scientists on Avionia Station, he could be quite longwinded when he got started on his specialty. As he wound into his finale, he said, "I must mention one final thing about the Avionians—their bowel functions. You know it is the action of their digestive system that produces the stones men are risking their lives to obtain. The average Avionian excretes a half a dozen times a day, and their output is highly toxic, gentlemen. The toxicity is the result of their diet, their digestive systems, and the food they eat. You probably know that the dung of terran birds is highly acidic and can ruin painted surfaces, for instance, if it's allowed to stay on them any length of time. Well, multiply the corrosive effect a thousandfold and you have an idea of what Avionian dung is like."

"Oh my." General Cazombi laughed. "All they need to do then is poo-poo on you and you're history."

"How do they stand it themselves?" Conorado asked.

Abraham smiled. "How did humans stand it before we developed sewer systems? The Cheereek, on whose lands the poaching is going on, are nomads. They move their camps several times a year. But they almost never excrete inside their camps. Each campsite has latrines far removed from the living area. They go there when they have to, uh, go. Each group has favorite campsites where they establish their villages year after year, as they move with the seasons. Gentlemen, some of the latrines at these frequently occupied sites—we've measured them—are in excess of ten meters deep. One final point. The stuff never seems to dry out. So don't fall in."

This last comment elicited polite laughter. General Cazombi smiled. But he was especially interested in how the Avionians communicated.

"I must defer to Dr. Gurselfanks, General," he said. "B.P. is our laryngopathologist with sub-specialization in languages. B.P."

A stooped, bearded man in a white lab coat worked his way through his seated colleagues to the front of the galley the scientists used as their conference room.

"B. Proteus, actually," he announced in a reedy voice. "General Zombie—"

" 'Cazombi,' actually," the general said. "What's the B in your name stand for, Doctor?"

"Excuse me, General. Uh, Benjamin. But everyone calls me B. Proteus, or just B.P. General Cazombi, you would've been better prepared for this mission if you'd read my doctoral dissertation, 'Speech Patterns of the African Parrot,' *Psittacus erithracus*."

"We did read it, Doctor. That's the African gray parrot, I believe," Nast volunteered.

"Yes, yes!" Gurselfanks answered brightly.

"Doctor, all of you," General Cazombi announced, "you should know that every book, every article, any of you have ever written—and that includes those on the other three shifts—were provided to us, and we scanned all of them during the flight. We also reviewed everyone's personal history file."

"And I remind all of you that our presence here is a law enforcement matter," Nast added. "We're here to stop the poaching, and I'm here specifically to dispose of the poachers and anyone else involved in their operation. I'll tell you right now, I don't think anyone on C shift is involved. Doctor, please proceed."

Gurselfanks swallowed. "Well, ahem . . . The Avionians, as

you already know from Dr. Abraham's lecture, are as intelligent as humans. You also know their brains possess a combination of avian and mammalian features. Now since you read my book, you also know how important song is to birds on Old Earth. But the Avionians do not sing, they talk. In Terran birds the songs and calls are produced in the syrinx, an organ posterior to the larynx, at the junction of the bronchi and the trachea. But—ah ah!—in the Avionians, sound is produced in the larynx, as—"

Cazombi interrupted and rephrased his question. "What kind of language do they speak?"

"Ah-hah, straight to the heart of the matter!" Gurselfanks cackled enthusiastically. "Well, we don't know," he answered, putting his hands behind his back and pacing back and forth. "We don't know how they learn language, for one thing. We've never, uh, taken an immature specimen, a baby you might say, and observed it in association with adults. But the Avionians have a very extensive vocabulary, that we do know. We have compiled a glossary of nearly six hundred Avionian terms. We haven't yet been able to figure out the grammar. Now mind you, what we know only represents a small portion of the vocabulary that the primitive tribes we study have developed. I suspect that, like us, the more highly developed societies have a very complicated and eclectic vocabulary, and undoubtedly the language used varies widely between groups. But we are prevented by law from having any contact with the more developed nations on Avionia, and since they haven't yet developed any sort of electronic communication, we can't eavesdrop on what they say to each other."

"So how do you communicate with the ones you've taken onto this station?" Nast asked.

"Holophrastically," Gurselfanks answered enthusiastically. "In other words, like infants. We can say 'tree,' and point to one when what we mean is 'I can see that tree,' or 'What a big tree,' or 'Let's climb that tree.' We have no idea how semantic, grammatical, or intonational nuances function in their languages. I'm sure the Avionians consider us idiots with very advanced technology. We use lots of sign language too."

"Ever heard of a guy named Herbloc?" Nast asked suddenly.

"Oh, yes, yes! Dr. Spencer Herbloc! He was on B shift but we exchanged notes on our research all the time! He's not with us anymore. Brilliant man. Shame."

"He was fired," Dr. Hoxey commented sourly. "He's a drunkard." Her eyes widened as a thought occurred to her, and she exchanged a worried glance with Abraham. Nast saw it and smiled.

Gurselfanks droned on for some time, lecturing on the significance of phonemes, morphemes, syntax, and semantics. A series of other specialists then spoke briefly about Avionia's geology, climate, the flora and fauna. A paleontologist said he was convinced by fossil evidence and anatomical studies performed on deceased Avionians that the creatures were once beginning to develop flight, but had moved away from that evolutionary path and adapted wholly to life on the ground.

"General, would you and your party like to see an Avionian?" Hoxey asked. "We have several here under study just now." The three men looked at one another and nodded. Smiling broadly, Hoxey led the way to the laboratory.

CHAPTER
THIRTEEN

In the lab, several Avionians perched disconsolately inside steel cages surrounded by elaborate arrays of instruments. There was a terrible smell to the place. "We have a hard time keeping the cages clean," a white-coated lab attendant apologized to the visitors. "In their native habitat these creatures usually excrete at some distance from their perches. But here . . ." He shrugged.

"We know. Dr. Gurselfanks told us all that. How do they like living up here?" Captain Conorado asked, though he could guess from the Avionians' posture. "How do you like working in here with that smell?" he added.

"You get used to it," Dr. Hoxey answered for the technician. "As to the Avionians, well, they don't like it much." She went on quickly, "But you see, there is nothing we can do about recreating their native habitats on board the station, and we *must* get on with our work." She gestured at the cages. "We collect these specimens from the uncivilized regions of the planet," she explained. "These savages have no idea of what's going on when we take them so there's no chance they'll ever figure out who we are or what we're doing here."

"But these are sentient beings," Nast pointed out.

"Yes, yes, but primitives, Mr. Nast, intellectually stuck in their Avionial-centric universe, hardly at a level where they can grasp the concept of space travel, much less extra-Avionian life-forms. Many of them aren't even aware that their planet extends beyond the lands of the next tribe or two. Most likely they think we are gods. In the case of those we have returned to Avionia, for example, I doubt many of their compatriots would believe them were they to speak of their adventures up here." She laughed. "Would the Attorney General believe you, Mr. Nast, if you told her you couldn't make it in to work because alien beings had kidnapped you, taken you to their ship and experimented on you?" The lab technicians laughed politely. Cazombi and Conorado avoided looking at each other. That story did not seem so preposterous to either of them, not with what they suspected about Society 437.

"They look somewhat, um, bedraggled, Doctor," Nast observed.

"Yes. Well, they don't take well to captivity," Dr. Abraham replied. "In fact, most of our guests so far have, uh, died." He and Hoxey exchanged hostile glances. The exchange did not escape Captain Conorado's attention. Obviously Abraham was not comfortable with some aspects of the creatures' treatment.

There was a moment of shocked silence. "But I thought we weren't even supposed to have contact with them," General Cazombi said.

Hoxey shrugged. "For scientific purposes, General, we must have some limited contact, in a controlled environment, of course. What we do here hardly upsets the social evolution of the Avionians, not like what the poachers are doing. In the long run it is better that a few of them succumb while in captivity, so we can learn more about them, and when contact finally is authorized, the transition will go more smoothly. You see, gentlemen, in science it is not the individual that matters so much as the whole—" She was interrupted by a terrible shrieking in one of the cages. The other Avionians began hooting and cawing in their own languages and the din became almost unbearable.

The hairs on the back of Conorado's neck stood up. The screaming was not so much an angry protest or even a reaction to physical pain as an expression of total hopelessness, a signal of despair such as he had never before heard from a living creature. The Marine officer had heard men scream and cry in the agony of battle, but this—this was terrible. "Jesus God," he shouted, and involuntarily took a step toward the instruments surrounding the screamer's cage. He stopped only when General Cazombi laid a hand on his shoulder. "Easy," Cazombi whispered, "easy. I'll take care of it.

"Stop it," the general's voice cracked in a tone that demanded instant obedience.

Hoxey started and shot a glare at him, then signaled to one of the attendants, who immediately twisted a dial on an instrument bank. The screeching ceased. Gradually the other prisoners quieted down. "We're performing gastrointestinal probes, gentlemen," she explained breezily, "and they occasion some physical discomfort. Now, some refreshments, perhaps?"

Conorado could not believe it: Hoxey acted as if totally unaffected by what had just happened. Worse, she was acting as if she was *used* to such incidents. "Wh-What were the other ones shrieking? Do any of you speak their language?" he asked as he ignored Hoxey's outstretched arm gesturing them to the doorway. Nobody spoke up for a moment. It was evident to Conorado that the lab technicians did understand at least some of the Avionians' speech but were reluctant to tell him what the aliens had been screaming. "I'm not moving until you tell me, Dr. Hoxey," he said slowly.

Hoxey could only stare at him open-mouthed. A military drudge addressing her like that? Intolerable! All she could think was that it had been a mistake to bring these men to see her work.

Dr. Abraham cleared his throat nervously. "They were saying that we were hurting their companion, and they begged us to stop. They asked us to take them home."

Conorado just stared at Abraham, his jaws working silently. "Home?" he managed to ask, getting control of himself. "Does that mean the same thing to them as it does to us?" It was if he were thinking out loud, not asking Dr. Abraham to explain.

"Yes, I think so," Abraham answered anyway, his face flushing. "I believe it does," he added.

"Well, nobody here is that well versed in the Avionians' languages that he can explain their psychology, gentlemen," Hoxey broke in. "We do no permanent harm to these creatures with our experiments. We cannot sedate them for the more intrusive procedures because we don't know what to use that would have the proper effect and we dare not try drugs that would work for humans because their physiology is so different from ours."

General Cazombi raised an eyebrow slightly. "Then why do they die on you?"

"It is not because of physical abuse, General. And as I alluded to before, we have returned some to Avionia, with no ill effects. Now, shall we move on?"

"Because they don't like it here," Abraham said as he walked quickly out into the companionway. "They shit in their cages, Captain," he said from the doorway, "because they simply don't give a damn anymore." His eyes blazed with anger directed at Dr. Hoxey. She ignored him.

"Doctor . . ." General Cazombi took Dr. Hoxey aside. "We would be delighted to share some of your coffee, but I wonder if you could give us some private place where I could discuss some matters with my party first. Would you mind? We'll join you later."

Shown to a nearby tiny but comfortable office, General Cazombi sealed the door and seated himself facing Nast and Conorado. There was really nothing he wanted to discuss with them that couldn't wait, but he wanted—and he sensed they also wanted—just to get away from the scientists for a while. He knew what was coming, but he addressed Nast first, to give Conorado time to cool down. "Let's take stock," he said. "Thom? Captain Conorado needs to know what you know."

Police intelligence was not the topic Nast really wanted to address either, but he understood what the general was doing. "Well, before we left, I received intelligence that this poaching operation is being led by Sam Patch, a very bad man, Captain. His consort, a woman known as Katrina Switch, is worse in her own way. I don't think Sam will be directly in charge of the poaching. He's got two ships. One of them is a Bomarc executive-class starship. The other's an older model freighter, one small enough to land on a planet's surface."

"What good is a freighter that small?" Conorado interrupted. "It can't carry enough cargo to be economically viable."

Nast's mouth twisted in a wry smile. "It was designed to carry exactly the kind of cargo it's hauling from here—objects of extremely low mass and extremely high value." He paused to see if there were more questions. When there weren't, he continued. "It's my guess he'll hand over day-to-day operations to a trusted subordinate. That man's name is Sylvestre Henderson, 'Sly' Henderson. He's a hard case himself and he's worked with Patch on dozens of jobs. Both these men are very dangerous, Captain. They are being backed by some very high officials in our government too. I can't tell you who. But Patch and his men are heavily armed and their ships have excellent stealth devices. They know what will happen to them if—correction, when—they are caught. When you run into them, be prepared for a fight. Save me a lot of work if you just waste the bastards." Shaking his head, he said, "I've been a cop too long to have much sympathy for men like these. Sorry if I sounded harsh." He sighed. "I will give you the full report on everything we know about these people.

"Any thoughts, either of you, about our hosts?" Nast abruptly changed the subject.

"If the Confederation wanted people kept off Avionia, the job should've been given to the navy, sir," Cazombi answered without hesitation.

"I agree, General. By the way, do you find these scientists to be a bit at odds with one another, especially over the issue of live experimentation?"

Captain Conorado smacked a fist into a palm. "General, may I speak frankly?"

General Cazombi raised an eyebrow a few millimeters. "I've been waiting to hear from you, Captain. Please proceed."

"Sir, I have been a Marine all my life. I have killed men and destroyed things. That's what we do. But that—that—" He gestured toward the lab a few compartments away, where the Avionians were confined. "—is wrong. It's flat wrong, sir. I have never knowingly hurt anyone who didn't deserve it. I think Mr. Nast will understand what I mean. Well, what we saw in that lab makes me sick. I mean we kill vermin, we eat animals to survive, but goddamnit, we don't *torture* them first. And these Avionians are not dumb animals! Their intelligence is as highly developed as ours is, they just don't know as much as we do. And frankly, sir, what we saw back there makes me doubt that the human race has really learned a damned thing over the past hundred thousand years except how to make itself an insult to the process of evolution."

"Whew!" General Cazombi said. The right side of his face twitched slightly, in a way that those who'd served with him would recognize as a smile. "I have no authority over how things are run on this station, Captain. We have our mission and it does not include interfering in any way with how things operate here. Dr. Hoxey's experiments have been going on for some time now and I assume someone back at the Confederation knows about them and hasn't seen fit to stop them. She's right, too, that the more we know about the Avionians the easier it will be when the time comes to reveal ourselves to them."

"General," Nast spoke up, "in my opinion we should just establish contact right now. Those poachers have probably blown the whole project anyway."

"You may have a point there, Mr. Nast. But again, we haven't been asked. Captain," he turned back to Conorado, "I have never believed that the individual is less important than the group, even though I've had to sacrifice individual soldiers in battle. But I suspect that none of the three of us would ever ask another man to do anything he wouldn't do himself. We all understand that every time a good man goes down it hurts like a knife in the heart. But we continue the mission. These scientists can never know that, and we cannot hold their ignorance against them.

"But, Captain, I agree. The experiments are an abomination, and that these people, ostensibly some of the best brains our society has produced, could tolerate such a thing makes me sick too. When this is over, I shall join you in filing a formal complaint on the matter." As the general spoke his face reddened slightly. "That said, I have only one question: Are you ready to land on Avionia?"

"Sir, my Marines are ready at your command."

"Good. Mr. Nast, you will accompany Captain Conorado's men and make arrests whenever possible. Are you ready?"

"I am, General. And I'll join you in that letter of protest."

"Well then . . ." General Cazombi stood and stretched. "Shall we get that coffee now?"

In the conference room refreshments were waiting. The visitors and the staff relaxed and discussed the briefings that had been given earlier. To the great relief of Dr. Abraham, the incident in the laboratory did not come up.

"Well, thank you all very much," General Cazombi said at last, standing up.

"One more thing, General." Dr. Abraham held out a specimen container. "The tiny capsules we found at the poachers' site. You might find them interesting. We found these on Avionia and we're sure they were left behind by the poachers—or the Avionians themselves. But if it was the Avionians, they had to have gotten them from the poachers. No culture of the Avionians is advanced enough to have manufactured anything like these things."

General Cazombi examined the tiny capsules. One or two had clearly been ignited; the others had been carefully pried open and their contents, a fine granulated powder, put into a tiny specimen bag. He picked up one of the tiny lead pellets that had topped the cylinders and examined it. "Looks like an old-fashioned bullet."

Abraham nodded. "And that granulated stuff is gunpowder, I believe."

Nast picked out one of the pellets and examined it. "Who uses this stuff anymore?" he asked. Obviously, police intelligence had missed something.

"Oh, it's still used on some worlds," Cazombi said as he inspected the brass casing. "On Elneal, for instance, the tribesmen use old-fashioned projectile weapons. Captain Conorado can tell you some interesting stories about Elneal." He inspected the bottom of the casing.

"So. The poachers are trading projectile weapons for gizzard stones. Dr. Hoxey, how will this affect the balance of power among the tribes down there, eh? These little things, Doctor, are capable of killing a man, you know."

"We don't know," Abraham answered for Hoxey, whose complexion had suddenly gone sickish. "But if the Cheereek—that's the tribe living in the area where we found these things—have guns—"

"Oh, heavens to Betsy," Hoxey exclaimed, "this makes useless everything we've been doing to protect the Avionians! It is essential they develop technology on their own. This could destroy them. What do we do now?"

"Now? Well, just now," General Cazombi answered, "I could use another cup of your coffee. And then, madam, then, well, I shall call in the Marines."

CHAPTER
FOURTEEN

Many of the Marines had never been on a space station before. It was huge, even bigger than a Crowe Class Amphibious Battle Cruiser. However, that size was where the station's resemblance to an amphibious battle cruiser began and where it ended. Avionia Station didn't have berthing and training spaces for the three thousand Marines of three FISTS; it was stressed to come up with space for the 120 Marines of Company L. Neither did it have a crew of thousands; instead it was run by a few hundred engineers and technicians aided by a small navy complement. Where an amphibious battle cruiser could single-handedly devastate a lesser planet, Avionia Station didn't even have defensive weaponry. Most of its nonengineering volume was taken up with living and recreational spaces for the hundred scientists who were aboard to study the Avionians, and mostly it had laboratories and other research spaces for those scientists. The ship even had a massive library of hardcopy scientific books, journals, and unpublished papers in addition to its electronic library, the content of which was larger by several orders of magnitude, though the space it took up was near infinitely smaller. And Avionia Station didn't turn its gravity off. But the surprises for the Marines of Company L began before they left the *Khe Sanh*.

"Say what?" Claypoole exclaimed when he boarded one of the two Essays ferrying the Marines to Avionia Station. The interior of the Essay wasn't like any he'd seen before: it had rows of seats instead of simply a large open space for three Marine-filled Dragons.

"The scientists who come here are civilians, Rock," Corporal Kerr said. "They don't make combat landings like Marines do, they travel in relative comfort."

Claypoole found his assigned seat and plopped onto it. He bounced. "Nothing 'relative' about this comfort," he said, and sighed contentedly.

Quickly, all the Marines riding the Essay filed in and found seats. In moments all were strapped in. A vid at the front of the cabin lit up and Captain Conorado appeared on it.

"Listen up," he said. The image seemed to scan the cabin, and it felt to every man in the company that the commander looked each of them in the eye even though he wasn't physically present. "I know you've heard this before, but I'm going to say it again. This is not a combat landing; it is not a combat assault. We are transferring from a military vessel to what amounts to a civilian city. A civilized city, not a liberty port. While we are aboard Avionia Station you are to conduct yourselves like gentlemen and be polite in your dealings with station personnel." He smiled wryly. "A lot of the people over there have spent their entire lives in ivory towers and think they're in another one. Real Marines might be too much of a shock for them to survive, so behave yourselves. This isn't Bronnys—the locals don't revel in fights. Now enjoy the flight."

The vid flicked off and almost everyone laughed. Gentlemen? Polite? Behave? Who? Marines?

"He meant you, MacIlargie," Kerr said.

"What? I didn't do anything." MacIlargie did his best to look innocent.

"Not yet," Kerr said dryly. "But you probably will. So don't; I'll be watching." He leaned forward to see past MacIlargie. "That goes for you too, Rock."

Claypoole spread his hands. "Come on, Corporal Kerr. You know I'm always the very model of decorum."

"Sure you are. And Schultz braids flowers in his hair and helps little old ladies across the street."

"But he does! The little old ladies, I mean. I've seen him do it."

"So have I, Corporal Kerr," MacIlargie agreed.

Kerr gave them a look of diminishing patience. "You know what I mean."

Then there was no more talk, the Essay's PA chimed and a carefully modulated female voice began speaking.

"Welcome aboard the Essay," the voice said, "the navy's most advanced shuttle vehicle, capable of both orbit-to-orbit and orbit-to-surface transport. If you look at the right upper corner of the front of the cabin, you will see a message board with numbers on it. These numbers are the countdown to launch. Right now they should read about thirty. When they reach zero, the shuttle will launch from the *Khe Sanh* and begin its transit to Avionia Station. When the Essay leaves the ship, there will be a brief period of weightlessness. Do not be alarmed by it; it's perfectly normal. Approximately fifteen minutes after launch you will begin to debark on board the space station Avionia Station. Please do not leave your seats until the Essay's pilot says you may. Speaking on behalf of your navy, I hope you have a pleasant trip." The PA chimed again, the message was over.

"Say what?" Claypoole said.

Kerr shook his head. "This Essay wasn't designed for us, it was designed for ranking civilians."

There was a slight jolt as the welldeck's bay doors opened below the Essay. The jets in the welldeck's overhead puffed so lightly the Marines hardly felt the Essay drop from the ship.

"Are we moving yet?" someone shouted to general laughter. The only way the Marines could tell they'd left the ship was by the sudden absence of gravity. The amphibious landing ship, CNSS *Khe Sanh*, hadn't bothered to turn off its gravity generators before the launch as it ordinarily would when it spit out Marine-filled Essays.

When the Essays were a safe distance below the ship, the coxswains—the voice had said "pilot" but the Marines couldn't help but think of them as coxswains—eased on their main engines. "Eased" was the operative word. The Marines weren't suddenly smashed into their seats by the many g's of acceleration they'd grown accustomed to; the gentle acceleration pushed them lightly and steadily into their seats until they reached what felt like a half g. A while later deceleration began just as gently, but they didn't return to full weightlessness. The Essay slid into Avionia Station's docking bay and the space station's gravity took over. The Marines looked at each other in surprise when they *heard* the clunks and clanks of the Essay being locked into place in the docking bay. Normally when Essays delivered them into an amphibious ship's welldeck, they only *felt* the clunks and clanks because the welldecks were in vacuum.

As soon as the coxswains gave the go-ahead to disembark, the platoon sergeants stood up and started barking orders. The Marines filed off the Essay into the docking bay.

"Gravity?" someone shouted.

"We're walking!" someone else shouted back.

"Hey, this is the way to do it!" a third Marine chimed in.

Navy vessels turned off their gravity when they launched or received Essays. Marines boarding a navy ship were strung together on long lines and towed by sailors from the welldeck to the troop compartments and never knew which way was up until the ships got under way and gravity returned. This was the first time for nearly all of them that they'd walked off a just-docked Essay.

"Right this way, gentlemen," boomed a chief petty officer in crisply pressed khakis as he waved the Marines past. "If you'll just follow that petty officer second class—he's the one with two chevrons under the eagle on his sleeve and a clipboard in his hand—he'll conduct you to your quarters." The chief's eyes twinkled as a PO 2nd was the equivalent of a Marine sergeant.

The Marines gaped. All the sailors in view wore sparkling white uniforms. On a regular navy ship, the sailors routinely wore dungarees and, more often than not, were sweaty and greasy. Sailors usually looked mildly annoyed about having to lead the Marines, as though they had more important things to do. These looked more nervous than annoyed.

"You and your sailors have been away from the real navy for too long, Chief," Charlie Bass said through a grin as he passed the chief petty officer. "A chief petty officer calling mud Marines 'gentlemen'?"

The chief grinned back. "This duty has its perks."

A hatch led from the docking well into a monorail station where four cars were waiting. The platoon sergeants took over from the sailors and got their men in the cars by platoon. As soon as each platoon sergeant reported all his men accounted for, the chief signaled the sailors to board the cars and the lead operator closed the doors. The monorail trip took longer than the transit between ships had. When the cars reached their destination, the platoon sergeants got their platoons into tight formations and waited for the sailors to tell them which way to go.

The second class found a spot where he could face the entire company and glanced at his clipboard. "First platoon, you follow Seaman Sumtow." He pointed at a sailor who raised his hand. The second class ignored the hoots that followed the seaman's polite call of "Follow me, please," and the platoon sergeant bellowed "Belay that, people!"

"Second platoon, go with Seaman Drake." The second platoon sergeant cut off his men's hoots quickly.

"Don't even think it," Staff Sergeant Hyakowa snarled at his men before the second class told third platoon to "Please follow Seaman Honor." Instead of hooting, the Marines snickered and nudged one another. A sailor saying "please" to Marines? That was too much. If they played their cards right, they could have a lot of fun with the local squids.

The Marines were assigned to suites normally occupied by technicians, who were grumbling about doubling up, four to a suite instead of the normal two, but their complaints slackened when they learned the Marines were packed eight to a suite. The Marines didn't mind the crowding; not only were the assigned spaces larger than their berthing on the *Khe Sanh*, they were more spacious than the barracks quarters back at Camp Ellis. The pleasure the Marines felt only lasted until they assembled in a small theater to meet the people in overall command of the operation and get the first of their detailed briefings. Then they became all business.

Captain Conorado stood at a dais on the stage. Four of the five chairs at a table next to the dais were occupied. Three of the four people were civilians, whom the Marines ignored. The fourth was an army major general. Most of the Marines glared at him. His presence meant the operation was probably being run by the army. Most of the men of Company L had been in the near disastrous war on Diamunde. The ground operations on that war were run by the army until the admiral in overall command relieved the senior army general of command of the ground operations and replaced him with the ranking Marine general. Convinced of the incompetence of army generals, the Marines of L Company never wanted to be under the command of the army again.

"On board the *Khe Sanh* you were briefed by Captain Natal," Captain Conorado began as soon as everybody was seated and looking toward the stage. "He gave you the bare outlines of this mission. First Sergeant Myer impressed on you why the mission is important. Now we are going to spend the rest of today and all day tomorrow getting the details of what we're going to do and how we'll do it. The next morning we will be issued whatever special equipment we need and head planetside.

"For the first order of business I will hand you over to Dr. Thelma Hoxey, the station manager. She will welcome you and introduce the other people at the table." He turned to the table. "Dr. Hoxey."

Giving Conorado a curt nod, the lone woman on the stage stood and strode to the dais. She faced the Marines. She was short and squat, with stringy gray hair. Frown lines marked her forehead and disapproval lines radiated from her slightly pursed lips.

"We are at Avionia Station on a scientific mission of gravest importance. Our mission is being jeopardized by unauthorized people who are planetside making contact with the indigenous population in violation of an Act of Congress and several Confederation laws. Your mission is to apprehend these people and remove them and all trace of their presence from Avionia. While you are on the surface of the planet, you are absolutely required to avoid any and all contact with the indigenous population. Anyone who makes contact with the indigenous population will be considered to be in league with the criminals who are already there and will be treated accordingly."

She paused for a moment, then said, "Now I will introduce Special Agent Thom Nast of the Confederation Ministry of Justice." She returned to her place at the table without so much as a welcoming glance at Nast, who nodded amiably at her as they passed.

"Well," Nast said, "I've worked with quite a few different law enforcement agencies during my career in the Ministry of Justice, but this is the first time I've ever worked with Marines. I've been looking forward to this ever since I got the assignment because your reputation as fighters is the highest. And I understand this company is regarded within the Confederation Marine Corps as one of the very best. A policeman working *with* fighters, that will be very different for me." He smiled broadly. "But I always enjoy working with the best."

Then he got serious. "You know what the basic mission is. I'm not going to waste your time or mine by reiterating what you already know. Your job is to apprehend the people down there and hand them over to me. I come here with police powers extraordinary. If you don't know what that means, just take my word for it, it's an extraordinary power for a policeman to have." He paused while some of the Marines laughed. "Later we'll get into the details of how we'll do this. Thank you for giving me your time and attention."

Dr. Hoxey didn't acknowledge Nast as he returned to his place at the table. Instead she said without standing, "The next speaker is Major General Alistair Cazombi, the C-1 from the Office of the Joint Chiefs of Staff. He's in command of the military aspects of this mission."

There were muffled groans from the Marines. Not only was he an army general, he was a staff officer.

"He hasn't been anywhere, hasn't done anything," PFC Rowe whispered to his fire team leader, Lance Corporal Chang. "He's only wearing two ribbons!"

"Yeah, I see," Chang whispered back. "Now take another look at them."

Rowe looked at the general's chest again and his jaw dropped. One was a star-speckled dark blue ribbon—it was the Army Medal of Heroism. Rowe hadn't been in the Corps for long, but he'd been in long enough to know that rear echelon officers in a combat zone sometimes awarded one another medals just for showing up every day, but you really had to do something to get the Medal of Heroism. Not everyone recognized the second ribbon, but for those who did, their opinion of the general went up even higher. The Army Good Conduct Medal was awarded only to enlisted men. Unlike the army, which commissioned its officers without requiring enlisted service, all Marine officers were commissioned from the ranks. The Marines thought their way was better because it virtually guaranteed that a new officer had a working knowledge of what he was doing.

Major General Cazombi casually stood next to the dais and looked at the Marines for a long moment, watching as their expressions changed from scowls to wonder to readiness to accept him.

"Good afternoon, Marines," he said, and paused for them to reply. "As Dr. Hoxey said, I'm the military commander here. I am here at the express command of the Chairman of the Combined Chiefs of Staff. My primary job regarding you is to enforce the Rules of Engagement the Combined Chiefs have drawn up for this operation. I'll brief you on them later. The ROE are stringent; the Confederation is quite adamant about no contact between humans and Avionians. But hear this: I've been where you are; I will look out for your interests."

Dr. Hoxey's head snapped toward him and she shot him a furious look which he ignored as he returned to his place. So she glared out at the Marines as though they were the cause of her displeasure and said, "Now Dr. Omer Abraham, our Chief Scientist, will tell you about the indigenous population."

Apparently lost in thought, Dr. Abraham stood and walked slowly to the dais. Unlike the others, who had simply introduced themselves to the Marines, he was about to deliver a detailed lecture. He still hadn't decided exactly how to begin it. He reached the dais and faced the 120 men looking at him. Oh yes, this might well be much harder than presenting a paper to a scientific conclave. Few of these men had advanced degrees, and they were apt to be practical in ways he couldn't conceive. How was he going to get through to them? Then he had it. These men were fighters. The Cheereek were fighters. He'd tell them about that.

"I'm sure you've all taken a survey course in the history of Earth. In it you probably heard of an ancient leader by the name of Temujin. He came out of nowhere to conquer almost all of Asia, a goodly part of Europe, and part of Africa before he ran out of steam. Until then all who stood in his way were crushed. Your job here is, in part, to stop a Temujin before he starts." He looked at his audience and saw he had their full attention. He smiled and started telling them about the Avionians of the steppes.

Quietly, Thelma Hoxey got up and left. Captain Conorado stayed; he needed the lecture as much as his men did. General Cazombi also remained at the head table; he wanted to see how the Marines reacted to Abraham's lecture. Nobody seemed to mind that Abraham took the rest of the day to tell the Marines about the Avionians.

The real problems didn't begin until late the next afternoon.

CHAPTER
FIFTEEN

RULES OF ENGAGEMENT

MISSION

1. Apprehend human personnel illegally on Avionia.
2. To the greatest extent possible, consistent with the General Rules of Engagement, remove all evidence of the presence of illegal personnel.

GENERAL RULES

1. Use the minimum force necessary to accomplish mission.
2. Illegal personnel who want to surrender will not be harmed. Disarm them and detain them for transfer to the ship.
3. Treat apprehended personnel humanely.
4. Collect and care for wounded or injured humans, whether Marine or illegal personnel.
5. Do not personally collect any personal property of apprehended personnel—do not steal.
6. Prevent and report all suspected violations of the law of armed conflict.

INDIGENOUS POPULATION

1. Contact with indigenous population is to be avoided.
2. Do not collect property or artifacts of indigenous population—no souvenirs.
3. Do not, using vid or any other means of data capture or storage, collect images of indigenous population.

SELF-DEFENSE

1. Only the appropriate nonlethal weapons may be used.
2. Use only the minimum force necessary for apprehension of illegal personnel.
3. Force in any measure against indigenous population may be used only in extremis.
4. If absolutely necessary, the minimum force may be used to avoid contact with indigenous population.

"What is this?" Claypoole demanded. "No pictures, no souvenirs, no contact! How are we supposed to do our job?"

"That's right," Corporal Kerr said to Claypoole. "This mission is secret, we don't take anything to show anybody that anyone's here."

"No force," Schultz said. A thunderhead seemed to gather over his brow.

"No force," Corporal Dornhofer said. "We're here to protect them, not kill them." He shook his head ruefully. Part of him understood exactly why Schultz was angry about no force. That part of him agreed.

General Cazombi stood at the dais in the same theater where he'd first spoken to the Marines. He made an unobtrusive gesture to Company L's leaders—let the men talk, give them time to study the Rules of Engagement. Each man had the rules on a card he was required to carry with him. The cards were printed on Avionia Station in place of the cards he'd brought with him from Earth. They were slightly altered because Dr. Hoxey demanded what she called a "semantic correction." The original cards said "native personnel." The modified ones said "indigenous population." According to Hoxey, *personnel* implied they were human. Personally, Cazombi suspected that for Hoxey *personnel* implied people, *population* implied animals. That would mitigate legal liability for her experiments on captive "research subjects."

"This is not a combat operation," General Cazombi announced when he thought the Marines had had enough time to digest the ROE. There was more mild annoyance in the company than anger. He even heard a few jokes cracked, followed by laughter. But nobody was going to find humor in what he had to tell them next. "Because it's not combat, you are going to turn in your blasters before you go planetside." He had to shout out the last few words.

Two other voices cracked over the shouts and protests from the Marines, the loudest and most violent of which came from third platoon. Captain Conorado bellowed, "AS YOU WERE!" and First Sergeant Myer boomed out, "COMP-nee, A-ten-HUT!"

The men immediately shut up and and rose to stand stiffly, facing the stage.

"This is a general officer addressing you," Myer shouted, glaring out at them from the front of the stage. "You *will* listen! You will *not* interrupt! You will *not* object! The next man jack to disrupt these proceedings will find himself in deep shit. His ass will belong to me until I feel like turning him over for court-martial. *Have I made myself clear?*"

There were murmurs from the company, but the first sergeant had made himself clear.

Myer turned to Cazombi. "Sir, I apologize on behalf of the men."

General Cazombi nodded at him, then looked stony-faced back at the Marines facing him. "Sit." They sat as rigidly as they had just stood. "You aren't going to be unarmed. Platoon sergeants and up will carry their normal hand-blasters. The rest of you will carry nonlethal weapons. I'll tell you about them in a moment. You aren't carrying your normal weapons because we don't want to kill smugglers or natives. You'll be wearing your chameleons; nobody on the surface is going to see you unless you want them to. Now, remember what Dr. Abraham told you—the Avionians have a very poorly developed sense of smell, they aren't going to pick up your scent. As long as you exercise reasonable caution, you are not in any danger of discovery." He held up a hand. "Yes, I know full well how many times 'no danger' has been said before a disaster. But I don't expect you to exercise reasonable caution; I expect *extreme* caution on your part." He stopped talking and looked at them for a long moment as agreement began welling up. Except in third platoon.

"All right," he finally said, looking directly at third platoon. "I know some of you are upset, and I know why. For right now, just take my word for it: the Avionians aren't like anything you've ever encountered before." Third platoon stared back at him. They didn't look like they agreed, but most looked willing to listen.

"Now," he reached under the dais, "this is what you are going to carry." He withdrew an odd-looking object a meter long. It was roughly a tube with a butt plate at one end and a blocky assemblage jutting out of it less than halfway from the butt plate to the business end. "The engineers who designed this call it a zapper. It's a neural disrupter. It fires a disruptive electric charge effective up to a distance of fifty meters. Its effect on a man is dramatic—it knocks him down and causes full-body spasms. It disables him long enough for the slowest person to run fifty meters to him and clap him in a restrainer. At closer range, it can knock a person out. Someone hit by a zapper is mobile again in five or ten minutes, but it takes several hours for all the effects to wear off. A shot from the zapper will render an Avionian unconscious for ten to fifteen minutes, longer if the hit comes from close range. It takes an Avionian a full day to fully recover." General Cazombi hadn't been told, but he had a pretty good idea how Dr. Hoxey had determined the zapper's effect on the Avionians. "Your platoon sergeants have already been familiarized with the zapper. When we are finished here, you will be issued these weapons and your platoon sergeants will instruct you on their use.

"We don't have much time. You make planetfall before dawn tomorrow morning. That is all."

"COMP-nee, A-ten-HUT!" Myer bellowed. The Marines jumped to their feet and stood at attention as General Cazombi left the stage.

Cazombi signaled Captain Conorado to follow him. "I want to meet privately with your third platoon," Cazombi said softly when they were alone. He looked uncertain, and somewhat embarrassed, when he said, "Third platoon only. Nobody from outside it, not even you or anyone else from your command group."

Conorado looked at him, stunned. For a general officer to exclude a company commander from a meeting with the company commander's own men was unheard of. And then he was angry. He guessed that Cazombi knew what third platoon had run into on its recent deployment and was going to talk to them about it. An army general was going to talk with his men about something he could only guess at, and he was banned from the meeting. And then he wasn't merely angry, he was furious. So he did the only thing he could under the circumstances. He said, "Aye aye, sir. Where does the general want to meet with them?"

Sitting with one haunch on the corner of the lecturer's desk in a classroom, Major General Alistair Cazombi waited patiently for the men of third platoon to file into the compartment. The first Marine in froze briefly then snapped to attention, blocking the door. Cazombi casually waved a hand, telling him to come in and take a seat. The Marine walked stiffly to the indicated chair and sat at attention.

"Come on in, have a seat," Cazombi said to the Marines who hesitated in the entrance. He waited until Staff Sergeant Hyakowa closed the door behind the last Marine and sat down himself before saying anything else. The hostility and anger in the platoon was palpable, and he knew he had to do something to defuse it.

"Relax," he began. "I may carry a lot of rank, but I started out as an enlisted man, just like you. At heart I'm a groundpounder, the same as every man in this platoon." A slight smile briefly cracked his face. "Well, not *quite* the same. I'm a dogface, and we do some things a bit different from the way you Marines do. Nevertheless, all of us in this room are field-ration-powered, foot-operated, multipurpose killing machines. Don't be fooled by the fact that my current job is personnel officer for the Combined Chiefs." He saw several Marines looking at the two ribbons he wore, and gave them time to consider the implications of an army major general who was a former enlisted man and had won the Medal of Heroism.

When the silence stretched long enough, he said, "There probably aren't many more than a dozen people in the Office of the Combined Chiefs who know what you encountered on Society 437. I'm one of them. I've seen all the vids, the trids, and read all the reports. I've also done extensive study of the Avionians—especially the Cheereek. The Cheereek aren't skinks." His use of the word startled many of them. Again there was a slight change in Cazombi's demeanor that those who knew him would recognize as a smile. "Yes, that's how thoroughly I studied your encounter on Waygone." He looked at each man and saw three who looked confused. He nodded and said, "That's right, not everybody here knows what we're talking about.

"You're a platoon. A squad is a family. A platoon is an extended family. I don't care who told you what before, I think it's time you filled in your family members on what happened. The way things are right now, you've got a rift in this platoon, a certain lack of trust between the veterans and the new men. The secrecy behind that rift will no doubt create stresses that can distract you from what you're doing, stresses that could get some of you killed. That would be tragic, particularly on an operation like this, which—once you get beyond the exotic aspects of it—is a pretty routine police procedure.

"Now, it's essential that you understand the differences between this operation and the one on Society 437 . . ."

General Cazombi then did his best to drum into the Marines of third platoon, Company L, 34th FIST the differences between the two missions, and why they were in little danger on Avionia. When he finished, he didn't ask for questions. By then he was thinking about something else. Whoever had made the decision that the Marines had to keep Society 437 such a deep secret that not even their immediate chain of command should know—well, they were wrong. He knew it might cost him his career, but the people who needed to know were going to find out. Beginning with Captain Conorado and his top people. Cazombi went to find the company commander.

Company L assembled by platoons in Avionia Station's docking bay at oh-dark-thirty hours to board the Dragons that were already on the two regular navy Essays assigned to ferry them planetside. They boarded, strapped themselves in, and the ramps were closed. When the Essays were secure, the atmosphere was pumped out of the bay and its hatch opened. Tractors nudged the two shuttle craft onto the launchpads at the lip of the opening and backed off. The launchpads' plungers lifted into position and seated themselves at the rear of the Essays. When all was ready, the plungers gave the Essays a quarter-g push then withdrew as the Essays floated free of the station's internal gravity. The webbing that held the Marines made quick adjustments for the transition to null-g. The coxswains used the crafts' vernier jets to maneuver to a safe distance from the station and pointed their noses at a slight tangent to the planet below.

"All right back there," said the coxswain of the Essay designated as *Lander Two*, "picnic's over. You're back with the *real* navy now."

With no further warning, the main engines blasted on and the Essays shot downward. Five seconds later the engines cut off and left the shuttles in an unpowered plunge at a velocity of more than 32,000 kilometers per hour. When the two Essays reached atmosphere, the shuttle craft deployed their wings and hit their retro rockets. The Essays shuddered violently, the men in the Dragons bouncing and rattling about in the acceleration webbing.

"High speed on a bad road," was how Marines described the fall from the top of the atmosphere to the beginning of powered flight, fifty kilometers above the surface. It was an apt description.

The Essays split from each other during the drop to the top of the atmosphere, so by the time the breaking rockets and deploying wings cut their speed and the angle of the shuttles' dives, the Essays were two kilometers apart. That gave the coxswains the space to bring their reentry vehicles under control without risking collision. Once the Essays' wings were fully extended, huge flaps extended from them to further decrease their speed. When the wings finally bit into the thickening air hard enough for controlled flight, the coxswains turned off the breaking rockets, fired up the atmosphere jets, and maneuvered the craft back toward each other and into a velocity-eating spiral that slowed their descent as well as the shuttles' forward speed. At one thousand meters altitude the coxswains pulled out of the spiral and popped drogue chutes. At two hundred they angled the jets' vernier nozzles downward. Seconds later the Essays came to rest on the surface of Avionia. Their rear ramps dropped. Three Dragons roared out from each and sped toward the area where the smugglers were suspected of having their base. The Essays launched and headed back to the *Khe Sanh*.

CHAPTER
SIXTEEN

The Nomads

"SSKKAARROOUUU!!!" screeched Guard Captain Cheerpt. He held his Clumsy Ones' weapon high over his head and kneed his eeookk into full galumph over the steppe. The fifty warriors of the raiding party lifted their Clumsy Ones' weapons and screeched victory cries as they galumphed behind him.

Cheerpt was beside himself with glee at the success of the raid. He and fifty warriors had attacked a hunting-roost of nearly four hundred Koocaah-lice, including more than a hundred armed hunters and warriors. Now they were nearly four hundred dinners for scavengers—and not a single Cheereek had fallen. He twisted his neck around to look again at the eighty captured eeookks that struggled to keep up with his raiding party under their heavy burdens of captured food and shinies.

"SSKKAARROOUUU!!!" he screeched again, and waved his weapon at his warriors. They waved their weapons and screeched victory back at him.

He brought his head back around and leaned forward, stretching his neck alongside his eeookk's so his head was next to his riding beast's—the posture of an attacking Cheereek warrior. Even though the fight was behind him, he still had energy to burn off. He continued the galumph until his eeookk gave signs of exhaustion. Only then did he sit upright and allow the beast to slow its pace. A few hops later he stopped and turned about. His warriors were strung out behind him, slowed by the eeookks with the booty.

"We roost here for the night," Cheerpt announced when all but the slowest stragglers had gathered around.

The late afternoon stillness was shattered by the cries and caws of the warriors as they set about arranging the roost. A few of them tethered the riding eeookks together, while the rest pulled the packs off the captured ones. The captured eeookks gobbled in protest as the Cheereek herded them into a tight knot, drew riding beasts into a circle around them, and tied off the last tether to complete the circle. The gobbling increased in volume and intensity when the warriors fed their mounts, increased again when the warriors tossed food into the captured eeookk mass to feed them. It ceased by the time the warriors had staked out small ground hollows or built small circles of stones and brush to serve as their individual nests.

Once their nests were ready, the Cheereek built fires and tore into the captured stores for food to cook. Meat was cut into small chunks, seared in the flames, then mixed in bowls with seeds and grain to be pecked at. Long throats rippled as food descended their length. As Aaaah sent his last rays slanting across the landscape, the warriors screeched their evening pleas for the god to return again then settled into their temporary nests. Aaaah hopped onto his nest, and everything became silent save for the hoos of early rising night hunters.

Aaaah's morning appearance woke the Cheereek, and they cawed and cried the dawn greetings to the god of life. The eeookks added their gobbles to the dawn cacophony. Prayers done, the warriors scattered to gloop their ablutions onto the sere ground. Then, in a frenzy of activity, the Cheereek pecked down the remnants of the evening's meal, fed scraps to the eeookks, broke apart the living fence, and reburdened the pack beasts.

Cheerpt, the first of the raiders to mount, looked again at the captured eeookks, piled high with booty, and cawed out in glee. Surely that proved his prowess as a raider. Surely that overcautious Graakaak would hear out his plans to find and raid the Clumsy Ones' roost. He screeched a command and his warriors bounded onto their mounts. Cheerpt led the happy raiding party at an easy trot. He calculated they would reach the shade of the High Tree before the great heat of early afternoon and rest from the heat in their own nests.

Less than halfway from the night roost to the High Tree, however, Cheerpt stopped the column to study unexpected markings on the rocky ground. Except for its width, it looked like the lines a fledgling with a straw might draw in sand. But no fledgling, not even the greatest warrior ever, was big enough to blow lines that wide. Cheerpt craned his neck high and looked at the length of the lines in one direction and then the other. He did not see what made the lines, but he knew what had made them: the strange mount of the Clumsy Ones. Only the topmost line was fresh. Others alongside or hidden, save for their edges below it, were older. Some were much older. Cheerpt's neck coiled as he scanned. Nothing moved in the distance other than a few sky-hunters drifting on thermals. Close by, the eeookks pecked at the ground. The warriors sat easy on their mounts, some wondering what their leader thought was significant about the Clumsy Ones' track.

What was significant to Cheerpt was that the track was *there*, not the direction from which the Clumsy Ones came with their marvelous weapons. It was not the direction in which they went when they took the gut-stones.

Cheerpt looked at the horizon and considered. The Clumsy Ones' mount could speed faster than the fleetest eeookk, and maintain that speed far longer than an eeookk could galumph. Yes, if the Clumsy Ones sped beyond sight when they left the Cheereek roost and then made a wide circle when they were on the Frying Rocks to leave them in another direction, *this* is where they would go. He cackled. They might be ugly, but the Clumsy Ones were clever. He remembered one time losing their trail in the Frying Rocks. He had not been able to find it again on the far side. Now he no longer had to wait on the far side of the Frying Rocks to see where they left it. Now when he confronted Graakaak with his demand that they find the

Clumsy Ones' roost and take all their weapons instead of getting only a few at a time, he could tell him exactly where the
roost was.

"Cheereek," he ordered his warriors, "go to the High Tree.
Tell the High Chief I will come later, I have found something
to investigate, something he will want to know. Say nothing
about this track."

The fifty warriors stretched their necks and pointed their
faces at the dome of the heavens. They would do as he said.

Guard Captain Cheerpt watched the warriors until they
dwindled and he could no longer distinguish where Cheereek
ended and eeookk began. Then he began following the track.

Hours later, when the distant Bower Curtain had grown
from a smudge hovering above the horizon to a towering
massif that marked the end of the world, Cheerpt admitted to
himself that he felt something akin to fear. The line drawn by
the Clumsy Ones' mount was as strong and wide now as it had
been when he first found it. There was no sign that the mount
tired or slowed its pace. Yet the distance traveled was great
enough that he found it necessary to dismount several times
and walk his tiring eeookk. Once, he had even stopped to rest
it. Cheerpt knew the Clumsy Ones' mount was not a beast,
that it was some kind of magically driven wagon. To make a
wagon that not only could go as fast as that one, but go that
fast as far as it went, told the Guard captain the Clumsy Ones
were more powerful than he might have guessed based on just
the marvelous weapons they gave to the Cheereek.

Now he knew much more, though he hadn't yet found their
roost. Perhaps Graakaak was right, perhaps it was best to go
slow with the Clumsy Ones.

No! Slow wasn't best. It could not be. The Cheereek were
the strongest people in the world. Soon they would be the
most powerful. No one, not even the Clumsy Ones, could be
greater than the Cheereek. Not if the Cheereek had a sufficiently bold and strong High Chief.

He urged his eeookk on.

Not long after, he found the Clumsy Ones' roost. It was

nestled in a curve of one of the many ridges that flowed from the side of the massif like the buttress roots of tall trees. Not that Cheerpt had any idea of what a buttress root was, and he had never seen a tall tree. Still, the ridges looked to him like they propped up the Bower Curtain. The plains nomads called them the Bower Boughs.

It didn't look like any tree or nest Cheerpt had ever seen. It was wider than it was tall, and longer than it was wide. It had no openings in it for the wind to blow away the heat. It was made of metal.

Metal. More metal than he imagined there was in the entire world. Cheerpt gaped at the Clumsy Ones' tree in awe, but only for a moment. He dismounted and hobbled his eeookk behind a ripple of rock that radiated from the side of the ridge, then crept forward, using as much concealment as he could find. He climbed a scree-fall to gain a better vantage and eased his head above the rock barrier he hid behind. There was no sign of nests on the ground around the Clumsy Ones' High Tree. It was so big and held so much metal he had to think of it as a High Tree, and only someone as powerful as a High Chief could possibly live in such a place. Did all of the Clumsy Ones live in the High Tree? It was certainly big enough. If he knew how many Clumsy Ones there were . . . He had only seen three—Heerk-kloock, Gun-chelk, and Chun-Oleeon. But they would need females and slaves, and there must be warriors, or at least guards—certainly they would not leave so wondrous a High Tree unattended in their absence. There had to be many more than three Clumsy Ones.

Cheerpt waited patiently and watched.

Aaaah was more than halfway down the sky when an opening growled into existence on the side of the High Tree and a branch grew downward out of it to the ground below. A Clumsy One appeared in the opening and walked agilely down the branch. Three more followed the first. They carried things in their hands, things that Cheerpt thought must be Clumsy Ones' weapons, but not the same as the weapons they traded to the Cheereek. The four Clumsy Ones came in his direction. He studied their faces; they were not the three he knew. They looked menacing. Somehow, they must have discovered that someone was watching their High Tree.

Cheerpt slid down the scree and, keeping behind concealment, ran to his eeookk and galumphed away.

Graakaak, High Chief of the Cheereek, sat in council with his chief advisers to discuss the matter brought to him by Guard Captain Cheerpt. The High Chief squatted, his feet wrapped around his stone-studded perch. In front of him, on a lower perch with merely a bowl of stones in front of them, were ancient Tschaah, chief councilor to the High Chief; the mighty warrior Oouhoouh, his Chief of Staff; and young Kkaacgh, Captain of Scouts. Guard Captain Cheerpt, as the one who'd brought up the matter, perched to the side facing between them. The bowl of stones in front of him was the same size as the bowl the other three shared.

"Tell them," Graakaak commanded.

"I have found the roost of the Clumsy Ones." Cheerpt puffed his chest and held his head menacingly at half the height of his neck. "Give me the same warriors I took on my raid against the Koocaah-lice and I will bring back all of the Clumsy Ones' weapons. We will no longer have to wait for them to bring us a few at a time."

"How many Clumsy Ones are there?" asked Tschaah.

"At least seven."

"How many at most?" asked Oouhoouh.

"They are clumsy, it doesn't matter."

Oouhoouh snorted. "What are their weapons like?" he demanded.

"They have Clumsy Ones' weapons," Cheerpt said derisively.

"Like these?" Oouhoouh waved a hand at the circle of guards and the Clumsy Ones' weapons they held.

Cheerpt twitched his head, a dismissive shrug.

"Even if they have the same weapons as we do," Tschaah said, "I have seen them fire the weapons. We all have. They work magic with them. They point the weapon and the bullet hits where they point it, not somewhere near, like when our warriors fire them."

Oouhoouh nodded agreement. "Even if there are only seven of them, and even if their weapons are the same as ours, they could kill the raiding party we sent against the Koocaah-lice."

Cheerpt glared at the Chief of Staff. His saying "we sent" rather than "you led" was a deliberate insult to the Guard captain.

Oouhoouh continued as though he hadn't noticed Cheerpt's reaction. "If we attack the Clumsy Ones' roost, we must send many warriors, not simply a small raiding party."

"And we risk losing many warriors," Tschaah added.

Like an old hen, Cheerpt thought.

"To what end would we lose so many warriors?" the ancient adviser went on. "Yes, we might get all of the weapons at once. But would we have enough warriors left to use them?"

"You have not yet spoken," Graakaak interrupted, speaking to Kkaacgh, Captain of Scouts, his newest adviser.

The Scout captain stretched his neck up and pointed his face at the ceiling. He was not yet used to the protocols of council meetings, therefore he behaved as he always had when speaking to the High Chief and exposed all of his soft parts. "High Chief," he said, a slight waver in his voice, "it is good that Guard Captain Cheerpt found the Clumsy Ones' roost. This is important for us to know. But Chief Councilor Tschaah and Chief of Staff Oouhoouh are right. We know so little about what the Clumsy Ones have at their roost that if we attack we risk greatly."

"No great gain is possible without great risk," Cheerpt snapped.

"You are on this council to give advice, Scout Captain," Graakaak said, ignoring Cheerpt's outburst. "What is your advice? And look at me when you give it so I can know you speak truth."

Kkaacgh lowered his face to look at the High Chief. It was difficult for the young Cheereek to speak his mind without exposing himself, but he managed. "High Chief, I can take scouts to the Clumsy Ones' roost. We can find out how many Clumsy Ones there are and how they are armed." He cast a quick, anxious glance at Cheerpt. "We can find the best approaches to their roost, approaches that will allow our warriors to get so close the Clumsy Ones cannot kill many before we are on them."

"I will think on it." Graakaak plucked four stones from his perch. He did not seem to examine them, but he tossed the best of the four to Kkaacgh and the least of them to Cheerpt.

Cheerpt left with the other councilors, but didn't speak to them. They were like Graakaak, old hens. If he were High Chief, he thought, he would have to replace all of them with proper Cheereek, aggressive warriors who wouldn't hesitate to take advantage of an opportunity.

The Philosopher

The honor at first seemed overwhelming to Waakakaa the Philosopher. The University of Rhaachtown was renowned not only throughout the realm of Rhaach, but in Gaagaahh as well, as the greatest of universities. Even Kcoock the Philosopher in Far Zheekeech knew of it with great respect. And Dean Ouoop was known throughout the world as a scholar of the highest perching. To think that Dean Ouoop would read his modest stickle about the New Glitterer, and then invite him to come to the University at Rhaach as a Visiting Philosopher!

Overwhelming as the honor might at first have seemed, Waakakaa quickly settled into the routine of university scholarship. In exchange for his honorarium, food, and lodging, he was required to teach one undergraduate course and conduct one graduate seminar per term.

The undergraduate course was a survey of the natural history of Aaaah and his cycles, a requirement for all first or second year students. Most Philosophers resented having to teach low-level survey courses, believing themselves to be above such mundanities which were best left to upper level students who were still so new to the arcana of Philosophy that they were not yet bored by constant investigation of the basics. But Waakakaa relished the time he spent with students so recently fledged. Their eagerness to learn and their ability to sop up knowledge astonished him and gave him great joy.

He tried to impart to those students his own enthusiasm to learn of the night sky. While most of the students seemed bored by that topic, and many looked at him with disbelief, there were a few whose crests flared and eyes glimmered when he told them of the wonders to be seen when Aaaah made his dark journey to dawn. Those few gave him encouragement that someday the puzzle of the New Glitterer might be solved—perhaps even within his own lifetime.

There were only four young seminarians in his seminar. But each of them had independently studied the night sky— and each had read his stickle on the New Glitterer even before they knew he was coming as a Visiting Philosopher. They had heard of his eyestretcher and greatly desired to see and try its wonders themselves. They were in his seminar because they wanted to learn, and they considered him to be the most knowledgeable Philosopher on matters that so intrigued them. Those four were Waakakaa's greatest pride. Every night at least one of them was with him in his study, peering through the eyestretcher.

Waakakaa the Philosopher took great pleasure in studying the night sky in his new surroundings. His lodging was far better than he was used to at home in Gaagaahh. So too was his food more nourishing. His pleasure in his lodging, his improved nutrition, the stimulating give and take with the barely fledged students, and the greater stimulation of his work with the seminarians, combined to improve his thinking. Early in his second year at the University at Rhaach he broached a new postulation to his seminarians.

The New Glitterer is not of the same nature as the other glitterers, he said. The New Glitterer is an artificial construct.

This postulation begged a question. Who sent it? Which was followed by more questions. Was it an eye, moved there by the gods to watch over the world? If so, to what purpose? Or might the glitterers be gods like Aaaah? If they were gods like Aaaah, there must then be other worlds with people of their own. If there were, when did they sleep? He told his seminarians about Kcoock the Philosopher and his belief that the world was a globe. If the glitterers were gods like Aaaah and had worlds populated by people, then might not one of those peoples have discovered how to travel among the glitterers? Then the New Glitterer would be an eye sent to observe the world. Why?

In talking with his seminarians, Waakakaa asked and listened as well as postulated, and as many of the questions were theirs as were his. The questions kept mounting until there were so many, they were a morass into which even the greatest of Philosophers might sink.

Waakakaa spent long hours with his seminarians, puzzling on the questions. Before the end of the semester they winnowed them down to two: Was the New Glitterer sent by the gods for reasons unknown or unknowable? Was the New Glitterer sent by people from another world for reasons unknown or unknowable?

The second of the two questions was the more problematic, for it required knowledge of the nature of the glitterers, which no one had. Yet the slow drifting of the New Glitterer and the small flames that shot from its side to move it back to its place near the split in the bole of the High Tree argued against it being a construct of the gods. The occasional small, tailed glitterers that visited also seemed to imply a construct from another world.

At the end of the academic year, Waakakaa and his seminarians were no closer to definitive answers than when he first made his postulation. After Waakakaa bid his seminarians farewell, he pondered the questions by himself as he prowled the nearly depopulated halls of the university. The postulation and questions ate at him. He lost his appetite and became slovenly in his dress. He considered taking the questions to Dean Ouoop, but the dean's field of Philosophy was the Natural History of Lice and he was quite ignorant of the night sky. When Waakakaa considered the entire faculty of the University at Rhaachtown, he realized he was the only one with more than the most passing knowledge of the glitterers. No, there was no use in discussing the questions or their underlying postulation with any of the local scholars. He needed to go elsewhere for help in solving the puzzle. But where?

After pondering all of his options, he decided the only viable one was to publish and hope someone would read it who might have an answer, even a partial answer, or a new question that would make him think in a different direction. It was a small stickle, even smaller than his first stickle on the New Glitterer.

Some months after the small stickle's publication, soldiers came from the palace of the High Priest and took Waakakaa the Philosopher away. The small stickle had come to the attention of the College of Priests. They intended to try him for heresy.

CHAPTER
SEVENTEEN

"Oh, hell! We've got a problem!" the *Marquis de Rien*'s radar tech shouted into the comm to the bridge.

Sly Henderson, the man in charge of the Avionian ground operations, hit the switch that gave him two-way communications with the comm shack. "What kind of problem?" he asked with no more than mild interest. All they'd seen near the ship's planetfall during the months they'd been planetside was an occasional wandering nomad. The nomads never stuck around for long, especially not when he sent out a few men with blasters to shoo them away.

"Someone's coming planetside, and I think they're looking for us."

Henderson shrugged, even though the tech couldn't see him. "So? Those eggheads up there come planetside sometimes."

"Not like this they don't," the tech said. Fear that edged on panic was audible in his voice.

"What do you mean?" Henderson stood as he asked the question.

"The eggheads loop down, take a couple orbits to get planetside. There are two shuttles coming almost straight down."

"Shit," Henderson swore under his breath. "I'm on my way."

A moment later Henderson strode into the comm shack, which was lit only by the displays linked to the surveillance units his crew had placed in a large circle around the ship when they first landed.

"What do you have?"

"Look at this," the tech said. He tapped a few keys on the control board under one of the displays and pointed a finger at the screen. The display replayed what it had recorded moments earlier. The streaks of two fast-moving shuttle craft angled downward across the screen.

Henderson felt his stomach knot up. "What's their location?"

"They'll touch down a hundred kilometers northwest of here."

"How soon?"

The tech peered at a scrolling column of numbers and swallowed. "Right about now."

"Damn!" Henderson had seen that kind of landing approach once before, when he was smuggling military hardware to some rebels on Fiesta de Santiago. Confederation Marines came in; that was the way they made planetfall. When the Marines had raided the smugglers' base, he was one of the few to escape. There was only one thing they could do now.

"Secure this place, we're getting out of here." As he raced back to the bridge he snapped orders into his pocket comm for the *Marquis de Rien* to launch.

Fifteen minutes later the *Marquis de Rien* launched.

Henderson knew that keeping the ship ready to go at a moment's notice was a good idea. Now, as he watched the local star swell through the polarized image in the forward viewscreen, he saw confirmation of his caution.

"This is where they were, all right, Skipper," Gunny Thatcher said when he caught up with Captain Conorado. "Looks like they left in a hurry." He nodded at Lieutenant Giordano, the company's executive officer.

Conorado grunted. He'd just finished checking the disposition of his men around the smugglers' base. The small vale in the side of the ridge was littered with the trash that always seemed to be left behind by civilized men. Without getting close enough to examine the detritus, he was sure some of it was still usable. Probably most of it was usable to less "civilized" people.

"How long?" he asked. From where he stood, the dents and scrapes on the ground where the ship had sat looked fresh, as did the scorching from its launch.

"Not long at all. The scorched ground is still hot to the touch." Thatcher considered for a moment. "Half hour or less." He made a face, which couldn't be seen behind his infra screen. "Someone must have told them we were coming."

Conorado shook his head. "If somebody told them, they would have left sooner—and in less of a hurry." He looked around as though he could see through the surrounding ridges and rock walls. The only thing his infra screen showed out of the ordinary that his unassisted eye couldn't see was the splotch of heat radiating from the scorched rock and dirt and the positions of the Marines. "They must have put out an array of sensors, or some remote radar units, and spotted us coming down."

Thatcher gave him a look from behind the infras. "That can be expensive."

Conorado nodded. "Whoever's behind this is well financed. They can afford it." He turned to Corporal Escarpo, his communications man. "Raise Papa Bear." Then to Sergeant Flett, the unmanned aerial vehicle chief, he said, "Get the birds up. See if they left anybody behind. Look for sensors and radars." The UAVs came in several sizes, all disguisable. For this mission, they used mid-sized UAVs that were outfitted to resemble local flying scavengers.

"Papa Bear, sir," Escarpo said, holding out the handset of the satellite comm unit.

"Papa Bear, Mama Bear Actual," Conorado said into the mouthpiece. "We didn't catch Goldilocks napping." He listened to General Cazombi's reply, then said, "Remote sensors of some kind—probably remote radars that picked us up on our way down. Has the *Khe Sanh* spotted their ship yet?" He listened to the reply, nodded, then glanced at Sergeant Flett and Corporal MacLeash, the assistant UAV operator. They were already launching the company's two spy-eyes. "They are in the air, sir." He listened again, raised an unseen eyebrow, said, "Aye aye, sir" when Cazombi signed off, and passed the handset back to Escarpo.

"Platoon commanders up," he said into the command circuit of his helmet radio.

Moments later his infra screen showed four man-size red columns approaching. He raised his left hand and let his sleeve slide down to bare his arm. The platoon commanders were almost certainly using their infras to locate him. The infra screens wouldn't show them that his arm was bare, but they'd see his arm raised and understand he meant for them to raise their infras. He removed his helmet. Thatcher did the same. By the time the four platoon commanders reached him, they were carrying their helmets. The five men looked at their commander expectantly.

"I just got off the horn with General Cazombi," Conorado said sourly. "It seems we accomplished our first objective. Even though we didn't arrest them, we got the smugglers off Avionia."

They were an eerie sight, six disembodied heads standing a man's height above the ground. Anyone looking at them the right way would spot an odd shimmer in the air, a peculiar off-setting of colors and shapes. And seen against the sky, or against a background of a distinctly different color and pattern from where they stood, they would appear to be man-sized pillars of dry dirt. But the Marines were used to the form of invisibility their chameleons gave them. Living, disembodied heads standing a man's height above the ground only bothered them if the heads weren't those of other Marines. Confederation Marines were the only people in Human Space who wore chameleons.

"We still have our second objective to accomplish," Conorado continued. "Remove all trace of the smugglers' presence—including artifacts."

Lieutenant Giordano looked at the debris left behind by the

smugglers. "It'll take one platoon maybe fifteen minutes to police that area."

Gunny Thatcher cocked an eye at him, but addressed his comment to Conorado. "Not much we can do about the gouges and scorching, though."

"You're both right," Conorado said. "However, that's not all of the artifacts."

The others looked at him. How were they supposed to get the projectile weapons away from the locals without making contact, which was forbidden by the Rules of Engagement?

"Sir." Bass had an idea. He didn't think it would be accepted, but it was the only idea any of them had. "The locals probably don't have a lot of ammunition. If we leave them alone until they use it up, they'll be left with nothing but a bunch of awkward clubs that they'll discard. Then we police up behind them and leave."

Conorado looked at him. "I hope you're making a joke, Charlie. We can't do it that way and you know it. And the joke's in bad taste."

Bass shrugged.

"Sir, Papa Bear," Corporal Escarpo interrupted.

Conorado accepted the offered handset. "Mama Bear," he said. "Go, Papa Bear." He listened for a minute, nodding occasionally, then said, "Thank you, sir. It isn't much help now, but it's good to know." He managed to keep any expression from his face as he listened again. "Aye aye, sir," he finally said, and handed the comm unit back to Escarpo. "Assemble the company," he told Thatcher. "Have each platoon leave a fire team out for security. Classroom formation." Then to the others, "I'll tell everybody at the same time." He found a shady spot to sit while he waited for Company L to assemble before him.

Conorado stood and told his men to sit. They did, in a semi-circle before him, removing their helmets so the company commander could see them all.

"As I'm sure you have surmised, the smugglers took off right before we got here. They went sun-side and the *Khe*

Sanh wasn't in a position to intercept them. That's right," he said to some murmured questions, "they took off and dove for the sun. I know, I know, that almost sounds suicidal. But think about it for a moment. The star's gravitational pull gets them away from Avionia faster, and think of the slingshot boost they'll get when they swing around it. They'll be far enough from a gravity well to turn on their Beam drive sooner than if they went perpendicular to the orbital plane like a normal launch.

"All right, we don't have to worry about them for now," he went on. "There are two things we have to do before we can leave. One is retrieve the weapons the smugglers provided the locals with." He held up a hand to forestall questions. "No, I don't know how we're going to do that. Rest assured, though, the best minds on Avionia Station are working on that problem. The other reason we have to stay is, just because we scared the smugglers off doesn't mean they're going to stay away. We're going to be here watching for them to return. If they do, we'll nab them.

"Yes, I know, that means we might be here for some time. If they go to the nearest human world and turn around right away, they could be back in a couple of weeks. It could take a standard year or longer if they go to the far side of Human Space. But it's more likely that their base is nearby than that it's remote from here. So I anticipate we'll be here for a couple of months. Don't anybody hold me to that. You know how Mother Corps is. We could launch tomorrow; we could be here until we've all retired.

"Now, I want each platoon to assign one squad to policing up this area. When you're through, I don't want to find even a strand of DNA to give evidence to whatever caused those gouges and the scorch mark. Everyone else is to return to defensive positions until further word. Platoon commanders, take your platoons."

Conorado turned away from his men and considered the middle distance. He wondered how his 120 Marines were supposed to get projectile rifles away from a few thousand war-happy Avionians without alerting those Avionians to their presence. Well, they were Marines. They'd do the merely difficult immediately; the impossible might take a little longer.

"Do you have any idea how improbable this is?" Lance Corporal Claypoole asked a short while later. He, Corporal Kerr, and PFC MacIlargie were watching out over the steppe, near the end of the ridge the smugglers' ship had been tucked against.

"What?" MacIlargie asked.

"Humanity's been out among the stars for how long now, three centuries? In all that time we've never run into another sentient species. Now, twice in a year's time, we've run into two different alien sentiences—and one of them's a space-faring species."

"So?" MacIlargie asked. He was bored by watching the barren plain and having trouble staying awake. Listening was too much bother.

Kerr tilted his head and listened without saying anything. Claypoole was always worth listening to; you never knew if he was going to come up with an absurdity to top his last absurdity or say something very astute.

"You ever hear of the Drake equation?"

"The who-what?"

"The Drake equation." Claypoole swatted at where he thought the back of MacIlargie's helmet was. He connected.

"Hey, what're you hitting me for?" MacIlargie spun toward his antagonist.

"Pay attention, Wolfman, I'm talking to you." Claypoole mock-glared at MacIlargie. MacIlargie glared back. Satisfied that the junior man was listening, he continued. "There was this astronomer back in, I think, the twentieth century, by the name of Drake. He was looking for evidence of other intelligences. He had this idea that he could work out the probability of their existence with a mathematical equation."

"You're shitting me."

"No! This is straight. Tell him Corporal Kerr."

Kerr nodded. "Frank Drake. Twentieth century American. I'm surprised you didn't learn about him in a History of Science course, Wolfman."

MacIlargie shrugged. There had been a lot of lectures he sat through without hearing anything—or at least nothing that he remembered.

"Keep talking, Rock," Kerr said.

Claypoole gave Kerr a suspicious glance, then resumed. "The equation had, oh, a dozen factors, or something. The problem was, they all had unknown values."

"All unknowns?" MacIlargie laughed. "How are you going to solve an equation with no known values?"

"Well, that was the problem. We know quite a few of the values now, though. One was, how many appropriate stars have planetary systems? Turns out just about all single-star systems do. How many have a rocky planet within the liquid water range? Again, most of them. On how many of them does life evolve? If it's got liquid water and a sizable moon, it's got life as we understand it. The tricky things, values that are still unknown, were questions about the likelihood of sentience evolving, the likelihood of that sentience becoming technological, and how long would a technological sentience survive."

"Say what? Survive?" MacIlargie looked like he was being asked to believe the incredible.

Kerr nodded again. "That's right. You should have paid more attention in class. If you had you'd know that during the twentieth century worldwide nuclear warfare was a real possibility. A lot of people were afraid humanity would destroy itself and all life on Earth."

MacIlargie's face worked as he considered the implications of that. "But . . . but that was before man went to the stars," he blurted. "If life on Earth got wiped out, that would have been it. That would have been the end of us!"

Kerr nodded again. "That's right. That's why the likelihood of survival was one of the factors in the equation."

Kerr nodded at Claypoole to continue.

Looking superior, Claypoole said, "So far, it's seemed like the values of those last factors was close to nil. We've colonized more than two hundred worlds and explored what, a thousand or more others? In three hundred years we've never found anything that resembled another sentient species. This bears out with historical thinking. I once saw a demonstration from the twentieth century of the Drake equation that gave the result that there was a point-five percent probability of there being one technologic sentience in the galaxy at any given time. In other words, it was fifty-fifty there were *none* at any given time. More realistically, plugging in the factors that we have values for now, it seems likely that there are thousands, maybe even a million or two, technologic sentiences in the galaxy."

"Then where are they?" MacIlargie demanded.

"Think about it." Claypoole waved a hand at the sky. "There are so many stars in the galaxy, a couple hundred billion or so, that even if there are a million technologic sentiences riding the spaceways, the odds against any one of them running into another might approach infinity. And now, in a year's time, we've run into two of them. Not humanity, *us,* third platoon, Company L, 34th FIST. Do you have any idea how improbable that is?"

"Very improbable," Kerr said. "But we have. So maybe sentience is far more likely an evolutionary likelihood than anyone has ever thought. Either of you want to place a bet on us running into another one in the next couple of years?"

Claypoole shook his head. MacIlargie peered out over the steppe.

"Wolfman, you want to make a bet?"

MacIlargie slid his infra and chameleon shields into place. "I don't know. But the way I understand it, you're telling me the odds are we shouldn't be seeing that birdman over there."

* * *

Kkaacgh, Captain of Scouts to the mighty High Chief Graakaak, struggled to quell his cloacal quaking and give no sign that he saw the demons. Not even with every fiber of his being shrilling *runaway-runaway* did he give sign. No one who ran from a demon survived, everybody knew that. When one saw a demon, one's only chance to survive the encounter was to pretend the demon was unseen. Demons hated to be seen, and killed anyone who saw them. Kkaacgh didn't know anyone who'd ever seen a demon—at least not anyone who lived to tell of it—but that was what the lore said and what the priests taught. He did his best to avert his eyes without being obvious about not looking at the demons. Even deliberately not looking at them could signal to them that he saw them, and they could kill him for that transgression. If he merely moved his head casually, they might think he was a lone hunter, even if his eyes did stray in their direction. If he gave no sign he saw them even when his gaze brushed across them, they might not think he saw them and might spare his life. He kept his eeookk moving at a lope and did his best to appear to casually look about for game.

Kkaacgh thought furiously. Where were his scouts? Exactly where were they? Were any of them in positions where they might stumble across these demons? He didn't think so. Not unless they came looking for him. He desperately needed to reach his scouts and warn them to stay away from this area. Ahead, less than half a foraging hop away, the next ridge tumbled its long way down from the Bower Curtain. If he could reach its shelter alive, he knew where there was a dry arroyo he could follow to reach the scouts who were even now climbing the other side of the ridge the demons were claiming as their own.

He wondered if the demons had killed the Clumsy Ones.

It took a quarter of the day for him to find all of his scouts and warn them of the demons. The last scout he found was at the top of the ridge above where Cheerpt had seen the Clumsy

Ones' roost. That scout was paralyzed with fear. The roost was no longer there and there was no sign of the Clumsy Ones. The place where the roost had been teemed with demons.

CHAPTER
EIGHTEEN

"You did what?" Kat screamed in disbelief, breaking into violent peals of laughter. Her face turned beet red and she doubled over, laughing so hard she began to cough. "You hired him?" She wheezed as she tried to catch her breath. "You hired him? Aw, Sammy, you stupid bastard," she shouted, still laughing, and grabbed him by the crotch—hard.

Patch grunted. Kat squeezed harder. Patch groaned. "Ah, the things you do for me, baby," he gasped. He bit down hard on her left nipple. She screeched and let him go. "Whew!" he sighed. "Thought you really had me there for a moment!"

Kat pushed Patch down on the bed and straddled him. "You drew blood, you bastard," she muttered, and held her injured breast out to him. He licked the droplet of blood that hung there.

"You deserved it, bitch. You almost ruined me."

She pinned his arms with her legs and slapped him—hard.

"Thanks," Patch said, "I needed that."

"And this," Kat answered, swinging her arm way up behind the back of her head. This time the smack of her hand on the side of Patch's face sounded like a shot in the landcruiser's tiny passenger compartment. The jolt of the blow traveled up her arm and turned her hand numb. They were both silent for a moment, sharing the pain.

Tears watered Patch's eyes. He licked at a tiny trickle of blood seeping from the corner of his mouth. "Lunchtime," Kat murmured, hitching her hips farther up onto Patch's chest.

"What's so damned funny about Herbloc?" Patch asked suddenly, his nose almost in Kat's "lunch."

Kat leaned back and studied Patch for a moment. "You'd hire a fool like that for an operation like this?"

Patch shrugged. "He's the only one who can talk to the Avionians. He's essential to the whole deal. Yeah, I know he's a fool, worse, a drunk, but I still need him. How the hell do you know anything about this guy?"

Kat hesitated before answering. "Okay. Older guy, round head, thin hair, always talking like a damn college professor?" Sam nodded. "I rolled the bastard the night before the *Marquis de Rien* left Luna Station. I picked him up in the Fifth Reich. Got nearly a thousand credits off him. I didn't know you'd hired him but I remembered that name. 'Herbloc,' who ever heard of anyone with a name like that? You need to tell me when you hire someone, Sammy."

"And you need to stay out of the Fifth Reich and you've got to stop rolling drunks. Goddamnit, you don't need the money! And you're supposed to be reformed. Besides, what are the boys going to think, they find out my squeeze is hanging out in places like that?"

"You own the damned place, Sam. And I was only having fun. What am I supposed to do, you takin' off on these capers all the time and leavin' me alone?" She pulled his right ear hard for emphasis.

Kat's real name was Sarah Goldfarb, but her "professional" name, the one by which thousands of desperate men knew her, was Katrina Switch. Still in her prime, she was reputed to be the most accomplished dominatrix of all time. She'd made a fortune before meeting Sam Patch, but she quickly realized life with him was more exciting, profitable, and satisfying than charging exorbitant fees to beat flabby old men into orgasms. And Patch, who could not be humiliated, at first challenged her professionally and then, by dominating the dominatrix, gave her what she had by then realized she'd always wanted.

He was different from any other man she'd ever experienced. For one thing, he was the strongest man she'd ever known. Kat prided herself on her own physical strength and conditioning. She could easily subdue clients much larger than she. But early in their relationship, to prove who was the real master, Patch just snapped the leather thongs with which she'd bound his arms behind his back and then used them to immobilize her.

As for Patch, he found Kat an excellent businesswoman. Her other talent was not lost on him either. Occasionally, Kat liked to "keep my hand in," as she expressed it, picking up stray men and humiliating them in special ways. Sam tolerated her forays, so long as they didn't go too far. She knew very well that if she ever became involved with another man the way she was with him, he would kill her without a second's thought.

Killing Patch, Kat knew, was the only way she would ever get away from him. It would be easy, she could just go a bit too far during one of their sessions. Been there. Done that. But she had no reason to leave him, and besides, she dared not cross him because he had a sixth sense for danger. She was convinced he could smell a threat. That was one reason he had survived and prospered so long. Kat wondered if he was fully human. Anyway, although she relished giving and receiving pain, she wanted very much to go on living. One good way to change that would be to cross Sam Patch.

After Henderson and his crew departed Luna Station in the *Marquis de Rien*, Patch had proceeded to New Carrolton, the closest human world to Avionia, where he established his headquarters. The previously agreed-upon date for his departure to take the first shipment of gems was still months away, so the pair decided to enjoy themselves in the interim.

New Carrolton was yet in the early stages of colonization, and the population was still small, not many of the "civilized" amenities were available yet. Nor were they likely to arrive anytime soon, because New Carrolton was a mining colony, and so long as the miners had reasonably comfortable places to live and properly rough places to spend their pay, they weren't concerned about museums and operas. Vast alien swamps and forests still covered much of the planet's surface. Animal and plant life there were still in a stage of evolution comparable to the late Permian period of Terra's geological history, so there were no species inimical to man on the planet.

Patch and Kat frequently rented all-terrain landcars to conduct long forays into the alien wilderness. Patch especially enjoyed driving through the swamplands, leaving an oozing trail of devastated vegetation behind him. He was a man who had to dominate, and for him the swampy excursions were a new experience, imposing himself like a god on nature itself. Occasionally they startled small groups of amphibians at their feeding and had great fun chasing them down. They laid bets, taking turns driving, on how many each could crush under the vehicle's treads. The things shrieked and gabbled hysterically while the pair tore up whole forests of fernoids chasing them, screaming and laughing and drinking Wanderjahrian wine.

Patch was into Kat for a thousand credits when, a hundred kilometers from Bowietown, New Carrolton's largest human settlement, they tired of the game. They'd headed for a nearby grove of coniferlike plants on a spot of high ground and parked there for the rest of the day. After lunch and a rest they'd taken up their favorite pastime in a bunk bed at the rear of the vehicle's passenger compartment.

Kat groaned with pleasure, Patch held firmly between her legs.

"Private communication for Mr. Patch," the communications console bleeped.

"What the hell? Kat, reach my communicator over there." Kat leaned over to the driver's console and retrieved Patch's equipment belt. She unfastened the communicator and held it to his ear.

"Speak," Patch commanded. A tinny voice said something. Patch's body went rigid beneath Kat. With one powerful movement he sat up, tossing Kat off his chest and onto the floor of the vehicle. She struck with a solid impact, momentarily stunned. Patch was up in a swift movement and fumbling into his clothes.

Kat got her feet under her and snarled up at Patch, anticipating an exquisite beating such as only he could administer, but when she saw the expression on his face, she knew the games were over. Patch used his anger as a tool. He could turn it on and off as needed to intimidate people but he never really lost control of himself when he was "mad," although his victims seldom realized that. But she saw that he really was mad; his face suffused with blood, the veins in his forehead and neck standing out like tree trunks.

"What's up?" Kat was careful to keep her voice small and her tone concerned. Patch cursed foully as he hopped in place, trying to remain upright on one leg as he stabbed the other at his utility coveralls. He braced himself against the wall with one arm and pulled the zipper up the front of his rig.

"Strap yourself in," he spit out, jumping to the driver's console and starting the power plant.

Kat quickly slid into her coveralls and sat in the passenger's seat. She looked questioningly at Patch as he put the powerful landcar into forward and accelerated to top cruising speed. They roared along for some distance in silence before he had regained enough self-control to speak.

"We're going back to Bowieville," he said.

"Sure," Kat answered agreeably. Well, where else would they be going at that speed after receiving a mysterious radio message?

Patch pressed the accelerator and the landcar surged forward at better than 100 kph. A tremendous rooster tail of muddy water sprayed out behind them as they roared along, leaving a wide swath of destroyed habitat in their wake. Patch's anger was mounting. "The *Marquis* is back," he said.

"You did what?" Patch screamed at the top of his voice. He was alone with Sly Henderson on the bridge of the *Marquis de Rien*, but Patch's shouting could have been heard in the empty crew compartment a deck below.

As soon as the *Marquis de Rien* had berthed, Henderson informed the port authority he would wait for the owner to arrive before requesting services. That was fine with the portmaster because the longer a vessel sat in his berths the more money he could charge in berthing fees—and on New Carrolton nobody asked questions about transiting spacecraft. Henderson dismissed the crew, telling them not to return for at least six hours. And then, after making the call to Patch's private number, he waited alone.

No doubt about it, Sly Henderson was nervous. He knew Patch's reputation for having a violent temper. But he also knew he'd made the right decision to abort the poaching operation.

Finally, Patch breathed heavily, getting control of himself. "Tell me again what happened," he rasped.

"The Marines showed up, that's what happened, Sam."

"Marines!" Patch roared. "Your ass, Marines! There aren't any Marines within fifty light-years of Avionia." Fists clenched, he moved in close enough for his breath to spray hot spittle on Henderson's face. "You got scared off by a bunch of dithering eggheads!"

Henderson stood his ground, determined not to be intimidated. "No way, Sam." He shook his head. "I saw them come down. Scientists don't make planetfall like they did. The Marines do."

"Sly, I never thought you a fool or a coward. I guess I was wrong. I'd know if Marines were sent to Avionia." He started to draw back a fist to pummel the other man.

"I recorded it, Sam. Take a look for yourself if you don't believe me." He turned far enough to push a button on a control panel, but maintained his close proximity to Patch. A radar screen lit up. Numbers scrolled up one side of the screen while two streaks drew rapid lines approaching the horizon indicator.

Patch's fist dropped, the blow he was about to deliver forgotten. "What—What's that?"

"That's two Confederation Navy Essays landing Marines."

"How do you know? Did they see you?" Patch's mind raced

back to how the ship looked as he approached it. He hadn't noticed any damage.

Still somberly looking at the replay, Henderson shook his head. "We didn't stick around. As soon as I saw that, I ordered the ship to launch."

"Then how did you know it was Marines?"

Henderson slowly turned his head to give his boss a level look. "Because I've seen the Marines make planetfall before. I was on Fiesta de Santiago a few years ago, supplying arms to some guerrillas. The Marines hit the group I was with, hit us hard. I was lucky to get away alive. Most of the people I was with didn't."

"But—But I thought they always came in over water. You weren't anywhere near water. You're saying they came in on top of you?"

Henderson shrugged. "I guess they faked it. They came down about a hundred klicks away. They could have been on us in minutes."

"A hundred klicks, you say?" Patch's eyes lit up. "Maybe they didn't even go to your base. Maybe they don't really know you were there."

"Sam, the Marines don't land on top of whoever they go after, not unless it's an accident."

Sam Patch thought for a long moment. He didn't like surprises, especially surprises like that one. They could be fatal. But how did Marines get there without any of his sources letting him know? Most likely it was Essays off a resupply ship, making a practice landing for when they would actually have to land Marines.

Patch was a cautious man. It was one reason he'd survived so long. But he was also a greedy man, and that operation promised more money than he'd ever made before. His judgment wasn't what it should have been.

"How did the trading go?" he asked, changing the subject.

"Fine." Henderson blinked at the abrupt change. "Art had all the rifles ready on time, and the Cheereek loved them," he said.

"Herbloc?"

"He did his job, Sam. Without him we would've had to

forage for the stones. He never let his drinking get out of hand. But, well, Herbloc is . . ." Henderson shrugged. "We did collect ten kilos of the finest stones you'll ever see," he continued. "Sam, we got enough to pay off the boys and set ourselves up for life. Let's just pull the plug on this operation. We can't go back now anyway, not with the Marines there. Your backers will just have to cut their losses."

Patch was silent for a moment. "Let's see them."

Henderson nodded and moved to a safe on the far side of the bridge. He swung the massive door open and hauled out several trays of stones. Patch was so surprised by the beauty of the things he caught his breath.

"My gemologists did a real good job, didn't they?" Henderson asked. They had cleaned, tumbled, and polished the stones beautifully. They glowed and sparkled on the velvet trays. Now Patch understood why people like Thigpen doted on the things.

Patch reached out and took one of the smaller stones, a gem that would fit nicely on any woman's little finger. "This one's for Kat," he said, putting it into a pocket. "Sly, we need more than this and we're going to get 'em. Get the boys back here now. Clear port as soon as they're back on board. We're going back there."

"But the Marines—"

"I think this was a fluke, Sly. It wasn't Marines looking for us. They had no way of knowing we were there. Anyway, my sources would have told me if Marines were on their way. We can make it back to Avionia and get a lot more of this stuff before anybody has any idea. Jesus, Sly, I can't believe you were scared off by a practice landing," Patch said, convinced by his own greed.

"Goddamnit, Sam, that was no practice landing! That was the Marines."

"Sly, there are times when a man's got to make his own decisions, according to the situation. If you'd worked this right, you could've bought us months of collecting before we'd have had to give it up."

"You mean if I'd let the Marines kill us? That's pretty heavy stuff, Sam."

"There weren't any Marines. Even if there were, they know we're gone and they won't be expecting us to come back. We'll sneak in, grab more of this stuff, and get away before the cavalry arrives. And there'll be a difference this time, Sly."

"What's that?"

"I'm going along with you."

Gunsel carefully nursed his glass of imported Reindeer Ale. "You're about in the bag," he remarked to Herbloc, sitting next to him.

"Boy-o," Herbloc responded, "we are all 'in the bag,' as you so prosaically put it, are we not? We have returned from our mission beforetimes, and our gallant captain is even now facing the unfaceable Samuel Patch." He raised his glass in a mock toast to Sly Henderson, and drank its contents in one gulp. "Ah! Barkeep! Another!" He held out the glass and an indifferent barman refilled it.

"Doc, your liver isn't going to take much more of that," Gunsel remarked, sipping his ale.

"Ah, me boy-o, who cares one whit for a liver? 'A liver, a liver! My kingdom for a liver!' quoth the Bard." He drank half his glass and sighed. "I have had three liver transplants already, Guns," he said sadly, "and I'll have another." He finished his drink and held out the glass for a refill.

In a strange way he did not understand, Gunsel came first to tolerate Herbloc's drinking and then to feel sympathy for the failed genius. With the possible exception of Jum Bolion, nobody else in the crew could stand Herbloc, but he and Herbloc had spent so much time together on Avionia that Gunsel had gotten used to him. Beneath Herbloc's drunken hyperbole dwelt a sad and broken little man who sometimes got out when the alcohol fumes dissipated a bit.

The bar they were in was not far from where the *Marquis de Rien* was berthed. Herbloc had found the place as easily as if he'd been there before. "I have an unerring sense of direction when it comes to watering spots," he'd said dryly as they entered the front door. The establishment was crowded with off-duty miners; it was smoky, raucous, and full of noise. "Ahhhh, the ambience of machismo, boy-o!" Herbloc called. A man at a nearby table, a burly, nasty-looking miner by his clothes, looked up sharply at Herbloc's voice. "Let us, sir, without further ado, find a spot at the bar and download some C_2H_5OH, as it is known among the educated classes. Rotgut, to you, Guns!"

They'd found a space at the crowded bar and Herbloc ordered whiskey. Time passed. Gunsel sat quietly for the most part, listening with half his attention to Herbloc, who rattled on and on about many things. Herbloc could actually be very entertaining when he was not too far into his cups. He was just about that far when someone pushed him violently into Gunsel's side. Herbloc's drink flew from his hand and splashed over Gunsel's face. The pair looked up, startled, as a burly figure forced his way beside Herbloc and loudly ordered beer.

"Whaddya lookin' at, gutbag?" the man asked Herbloc, who sat on his stool, mouth hanging open in hurt surprise. "Wipe your face off, you little prick," he said to Gunsel, and turned back to the bar.

"My dear sir," Herbloc protested, "I must say, you jostled me. Quite by mistake, I'm sure. But my drink is, alas, spilled, gone, kaput," he said, a plaintive tone to his voice.

The big man turned and glared down at Herbloc. "Speak English, you fat fart," he said, and shoved the little man hard. Again Herbloc bounced off Gunsel's shoulder.

"Hey!" Gunsel protested.

The miner swiveled on his stool, grabbed Herbloc under both arms, lifted him bodily and tossed him to the floor like a sack of rags. The old man sprawled in the filth and lay there stunned. Someone nearby laughed but none of the other patrons took much notice. "You're next," the big man said and half rose off his stool.

Gunsel blanched, then whipped out the knife he carried in his boot and buried the blade about four inches below the big man's sternum, thrusting upward. The man shrieked and staggered away from the bar, his hands clutching the gaping slit in his middle. He made a sound like "Gaaaaw, gaaaw," and stumbled over a nearby table, sending the occupants sprawling. Several men laughed and someone cursed, but only a few other heads turned.

Gunsel stooped down and helped Herbloc to his feet.

"Damned impertinent of the rascal!" Herbloc said, brushing himself off. Then he noticed his assailant lying beside the overturned table, a large pool of blood forming on the floor. "Oh," he muttered, and Gunsel had to hold him up as he vomited.

"Time to go, Doctor," Gunsel whispered. Trying to wipe the last of the vomit from the old man's mouth, he hustled Herbloc away, through the crowd and out the door. No one followed them and nobody sounded the hue and cry. It was Bowietown after all. Firmly gripping Herbloc by the arm, Gunsel walked him swiftly away from the bar.

"You're hurting me," Herbloc protested.

"Sorry, Doc. Damn, that was a good knife," Gunsel said, wiping blood on his trousers as they hurried along.

"Art! Gunsel!" someone shouted from behind them. Gunsel turned. It was the chief engineer from the *Marquis de Rien*. "Back to the ship! Henderson says we're leaving! I've been looking all over for you two. Come on, come on!" He took Herbloc's other arm and helped him along.

"Where we going?" Gunsel asked.

"Back to Avionia," the engineer replied in a low voice, his eyes wide with trepidation. Then he noticed Herbloc's condition. "Boy, Doc's sure tied one on, hasn't he?"

"Not at all, dear sir, not at all! I am only marginally incapacitated. So, it is 'Once more into the breach, dear friends, Once more!' as the noble King Hal once said. Once more into the shit, dear friends, once more! But remember this: under each pile of birdshit there is—more birdshit!"

Madam Piggott Thigpen lolled in her enormous bath, luxuriating in the warm water, absorbing the delicious aroma of the various salts and soaps the servo had mixed for her. The water was beginning to cool. "Two more degrees," she muttered, and swiftly the temperature of the water increased by two more degrees centigrade. The infusion of warm water caused her skin to flush a rosy pink. She sighed. Supported by the water, liberated from the tyranny of gravity, her enormous bulk floated lightly in its warmth. Sometimes she wallowed in the tub for hours. Not even sex pleasured her as much as one of those baths, and sometimes she even thought a bath might be preferable to the ultimate physical indulgence of her life—food.

Piggott Thigpen allowed herself to engage in a brief moment of whimsy. What if she slipped giving verbal orders to the computer that controlled the bath and said, "One thousand degrees"? She laughed aloud at the thought of being boiled alive in her own bathtub. That could never happen, of course, because the computer had been programmed to shut down automatically if ever given a command to produce dangerously hot water. Nevertheless Thigpen, always the plotter, wondered if somehow the program could be sabotaged. She made a mental note to find out. Such information could be useful, if it turned out an enemy owned a tub like this.

Piggott Thigpen chuckled. Sex? Food? Long, hot baths? Wonderful. But power and money were her ultimate pleasures. Time to go to work, she thought, and commanded the tub to drain. As the water flowed out, plastic cushions gently inflated about her body as it settled toward the bottom, slowly adjusting to support her weight as gravity reasserted its imperative. Like the orthosofas she loved so much, the bath cushions slowly shifted and adjusted to stand the big woman upright without the expenditure of her own energy. As she stood naked on the tiled floor, soft breezes sighed up through carefully disguised vents and caressed her gently, drying her thoroughly and effortlessly. A servomechanism rolled from its niche and draped her with a huge terry-cloth robe. Fastening it about her girth, she strode heavily into the living room.

Thigpen could have taken advantage of several different proven and completely safe medical procedures to rid herself of the fat that encased her body. That she did not was due to her desire to be bigger than life. Her physical size, she believed, should match her power and influence in the political life of the Confederation. And she was very powerful in politics.

So Patch had gone back to Avionia himself, to oversee operations there? Her informants had done their work well. That would mean he planned a quick grab to supplement what Henderson and his crew had managed to collect and then he would pull his coup, screw everyone at once. Very well, it was time to put her own plans into motion. Thigpen laughed aloud. Oh, this game was a good one! How dearly she loved matching wits with worthy opponents. Patch was worthy, very worthy. But she'd seen through his schemes from the first and—

"Madam?" Thigpen started. It was Michelle, the security servo. "A gentleman has requested entry."

"What? Who?" She did not remember scheduling a visitor at this hour.

"A technician from the Brooklyn Orthosofa Company, Madam. The sofas are due their six-month maintenance check, he says."

"Call Brooklyn. Verify his ID. Then let the bastard in. But wait until I am in the bedroom suite. I do not want to see him." Damn! Maintenance men always picked the most inconvenient time to do their work. But it was in the contract, and the maintenance had to be performed to keep the sofas in tip-top condition.

Juan Borders, Brooklyn Orthosofa's senior technician, waited patiently in the hallway outside Thigpen's suite. At five feet eight inches tall and carrying 140 kilos, Borders understood why people like Thigpen loved the orthosofa so much. Thigpen could afford them. Well, Borders reflected, he would very soon be able to afford several—and a one-way ticket to New Brooklyn and retirement. Sam Patch had paid him well—and in advance—for the work he was about to perform.

The door to Thigpen's suite hissed open and Michelle invited Borders in.

"Madam would like to know how long this will take."

"Oh, about an hour. Show me where the orthosofas are."

Borders waddled to the nearest one and began to unpack his equipment, a tiny laptop computer and a small kit of tools, spare parts, and lubricants. Michelle stood silently by. "You are disturbing my concentration. Leave," Borders ordered.

It took seventy-two minutes to maintain and reprogram the orthosofas and install eavesdropping devices. By the time anyone detected his unauthorized modifications, Juan Borders, fifty kilos lighter, with a new set of fingerprints and retinas and a new identity, would be living comfortably far, far away.

As he waddled happily toward the elevators, Borders could not help snapping his fingers and whispering the lyrics of a hit tune from *Dagon*:

"I am the very model of a literary critic
I have a nasty temper and a wit that is acidic.
I do not care a whit for
Writers just a bit more
Talented than this nasty-tempered literary critic."

CHAPTER
NINETEEN

"It was peculiar," Corporal Kerr said, shaking his head at the memory of what he'd seen. He had reported the Cheereek sighting to Gunnery Sergeant Bass, who then took Kerr and his fire team to Captain Conorado to repeat the story. "He's not human, so I can't say what was going through his mind or what he was really doing. But if he were a man, I'd say he was trying real hard to act like he didn't see us."

"How could he have seen you? Were you in the open with your helmets off?" Conorado asked. Everyone in the group—Kerr's fire team, Conorado, Lieutenant Giordano, Gunny Thatcher, and Charlie Bass—had their helmets off so they could see one another's expressions. All the other Marines in the secured area wore their helmets, and most of them had their chameleon shields down as well, so not even their faces were visible.

"Negative, sir. Our helmets were on and we were mostly in defilade." He considered, then amended his statement. "We had our shields up at first."

"So it's possible he saw your faces?"

Kerr nodded uncomfortably.

"But he kept going and you didn't see him again after he passed the end of the next ridge?"

"That's right, sir."

"Sir," Bass interjected, "Corporal Kerr called me right away. I was there in time to see the nomad. He disappeared beyond the next ridge, just like Kerr said. We waited for fifteen minutes and didn't see him again. Then I called in a replacement fire team to cover the OP and brought these men to you."

Conorado nodded. He hadn't needed that; Bass had reported the sighting to him as soon as he got it. The rest of what Bass just told him had been done under his orders. He asked Kerr, "What did he do that made you think he was acting like he hadn't seen you?"

"It's hard to say, sir. He didn't make any sudden movements, or stare at us, nothing like that. Even though his head occasionally swung in our direction, it was more like he was trying real hard to look everywhere *but* at us."

Conorado looked at Claypoole and MacIlargie to see if they had anything to add to Kerr's account. Both kept quiet, more than content to let Corporal Kerr give the report. Both of them respected and admired Captain Conorado, but he was an officer. Even though Marine officers always started off as enlisted men, just like them, when a man got that commission it did strange things to him. No matter how good an officer was, you could never tell when he might get some strange idea in his head and take radical action. No officer, not even Captain Conorado, could be fully trusted. It was better to avoid saying anything to officers if at all possible.

"Describe him."

"He looked just like the pictures we saw on the station. Hard-looking mouth, very long neck, fleshy crest laid back on his neck, a protrusion at the base of his spine that looked like a knobby tail, very thick thighs, skinny lower legs." Kerr shook his head. "The pictures we saw showed them wearing shiny clothes, sort of shimmery. His were dull, matte. He looked like he could blend into the background if he wanted to. He was carrying one of those projectile rifles and a short spear."

"What do you think he was doing?"

Kerr shook his head. "I don't know enough about these creatures to hazard a guess."

"What would you guess if he were human?"

Kerr shrugged. "Either hunting alone or scouting for something."

"And no one else came along?"

"That's right, sir. Not while we were there. We used all three visuals to improve our chances of spotting anyone. I was using naked-eye, Claypoole used his infra, and MacIlargie used his magnifier." That was standard procedure for a three-man OP.

Conorado looked at Bass.

"Lance Corporal Chan's fire team is manning the OP. They haven't reported seeing anything."

Conorado knew how conscientious Chan was. If he hadn't reported anything, there was nothing to report.

"Thank you, Corporal Kerr. Carry on. Charlie, stay here."

"Aye aye, sir," Bass said. Then to Kerr, "Report to Staff Sergeant Hyakowa."

"So what do you think?" Conorado asked when Kerr and his men were gone.

It took a moment before anyone said anything; nobody knew what to think about it. Bass was the first to come up with anything.

"Maybe the Avionian saw a face. If it saw a hovering face, it might have thought it was hallucinating."

"Say 'he,' " Conorado interjected. "They're sentient, not dumb animals."

Bass nodded. "Maybe *he* saw a face and thought it was one of the smugglers," he continued as though he hadn't been interrupted. "This site is pretty remote from the Cheereek village. Maybe they aren't supposed to know where it is, and he didn't want to give away that he'd discovered it. Maybe he saw something else that he didn't want to look at." He shrugged. "They're plainsmen. Maybe that's the way they always act near mountains."

"Any other ideas?"

Neither Bass, Thatcher, nor Giordano ventured any.

"Well, I guess that covers the spaceport. Make sure everybody knows Cheereek might be in the area and we need to avoid being seen." He looked at Thatcher. "Get some passive sensors out. That is all." They put their helmets back on and split up. Bass went to rejoin his platoon and give them the word. Thatcher took off to talk privately to each of the platoon sergeants and see to the placement of sensors. Giordano turned to tell the enlisted men in the command group—needlessly, as they had eavesdropped on the meeting. Conorado flicked on his helmet radio's command circuit to pass the word to the other platoon commanders.

"Demons," Guard Captain Cheerpt sneered. "There are no demons. Demons are stories told by old hens to make fledglings behave."

"There were demons at the Clumsy Ones' roost!" Kkaacgh snapped.

Graakaak was perched in council again. This time Cheerpt was on the long perch with Chief of Staff Oouhoouh and Chief Councilor Tschaah; Kkaacgh squatted alone on the side perch, facing between Graakaak and the other councilors.

"Describe them again," Tschaah interrupted when he saw Cheerpt's shoulders begin bunching to move into threat posture.

Kkaacgh took a deep breath to steady himself. He wanted to ruffle his shoulders but didn't dare, it could be taken as a challenge, and he didn't want to provoke a fight with the Captain of Guards.

"They were very hard to see," Kkaacgh said. "They had no true colors to them, just a red that flared slightly and faded almost to invisibility as they moved. Neither did they have true forms, instead they blurred around the edges, like they were halfway between here and the nether world. They seemed to have no necks, but had large lumps above their shoulders that I took for heads. Most of them carried objects that slightly resembled the Clumsy Ones' weapons, but had no more color or form than they did."

"How many were there?" Oouhoouh asked.

"I counted more than a hundred."

"You watched long enough to count that many?" Tschaah asked in awe tinged with fear.

Kkaacgh stretched his neck to its full height to emphasize his reply. "Yes."

"You are either very brave or very foolish," Tschaah said. "If you watched that long, I'm surprised the demons didn't see you and kill you for seeing them."

"I am a good scout. When I know the location of who I am scouting, they do not see me."

"But some of them did see you."

"Yes. When Guard Captain Cheerpt told of how he went along that Bower Bough to the Clumsy Ones' roost, he said there was nobody watching, nobody outside their tree. I had no reason to expect anyone to be there." This time his shoulders ruffled before he could catch himself. "I had no reason to expect demons."

Cheerpt hissed. "Demons! You went and and saw the strength of the Clumsy Ones' tree and it frightened you. You fear what you think their weapons might be like. So you come back and tell us stories of the tree not being there anymore, and stories of demons in its place so we will not attack and expose your fear by our victory."

Kkaacgh hissed back at him. "I do not lie! Three of my scouts saw demons as well. You can ask them. They will tell you the same."

Cheerpt began to say the scouts would give whatever report their captain told them to, but Chief of Staff Oouhoouh cut him off.

"There was no sign of the Clumsy Ones' tree?"

"No. There was only burned ground where it had been."

"The demons destroyed it with their hellfire?" Tschaah asked.

"I cannot say, but that's what it looked like."

"The demons do not like the Clumsy Ones," Tschaah said, addressing Graakaak. "We must take care they do not come after us for trading with them."

"What do you propose we do so that the demons do not come for us?" the High Chief asked his chief councilor.

"Get rid of the weapons. Hide them someplace away from

our rookery. Then if the demons come to see if we have any-thing from the Clumsy Ones, they will find nothing and leave us alone."

Graakaak stroked the many-tiered necklace of shinies that hung over his chest, the shinies that were left over from the Clumsy Ones' ammunition. If he followed Tschaah's advice, he would have to hide it as well.

"Do you say I give up my weapons and my conquest of the world?"

"No, High Chief." Tschaah smiled. "After the demons go away we can retrieve the weapons."

"No!" Cheerpt bolted upright on the perch and thrust his body toward Tschaah, arms spread wide. "We do not hide the weapons from demons that do not exist. We attack the Clumsy Ones' roost and take all of the weapons. Then we con-quer the world!"

"Cheerpt!" Graakaak bellowed, jumping to threat posture himself. Several guards aimed their Clumsy Ones' weapons at their captain.

Cheerpt looked at Graakaak and quailed; he had just done something very wrong, something taboo. Graakaak could have him killed for his outburst. In his peripheral view he saw the weapons pointed at him and knew he would stand no chance if he launched himself at the High Chief. Shivering, he raised himself from the threat posture and stretched his face toward the roof of the tent.

"I beg your pardon, High Chief. I think only of Cheereek conquest—and the greater glory of the great High Chief Graakaak."

Graakaak maintained his threat posture for a long moment before settling back and saying, "Sit, Cheerpt."

Cheerpt eased down.

Graakaak thought of all that had been said. Oouhoouh and Tschaah believed what Kkaacgh said about demons. Tschaah said they should hide the Clumsy Ones' weapons and all the shinies that came from them until the demons went away. He again fingered the glittery pectoral he wore so proudly.

Cheerpt thought Kkaacgh was lying. He wanted to attack the Clumsy Ones' roost and take all the weapons at once. Who should he believe? What should he do?

He decided.

"We will send another scouting party. This time it will be accompanied by two hundred warriors so if we find that we can attack we can do so immediately. I will lead." He did not pluck stones from his perch for his advisers.

"They should have killed him."

"Who should have killed who, Hammer?" Corporal Dornhofer asked.

"Corporal Kerr and his men. The alien."

Hayes tried to keep from looking at Schultz. He found the man's constant, barely contained violence a strain to be around. He was afraid he'd start shaking and drooling if he looked at Schultz and Schultz looked back at him. He managed to keep watching the desert, rotating his screens through naked-eye, infra, and magnifier. The three Marines were manning an observation post at the end of the next ridge to the east, a couple of kilometers away from what the Marines were beginning to call Smuggler's Ridge. Even wearing their chameleons and effectively invisible, they were behind a low ripple of rock. Directly behind them the rock rose a meter and a half to a narrow ledge, then continued up in a steep cliff.

"Not a good idea, Hammer," Dornhofer said laconically. "We're not supposed to let them know we're here, remember? If we flamed one of them, others would come looking for him and might find us."

Schultz raised all shields and spat. "Can't see us." He dropped his chameleon shield back into place, left the others up.

"Kerr thought that one saw them."

Schultz grunted, but didn't say what he was thinking—that Kerr's mind wasn't right yet, and it might never be right again. He had been very nearly killed a while back, and his physical recuperation had taken a long time. The experience had left his self-confidence shaken and made him too susceptible to fear. When a combat Marine lacks self-confidence and has a tendency to fear, he makes mistakes. Mistakes in a hostile situation can get Marines killed. Schultz had once admired Corporal Kerr. He no longer thought Kerr could be fully trusted.

Instead of saying what he thought, Schultz said, "They're aliens. We have to kill them before they have a chance to kill us."

"Hammer," Dornhofer said, his patience wearing thin, "you were at the same briefings and classes I attended. Weren't you listening? These birdmen are way behind us. In technology, in philosophy, in basic science. Everything. They don't even know the stars are suns and have planets. They aren't like the skinks. There's no way they can get to us. The scientists on the station never have any problem when they come planet-side. They aren't a danger to us." He watched Schultz raise his screens to spit again and then lower the chameleon back into place. That bothered him. In the years he'd known him, he'd only known Schultz to use his chameleon screen twice before. The first time was when 34th FIST was on Wanderjahr and Schultz saw the horrifyingly large animals of that world. The second time was when they fought the skinks on Waygone. Schultz had to be afraid, and that scared Dornhofer. Schultz was never afraid of anything.

"Human-designed projectiles," Schultz said in the short-hand in which he normally spoke.

"So they've got projectile rifles. Big deal. You can't shoot something if you don't know where it is. We're in our chameleons. They can't see us."

"Kerr thought that one did."

Dornhofer went to lift his shields to spit in disgust. His hand froze just short of the shields. "Traffic," he said to his men, then concentrated on the message coming over his helmet radio. He rogered his receipt of the message and in-structions, then said to Schultz and Hayes, "Look alert. Sensors picked up a large number of bodies headed our way from the east." He paused, then added, "Might be a couple hundred of them."

"How far away are they?" Hayes asked. Now that Schultz wasn't talking about the need to kill the aliens, he felt able to talk.

Dornhofer looked at the heads-up display that was transmitted to him as part of the message. "About four kilometers. If they keep coming, they should reach us in about fifteen minutes."

"They're moving pretty fast," Hayes said. "Any identity on them?"

"No. We shouldn't worry, though. They could be grazers, migrating to a new feeding ground."

"That's fast for migrating grazers." Schultz's fear had rubbed onto him.

"Maybe they're running from a predator."

"That's slow for running from predators."

Dornhofer sighed. "They're aliens. We don't know how fast or slow they move for whatever reason."

Hayes thought about that. Avionia was only the fourth world he'd been on. Like most Marines, he'd never left home before he enlisted. He really *didn't* know from experience or personal observation how fast animals traveled when they were migrating or fleeing predators. But he'd read and studied. On most worlds colonized by humans, grazers migrated much more slowly than this group was approaching, and ran much faster when trying to avoid becoming dinner. He hunkered lower. Those weren't grazing animals approaching them. In addition to learning about grazers, Hayes had spent a goodly part of his childhood and youth watching histo-entertainment vids. A couple hundred, Dornhofer had said. They had to be a Cheereek war party. Was he about to get into his first combat? He ran his hands over the not-very-familiar weapon he'd been issued, to make sure it was ready—a nonlethal weapon, he reminded himself uncomfortably. Three of them and two hundred nomadic warriors. He didn't think that many Cheereek had to be able to see the Marines in order for their bullets to hit them. And the Marines weren't wearing body armor.

Kkaacgh, Chief of Scouts, reined in his eeookk at the end of a ridge and twisted around to see how close Graakaak was. The High Chief was pulling up beside him.

"The next Bower Bough, High Chief," Kkaacgh said. He stretched his neck high in speaking to his leader, but didn't aim his face at the sky. "When we reach its end we will be able to see the Bower Bough where the Clumsy Ones had their roost."

"Why do we stop?" Graakaak demanded.

"High Chief, I stopped so if you wanted to send scouts ahead to see if any demons are where they can see the toe of the next Bower Bough, I can send them forward."

Cheerpt joined them in time to hear Kkaacgh explain the halt. "There are no demons," he said.

Graakaak looked to the next ridge and tried to picture the Bower Bough beyond it. Today was the first time he'd ever been close enough to the Bower Curtain to see the true size and texture of a Bower Bough. He was too unfamiliar with them; he couldn't picture something he'd never seen.

"What difference does it make if two or three scouts go to the next Bower Bough or we all do? If there are demons, they will see us however many come."

"High Chief, I would send scouts along the side of this Bower Bough." Kkaacgh pointed along the base of the ridge where they had stopped. The foliage there was higher than the spotty scrub of the steppe floor. "My scouts could go around until they reach a place where they can climb the side of the next Bower Bough and not be seen. Then, if there are no demons that can see us here, they will cross directly back, or stand where we can see them and signal us to advance. If demons are there, the scouts can come back unseen and we make a different approach." Or go away before the demons see us, he thought.

Graakaak regarded the length of the ridge to where it met

the mountainside and saw how long the roundabout was. He estimated how long the scouting trip would take.

"You make us wait for nothing," Cheerpt shrilled.

Graakaak glanced at his Captain of Guards. He agreed. "Too long," he said to Kkaacgh. "We cross. The demons have no reason to be looking here." Graakaak, High Chief of the Cheereek, raised a hand and dropped it forward. The mass of warriors and their thin screen of scouts surged forward.

Kkaacgh gulped and led the way. Who knew what demons had reason to do or not to do?

"Here they come." Dornhofer dropped his magnifier into place. The Cheereek were more than a kilometer and a half away, but the shield made them appear less than a hundred meters distant. "Looks like Cheereek," he said. He toggled on the command circuit and reported the sighting. "They're just trotting in the open like they don't have a care in the world," he finished. Then, "Roger," in reply to the instructions Bass gave him.

"The Skipper wants a head count," he told Schultz and Hayes when he got off the radio.

Schultz made a noise deep in his throat. He sounded like he wanted to spit, but wasn't about to raise his chameleon shield with the aliens in sight. He glared at the zapper he twisted in his hands, furious that it wasn't a killing weapon. Well, he still had his knife, still had his hands. When the aliens got close enough, he could still kill them.

When the distance closed to less than a hundred meters, Dornhofer hopped onto the ledge behind their position and stood up against the face of the cliff. He needed the elevation to be able to count the Cheereek. The way the chameleon effect worked, he should be completely indistinguishable from the rock face, even to someone who knew how to see a chameleoned man.

Kkaacgh resisted the impulse to spin around and flee when the demon hopped up on the face of the Bower Bough. "High

Chief," he trilled, "do not look at the toe of the Bower Bough. A demon stands there."

"I saw it," Graakaak trilled softly in a high, startled register. "Yet we live!"

"Don't let it know you saw it," Kkaacgh chirped back.

"There are no demons!" came Cheerpt's angry voice from only a few strides back. "If that was a demon, we'd be dead." But he had also seen it, and was now looking directly at the reddish blur that showed where it was. One-handed, he pointed his Clumsy Ones' weapon and pulled the trigger. The weapon roared thunder and bucked in his hand. His eyes followed the shiny it kicked out to the side. When he looked back, the demon wasn't there—and he was still alive!

"It's a Clumsy Ones' trick!" Cheerpt cried in triumph. He heeled his eeookk into a full galumph toward the toe of the Bower Bough.

Before he reached it, two sizzling pops sounded and he tumbled backward off his eeookk. At the same time, the riding beast was flung forward as though one of its legs hit a trip wire. The eeookk landed with a thud, bounced once, and momentum slid its body forward. Its outstretched neck and head caught against something and didn't move with its body—there was an audible crack as its neck broke. The eeookk's body spasmed and it emitted one feeble "eeookk" before it became silent. But its legs kept scrabbling at the ground as though it was trying to stand.

The Cheereek had never before heard sounds like the two sizzling pops. They saw the Captain of Guards tumble backward and his eeookk fly forward to its death. They cried out in fear and spun their mounts about to flee. They got in each other's way in their panic and briefly milled about, slamming into each other, before they untangled and raced away. During that brief moment three more sizzle-pops sounded and three more Cheereek fell to the ground. One was trampled into mush under the feet of the eeookks.

The Cheereek were so terrified by the demon's wrath that none of them saw Cheerpt rise to his feet and lurch about disoriented. Cheerpt's head cleared quickly enough for him to realize his scrabbling eeookk was dead and the rest of the party was abandoning him. He staggered after them, still so dazed he didn't even realize he didn't have his Clumsy Ones' weapon in his hand.

CHAPTER
TWENTY

Corporal Dornhofer was concentrating so intently on mentally sorting out the weaving, trotting Cheereek to count them that he didn't immediately notice the one pointing a rifle at him. When he did, he instinctively stepped off the ledge and went for cover. The move might have saved his life; it certainly lessened the injury. Just as he began dropping, a bullet slammed into his shoulder—it would have hit him in the chest if he had stayed on the ledge. When his feet hit the ground he staggered and dropped to his knees. He gritted his teeth against the pain and groped one-handed for the first aid kit on his belt. He didn't know how badly he was hurt, but blood was pumping from the wound and flowing down his arm so he knew he had to stanch the flow quickly. At the moment, he wasn't paying any attention to what his men were doing.

Schultz couldn't make out enough details in the milling mass of riders. Their constant movement and countermovement confused the eye and made it difficult to concentrate on any one of them, so he didn't see the alien point its rifle. But he heard the *crack* of the shot, then saw one alien burst from the flock and charge their position. He snapped his zapper around to bear on the alien and fired. The alien flipped backward. Next to him, he heard the sizzle-pop of Hayes's zapper and saw the now-riderless biped fall forward, vestigial wings flailing. The other aliens suddenly began twisting and weaving in an even more confusing pattern, meanwhile emitting sharp cries that sounded too much like the screeches of startled birds. He tried to shoot another of the creatures, but their rapid movement kept him from drawing a bead on any of them. In frustration, he fired without aiming—even a random shot into that flitting mass had a good chance of finding a target.

An alien pitched from its mount. Schultz fired again, and a second alien flipped to the ground. He heard Hayes fire again, and a third alien went down. Then he stopped at a weak cry behind him.

"Cease fire," Dornhofer croaked. "Cease fire." He held a field dressing to his wounded shoulder but was unable to pull the adhesion tabs on the bandage. He watched the Cheereek flee, then turned his attention to Hayes, who saw the blood oozing around the edges of the bandage. Hayes immediately put his zapper down and reached to complete the bandaging of Dornhofer's wound.

Schultz, seeing that his fire team leader was being taken care of, turned back to the aliens, ready to zap more of them.

"I said cease fire, Hammer," Dornhofer said. "They're running away. Let them go."

"We have to kill them before they come back," Schultz snarled. But he turned back to Dornhofer and locked eyes with him.

"You know the rules, Hammer. Force only 'in extremis.' They're running now. It's no longer extremis."

Schultz lifted his shields to spit. Except for a brilliant swath of crimson that painted his upper left arm, Dornhofer was invisible in the visual.

"That's a bullshit rule and you know it."

"Maybe, but it's still the rule." Dornhofer's voice was stronger now that he wasn't concentrating on holding the field dressing in place. It also helped that an analgesic flowed into his system from the bandage to dull the pain, along with the usual battery of antiseptics. "We let them go." His gaze briefly flicked past Schultz and he saw three of the Cheereek who'd been zapped stagger away—and a bloody mass that might be another. One of the riding beasts lay closer. He didn't want Schultz to see the fleeing Cheereek and take off after them so he kept talking to focus Schultz's attention on something other than the Cheereek who were still in range of the zappers.

"We have to report this," he said. "Somehow, either they saw us or they knew we were here. Then we have to stay here until someone comes to relieve us."

"We have to move," Schultz snapped. "They know where we are."

"Negative on moving. I don't think they're coming back anytime soon, not the way they ran away." By then the staggering Cheereek were well beyond zapper range. He flicked his radio to the command circuit to report.

Schultz swore when he turned and saw the last of the aliens making their stumbling retreat. He could have gone out there and killed them with his knife; he'd had time when they were closer. He ignored the eeookk; it was dead. He spat again and glared at the aliens. Why didn't the fools up the chain of command realize the danger the aliens represented? Some day a lot of Marines and other people would get killed because they weren't allowed to kill the aliens *now*. He glared at Dornhofer for distracting him while the aliens got away, but he didn't say anything.

Hayes shifted his position, drawing back from Schultz.

A Dragon roared up minutes later, throwing up a cloud of dirt and dust from under its skirts as it settled. Captain Conorado was the first man off. He quickly scanned the area, then went to Dornhofer. Gunny Bass and Sergeant Ratliff, the first squad leader, joined them.

"That it?" Conorado asked, jerking a thumb on an uncovered arm toward the bloody mass sixty meters away.

"Yessir." Dornhofer's voice was weak, the drugs supplied by the field dressing kicking in full force.

"Tell me what happened." Conorado stepped aside for one of the two corpsmen who came with him.

Dornhofer shook his head. "They saw me. They had to have seen me or it wouldn't have known I was there, wouldn't have been able to shoot me." He described what happened.

The corpsman ignored the conversation and gave Dornhofer a quick exam and treatment while he reported. "You'll live," the corpsman said when Dornhofer had completed his report to the company commander's satisfaction. "Hell, Dorny, I don't even know why you wanted a house call. I've seen Hammer cut himself worse shaving." He splinted Dornhofer's arm and bound it to his side while he talked.

Dornhofer chuckled. "Hammer could probably shake off a traumatic amputation."

"You could be right." The corpsman stood. "Let's get you aboard that Dragon. Take you someplace where we can check for broken bones." He looked around for Lance Corporal Chan, whose fire team had come along, and signaled him for help getting the wounded man into the Dragon.

While Conorado and the corpsman were dealing with Dornhofer, Bass and Ratliff were talking to Schultz and Hayes. Schultz complained bitterly about the ineffectiveness of the zapper.

"It's supposed to knock them down and keep them down. It didn't do squat."

Bass looked at Hayes.

Hayes swallowed. He was afraid to contradict Schultz, but Schultz hadn't given an accurate report of what happened. "It knocked them down for a few seconds," he said with a sidewise glance at Schultz, "then they got up and staggered away."

"Were they in fighting shape when they got up?"

Hayes shook his head. "I don't believe so. They forgot to pick up their weapons."

Schultz didn't say anything. He locked his jaw and glared at the one corpse, wishing it were a couple hundred flamed crispers.

Bass looked toward the observation post and saw two infra shapes coming their way. He removed his helmet.

"How does it look from here?" Captain Conorado asked as he reached them and removed his helmet. So did the second corpsman, who accompanied him.

"The zappers don't work as advertised. They knock them

down and take them out of the fight for a moment or so, but don't keep them down for as long as the scientists said."

Conorado grunted. That fit in with his idea about how the zappers were tested and told him why the tests might be flawed, but he didn't want to say anything about it yet. "Let's take a closer look," he said.

The eeookk was only twenty meters away. They went to it first. Its limbs still twitched and an occasional spasm rippled through its body, but its unmoving head showed it was dead.

"Damnedest thing I ever saw," Conorado said when a spasm made the corpse jump slightly.

"You never saw a chicken on a farm," Bass said, looking at the eeookk. "You go out and catch one for dinner. You cut off its head and let it go. Then watch the body run around for a few minutes. When it falls down you pick it up and hang it by its legs until all its blood drains out and it stops moving. This looks like pretty much the same thing."

Behind them the Dragon roared off, ferrying Dornhofer back to the camp for transfer back to Avionia Station and any surgery that might be necessary.

"They can keep fighting after we kill them," Schultz said accusingly.

"We don't know that," Conorado said.

"Maybe they'll run around," Bass added with a shrug. "Maybe their fingers will even jerk on the trigger and fire random shots. Or maybe they'll fall down just like we do. But either way, they won't be fighting, they'll be dead." Cheerpt's rifle lay a few meters away. "Secure that weapon," Bass ordered Schultz. He knew he had to find things to occupy the man or there could be trouble soon.

"Let's go," Conorado said as soon as Schultz picked up the rifle. He headed toward the Cheereek corpse.

Unlike the eeookk, the Cheereek corpse was motionless. The corpsman knelt next to it and opened his medkit. The corpsman began laying out the instruments and containers he thought he'd need to examine the body, then slipped on a pair of impermeable gloves to protect himself from possible pathogens.

Bass looked at the area around the corpse. The gouges and scuffing on the ground made it obvious what happened. The Cheereek—or more likely their mounts—had panicked. They jostled one another as they scrambled to flee. This Cheereek was either knocked off his mount in the melee or was zapped by one of the two Marines. Whichever, it got trampled to a pulp. He saw three more rifles in the area.

"Lance Corporal Schultz, secure those weapons."

Schultz shot him an angry look and darted a glance at Hayes. He thought the junior man should be given the job of policing up the dropped weapons, but went to gather them without giving voice to his thoughts.

"Bring them here," Bass said when Schultz picked up the last rifle.

Schultz made to offer a rifle to Bass.

Bass shook his head. "See if you can field-strip it," he said.

"Field-strip." Schultz sighed softly. He put the rifles on the ground, then sat cross-legged and picked one of them up to examine closely. He quickly figured out how to unload it, then set about pulling and twisting various parts to see which of them might separate from one another. In three minutes he had it broken down into half a dozen parts. Each of the parts looked like it would require specialized tools for further disassembly.

"Kind of slow, Hammer."

Schultz gave Bass a hard look. "Different technology." He was unfamiliar with how the rifles functioned, but he knew picking up something he'd never handled before and figuring out that fast how to take it apart was pretty good.

"You're right." Bass acknowledged what Schultz hadn't said. "Now how fast can you put it back together?"

It took him less than thirty seconds.

"You might have just earned yourself a souvenir."

Schultz nodded once, sharply. He stood up with the reassembled rifle and tried its feel. "Wasn't made for humans," he said.

"But it was made by humans," Bass said. "Take them back to the OP."

Schultz looked pointedly at where Conorado stood over the

corpsman who was still working on the corpse, with only Hayes nearby guarding them.

Bass nodded in the direction the Cheereek had taken off. "It's all right. We'll be able to see anyone coming long before they get here."

Schultz grunted, then turned and headed back to the observation post with the four rifles.

Bass joined Conorado. "What do you think we'll learn that the scientists didn't already tell us, Skipper?"

Conorado shook his head. "Probably nothing. Maybe something. The scientists didn't know these creatures would be able to see us in our chameleons, so there are things they don't know that we need to know." He gave Bass an odd look. "How much did you find out about the physiology of those aliens you ran into?" He was still angry that one of his platoons had fought aliens several months earlier, on what should have been a nothing deployment, and that he'd only just found out about it. And here his whole company was confronting a totally different alien species. Three centuries of humanity riding the spaceways without running into a single alien sentience, and now Marines from his company encountered two different—and very different from each other—sentiences in only a few months' time.

"I didn't find out a damn thing about them," Bass said. There was a haunted look in his eyes. "We never even found out why they vaporized when we flamed them." He turned his haunted look on the captain. "Anywhere we hit them, even glancing, they flared up."

Conorado shook his head. He couldn't visualize an entire body flashing into vapor from a direct blaster hit, much less a glancing one.

Both Marines looked at the corpsman, who was putting his equipment back in his medkit. He stood.

"Well, sir, it was hard to tell, he's got a lot of broken bones, but from what I can see, what we were told on Avionia Station about their gross anatomy and movement is accurate. I took a few fluid and tissue samples. Maybe I can learn something from them." He shrugged. "If for no other reason than to verify what we were already told."

"That's all we can ask of you, Doc." Conorado clapped the corpsman on the shoulder. "Let's go back to the others. The Dragon should be on its way to pick us up." He looked west and saw the dust cloud raised by an approaching Dragon.

While the rest of his men boarded the Dragon, Conorado spoke briefly to Sergeant Flett on his helmet radio and told him to send one of the UAVs east along the foot of the ridges.

Back at Smuggler's Ridge, Captain Conorado made a detailed report to General Cazombi.

Cazombi sighed deeply. "One incident of the Cheereek seeing one of your OPs could mean anything. Probably one of your Marines had his chameleon shield up, or they had some equipment out where it could be seen. Two incidents, the second where the men knew about the first, that sounds like, yes, the Cheereek can see in the infrared. This is a hell of a way to find out."

Conorado didn't comment. Ground commanders on his level found things out in "a hell of a way" entirely too often.

"Well, they know you're planetside and where you're at," Cazombi continued. "I want you to move out ASAP. I'll have Essays on the ground in an hour. Use them to move your people in their Dragons to a point halfway to the Cheereek encampment. Ride in as close as you can, then go by foot the rest of the way. See if there's an armory where they store the rifles. If there is, see if you can get someone into it to get some of those weapons out." He paused in thought for a moment before continuing. "I think we have to forget about getting all of them. Whatever else you do, don't let the Cheereek see any of your people. Don't put any of your people in jeopardy to get the weapons; we don't have body armor for them. Questions?"

"Sir, why wait for Essays? By the time they get here, I can have my Dragons at the Cheereek encampment."

"The Dragons leave traces on the ground, the Essays don't. Understand?"

"Yessir. Good idea."

"Then let's do it."

"Aye aye, sir."

An hour later the Dragons boarded the Essays for the short hop. Three hours after that, when scouts led by Scout Captain Kkaacgh checked the demon-home, where Graakaak's war party had seen the mighty stones fall from the sky and magically fly away again, the place was empty. The only sign the scouts found to show the demons had ever even been there was a few spots of blood where Cheerpt had shot one. Graakaak gave the order to return to the rookery.

General Cazombi's brow furrowed deeply when he finished his conversation with the Marine commander. *The Avionians can see in the infrared!* That was the only way he could imagine them being able to see the Marines. Unless they had some sort of radar sense, or something like the echo location of bats. Or could sense electromagnetic radiation the way some fish did. And why shouldn't they have a nonhuman sense, when they weren't human? And why hadn't the scientists studying them discovered it? Or did they know about it and simply not think to include that tiny bit of information in their briefings and data packets? No, he thought, they wouldn't have neglected to tell him and the Marines about it, not if the lecture the laryngopathologist gave him on the biomechanics of Avionian speech—when all he wanted was information on their language—was any indication of their thoroughness.

No point in worrying about why they hadn't discovered this sense. That would be as much of a time and energy waster as agonizing over the Combined Chiefs decision for the *Khe Sanh* not to deploy its string-of-pearls. Either you accept reality and deal with it or reality will kill you. The reality he had to deal with was that the Marines had no advance knowledge of the Avionian ability to see in the infrared. The reality was that the Marines had to move across a sparsely vegetated flatland without being detected by beings who could see them. The reality was that he didn't have a string-of-pearls to feed the Marines the information they would need to make that move undetected.

The general thought about all the resources he had available. There were enough. All he lacked was permission to use them. Getting permission would be tough if not impossible; he doubted any of the scientists on Avionia Station understood enough about military necessities to realize how important detailed information about the steppe landscape was to those Marines down there. No matter how bluntly he said it, they probably wouldn't believe him if he told them they could have 120 dead Marines on the surface without a proper ground survey. Too damn many ivory tower scientists—and these scientists were definitely ivory tower—couldn't see one mil beyond their own specialties. But he wasn't about to risk the lives of those Marines on anyone's myopia.

He headed for the docking bay, sure that an Essay was in it. The chief petty officer who rode herd on the shuttle craft might be station personnel, but he was still a navy noncommissioned officer. Cazombi had no doubt the chief wouldn't hesitate to do the right thing when a general asked him for a small favor.

General Cazombi was right. Fifteen minutes after making his decision, he was in a shuttle headed for the *Khe Sanh*. Convincing Captain Natal took less than a minute. Convincing Commander Spitzhaven, the *Khe Sanh*'s captain, took no time at all—he was under Natal's operational command and didn't need to be convinced, merely ordered. Natal didn't simply order Quantex, though, he took half a minute to convince the ship's captain. It took an hour longer to prepare and launch a ground-survey satellite.

Dr. Hoxey might not like it, and the Combined Chiefs might get their knickers in a bind over it, but it was done. The only thing Hoxey could do was order the satellite retrieved. By the time the surveillance crew solved the "technical problems" Commander Spitzhaven assured him they'd have in retrieving the satellite, its work would be done. The Combined Chiefs, a hundred light-years away, were even more impotent. They couldn't do anything at all unless somebody told them about it, which Cazombi had no intention of doing—and both Captain Natal and Commander Spitzhaven were adamant that no sailor would volunteer the information to the Combined Chiefs.

General Cazombi had no illusions that he was home free on his possible breaches of the Rules of Engagement, but he wasn't going to have dead Marines on his conscience.

CHAPTER
TWENTY-ONE

"I killed one," Cheerpt snapped. "They cannot be demons."

Graakaak jerked into threat posture, his mouth a head's length away from the Guard captain's outstretched throat.

"You shot it and it disappeared. That does not mean it wasn't a demon. Nor does it mean you killed it." Graakaak's breath was hot and threatening against Cheerpt's throat.

"It did not kill us. That proves it was not a demon."

"What did it do after you shot it?" Oouhoouh demanded. "It killed your eeookk and took your mind," the Chief of Staff said, answering his own question. "When the rest of us fled its wrath, it took the minds of two warriors and killed another one."

Cheerpt swallowed but bravely plowed ahead. "A demon would have killed all of us. The scouts said our dead was trampled, not killed by demon power."

Kkaacgh shifted uncomfortably on his perch. When he first saw the strange apparitions, he believed they were demons. He did not want to join Cheerpt in arguing with the High Chief, but . . . He stretched his neck up but remembered to keep his face level so the truth of what he said could be seen. "High Chief, I believe Guard Captain Cheerpt might be right."

Graakaak's head darted from nearly touching Cheerpt's throat to threateningly close to the Scout captain's. "You were the first to say they were demons. Explain yourself."

"High Chief—" Kkaacgh struggled internally and managed not to swallow. "—Guard Captain Cheerpt is right when he points out the demons did not kill us. All the stories say demons kill everyone who sees them."

Graakaak slowly withdrew from his threat posture and settled back on his perch. He cocked his head at Tschaah in question.

In agreement, the ancient Chief Councilor reluctantly lowered his head to chest level. "The Captain of Guards is right, High Chief. All the stories say the demons let none who see them live."

"If not demons, then what are they?" Graakaak demanded.

The four advisers exchanged glances. Even Cheerpt turned his head to look at the others.

At length, Kkaacgh ventured a guess. "Their heads are large and sit directly on their shoulders," he said. "They balance on top of their legs instead of between them like proper people. I have seen the images of demons Tschaah sometimes draws in the sand. The demons he draws resemble proper people. Perhaps these are Clumsy Ones' demons." The others all cackled at once, demanding to know why he thought that.

"I first saw them where the Clumsy Ones had their roost, and the Clumsy Ones' roost was no longer there. Perhaps they came to punish the Clumsy Ones."

"I was right," Tschaah said. "These demons disapprove of the Clumsy Ones trading with us. They fear to have the Great High Chief Graakaak armed with such weapons. We must hide the Clumsy Ones' weapons until the demons are gone."

"They are not demons!" Cheerpt interrupted. "And they are gone. We saw the sky stones that came and took them away."

"We saw the sky stones come and leave," snapped Tschaah. "We do not know what happened to the demons."

Graakaak considered his advisers and what they had said. Young Scout Captain Kkaacgh was astute, very astute. Why hadn't he noticed that much earlier? He would bear watching to learn what his ambitions were, to see if he presented a potential threat. And he might be right about the nature of the demons, or whatever they had encountered near where the Clumsy Ones' tree had been. Guard Captain Cheerpt had obvious ambitions, but he recently proved himself a worthy leader of warriors. Perhaps there was another use for him. Chief Councilor Tschaah was wise, as the old ones are supposed to be, even if he was as cautious as an old hen. But Graakaak knew if he followed Tschaah's advice too closely, he would never rule the world. Chief of Staff Oouhoouh was a puzzle. He had been too quiet during the deliberations. He had not stepped forward to take the lead in raiding the Aawk-vermin or the Koocaah-lice to prove the value of the Clumsy Ones' weapons. Very strange behavior for the war chief of the Cheereek. Perhaps he was getting too old for his position and should be removed as Chief of Staff. Maybe Chief of Staff would satisfy Cheerpt's ambitions. If not, he would have to die.

"I will think on these matters," Graakaak said. "One thing doesn't need thinking about." He fixed his gaze on Kkaacgh. "I must know if the Clumsy Ones or their demons return."

"High Chief, I will dispatch scouts to watch. I will place them myself. We will know swiftly if the Clumsy Ones or their demons return to that place or to a place near it." His chest was puffed out because the High Chief accepted his idea of the Clumsy Ones' demons.

Graakaak plucked four lesser stones from his perch and flipped them at his advisers.

Shortly after, Kkaacgh led twenty scouts out of the rookery. When they reached the place where the Clumsy Ones' roost had been, they found no sign of the Clumsy Ones' demons.

When the Essays picked up the Marines, they shot to sub-orbital altitude before diving back at an angle calculated to bring them down so the descent wouldn't be seen by the Cheereek. Then they zoomed nap-of-the-earth until they reached their LZ, a low place in the steppe. The Essays touched down for less than half a minute, discharged their Dragons, then headed back to orbit and Avionia Station.

The Dragons were roaring out over the steppe even as the Essays lifted. Ten kilometers from the last known location of the Cheereek camp, they stopped in a small pan and drew into a defensive circle. Their ramps dropped open and the Marines boiled out. The platoons had their assigned security sectors already, and every man in the company knew exactly where to go when he ran off the Dragons.

Then they waited for General Cazombi to get back to Captain Conorado with further orders. Two hours passed before the call came.

Seen from the height of a standing man—or from the stretched-neck height of a Cheereek—the arid steppe looked billiard-table flat, a plane broken only by occasional spikes of vegetation. But the appearance was deceptive. Eons of wind had sculpted shallow dips in the flats, and rains had slashed channels into its surface.

The scientists on Avionia Station had many and varied duties to perform in their study of that alien world. None of them, though, had the same interest in the minutiae of the surface that an infantryman had. So the staff hadn't developed the kinds of maps an infantryman needed to move from one place to another. Their maps of the Cheereek home range showed no details smaller than three meters in diameter. They were sufficient for a Dragon racing cross-country, or for a man who simply wanted to walk from here to there. But the maps were absolutely inadequate for an infantryman who needed to travel undetected.

Most times that would present no particular problem for the Marines. Most places they went they either had maps with the necessary level of detail or they moved through areas sufficiently foliated that they didn't need to concern themselves with every ripple or irregularity in the ground. Or the string-of-pearls could transmit real-time maps down to the infantrymen. But they had no string-of-pearls now. The lone satellite General Cazombi had launched was a poor substitute.

Captain Conorado studied the heads-up display map he received from the orbiting satellite. Its resolution was much finer than Avionia Station's maps—thirty centimeters. He would have preferred fifteen centimeters, but thirty was good enough so many kilometers from the Cheereek encampment. He sketched out a proposed route of march for the first five kilometers, then magnified it section by section to make sure it gave adequate concealment all the way. It seemed to. He called for a meeting of the platoon commanders and sergeants, and Lieutenant Musgrave, commander of the reinforced Dragon platoon, joined him. Gunnery Sergeant Bass brought Sergeant Bladon, whose squad would have the point on the movement. The face-to-face meeting wasn't absolutely necessary, not with the helmet radios. But no matter how sophisticated communications became, Conorado believed that nothing could ever replace looking men in the eye.

When the platoon commanders and sergeants gathered, Conorado looked at each one, then glanced at Sergeant Bladon and back at Bass for a moment before he began by informing them that second squad, not first, was going to have the point. Schultz was in first squad. He was almost always the pointman in a company movement. In addition to having first-rate field skills and uncanny instincts, the career lance corporal didn't trust anybody else with the most dangerous job in a movement. Conorado wondered how Bass was going to handle Schultz's inevitable explosion about not having the point. Well, Bass could handle it.

"Don't ask how, I don't know," he said, moving on, "but we've got detailed topography. Take a look." He transmitted the satellite map to the Marines. At first glance the map wasn't much, displaying a strip twenty kilometers long by little more than one wide. It became more impressive when they magnified the scale.

Bladon whistled softly. He hadn't been a squad leader long, and this was the first time he'd ever seen a fresh satellite map on a HUD.

Staff Sergeant Hyakowa chuckled and nudged him. "Bet you didn't know you were having your picture taken, did you?"

Bladon didn't answer, he just stared at the image in the display. He was looking at the platoon's position. Not only could he see nearly every ripple in the ground and about half of the studs of vegetation, in infrared he saw each of the Marines.

"We are going to make a reconnaissance in force," Conorado said after a moment. "This map shows the first part of our approach to the Cheereek encampment." He had no need to elaborate, they already knew what they were doing; all that they lacked was some few details, and he didn't have many to tell them. "I don't know how much of the company will get closer than five kilometers from the camp. Right now I don't even know how many men I'll send in closer once I decide where the company waits. The Avionians have extremely sharp vision, and we found out the hard way that they can see us in our chameleons. So we absolutely need to stay out of sight." Conorado looked at Bladon. "Is there anything about that route you don't understand?"

Bladon looked the captain in the eye. "Nossir, it's clear."

"Then let's move out. Take care of it, Charlie."

Bass nodded with a wry grin. The others cast sympathetic glances at him. None of them would want to deal with an unhappy Hammer Schultz, and Schultz had been unhappy to begin with on this mission.

They took their time, keeping to hollows and deeply cut channels. There was only one spot where they had to rise to level ground, and it had enough vegetation that they were able to crawl one at a time across the four-meter flat without exposing themselves. The sun was going down by the time they reached the five kilometer midpoint to the Cheereek encampment. By then the ground surveillance satellite had completed three orbits and gathered more data.

Captain Conorado studied a new map, one displaying twenty kilometers by nearly three. He saw that a platoon could get close enough to the camp to hear the voices in it—and avoid the sentries the map showed. It showed him the same for the opposite side of the encampment. But the map wasn't sufficiently wide to show enough of the landscape to its flanks. Two more passes would do that. He checked the time data on the map. Another pass was due in forty-two minutes. Then a ninety-six minute wait for the next one. Nearly an hour and three-quarters before he had a map that would show all the approaches. He wanted, needed, his men to be in positions where they could observe the entire encampment.

He toggled on his helmet radio's command circuit and said, "Hold positions. All platoons, put out observation posts. Chow down."

It was full dark by the time Conorado had enough data from the satellite to make his night plans. He moved the whole company forward to within two kilometers of the encampment. First platoon sent one squad forward to a spiderweb of runoff channels half a kilometer closer. Second platoon sent a squad more than halfway around the camp to the right. Third platoon sent one squad more than halfway around to the left. The nocturnal habits of the Cheereek helped greatly—most of their sentries were called in; the few still left on watch were withdrawn to within a hundred meters of the encampment's boundaries. He had people in position to observe the entire encampment when the sun rose.

When day dawned, the Marines quickly learned there was no central storage, that the Cheereek took their rifles home with them at night. The Marines waited until after sunset to withdraw. They returned to Avionia Station.

"They're gone," Dr. Hoxey said. "Your mission is over. How soon can you leave?"

General Cazombi shook his head. He had a feeling the smugglers, whoever they were, weren't finished yet. "If we leave, there's nothing to keep them from coming back. Our mission isn't over until we know they're through here." He looked at Special Agent Nast.

Nast nodded. "The mission isn't over until we've found and arrested them."

Dr. Abraham spread his hands. "How can you catch them if they're gone and you're here?"

"By being here when they return," Cazombi said.

"And being ready for them," Captain Conorado added.

"But the Avionians," Abraham objected. "The Marines on the surface, surely they'll be seen. Think of how that will disrupt Avionian development!"

Cazombi shook his head. "Don't worry, Doctor, the Marines won't disrupt the Avionian development."

Hoxey was angry. "How can they not?" she shrilled. "We know they can see your Marines in their—what do you call them—chameleons."

"I'm keeping the Marines in orbit until the smugglers return."

"You can't! Why—Why there isn't space for them on the station. We won't be able to get any work done."

"Don't worry, they won't be underfoot. I'm going to return them to the *Khe Sanh*. It has the training and recreation facilities they need that Avionia Station doesn't."

"You mean that—that warship is going to remain here?"

"Yes, ma'am. For as long as I believe the Marines might be needed."

Hoxey glared at the general and the Marine captain. She'd see about that. As soon as the meeting was over, she'd have Markoney prepare another drone. It would demand the recall of the Marines. It didn't matter to her that the drone would take months to make the round trip to Earth and the Marines would probably be gone by the time it returned; they might not be gone by then, and she had to get them out of her way so she could continue her essential research without fear of outside interruption or meddling.

CHAPTER
TWENTY-TWO

The *Lady Tee*, Patch's private ship, made a perfect landing less than a kilometer from where the *Marquis de Rien* had touched down.

Henderson and his men waited nervously for Patch to join them at their new planetfall, about five kilometers from where the *Marquis de Rien* had first come down. Most of the men stood about nervously outside the ship, waiting for the boss to arrive. Herbloc, dreading every contact with Patch, had retreated inside, where he lay in his bunk, his flask within easy reach. He knew Patch would want him to go to the Cheereek encampment, and he needed to prepare himself for that. After a few moments he dozed off.

"Heeer-bloc!" a voice roared over the ship's intercom. "Get your fat ass out here on the double!"

Herbloc started awake. "His master's voice," he whispered, swinging his legs out of his bed. He took a long nip from his flask and sighed.

Emerging from the ship's passenger elevator into the steamy Avionian sunlight, Herbloc froze. *That woman!* She was the one he'd encountered on Luna Station before they left to come to Avionia the first time. What . . . ?

"Well, well," Katrina Switch said, smiling viciously, "who do we have here? Why, it's Dr. Fatass. We meet again." She swaggered over to Herbloc, who stood rooted with embarrassment, and rubbed her riding crop gently between his legs. Herbloc's face turned a deep red.

"Madam . . ."

She grabbed Herbloc's ear—hard—and dragged him to

233

where Patch was standing. As he stumbled along, she swung her crop hard against his copious posterior. The men gathered around roared with laughter. "The boss wants you, needle dick." Kat laughed and pushed him forward. Herbloc lost his balance and fell to his knees in front of Patch. He was overcome by a feeling of terrible desperation: he had been coerced into a dangerously illegal operation that could get him a life sentence with no chance of commutation; none of these professional criminals cared for him; and now this bitch had made his humiliation total.

"Sam—" Gunsel protested. Kat flashed him an evil look and he let his protest die. Nobody dared cross Kat in front of Sam Patch.

"On your feet, gutsack." Patch hoisted Herbloc to a standing position. "Okay, Jum, you drive. Art, get your tool kit and any remaining rifles. Don't worry about the trinkets, we won't need them. Doctor, you've been talking the talk, so I hear. Well, now you're going to walk the walk. Get in the landcar." He turned to Henderson. "Sly, you and the rest of the boys secure the area while we're away."

"Sam, what are you going to do?" Henderson asked. He felt he knew and he didn't like it.

"I'm going to kick some birdbrain asses, Sly. We're going to that camp and get all the goddamned stones the birdies can shit in a day. Then we'll blow this hole."

"Sam, be careful. These Cheereek can be dangerous. You should take more men and better weapons than your sidearms. The Cheereek have Art's guns and know how to use them."

Patch snorted. "Goddamned popguns, Sly! I planned it that way." He patted his holstered hand-blaster. "This is all the persuasion I'll need. I'm taking personal charge of this operation now and I don't take no crap off nobody, especially a bunch of goddamned birds. Just leave this to me." He turned to Kat. "Katrina, come along with me and bring your toy collection. If things slow down, you can practice on the good doctor here." He roared with laughter and climbed into the landcar.

                              * * *

Cheerpt, Captain of Guards, was enjoying a warrior's trail meal, a living gwak. The small ground-burrower, held firmly in Cheerpt's powerful hands but not yet quite dead, protested loudly, appendages flailing feebly as Cheerpt's powerful mouth tore into its innards. Gwaks were delicious. Cheerpt looked up suddenly. A messenger stood before his perch and held his head high, face pointed at the sky. Annoyed by the interruption, Cheerpt expressed a long white stream of goop from his cloaca. This was not only a sign of his displeasure but also an affectation of his position; only someone of his perching could get away with excreting within the confines of the rookery. A stone squished to the ground in the midst of the goop. He gave the unremarkable stone a quick glance. Every time he saw one of the things now he was reminded of the Clumsy Ones. Cheerpt shifted angrily on his perch.

"Yes? Be quick!"

"The Clumsy Ones, Captain. They come again."

Cheerpt stiffened. Lifeless, the gwak fell from his hands. "Which ones? How far away are they? How many? Look at me so I know you speak the truth."

"One swift-mover, Captain, the kind Heerk-kloock uses, not the kind the demons use. When I saw it, it was too far away to tell how many Clumsy Ones are in it. They will be here by the time the sun touches the top of the High Tree."

Cheerpt calculated. It was mid-morning, he had plenty of time. "Did anyone see you come to me?"

"No, Captain. I entered the rookery quietly and told those who greeted me that I was returning from the training roost."

Cheerpt had posted guards on the far edge of the dry lake bed to warn of the approach of the Clumsy Ones. True, they had not been seen since the arrival of the others, the ones some thought were demons, but Cheerpt knew the Clumsy Ones would be back. He was patient. He needed them to put his plan into operation.

On the ancient lake bed's far side, a hundred of Cheerpt's most trustworthy warriors were at a post he called a training roost. It was a few kilometers from the encampment. Graakaak

had ordered him to prepare them for a full-scale assault against
the Aawk-vermin's rookery, to wipe them out entirely. Cheerpt
protested that he needed time to develop new tactics neces-
sitated by the introduction of the Clumsy Ones' weapons.
Graakaak had conceded the point reluctantly. They had attacked the Aawk-vermin several times before using the
weapons, the High Chief pointed out, and those raids had
been great successes, so he wanted to move at once. Cheerpt
had convinced him that an assault on a rookery demanded
different tactics than an ambush of a hunting party. He added
that the possibilities for extending the Cheereek territory—
and Graakaak's grandeur—were guaranteed if he could be
allowed to exploit to the maximum the use of the new weapons. And who knew what tribes lived beyond the horizon?
They might not all be so despicable or as easy to defeat as the
Aawk-vermin.

Lands beyond what they knew! The idea of going so far and
attacking those who lived in the far regions fascinated the
High Chief. "How do you propose to march farther than any
others have ever marched?" he asked.

"I have a plan, Great One," Cheerpt answered evasively,
"but I would rather you permit me to develop it fully before I
announce the details to you." That was precisely why
Graakaak had to be replaced as High Chief. He could not
think ahead. He could not think *big*.

So far Graakaak had been patient with the delay. Cheerpt
was gambling the Clumsy Ones would return before he was
forced to attack the Aawk-vermin roost. He needed the more
powerful weapons he was convinced the Clumsy Ones kept to
themselves. The wait had paid off.

"Return to the training roost. Tell the lead guard in command to prepare the ambush. I shall be there shortly to take
charge."

"I go, Captain," the messenger said. He bounded onto his
eeookk and galumphed toward the training camp.

The route the Clumsy Ones always took to the rookery
passed through a deep defile on the plain just above the shore-

line of the dry lake bed. It was there Cheerpt planned to trap the Clumsy Ones and kill them all.

Patch was in a very jovial mood as his landcar sped along at more than a hundred kilometers per hour, kicking up a vast cloud of dust as it crossed the ancient lake bed. Jum Bolion was silent, paying strict attention to his driving. Kat toyed with Herbloc, telling him in graphic detail how she would use him once they were back on board the *Lady Tee*. Herbloc had to admit he was a little interested at first, but after a few moments of the most vile descriptions of sexual perversions, he tried unsuccessfully to concentrate on other things. He dared not even take a nip from his flask. He watched Gunsel out of the corner of his eye. The artificer sat morosely silent himself, looking out the nearest viewport, toying with the hilt of the knife strapped to his equipment belt. He was the only person in the world Herbloc could call a friend. A wave of self-pity welled up inside the forlorn old mountebank.

"Lay off a bit, Kat," Patch said over his shoulder, "I think the old bastard's enjoying it too much." Kat's cynical laughter joined Patch's. Herbloc suddenly realized he would never get out of his situation alive. The two of them were going to work him over after they had gotten all the stones they wanted. He shuddered. There was no escape.

The landcar began to slow down. "There's the old shoreline, just ahead," Jum Bolion said. "Once we're up and over that, we go into the woods, through a short defile, and then there's the hardpan of the old lake. That'll lead us straight to the camp."

"How long is that defile, Jum?" Patch asked. "I don't like defiles."

"A hundred meters, maybe, and two meters deep at the deepest part. It's the most direct route to the camp."

The landcar crawled up the slope and then plunged onto the plain. A few hundred meters along it roared down into a gully that grew narrower as they proceeded. Jum Bolion abruptly slammed on the breaking lever and the vehicle skittered to a dust-billowing halt. "What the hell?" he exclaimed.

Patch leaned forward and peered out through the windshield. A huge boulder, easily two meters in diameter, blocked their way forward. "Must've come down since we were last out here," Bolion said, putting the vehicle into reverse.

Kat screamed from the rear of the passenger compartment, "Look out!" A tremendous crash sounded behind them and the vehicle was momentarily engulfed in dust and debris. "There's another boulder behind us!" she shouted.

"You damned idiot," Patch screamed at Bolion. "We've been ambushed! Drive over the goddamned thing!"

"I can't, boss. The boulder's too steep. We're trapped!" Bolion screamed back.

"Kat, Art, Jum, draw your weapons," Patch ordered. "We're going to get out and slag a way through that rock. Anybody shows his head over the embankment, flame his ass."

They clambered out into the narrow defile, weapons at the ready. All was quiet in the gully. "They thought better of it." Patch grinned and confidently stepped toward the boulder. Then a hundred Cheereek warriors descended on the quartet in a solid mass. Not a single shot was fired, but even disarmed, Sam Patch was still a tough customer. Dust flew everywhere as Patch lay about him, smashing faces and breaking arms and cursing. A well-aimed spear-butt to the back of his head finally brought him to the ground.

"Secure them firmly!" Cheerpt ordered. He picked up Patch's weapon and examined it carefully. He pressed a stud where a trigger might have been and a small ball of flame shot out of it. The ball bored a black-rimmed hole through one of his warriors, bounced straight back off the defile wall behind him and engulfed him in a ball of flame. The warrior flapped his arms in agony and rolled on the ground, blazing intensely. A pall of burnt roast filled the air.

Cheerpt watched the dying warrior in wide-eyed astonishment. "I knew they kept better weapons to themselves," he mused. "Now I know how to use them. Excellent!"

Two of the Cheereek emerged from the landcar, Herbloc in tow. "Heerk-kloock!" they announced victoriously. Another displayed his soft parts to Cheerpt. "And we have the Gun-

chelk, Captain. And his tools." Cheerpt's guards had watched
Gunsel closely as he repaired weapon malfunctions, noting
which tools he selected for each job and how he used them.
They understood perfectly the concept of interchangeable
parts, and with the tools in their possession, Cheerpt was confident he could always maintain a corps of riflemen whose
weapons would function.

Patch had now recovered from the blow that knocked him
out of the fight. Blood streaming down the side of his head, he
shouted at Herbloc, "Goddamnit, fatass, tell these stinking
birdmen who I am. They'd be nothing without me, I supplied
the goddamned rifles! Tell them they're making a big mistake,
Herbloc, a *big* mistake. Tell them, goddamnit, tell them! What
am I paying you for, you silly old bag of farts?" An unfamiliar
tone of panic had crept into Patch's voice. Herbloc enjoyed it.

"Ah, Heerk-kloock," Cheerpt said, addressing Herbloc who
now stood before him, his arms firmly secured with cords.
"What is that loud Clumsy One saying?"

Herbloc answered without hesitation. "Honorable Guard
Captain, he says you are the entrails of a Gwak, your anus is
plugged with stones, and you have the sex organs of a dis-
eased female fledgling. He says you reek of the excrement of
the Aawk-vermin, which you eat with great relish, and that
your own excrement—"

"Cease, Herrk-kloock!" Cheerpt squawked imperiously.
He heaved his shoulders and ruffled his feathers. "You come
for the stones, Heerk-kloock? You shall have them, then. For
his insults, the loud Clumsy One shall have all he wants, if he
can find them. Strip them of their coverings," he ordered his
warriors. In seconds the five humans stood naked before the
Captain of Guards. "What is this one?" he asked, gesturing
toward a seething Kat.

"That's a 'woman,' a female of our kind, Captain. Its function is to provide pleasure, domestic comforts, and fledglings
for our warriors." He couldn't help breaking into a grin as he
spoke.

Kat did not miss the grin. "What are you telling him, you

limp-dick bag of turds?" she shrieked. Herbloc grinned even wider.

"It is surpassingly ugly, Herrk-kloock, uglier than you even," Cheerpt observed.

Herbloc stretched his neck as high as he could. "That is indeed ugly, Greatest of Warriors, Most Generous and Wisest Councilor."

Cheerpt preened himself for a moment, deeply pleased by Heerk-kloock's words, which all of his men had heard and understood. And fully agreed with, of course.

"Bring the eeookks!" he commanded, "We are going to the pit!"

"Where are they taking us?" Patch shouted.

"Where you will get what you want, Sam, boy-o, what you came here for," Herbloc answered, and then laughed outright. Patch lunged at him but was instantly restrained by his guards.

"Herbloc, you worthless shit, when I get loose I'll cut your goddamned cock off and feed it to you!"

"Indeed, boy-o? Indeed?" Herbloc laughed.

They smelled the pit long before they reached it. Here and there, Cheereek squatted on the latticework erected over it. A few looked up in surprise. Cheerpt's guards seized them. A platoon spread out to watch the trail approaching from the rookery. He could not afford now, so close to success, to have someone blunder into them and warn Graakaak of what was going on.

The humans stood on the edge of the vast stew, gagging on the acrid stench that rose from the viscous lake of excrement accumulated over generations.

"Throw the loud Clumsy One in!" Cheerpt ordered. The guards holding Patch lifted him up and tossed him lightly over the edge. The humans watched in horror as he plopped feet first into the effluvia and went right under. An instant later his head burst through. His entry had released a wave of indescribable stench that now wafted over the onlookers, who choked on the acrid fumes that burned their eyes and made them cough. His bonds had separated and Patch flailed about in the muck helplessly. He screamed once and went under a second time, but he managed to break through to the surface again. This time his hair was gone, eaten away by the caustic guano.

Kat watched her partner, fascinated by his agony; his screams sent shivers of pleasure through her body. She twisted free of her guards, stepped close to the edge and shouted down to him. "Not such a big man now, are you, Sam? How's that big cock of yours doing, little man? Shriveled up, I bet. I can hear those big nuts of yours singing a different tune now. You're screaming beautifully darling, far better than when I used to whip your bony ass. How sweet it is, how sweet it is!" She laughed.

Herbloc, standing behind her, lurched forward, placed his foot on her rump and shoved hard. Kat teetered on the edge of the pit. Lithe and athletic, she managed just barely to keep her balance. "Aaah, aaahh!" she screamed.

"Fair return is fair play," Herbloc said, nudging her gently with his shoulder, pushing her finally over the edge.

Gracefully, like a pirouetting ballerina, she plunged down into the jakes. She landed face first with a loud splat. Her bonds separated and she spread her arms and legs wide in an effort to keep herself afloat. By then Patch had gone down for the last time. Kat managed to roll over and rise to a half-sitting position as she too sank quickly into the bowelage. With one hand she clawed wildly at the feces burning her eyes, nose, and mouth; with the other she beat in futility at the rising excrement. Great patches of her hair began to fall away from her head. As the tide engulfed her magnificent breasts, she stretched her neck to take in one last breath of fetid air, and in a pure ecstasy of terror Katrina Switch slowly commenced her final sadomasochistic epiphany.

Her last scream echoed for a long time, it seemed to the three men standing above the pit.

"It's our turn now," Gunsel whispered, his voice quavering. "Godawful way to go."

"Maybe not," Herbloc answered. He had never felt more confident in his whole life than he did right now. "Great One," he addressed Cheerpt, aping as best he could the Cheereek submission posture and speaking in a powerful voice. "Eagerly, we await your pleasure! Should you deign to spare us, which you shouldn't because we are totally worthless creatures, we shall never trouble you again." The warriors murmured approvingly. Heerk-kloock had courage, and he knew the proprieties of dealing with a great leader.

Cheerpt did not respond at once. "Go!" Cheerpt ordered the trio at last. "Go and never return! Tell your kind the Cheereek wish never to see them again. Tell them Cheerpt rules in this land now and he is a terror and an avenger and any of your kind who come here again shall end like those two in there." He gestured toward the pit. "Go! Go, before the Mighty Cheerpt changes his mind."

"Beat feet," Jum Bolion whispered as a guard released his bonds. He wasted no time trotting off in the direction of the ancient lake bed. Gunsel and Herbloc turned and followed him. It was a very long walk back to the *Marquis de Rien*, and they might die of dehydration before they reached it. But even that was better than the pit. Bolion and Gunsel hardly noticed that Herbloc chuckled to himself almost all the way back.

CHAPTER
TWENTY-THREE

"They'll be back," General Cazombi said.

"How do you know?" Dr. Hoxey snapped. "Do you know who they are? Are you in touch with them that you know their plans?"

Cazombi gave an eyebrow a quarter raise. "Doctor," he said in a very soft voice, "I don't need to be in contact with them to know they'll be back. They are greedy men who see the chance to gain incalculable riches. No risk is too great for them to take. Besides, they probably think the Marines left when we found the smugglers had gone. They might think it's safe to come back."

Hoxey snorted. "Poachers are cowards. They sneak around and only go where they think there is no danger to them."

Poachers aren't cowards, Cazombi thought, they're hungry, desperate people. He knew that poaching was often the difference between life and death for them. And smugglers were willing to take huge risks for huge gains. Both could be very dangerous. He gave Hoxey a speculative look and wondered if she knew the difference between poachers and smugglers, if she deliberately used the term that originally meant hunting on a royal preserve instead of the term that meant traffickers in contraband. He wondered if the official charges against them meant poaching in that classical sense.

"I'll have the Marines ready for them when they come back," Cazombi said. "But I have to launch more satellites to spot them if the Marines aren't allowed planetside."

"*No!* Absolutely not. You simply cannot put out that 'string-of-pearls.' There's too great a chance of the indigenous population seeing the satellites and realizing they're being observed. Think of the devastation that would cause, how horribly their cultural development would be disrupted!" She glared at him, remembering how he had already launched a satellite without her authorization, and how much trouble the navy seemed to have withdrawing it when she learned of the device. She believed the navy was in league with the general and deliberately delayed retrieving that satellite—but she couldn't prove it.

Cazombi nodded. "Yes, I understand why we can't deploy the string-of-pearls. That's not what I want. A half-dozen orbiters and one geosync stationed over the smugglers' area of operation will do everything we need."

Hoxey's eyes popped. Did he really think she'd give permission for so many satellites? "Don't be absurd. You can't launch satellites. There's entirely too much danger of their being seen and upsetting the development of the indigenous population."

He again quarter-raised an eyebrow. Even if seen by the creatures, who were rarely awake at night, a satellite could easily be taken for a meteorite shooting across the night sky. It would certainly be less disruptive than a clearly visible "new star" that suddenly appeared and wobbled against its background—and might even show a disk to the Avionians' sharp eyes.

"All right, then, four orbiters and a geosync."

"Nonsense! It can't be done. No satellites. None at all."

In the end Cazombi got Hoxey to agree to two satellites in high orbits. It was less than he wanted, but the worst case scenario was the smugglers wouldn't be spotted until it was too late to intercept them.

On the *Khe Sanh*, the Marines trained for a rapid launch. General Cazombi had Captain Conorado set up a rotation. One blaster platoon, reinforced with a corpsman, was on standby at all times, in chameleons with all combat gear, in a compartment near the ship's welldeck. The ready platoon could launch on fifteen minutes notice.

Third platoon was on its third rotation as the ready platoon when one of the satellites detected a ship touching down. Twelve minutes later an Essay holding third platoon in two Dragons and a third, passengerless Dragon ejected from the *Khe Sanh*'s welldeck and headed for that "high speed on a bad road" that was a Marine planetfall. The Essay touched down seventy-five kilometers from the spot where the satellite showed the smugglers' ship had touched down—only a few kilometers from Smuggler's Ridge.

The original plan was for the ready platoon to head straight to the smugglers' ship, apprehend everyone aboard, and hold them for Special Agent Nast. But the satellites showed the smugglers had almost immediately headed for the Cheereek encampment in a landcar. Third platoon set out to intercept them. But Guard Captain Cheerpt sprang his ambush while the Marines were still three klicks away.

"Do not intervene," General Cazombi ordered. "Stay out of sight and see what they do. First platoon is ready to launch. Special Agent Nast is with them."

The Marines dismounted and followed irregularities in the steppe floor to where a few of them could watch the encampment while the rest of the platoon remained out of sight.

Gunnery Sergeant Bass set two flank observation posts, each a hundred meters from where the platoon waited in defile. Sergeant Ratliff took Schultz and Hayes to man the one to the left—Corporal Dornhofer's wound was severe enough to keep him out of action for at least two weeks. Sergeant Bladon sent his second fire team—Corporal Kerr, Claypoole, and MacIlargie—to the right. To augment the satellite coverage being fed to him, Bass himself used a collapsible periscope from his position in the middle. The Marines watched helplessly as Cheerpt's guards manhandled the captive humans.

"What are they doing?" PFC Hayes asked when he saw the Cheereek line up the five naked humans at the edge of the pit. Even at that distance they could detect the stench. He gasped when they picked up a man and threw him into the muck. Next to him Schultz bit off a howl of fury and twisted his hands on his zapper as though he were strangling the ineffective weapon.

Hayes was so shocked he couldn't make a sound when one of the men kicked the woman into the pit. A moment later he looked at Sergeant Ratliff for an explanation when the Cheereek appeared to send the remaining humans away.

Ratliff shook his head; he had no explanations. They watched the three naked men shrink into the distance.

"What are we waiting here for?" Schultz snarled. "We should be going after them."

Hayes couldn't tell from Schultz's voice whether he meant the men or the Cheereek, and didn't know whether Schultz wanted to rescue the humans or arrest them.

Then Gunny Bass's voice came over the all-hands circuit: "Look alert. Something's happening down there."

In the encampment, in an open area a short distance from the pit, a gaudily ornamented Cheereek accompanied by a phalanx of Cheereek armed with the human-manufactured rifles, confronted the group that had held the humans. An iridescent sash shimmered across a massive pectoral that glittered and flashed in the sunlight on his chest. A bonnet of brilliantly dyed feathers adorned his head, and more iridescent material bound his loins. Obviously the chief, he stood with his feet planted wide apart, legs straight, torso and long neck stretched parallel to the ground, arms splayed. One hand gripped a rifle, the other a short spear. The Marines could just hear his shrill cawing.

One of the Cheereek who'd killed the two humans hopped out of his group and mirrored the chief's stance. His pectoral was smaller than the chief's but larger than any of the other Cheereek present. His hands were empty but his shrill caws no less loud than the chief's.

"You killed two Clumsy Ones!" Graakaak bellowed. "I did not tell you to kill Clumsy Ones! For that, you die!"

Cheerpt hissed at the High Chief. "No, Graakaak, you old hen's dropping. I do not die, you do! You are content to perch quietly and let the Clumsy Ones bring what droppings they deign to give us. We should attack them as I have said. Then we would have their even greater weapons, the weapons that will allow us to attack and conquer the entire world, not just the Aawk-vermin and the Koocaah-lice."

"Back!" Graakaak snapped at the guards who'd begun to advance to arrest their captain as soon as they heard his treasonous words. "Cheerpt is but a frill-mite, yet he dares insult the High Chief. If he were a fledgling, I would give him to the females to discipline. But he has masqueraded as the Captain of Guards for too long to give to the females." He shook the weapons he held. "I will kill him myself!"

The guards who supported Graakaak formed a semicircle behind him, facing the guards who stood with Cheerpt. More guards skittered to the commotion, saw what was happening, and took sides. The sides were about evenly matched, most of them carrying short spears as well as Clumsy Ones' weapons. Oouhoouh arrived with a cohort of warriors. Graakaak gave him a quick sign, and the Chief of Staff ordered the warriors to form a circle at a distance around the two groups. Chief Councilor Tschaah joined Oouhoouh.

Silence settled over the Cheereek rookery as word got around and everyone rushed to the pit to see. It seemed that everyone wanted to be present when the drama played out.

"The Clumsy Ones do not have more powerful weapons!" Graakaak cawed when the silence had filled to breaking. "Cheerpt the frill-mite spins old hens' tales. We have seen their demons, and not even their demons have weapons as powerful as these!" He shook his rifle again.

Cheerpt smiled and curved his neck back. His tongue protruded mockingly between his hard lips. "You are wrong, Graakaak. They do have more powerful weapons. I have some of them. Here is one." He pulled the hand-blaster he'd taken from Sam Patch from his sash, pointed it at Graakaak, and pressed the firing stud.

The plasma bolt passed close enough to blister the High Chief's shoulder, and Graakaak leaped backward, screeching in pain. To his rear a guard squawked in agony when the bolt struck his shoulder. The aroma of freshly cooked meat filled the air. The two groups of guards instantly sprang at each other, wildly firing their rifles and jabbing with their spears.

Tschaah put a gnarled hand on Oouhoouh's arm to stop him from ordering the warriors into the fray. "Let them fight," he said. "If we back one and the other wins, we will be slaves."

"But—" Oouhoouh protested.

"Whichever wins will still need a Chief of Staff and a Chief Councilor," Tschaah said. And if both die, he added to himself, no one will challenge Oouhoouh's right to be High Chief. And I can control Oouhoouh.

Oouhoouh signaled his warriors to keep their positions and not let any of the combatants break out of their circle.

Graakaak craned his neck to look at the red blisters on his shoulder. He saw the injury was superficial and snapped his head toward his antagonist. A group of guards loyal to Graakaak had charged Cheerpt as soon as he fired the hand-blaster, but a knot of guards loyal to their captain bounded to form a shield in his defense. The two groups were unable to take the time to reload the rifles after their first flurry of fire. Some swung their Clumsy Ones' weapons like clubs, others dropped the rifles and fought using the short spears. All cawed or screeched battle cries. They collided with thuds and clashes of weapons. Dust bellowed in clouds around them.

Looking for Graakaak, Cheerpt hopped up and down behind the milling guards. Just as Graakaak screeched his war cry and began running around the melee that protected him, Cheerpt saw him. He pointed the hand-blaster and pressed the firing stud. The plasma bolt went high and struck the top of Chief Councilor Tschaah's tree, bursting the roof into flame.

An attacking guard leaped to intercept Cheerpt, but the attacker's side was momentarily exposed and one of Cheerpt's guards sliced deeply into the muscles of his side. The attacker was spun about by the force of the hit and lost his balance. Spewing blood, he sprawled into Cheerpt's path.

Cheerpt tripped and fell heavily just as a bullet from Graakaak's rifle shot through the space his chest had occupied. Cheerpt wasn't aware of the near miss, he only knew he'd been tripped. He savagely kicked the head of the near-dead guard whose fall inadvertently saved his life.

Graakaak had seen Cheerpt fall when he fired the Clumsy Ones' weapon, and he lifted his head to crow victory to the sky just as two guards, grappling bare-handed, slammed into him. All three tumbled to the ground, with the High Chief on the bottom.

Cheerpt's follower, seeing who was under him, let go of his antagonist and thrust his hands at Graakaak's throat to strangle him, but the loyal guard plunged his short spear into the traitor's back. Two loyal guards pulled the corpse off the High Chief and helped their leader to his feet.

Graakaak brushed them off without thanks and looked again for Cheerpt to make sure the usurper was dead. When he held Cheerpt's disembodied head high in his hand, that would stop the fighting.

Cheerpt saw Graakaak first. He whipped his blaster around, but the plasma bolt bored through the chest of the guard standing next to Graakaak and went on to hit another in his pectoral of brass cartridges, which absorbed enough of the bolt's energy to melt, charbroiling the guard's breast well-done. He died shrieking in horrible agony.

Graakaak screamed and leaped at Cheerpt. The two collided and went down in a frenzy of flailing arms and stabbing, poking, hammering weapons. Graakaak tried for a quick victory, spearing his head at Cheerpt's throat, but Cheerpt jerked his neck into a loop and Graakaak's mouth bit the hard-packed dirt. Sensing his opportunity for a quick victory of his own, Cheerpt twisted his arm around and pressed the hand-blaster's stud. The plasma bolt flashed through the High Chief's arm frill and burned half of it away. Screaming more from shock and surprise than from pain, Graakaak rolled away.

The weapons held at the ends of their outspread arms momentarily forgotten, the two scrambled to their feet and spun to face each other, instinctively dropping into the threat posture and darting their heads in and out, trying for bites on one another's head and neck, poking at eyes.

The melee around them dissolved into paired combats. The

weaker—or less lucky—fighters among the guards were down, dead or dying, and the survivors were more evenly matched; none of them could spare any attention to the central fight between Graakaak and Cheerpt. Their caws and battle cries combined into a cacophony that absorbed and obliterated individual cries.

Graakaak was the first to remember his weapons. In a movement almost too fast to see, he jerked his neck into an S curve to pull his head and neck out of danger, stepped forward and swung his arms together so the weapons would meet in the middle of Cheerpt's neck. As fast as Graakaak moved, Cheerpt saw what he was doing and jerked himself erect. Graakaak's rifle and spear clanged together harmlessly. Cheerpt cackled as he brought his hand-blaster around and fired.

Again the bolt missed its intended target. It flashed into the rookery and set another tree aflame. By then the flames from Tschaah's tree had spread to others. Hens and fledglings raced about the rookery shrieking and squawking in panic. The few warriors and other males who were still in the rookery tried to contain the growing conflagration, but they were too few and there wasn't enough water, so the blaze grew.

Graakaak saw that Cheerpt had fired the Clumsy Ones' terrible fire weapon at him several times and the only injuries he suffered were a scorched shoulder and a singed arm frill. The gods meant for him to win—Cheerpt could only lose this fight! He shrieked and threw his rifle at Cheerpt. Cheerpt had to duck out of the way just as he fired the hand-blaster again, frying a pair of fighting guards, killing one and leaving the other to writhe on the ground in terminal agony. Before Cheerpt could regain his balance, Graakaak sprang and skewered him with his short spear.

Shocked by the sudden strike, Cheerpt looked at the spear protruding from his belly just below his ribs and knew it was a fatal wound. His face twisted with hate, he looked the victorious Graakaak in the eye and raised the hand-blaster. He wasn't going to die alone.

Graakaak contemptuously slapped the weapon from his

hand. Then he jerked the spear from Cheerpt's belly and plunged it into the top of his chest, just above the pectoral.

Cheerpt staggered back, then slowly toppled.

Graakaak straddled the corpse and used his spearpoint to sever Cheerpt's head from his neck. He rammed the spearpoint into the head from the neck hole, thrust it high into the air, and cawed his mightiest victory cry. It was loud enough to cut through the cacophony of battle.

All the guards looked to see who had won. Graakaak's loyal guards joined in his victory cry, then turned furiously on the disheartened traitors. It was over in moments.

CHAPTER
TWENTY-FOUR

"I told you I saw the demons' mounts," Captain of Scouts Kkaacgh said to Lead Warrior Ctweeleer. "There are their tracks." He pointed at lines in the dirt.

Lead Warrior Ctweeleer didn't look at the marks. His neck was craned around and he was looking back toward the rookery. He was sure Guard Captain Cheerpt was up to something. There had to be a reason Cheerpt took the Clumsy Ones captive, and that reason couldn't be good. He didn't want to be out with two hundred warriors looking for the "demons" the Scout captain thought were there, he wanted to be back at the rookery where Chief of Staff Oouhoouh could tell him what was important, what to do.

"Lead Warrior," Kkaacgh snapped. "Look at the marks."

Ctweeleer slowly turned his head. "Scouts don't give orders to warriors," he sneered.

"Captains give orders to leads." Kkaacgh half lowered himself into threat posture.

Ctweeleer curved his mouth parts with disdain. Later, he would talk to Oouhoouh, ask if the Scout captain did indeed outrank a lead warrior. For now, he looked at the marks. Yes, they were much the same as the marks left by the mount of the Clumsy Ones. They were wider, that was the only difference he saw. But that didn't mean they were made by the demons' mounts.

"The Clumsy Ones' demons went away."

"They went away when the Clumsy Ones went away. The Clumsy Ones came back. So did their demons."

"You don't know that."

Kkaacgh stared hard at Ctweeleer. "We will follow their tracks."

Ctweeleer bobbed his head at the sky in reluctant acquiescence. Oouhoouh *had* told him to go with Kkaacgh. Still, he thought he should be back at the rookery.

Kkaacgh had thought long about the Clumsy Ones' demons. When Cheerpt attacked them at the Bower Curtain, he might have killed one. That would explain why it disappeared as it did, and the blood. The demons had fought back, but only managed to stun the Cheereek. If it was true that Cheereek armed with Clumsy Ones' weapons could kill Clumsy Ones' demons, and the demons did not have weapons that killed Cheereek, it should be possible for a Cheereek war party to attack and kill the demons. This was his own idea. As soon as one of his scouts reported seeing the demons' mounts, Kkaacgh had gone to Chief of Staff Oouhoouh and told him a scout reported the approach of a Koocaah-lice war party. Oouhoouh told him to take a party of warriors under Lead Warrior Ctweeleer to find and stop the Koocaah-lice. They left just as Cheerpt and a group of guards neared the rookery with naked Clumsy Ones. He would have liked to stay and see what the Captain of Guards was doing, but he had to find the Clumsy Ones' demons. If he returned to the rookery with the heads of Clumsy Ones' demons, no one would object that he had lied about the Koocaah-lice.

Kkaacgh sent scouts ahead on fast eeookks to find the demons. It didn't take long. The demons had dismounted and gone on foot to where they could watch the rookery without being seen—from the front. They were fully visible from the rear. Including the few who were off to the sides, there were a little more than thirty. It was easy for the Cheereek war party to move into position behind them.

"They've got blasters!" Hayes exclaimed when he saw a plasma bolt flash through the mass of Avionian nomads.

There seemed to be a momentary pause, then the Cheereek in the flat rushed together. Seven seconds later an irregular rattle of gunfire faintly reached the Marines across the two-kilometer distance to the camp.

Schultz lifted his magnifier shield to spit. "Only one has a hand-blaster," he said after watching the battle for a moment. He glared futilely at the zapper in his hands. The way those aliens were bunched up, third platoon could quickly slip into position eight hundred meters from them and cook most of them before they even figured out what direction they were being attacked from. Then head back to orbit and have the *Khe Sanh* nuke the whole damn planet! Slag the aliens, all of them. And if those damn scientists on Avionia Station didn't like it, slag them with the aliens.

In all their positions, the Marines were watching the battle in the Cheereek encampment. None of them paid any attention to the sensors they'd deployed, sensors that were trying to alert them to the arrival of a large group of man-sized bodies a hundred meters to their rear. The first any of them knew about the war party behind them was when an irregular volley of rifle fire stuttered past them and into the ground around them. Except for PFC Hruska in second squad; before he knew anything, a bullet thudded into the back of his neck, entered his skull, and turned his brain into mush.

The Marines spun about, ready to fight back. The Cheereek were out of range of the zappers. But not for long.

Lead Warrior Ctweeleer cawed a loud command and the Cheereek kneed their eeookks into full galumph. Most of them fumbled fresh magazines into their rifles as they charged and got off another shot before they reached the Marines. Their aim, poor to begin with, was worse from the backs of their galumphing mounts, and all their shots missed.

"Hold your fire," Gunny Bass ordered on the all hands circuit, calm despite his surprise. "On my order." He watched the approaching Cheereek, judging their distance, while he drew his hand-blaster. Only three of the humans had hand-blasters— he, Staff Sergeant Hyakowa, and the corpsman. Everyone else had zappers. He waited until the ragged line closed to within fifty meters, then shouted, "Fire!"

Thirty-one zappers and three hand-blasters fired instantly in a hum of simultaneous sizzle-pops from zappers, punctuated by the louder cracks of plasma bolts. Three Cheereek were thrown from their eeookks, black-rimmed plasma holes charred through their torsos. A dozen and a half others wobbled or fell from zapper hits, or were tossed when their eeookks were hit and tumbled to the ground.

The Marines shifted aim, fired again, shifted aim once more, fired a third time. Eight Cheereek warriors and one eeookk lay dead with the aroma of overcooked meat wafting from the plasma holes bored through them. Two lay twitching, cawing softly, their necks broken in their falls. Many others staggered to their feet and stumbled about, disoriented from the zapper hits. But the great majority of them reached the Marines and raced through, jabbing and slashing with their short spears.

The Marines fought back.

Three Cheereek were surprised by a maneuver a few of the Marines used. Lance Corporal Claypoole had an instant of déjà vu when he saw a Cheereek coming straight at him, leaning over his eeookk's neck, spear jutting straight forward to skewer him. He'd seen something very like this once before, and his body remembered what happened then. He dropped his zapper and drew his combat knife, then stood his ground until the charging Cheereek was too close to change his spear's aim. Claypoole simultaneously twisted and dropped onto his back on the ground, slashing upward with the razor-sharp blade. It sliced through the eeookk's thigh. The animal shrilled out in pain, staggered a couple of steps and collapsed, sending its rider tumbling. Claypoole was already back on his feet and moving. He leaped and landed full-length on the fallen Cheereek. His knife darted out and the warrior bucked violently once, then settled into spasms as blood gushed out of his neck onto the thirsty ground, which eagerly drank it. Claypoole rolled off the dead Cheereek and spun away, looking for another. They were all past the Marines.

In other places Dean and Chan used the same maneuver to dispatch Cheereek.

Schultz was more direct. He spun aside, grabbed the spear thrust at him and used its leverage to yank the rider off his eeookk. He dropped his knees heavily onto the Cheereek's chest to knock the wind out of him and pin him, and heard and felt bones shattering from the force of his landing. He was surprised, but only for an instant. Then he was on his feet shouting into his helmet-radio, "Hit them hard, their bones are weak!"

Corporal Goudanis saw a knot of riders charging his fire team's position, saw the length of the eeookks' stride, and realized the Marines could roll under them without getting stomped on. He shouted at his men to dive under the galumphing beasts. He made it and came up to zap a warrior in the back. PFC Quick lived up to his name and also came up shooting and staggered an eeookk, which almost threw its rider. Lance Corporal Van Impe wasn't as lucky—he dove right into the forward swinging foot of an eeookk. He fell heavily and rolled, but the agony of broken ribs and clawed flesh tore through him. The eeookk also felt the collision—the bones of its foot shattered and it flipped, landing on its rider and knocking him senseless. Goudanis bounded to the insensate warrior and killed him with his knife. Quick dashed after the staggering eeookk and managed to grab its rider before he recovered his seating. He flung the Cheereek to the ground and smashed a fist into his throat. The warrior clutched his throat and struggled for breath that wouldn't come through his crushed windpipe. His face turned purple and his feet thudded helplessly against the ground until Quick drew his knife and plunged it into his heart.

A short distance away, the rest of the Cheereek reined their eeookks around and prepared to charge again. Most of the Marines took advantage of the momentary pause to fire at them. Three fell from blaster hits, more staggered from zaps, then they charged, cawing their war cries. Eight more were staggered by zapper hits or thrown from stunned eeookks before they reached the Marines.

But the Marines now knew the physical weakness of the warriors. They swung their zappers like clubs and had the satisfaction of hearing bones shatter and the screams of injured Cheereek. All about the Marines, bodies thudded to the ground, and they fell upon the Cheereek with their slashing, jabbing knives.

The second charge wasn't a totally one-sided victory, though.

Corporal Pasquin was stabbed in the back as he crushed the head of a warrior he'd knocked to the ground.

Corporal Linsman killed a Cheereek who'd thrust a spear into Lance Corporal Watson and then been pulled from his mount when the spearpoint jammed between two ribs.

Lance Corporal Neru from the gun squad suddenly found himself surrounded by a trio of Cheereek He grasped his zapper like a bat and twirled, flailing, to keep the Cheereek at bay. But one warrior managed to fumble a fresh magazine into his rifle and made the shot of his life. The bullet struck Neru in the sternum and holed his heart. The three warriors raced on to join the next charge.

Still, only half of the Cheereek were still mounted when they turned to charge a third time. But those who had been zapped at the greatest range had already recovered enough to begin looking for riderless eeookks so they could rejoin the fight.

Before leading his warriors at the Clumsy Ones' demons again, Lead Warrior Ctweeleer trilled out orders. Since many of the demons were down, the Cheereek would not charge through; they would melee. He signaled and they galumphed into a thin rain of hand-blaster bolts and zapper shots.

A clump of twenty Cheereek sped toward the OP where Sergeant Ratliff waited with Schultz and Hayes. Ratliff and Hayes methodically fired their zappers. Ratliff picked targets for both of them to shoot at; if one hit wasn't enough, maybe two simultaneous hits would be. They were. Schultz couldn't fire, he'd battered his zapper so badly on the Cheereek he broke its firing mechanism.

Seventeen Cheereek reached the trio.

Schultz bellowed, stepped inside a thrusting spear, and rammed his zapper into the eeookk's chest so hard he shattered its ribs and sent a spew of guts from its cloaca. He grabbed the rider by the throat and threw him to the ground then stomped his chest, crushing his rib cage and sending splinters of bone into his heart. Almost casually, he swept his zapper in a roundhouse at another Cheereek and broke his back. He felt a sudden burning in his shoulder and turned to see what had stung him. The Cheereek who'd just stabbed him was darting his head forward to bite the Marine. Schultz slipped to the side and shot out a hand to grab the warrior's neck just behind his head. Grunting as he yanked the Cheereek from its seat, he spun it around his head, its body like a weight in the middle of a rope, knocking down two eeookks and their riders and sweeping a third off his eeookk before the abused Cheereek's head separated from its neck and its body flew away.

Ratliff ducked and weaved and bobbed as half a dozen Cheereek milled about him, getting in the way of each other's jabs and thrusts. He swung his zapper at one eeookk that danced out of the way, but his swing was hard enough to throw him off balance and he tumbled into the legs of another who didn't dance away quickly enough. It fell, both legs broken, and pinned its rider. Another eeookk pranced over Ratliff, who jammed his zapper upward into its abdomen, rupturing something just as the rider jabbed his spear into Ratliff's thigh. The injured eeookk shrilled and bolted, its rider unable to control it. Ratliff pulled the spear from his thigh and dropped his zapper in favor of his new weapon. He thrust the spear at a Cheereek who came in too close. The warrior jerked back and avoided the point, but his eeookk didn't manage to avoid the backswing and the spearpoint sliced through its neck. Out of the corner of his eye Ratliff saw another spear flashing toward him. He slapped it out of the way but it sliced a long gouge from his hand to his elbow. He slammed the point of his spear into the side of the Cheereek and looked around for the others. They were prancing back out of range.

Hayes ran and jumped, kept moving so he wouldn't be a stationary target. He fired his zapper time and again, doing his best to hit a Cheereek two or three times before he had to pay attention to another attacker. Sometimes he missed the rider and hit the mount instead. The eeookks staggered more than their riders did. When Hayes realized that the eeookks were more susceptible to the zapper than the Cheereek, he aimed at them. The animals he hit stumbled and responded sluggishly to the commands of their riders; two of them fell, and one of those didn't get back up. In moments Hayes was faced by only four dismounted warriors. He managed to hit one of them three times and knock it out of the fight before the other three closed to spear range. He parried one jab, but a second coming at almost the same instant hit him in the side. It glanced off his ribs but cut deeply enough to send a cascade of blood flowing down his side. That Cheereek darted in to finish him off with a bite, but Hayes broke its neck with the zapper before its hard mouth could reach him. The remaining warrior, realizing he was facing his demon alone, ran. Hayes calmly raised his zapper and shot him three times.

The fight was over. A few dozen warriors were in full, screeching flight, mounted or on foot. The survivors, dazed from zapper hits, were beginning to stir. Many of the Marines methodically began to kill them.

"Belay that!" Charlie Bass roared into his all-hands circuit. "Remember the ROE!" He looked around the battleground through his infras and saw his men backing away from the Cheereek survivors. Despite the distance, he even saw first squad's outpost 150 meters away from his position. No one there was moving away from the alien red splotches. Either those aliens were all dead, or those three Marines had already finished killing them. "Squad leaders report." Without paying much attention to what he was doing, he slapped a field bandage high on his left chest and pressed it into place to stop the bleeding. He ignored the lesser cuts on his hands and arms.

The reports came in. Everyone except the corpsman and PFC Kindrachuck in the gun squad had suffered at least one wound. The gun squad's Lance Corporal, Neru, was dead. So were PFCs Hruska and Rowe from the second squad. There were no fatalities in the first squad.

Bass called for the Dragons to come up. "I don't give a good goddamn if the locals can see them," he snapped when the Dragon squad leader reminded him they weren't supposed to get close to the Cheereek encampment. "I've got too many people who can't walk. Get to my location as fast as you can."

Then he called Captain Conorado, on the *Khe Sanh*. At the end of his report he requested to be relieved of command. "Sir, it's my fault they got so close before we realized there was anyone around. I failed miserably in my responsibility as platoon commander. I should have made sure someone was watching the sensors."

"Not a chance, Charlie," Conorado replied. "You're the man on the scene. You have an unfinished job. I'm not relieving you until that job is done."

"Staff Sergeant Hyakowa can finish the job, sir."

"Not as well as you can. The smugglers still have two ships down there. It's your job to secure them until someone arrives to relieve you. Now do it."

"But—"

"I said do it, Gunnery Sergeant."

"Aye aye, sir."

Bass looked around at his men. Those with lesser wounds were bandaging each other. The corpsman was tending to the more seriously wounded. He looked north and saw the dust clouds raised by the rapidly approaching Dragons.

"Platoon Sergeant, get the platoon ready to mount up," he said into his radio's command circuit.

"Aye aye, boss," came Hyakowa's reply.

Bass raised his shields as his men approached. Sergeant Ratliff's disembodied head was bobbing irregularly, blood staining his invisible trouser leg. Hayes's face was rigid; he seemed to be in pain from the wound in his side, which was visible only as a red blot in the air a foot and a half below his face.

Then Bass blinked in surprise. Beyond the three Marines he saw Cheereek struggling to their feet—Ratliff must have managed to keep Schultz from killing the wounded. He looked at Schultz's face to gauge his state of mind.

Schultz saw where Bass had looked and knew what he saw.

He spat to the side and said in passing, "They're weak. Fragile. No threat to us."

Scout Captain Kkaacgh looked at his Clumsy Ones' weapon with hatred. The Cheereek had just lost a mighty battle because of it, and many warriors lay dead, killed by the Clumsy Ones' demons. The weapons so effective against his kind had been almost worthless against the foreign demons. Except to make them angry. Gods! The demons had fought like furies. He'd seen them kill warriors with one blow of their bare hands.

If only the Clumsy Ones had never come! Their demons wouldn't have followed them, and all those warriors who died that day would still be alive, still be able to fight for the glory of the Cheereek.

Now he had to go back to the rookery and face High Chief Graakaak. If he was lucky, the High Chief would have him killed. Otherwise he'd be made a slave. As soon as . . .

Wait. Lead Warrior Ctweeleer went down, slit open by a blade wielded by one of the demons. He thought furiously. Who else knew that finding the Clumsy Ones' demons was his idea? His scouts knew, those who were with the war party. Could he talk to them, convince them they should not tell Graakaak what really happened, tell the High Chief the attack on the demons was Ctweeleer's idea? He thought. Three of the four scouts were dead, he'd seen them killed. Where was the fourth? He had to find him before he returned to the rookery. Was there anyone else, any of the warriors?

Yes, there were three. Two of them he knew had died. One with Lead Warrior Ctweeleer, the other alone. Who was the third? Yes, he knew who that was. He remembered seeing that warrior running at the end of the battle. Where was he?

"My captain."

Kkaacgh spun toward the voice, pointing his Clumsy Ones' weapon. He saw who it was and lowered the weapon. Of course, it was his remaining scout. No one else could have slipped up on him unnoticed like that.

"Yes, Cheererere."

"It was a bad loss."

Kkaacgh barely acknowledged the obvious statement.

"When the High Chief learns this attack was our idea, it will be death or slavery for us."

Our? It was interesting that the scout seemed ready to share the blame. Kkaacgh bobbed his head at the sky.

"There are few who know."

Again Kkaacgh bobbed agreement.

"You and I and one warrior are the only ones to survive the battle who knew."

"Yes, and I know who that one warrior is."

"Is this him?" Cheererere reached behind himself and brought forth a head.

"That is him, *Lead* Scout Cheererere. The High Chief will know that the attack was Ctweeleer's idea."

Cheererere preened. He'd never before heard of a battle-field promotion among the Scouts.

CHAPTER
TWENTY-FIVE

The trek back to the *Marquis de Rien* naked, on foot, proved to be a terrible ordeal for the three men. They stood on the edge of the dry lake bed, considering their chances. The relatively short walk from the pits to the arroyo where the hulk of the landcar still smoldered had just about worn them out, especially Herbloc, who was far older than the other two and in much worse physical shape.

"Leave me," Herbloc panted, "I cannot walk another meter." He collapsed to the ground in a heap.

"He's right, leave the worthless old shit," Jum Bolion said, falling to the ground himself. He inspected his feet and groaned. They were cut to ribbons already. Gunsel hobbled to some nearby bushes and began gathering leaves. "Guns, are you crazy?" Jum Bolion shouted weakly from where he lay.

"We're not leaving Herbloc," Gunsel said as he plucked the leaves.

"Oh, yeah, you're asshole buddies. I forgot," Bolion replied sarcastically.

Gunsel turned and stared at Bolion silently for a few seconds and then went back to plucking fronds. "You didn't send a message to Henderson when the Cheereek ambushed us, did you?" he said conversationally.

"There was no time! They were on us too quick."

"Uh-huh. Yeah, yeah." Gunsel sat down next to the other two, a pile of leaves and some long, stringy rootlike fibers piled beside him. "Well, Jum, far as I'm concerned, you're chiefly responsible for us being in this shit in the first place. Sly'd have been here hours ago if you hadn't panicked. As far as assholes go, you're the only one I can see within thirty klicks of here. So shut up and let's get out of here."

"What's all that stuff for?" Bolion asked, pointing at the vegetation Gunsel had gathered.

"A new suit of clothes."

Herbloc sat up. The brief rest had restored him somewhat. "Brilliant, boy-o!" he gasped. "Brilliant!"

Jum Bolion looked at Herbloc as if the scientist had just lost his mind. Herbloc got painfully to his feet and began gathering leaves and fibers himself. "Lend a hand, boy-o! We need more of them!"

"What the . . . ?"

"Look," Gunsel said, holding up one of the leaves. "These leaves are sturdy and flexible, see? And these roots or whatever are strong. We can make shoes out of the leaves by tying them together and wrapping them around our feet, and we can protect our skin from the sun by making cloaks out of leaves and putting them over our heads and shoulders. Get to work."

"Aw shit, Guns, can't we just wait till dark and follow our tracks back across the bed?"

"You won't make it one klick with your feet in that condition. Besides, do you want to lay around here until the Cheereek change their minds and toss us into the pit too?"

Jum Bolion leaped to his feet and began gathering leaves.

"They're back!" the radar tech, a man named Flinders, shouted as he burst into Henderson's cabin.

"Sam?" Henderson said, thinking Patch and his party had already returned from their expedition to the Cheereek encampment. He sat up in his bed and swung his feet to the deck.

"No, Sly, the Marines are back!"

Henderson froze. "Where? When?"

"The sensors just showed an Essay landing about seventy-five klicks to the southwest. Same as before, Sly, a damned Marine combat landing. No mistake about it then, none now." Flinders was perspiring heavily. "Goddamn, Sly, they'll be here any minute!" Clearly, the radar tech was losing control of himself. Henderson couldn't blame him. If the Marines got them, it'd be Darkside for sure. If they weren't all killed first. They didn't have a chance on the ground, but if they could launch the *Marquis de Rien* first . . .

"Send a message to Patch—"

"Tried that," Flinders shouted. "Tried that! Goddamnit, I couldn't raise anybody. We gotta get outta here—now!"

"Get Hanks and meet me on the bridge," Henderson said, pulling on a pair of coveralls. Flinders was out the door immediately. Henderson punched the ship's intercom. His voice boomed throughout the vessel. "Now hear this," he said in his most commanding voice. "All hands secure for takeoff. Get a move on!"

In the companionway outside Henderson's compartment, Hanks, the ship's engineer, almost ran into him. "What the hell's going on?" he demanded.

Hitching up his clothes and heading for the bridge, Henderson said, "The Marines are back. We're getting out of here. Right now."

Hanks reached out and lay a restraining hand on his shoulder. "But what about Sam?"

Henderson turned and faced the engineer. "How long you known me, Hanks?" he asked.

Hanks shrugged. "Thirty years?"

"We've done a lot of jobs together, ain't we?" Hanks nodded. "The Marines have landed, you can bet on that, and if they get us on the ground, we're all dead meat. Patch'll have to look after himself. He's got his ship parked over there, if he can get to it, but I ain't waiting around. Besides, old buddy, I don't think he's ever coming back." Hanks stared at Henderson. "Nobody screws with the birdmen, Hanks," Henderson explained, "not even Sam Patch."

"But the stones—"

Henderson placed his hand flat on Hanks's chest. "Hanks, give me all the power you got. Sam Patch is on his own. If we can get off this rock and to our jump point, we might live to cash in on the stones we've got. Now get a move on. We're getting out of here."

* * *

"Gone! Gone!" Herbloc wailed. He collapsed to the ground, weeping like a motherless child.

From several kilometers away they had seen the *Marquis de Rien* rise. They screamed and waved their arms even though nobody aboard her could possibly see or hear them. They gathered their last reserves of energy and ran and stumbled until they burst into the clearing where the ship had been. They told themselves the *Marquis de Rien* had just changed positions for some reason and a shore party would be waiting for them.

There was no one there.

Jum Bolion and Gunsel gaped helplessly at the empty clearing. The ground where the *Marquis* had sat was still warm. They hadn't missed her takeoff by much.

All hope completely drained away, Gunsel sank to his knees. Bolion ripped off his cloak of leaves and threw it down. "For what?" he shouted, his voice breaking. "They left us! The bastards left us! Oh, Jesus Christ!" He too sank to the earth. They were naked, abandoned on a hostile alien world, and worst of all, had missed being saved by only a few minutes. The trio lay there, panting and muttering ineffectual curses for a long time.

"Why? Why did Sly abandon us?" Gunsel asked at last.

"Who knows?" Jum Bolion answered. "It don't make no difference now, does it?"

"A purely rhetorical question," Herbloc gasped. "There must've been a good reason Henderson took off, is what Guns meant."

" 'A purely rhetorical question,' " Bolion mimicked, "Jesus, what muck! You guys reading each other's minds now?"

Herbloc paused to catch his breath. "Don't you see? He took off thinking Patch was still alive! There must've been a very good—"

Bolion gave a shout and slammed the palm of one hand into his forehead. "The *Lady Tee*!" he shouted. "Patch came in the *Lady Tee*! She's, uh, she's right—over there." He pointed off to the northeast. "I think," he added lamely.

"Oh, my God," Gunsel exclaimed. "How could we have forgotten? Sly knew Patch had the other ship. He wasn't abandoning us after all!"

Herbloc sat up. "But that doesn't answer the question: *Why* did he leave?"

"Well, he left in a mighty big hurry," Bolion said. "It couldn't have been the scientists or any of the birdmen, so . . ." Bolion's face turned white and he gasped. "It has to be the Marines! They waited for us to come back."

Gunsel was on his feet instantly, pulling Herbloc up with him. "Then we'd better find the *Lady Tee* and get the hell out of here in a hurry!"

"Right!" Bolion shouted. "It was over this way."

"No! That way!" Gunsel pointed in the opposite direction.

"You're both wrong. Patch and Kat came out of the woods over there. I remember," Herbloc insisted.

"You can't know that!" Bolion shouted. "You were in the ship when they came out of the woods. They came from over there!"

The three stood there, staring at one another. "Okay," Gunsel said, taking charge. "Look for signs in the vegetation, where they'd have come out of the woods. Split up and look around the perimeter of the landing site. Look close and careful."

After a few minutes Herbloc saw what he took for crushed brush. "Here! They came out here!"

"How do you know it wasn't the security party?" Bolion asked.

The three stared at one another again. "We don't," Gunsel said at last, "but it's the only lead we got. Let's go."

Five thousand meters through the scrub that lined the ridges flowing down from the massif, they discovered Patch's executive starship.

"Now let's see if he locked the damn thing up on us," Bolion said. He touched a keypad mounted beside the passenger hatch. Nothing happened. "It's coded! The Enter key won't work without the damned code!" Bolion pounded his fist into the hull of the spacecraft in frustration.

"Oh, no," Gunsel moaned. "We come this far and now

we're finally screwed." He sat down in the shadow of the small craft. "May as well wait until the Marines come and find us. At least they'll give us some clothes and something to eat."

Jum Bolion plopped down beside him. Herbloc, however, examined the pad. He pressed several keys experimentally. Nothing happened. He pressed some more with the same results. The third time the lock hissed open.

"How the hell'd you do *that*?" Jum Bolion asked in an awed voice.

Herbloc chuckled. "Obviously Mr. Patch did not bother to change the combination when Tweed handed this ship over to him. You can see where the keys are worn from constant use. I guessed the right sequence, is all."

"Doc, I take back everything I ever said about you," Bolion said as he got lightly to his feet.

"And I you, old chap," Herbloc answered under his breath.

Once on the tiny bridge, Bolion easily initiated the ship's preflight sequencing. "This thing is programmed so even an idiot could fly it."

"As we all can see," Herbloc muttered.

"Doc," Bolion said over his shoulder, "is there any doubt why nobody likes you?" He fiddled with the instrument panel a bit longer. "It'll take a few minutes for the computer to complete the preflight sequencing. Anything to eat around here? How about something to wear?" The three began rummaging eagerly through the ship's comfortable passenger compartment.

Then Herbloc gave a shout of delight. He emerged from the living quarters with a large brown bottle in his hand. "Invergordon!" he exulted. "Scotch! The finest Scotch there is. Inver-goddamn-gordon!" He took a long swig and closed his eyes in ecstasy. "I must say, whatever his faults as a social being, old Sam Patch had good taste in booze. Have some?" He held the bottle out to Jum Bolion.

"Well, we have a few minutes before takeoff. If the Marines get here before then, at least we'll have a buzz on. Why not?" He drank from the bottle and made a face. "Tastes like—

like—burnt cork. But—damn!" He handed the bottle to Gunsel, who drank.

"Goddamn, Spence," he said to Herbloc, "if this is 'the finest Scotch there is,' I'd hate to drink the inferior stuff! Nevertheless . . ." He drank again and handed the bottle back to Herbloc. It made another round.

"The taste for Scotch, my lads, is an acquired one," Herbloc said, lifting the bottle to his lips, "and as you can see, I have acquired it."

"Well, let me acquire some more of it," Bolion said, reaching for the bottle. He drank. Herbloc took it back and drank and then Gunsel took another swig. One by one it made the rounds until it was empty.

"More!" Herbloc shouted. " 'More, more, more, cried the pirates! Merry men are weee!' " he sang, staggering back into the living compartment. He emerged a moment later with a joyous shout. "Bourbon, me lads! Kentucky sour-mash bourbon! Tim Breem, too. Green label! The finest bourbon there is! No branch water to accompany this wonderful ambrosia but, taken neat—" He swigged out of the open bottle and sighed deeply. "—who needs a mixer?"

He handed the bottle to Bolion, who drank. "Whew!" Bolion shook himself, passing the bourbon to Gunsel. "Man, that is sooo much better than Scotch!"

The instrument console on the bridge blinked. "Preflight sequencing is completed," the computer announced in a pleasant female voice. "All systems are go. Ignition sequence on your command. Passengers and crew should now prepare for takeoff."

"Ah-ha!" Bolion exclaimed as he staggered to the console and sat down heavily in the captain's chair. The instrument panel seemed to wobble before his eyes and go out of focus, but that did not dim the euphoria that possessed him. He could fly that thing to the edge of Human Space and beyond if they wanted him to. Why hadn't Herbloc shared his secret juice with him before now? Gotta treat the doc better after this, he thought. He stared at the instruments. Where the hell was the ignition switch? "Gadfrey," he muttered, and pressed a button. Nothing happened. He stared at the panel. The readings swam before his eyes. "Whew," he said, shaking his head to clear it. "Um," he nodded, finally realizing he'd opened the cargo hatch by mistake. Suddenly the ignition switch swam into focus. "Ahhh," he sighed, "time to go." He reached out a finger. "No, no," he muttered. "Gotta close the goddamn hatch first!" he said, striking the palm of one hand into his forehead. Now where the hell did that hatch relay get away to? He stared at the panel in confusion. It had moved! "Aw, the hell with it," he mumbled, turning back to the others.

Herbloc was raucously singing a song about whiskey growing on trees. "Another drink, my friends, and then we're out of here!"

First platoon made planetfall and their Dragons sped toward the smugglers' landing site. The *Marquis de Rien* was gone by the time they got there. The *Lady Tee* seemed to be unoccupied. Special Agent Nast used a skill he'd picked up along the way—a highly unauthorized skill, but one sometimes necessary for an isolated agent far from proper backup—and bypassed the Bomarc's lock.

"So what do we do with it?" Ensign Llewellyn, the first platoon's commander, asked once Nast determined that the ship was indeed untenanted.

"We have three men still on the surface, and I'm going to arrest them," Nast replied. He gave a Gallic shrug. "But they're naked, and it will take them time to get here. You have another platoon down here, and they've suffered quite a few casualties. I propose we go to their aid. We'll be back in plenty of time to apprehend the naked fugitives."

"Are you sure? Llewellyn asked.

"One of them is Art Gunsel. They'll get here. Eventually. Let's go help your wounded Marines."

Ensign Llewellyn gratefully gave the order for first platoon to mount up. Taking care of wounded Marines was more important to him than intercepting criminals who might die of exposure and save everybody a lot of trouble if they weren't picked up quickly.

Nast planted a transmitter in the locking mechanism, just to be on the safe side. If anybody opened the ship, the transmitter would notify him.

Art Gunsel proved even more resourceful than Nast had assumed, and the trio reached the landing site much faster because he came up with the makeshift clothing. The agent was surprised when the transmitter signaled him that someone had opened the *Lady Tee*'s lock. At that time, the two platoons were on their way back to orbit. First platoon's Essay got instant authorization to return planetside, but had to reach orbital altitude before it could turn around. Nast began to worry. If any one of the three was a properly trained Bomarc pilot, the ship would launch long before he and the Marines reached it.

But the three men were hungry and needed to get dressed in real clothing, none of them had ever piloted a Bomarc before, and Herbloc found the liquor. So they were still there, barely into the launch sequence, when first platoon returned to the landing site.

Special Agent Nast felt a surge of elation when they found the *Lady Tee* still on the ground.

"Shouldn't we go in first?" Ensign Llewellyn asked as Nast stepped into the ship's airlock.

Nast laughed. "If that were Sam Patch or even Sly Henderson in there, Ensign, I'd call for artillery preparation, but not this trio. I'll go in first and make the arrest. You back me up. I may need some help getting them outside, though. Especially Herbloc." He laughed again.

Nast calmly ambled onto the bridge, hands clasped behind his back. A squad of Marines rushed in behind him and took positions around the bridge's bulkheads.

Nast casually looked around the bridge and slowly shook his head. A man lay slumped over the instrument panel, apparently sleeping, another lay curled up on the deck, an empty brown bottle grasped in one hand. A third, a fat, balding old man stood swaying slightly, a nearly empty bottle with a green label clutched tightly in one fist.

"Gentlemen," Nast said softly, "I am Special Agent Thom

Nast of the Confederation Department of Justice. You are under arrest for violation of Chapter Six, Section 3103 of Title Eighteen, and Chapter . . ." He paused and stared at Herbloc. It didn't make any difference, Nast realized. These men had no rights and there wouldn't be any trial. "You are under arrest," he said at last.

"Wel—" *Hiccup!* "—come to my humble but very tempor-ary abode, Mish-Mister Sh-Shpeshal Agent Nashhht!" the old man said, pronouncing every word carefully. He blinked at Nast, belched, and slowly, gracefully, crumpled to the floor, where he passed out.

CHAPTER
TWENTY-SIX

The *Khe Sanh* got under way as soon as first platoon was secure in its compartment and the three prisoners were in the ship's brig. Commander Spitzhaven wasn't concerned about the several hour head start the *Marquis de Rien* had. The *Marquis* was a small, old freighter, it simply didn't have the acceleration of a Confederation warship and would need several days to reach its jump point—even with the slingshot effect imparted by swinging close to the local star. The *Khe Sanh* would have no problem catching it before it got too close to the star, where heat and radiation would prevent the Marine boarding party from launching a breaching operation. Spitzhaven was glad his ship still carried the obsolete breaching equipment that ripped off airlock hatches. Captain Conorado had assured him the Marines were well trained in the use of the old equipment. They certainly couldn't use the new Tweed Hull Breacher, not after Fleet put its use on indefinite hold until its technical problems could be worked out.

Spitzhaven hadn't figured on the modifications Sam Patch had made on the *Marquis de Rien*, however. The *Marquis* may have been old and small, but it had an up-to-date powerplant. It couldn't accelerate as fast as the *Khe Sanh*, but it was still faster in-system than its size and age indicated. It wasn't long before Navigation reported to him that the ships were going to be perilously close to the local star by the time they closed. The Marines would have to board the *Marquis de Rien* quickly or it might well reach its jump point and get away.

Spitzhaven put the engineering department to work on finding a modification for the Marines' armored vacuum suits that would keep them from getting fried while they were close to the star. Keeping the suits cool and radiation-proof wasn't the problem, the engineering department assured their skipper. They could modify the suits easily enough. The problem was keeping the suits small enough to fit into the *Marquis de Rien*'s airlock.

Commander Spitzhaven's engineering department wasn't alone in working on the problem, though. True to their ancient heritage, the Marines weren't without their ability to improvise.

"Top?" Corporal Doyle's voice was hesitant. Even though as Company L's senior clerk he worked directly for First Sergeant Myer, he had the same uncertainty about approaching a first sergeant that just about all Marines under the rank of staff sergeant seemed to have. First sergeants were entirely too unpredictable.

"Speak, Doyle." Top Myer didn't bother looking up from the reports he was scanning.

Speak, Doyle. A Marine's rank, especially for corporals and up, was his first name, and everybody was called by rank as a sign of respect. But not many called Corporal Doyle "Corporal," even though he had a bona fide hero medal, a Bronze Star, to go along with his stripes.

"Uh . . ." Doyle had second thoughts about talking to Top Myer.

Myer flipped down the vidscreen, leaned back in his chair, and fixed Doyle with a steely gaze. "You have something to say, Corporal Doyle?"

"Uh, yeah, uh, I mean, yes I do, Top." He paused.

"Well, what is it, Doyle? Spit it out. I've got a boarding operation to plan."

"Well, Top, it's about that boarding operation." He hesitated again.

Top Myer drummed his fingers on the top of his tiny desk. "Yes?"

"I've been thinking about the Tweed Hull Breacher," Doyle blurted.

"We can't use it," Myer said sourly. "It's defective and kills Marines."

"I think I know how to fix it."

The first sergeant's fingers stopped drumming and he looked speculatively at his senior clerk. Corporal Doyle was usually a supercilious little twit, but there was more to him than met the eye. Myer gestured at a small, wall-mounted seat. "Tell me about it, Corporal Doyle."

Doyle plunked his bottom onto the seat and leaned forward eagerly. "Top, I reviewed the development and testing documents for the Tweed."

Myer cocked an eyebrow. That was classified material, and he was pretty sure Doyle didn't have high enough clearance to access it. Well, if a clerk was going to be really useful to his first sergeant, he had to find ways around things. He nodded for Doyle to continue.

"The breacher was developed by Tweed Submersible Recovery Operations. I looked into them. All their expertise is in deep-sea operations. They make and operate equipment that works on the bottom of oceans."

"I know that. Tell me something I *don't* know." He made no indication that he noticed Gunny Thatcher slip into the small compartment used as Company L's office. Thatcher stood quietly where Doyle couldn't see him without turning around.

"The breacher was tested in a one-atmosphere, one-g setting. Top, don't you see? This equipment that was meant for use in a null-g vacuum was tested at the bottom of a gravity well in full atmosphere."

Myer waved his hand in a circle, meaning move on—he knew all that too. He ignored Gunnery Sergeant Bass, who leaned on the hatch cowling behind Gunny Thatcher.

"It's simple, Top. Just like their engineers had to adjust their thinking to allow for the reduced pressure and changed temperature of deep-sea to make the breacher work at one atmosphere, one g, we need to make adjustments to make it work in a null-g vacuum."

"Doyle, do you think nobody else has thought of that? And how'd you come up with it?"

Doyle blanched. "Uh, well, uh, I studied mechanical engineering in college—it was my minor. And I'm sure someone else thought about it, Top. But they haven't done it yet, have they?"

Myer didn't answer with words; his look told Corporal Doyle he had no way of knowing what someone did or didn't do several months' travel away. He didn't acknowledge Captain Conorado, who was now standing behind Bass.

Doyle flinched from Myer's look but kept talking. "The gases went into the burners with too much pressure, the flame came out too fast for the nozzles to control. Then they lit off the atmosphere in the chamber. All we have to do is damp down the pressure so the gases enter the mixer slower, and not pump atmosphere into the chamber until the hull is breached."

"No atmosphere in the chamber means atmosphere will slam into it from inside the ship as soon as the hull is holed. Do you want to stand in that kind of maelstrom?"

"But Top, close the inner hatch as soon as the cuts are through! There won't be much evacuation of atmosphere from the ship to the chamber."

"Corporal Doyle, come with me," Captain Conorado said, and Doyle spun about. "We're going to see Captain Spitzhaven and pitch your proposal, see if his engineering department can come up with your modifications."

Doyle, jaw gaping, merely stared at his company commander.

"Don't just sit there, Corporal," Conorado said. "We need to see the Skipper." He turned and strode away.

Corporal Doyle jumped up and skittered after him.

"Corporal Doyle," Bass called after him, "if you ever want to change MOS, come and see me." Then, in a lower voice because Doyle was too far away, "I'm sure I can find a way to fit a corporal into a lance corporal's slot in my platoon."

Myer and Thatcher exchanged a glance. Doyle had won his Bronze Star on a patrol Bass led, so they assumed Bass knew what the clerk was capable of. Maybe . . . Nah, not that supercilious little twit, Corporal Doyle.

* * *

Commander Spitzhaven listened without interruption as Corporal Doyle repeated his idea. Then he made him repeat it again for his engineering head and the engineering chief. General Cazombi quietly joined them during the retelling.

"Why didn't I think of that?" groaned Chief Petty Officer Magruder when Doyle finished.

"For the same reason I didn't," Lieutenant Haselrhampti snorted. "I'm a nuclear engineer; you're an electronic engineer. That's a mechanical engineering solution."

Chief Magruder nodded. "Right. The navy's heavy on nuclear and electronic engineers, light on mechanical and civil engineers." He looked around for a place to spit, didn't see one, made a sour face. "This here jarhead might be the only man jack in all the naval services to have come up with the solution."

"How long will it take?" Spitzhaven wanted to know.

"Less time than coming up with modified armored vacuum suits that'll fit into a standard freighter airlock," Chief Magruder replied.

Lieutenant Haselrhampti agreed with his chief.

"Then do it," Spitzhaven ordered.

"Aye aye, sir."

"Good job, Corporal," Spitzhaven said to Doyle. "That is all."

"Thank you, sir," Doyle said. He executed a sharp about-face and headed briskly back to Company L's offices. Even though it was sometimes interesting to listen in while officers talked, it was never interesting when they were aware of his presence.

"Too bad you Marines are so fixated on battle that you only give medals and decorations for combat," Spitzhaven said when Doyle was out of earshot. "If his idea works, that corporal of yours just earned himself an 'Atta-boy' medal."

Conorado nodded. "It does sometimes seem unfair," he agreed, "but long ago, when we Marines did give out Atta-boys, too damn many people who didn't deserve more than a pat on the back for a decently done job got a chestful of medals for little more than just doing what they were supposed to do."

"You're right, but sometimes . . ." Spitzhaven's voice trailed off. It might not be fair, but there wasn't anything he could do about it.

"Actually," General Cazombi said, speaking for the first time since joining them, "I'm the nominal commander on this operation. That makes this, technically, an army operation. The army *does* give out Atta-boys. If this works, I'll give him one myself."

Captain Conorado gave him a bland look. While he privately agreed that Doyle deserved an Atta-boy, he thought it might set a bad precedent. He didn't want to see the plethora of commendation medals return to the Marine Corps; he thought they cheapened the decorations for combat heroism. The Marine Corps wasn't about doing desk or other support jobs well, it was about fighting.

Lieutenant Haselrhampti and Chief Magruder were back to Commander Spitzhaven in a matter of hours.

"Got it, sir," Haselrhampti reported. "The cutters work in null-g vacuum now."

"Will they be able to cut through the hull fast enough?"

Lieutenant Haselrhampti nodded. "Like butter, sir. That class of freighter has a single-skin hull."

"Single-skin?" Commander Spitzhaven blurted out. "What kind of fool designed a starship with a single skin?"

"It's a planetary lander, sir." Haselrhampti understood his captain's surprise. "They had to sacrifice a lot of mass. Not having a double hull saves a lot of mass. It's like the chief said, it wasn't a popular model."

Spitzhaven shook his head at the sheer stupidity of some people. Well, it wasn't his problem. "What about the atmosphere-exchange problem?" he asked, turning the subject to something that was his problem.

Chief Magruder sighed. "I'm afraid we'll have to test that one in live action, sir." One of his sailors would have to do it, and he didn't like risking a man's life that way. He'd have to make the danger clear when he asked for a volunteer.

The Marines solved the problem of a volunteer.

"Your sailors are all engineers, right, Chief?" Gunny Thatcher asked.

"Of course they are. They wouldn't be in engineering if they weren't."

"Mostly nuclear and electronic?"

Magruder thought for a moment, then nodded. "Every last one of them."

"You need a mechanical engineer for this job. We've got one. Corporal Doyle will operate the interior controls if we have to breach the hull."

Chief Magruder stared at him for a moment. "All right," he finally said. "Send him down to Engineering. I'll start training him on it immediately." He headed for Engineering himself, muttering something about "Marines, they've always got to be goddamn heroes, doing shit that ain't their goddamn jobs, just so long as it puts their goddamn lives on the line."

"Say what?" Corporal Doyle squawked when Top Myer told him Gunny Thatcher had arranged for him to operate the controls of the Tweed Hull Breacher if they had to conduct a hostile boarding of the *Marquis de Rien*. "That's a squid's job, Top. I ain't no sailor-boy, I'm a Marine!"

"You're not a . . ." Myer reconsidered what he was about to say. Doyle might only be a clerk, but, yeah, he was a Marine— and he had that damn Bronze Star to prove he was just as tough a fighter as any blasterman in the company. Damn that Charlie Bass for giving Doyle the chance to earn it. The first sergeant conveniently forgot that he was the one who'd assigned Doyle to that patrol, and that Bass hadn't been particularly gracious about the whole business.

"You're not a squid," Myer corrected himself. "But you are a mechanical engineer. The job requires a mechanical engineer, and you're the only one on board ship."

"No I'm not, Top! I'm not a mechanical engineer. That was my minor. My major was accounting. I'm an accountant, Top, not an engineer!"

"But Corporal Doyle, you came up with such an elegant so-lution to the problem," Myer said, holding his hands out. "It's only right that you should demonstrate it."

"But, Top—"

"Corporal Doyle!" Myer snapped; his patience, never great, was totally gone. "You volunteered for this job. That's an order. Do you understand?"

Corporal Doyle pulled himself into something that vaguely resembled the position of attention.

"Aye aye, Top." He looked about uncertainly. "Uh, which way is Engineering?"

"Ahoy, freighter *Marquis de Rien*." The voice crackled from the comm speakers on the bridge of the *Marquis*. "This is Confederation Navy Starship *Khe Sanh*. Spin down your engines and prepare to receive a boarding party."

Sly Henderson slapped the button that gave him a visual to the rear. Most of the view was blotted out by glare from the star they were rapidly closing on. Only the very brightest of the stars in the heavens were visible. And one that showed a disk—the *Khe Sanh*.

"My God," the radar tech cried, "they're right on top of us!"

"Give me a reading, Flinders," Henderson snapped.

Flinders pulled himself together and looked at his display. "They're a hundred kilometers and closing."

"What's their relative speed?"

Flinders calculated. "Twenty-five kph," he said.

Henderson tapped a few keys on his console. "We reach the slingshot in five hours," he said. "We're in good shape."

"Five hours? But they'll be next to us in four!"

Henderson shook his head. "Do you know how they con-duct hostile boardings? They send men in armored vacuum suits with equipment that breaks through airlock hatches, that's how. It's a slow process." He barked a laugh. "We're so close to this star that all we'll have to do is spin around our long axis. The boarding party will spend so much time in di-rect sunlight, eating that radiation, they'll cook before they can blow a hatch. And that's if they can manage to latch onto our hull at all!"

"Marquis de Rien." The speakers crackled more than before. "This is the CNSS *Khe Sanh*. I say again, spin down your engines and prepare to receive boarding party."

Henderson picked up a comm set and said into it very clearly, "CNSS *Khe Sanh*, this is the *Marquis de Rien*. Eat my vacuum." Then he turned the planetary space comm off. "Won't be long before all we get out of it is static anyway."

"But—"

"It's too late for 'buts,' Corporal Doyle. You volunteered for this, and there isn't enough time to train someone else."

"No, I—"

"Yes you did, I heard you volunteer. Didn't you hear him, Gunny?"

"I sure did, Top," Gunnery Sergeant Thatcher said, nodding vigorously.

"See? It's settled. Now cooperate with this nice sailor. He's trying to fit your armored vacuum suit so nothing leaks out and nothing nasty gets in."

"But—" Corporal Doyle's protest was cut off by Engineering Mate Second Class Goldman, who settled the suit's helmet into place.

The modifications made the armored vacuum suit twice as bulky as normal. There was extra radiation shielding all around it, an outsized cooling unit was mounted on its back, and shallow fins protruded from all surfaces to radiate excess heat.

"I'm going to have to turn his comm on, First Sergeant," Second Class Goldman said apologetically.

"Whatever you have to do. It's too late for him to back out, and he knows it."

Goldman opened a panel on the suit's chest and briefly fiddled with the insides. "Can you hear me, Corporal Doyle?" he asked.

"Yeah, I can hear you fine, but—"

"All right, you've got atmospheric audio pickup. Now I'll test your radio." Goldman fiddled with the inside of the panel again to turn off the atmospheric speaker—Corporal Doyle could still hear what they were saying, but they couldn't hear him—then Goldman donned a helmet and adjusted it on his shoulders. He looked at the two Marine senior NCOs and said, "Somebody say something," through his atmospheric speaker.

"Testing, testing, one-two," Top Myer said, looking into the faceplate.

"Thanks." Second Class Goldman hadn't heard anything; Doyle's helmet was properly in place. He toggled on the suit-to-suit radio. "Corporal Doyle, how do you hear me?"

"I hear you five by, but—"

Goldman missed the rest of what Doyle said; he popped his helmet seal and toggled off the radio as soon as Doyle said "five by." He busied himself for a few moments attaching wires and cables to Doyle's suit. A low, almost inaudible chugging and humming filled the small engineering compartment they were in.

"Raise your right arm straight up, Corporal Doyle," Goldman said. Doyle reluctantly raised his arm. "Now rotate it in a full circle, down to the front, up to the rear." He watched a gauge while Doyle rotated his arm.

Top Myer and Gunny Thatcher mostly watched Second Class Goldman. Looking at the dials, gauges, and blinking lights on his instruments wouldn't tell them anything, and neither of them had the heart to watch Corporal Doyle silently mouthing objections and complaints behind the face shield of his helmet.

"Now hold it straight out to the side." Goldman said. Doyle did. "Swing it fore and aft." Satisfied with the movement of the suit's right arm, Goldman had Doyle repeat the movements with his left arm. "Stop!" he ordered when Doyle's left arm was halfway up the back of the circle movement. He stepped close and made an adjustment. "Do it again." This time he nodded, satisfied. "Now walk forward two paces." He nodded at his instruments. "Go there, please." He pointed at a mock-up of the cutter controls of the Tweed Hull Breacher. "You know the sequence, I want you to go through it now."

Clumsily, reluctantly, Corporal Doyle went through the motions of operating the cutters and closing the hatch.

"Your suit fits properly, Corporal Doyle," Second Class Goldman finally said. "Good luck out there, Marine." He grabbed one of Corporal Doyle's gloved hands in both of his and shook it. He reopened the chest panel to turn the atmospheric speaker back on.

"Thank you, Second Class Goldman," Myer said. Then to Thatcher, "Let's go see how those men from second platoon are coming along."

"Second platoon?" Corporal Doyle squawked. "What men from second platoon?"

Myer looked at him quizzically. "The boarding party."

"I'm not going!"

"What did you say?" Myer asked in an ominously low tone. He clenched his fists and advanced on Corporal Doyle.

"I said I'm not going." Corporal Doyle awkwardly folded his armored arms across his chest and leaned back against the mock-up.

Engineering Mate Second Class Goldman looked at them nervously. "Uh, First Sergeant, I advise you don't try to do anything physical."

Myer speared him a withering glance and continued to advance until his nose was millimeters from Doyle's faceplate.

"You're going, *Corporal* Doyle, if I have to suit up and take you myself."

"Nossir, First Sergeant," Doyle said in the firmest voice Myer had ever heard him use. "Not with second platoon, I'm not. You want to court-martial me, then court-martial me. I'm not going with second platoon."

Myer glared, unable for a moment to think of anything to say.

Thatcher noticed Doyle's emphasis on second platoon. "What's wrong with second platoon?" he asked.

Corporal Doyle turned his head slightly to look at the company gunnery sergeant. "I've never been in combat with second platoon, that's what's wrong with them. You want me to go?

Make third platoon the boarding party. I'll go with third platoon."

Myer exploded, waving his arms and spraying spittle on the suit's faceplate. "Third platoon! Third platoon can't go. They've seen more than their fair share of the action on this mission. And they're shot to shit! Everyone in that platoon is wounded."

Corporal Doyle shook his head. "I visited them a few hours ago. The ship's surgeons and corpsmen have done a real good job fixing them up. Some of them are a bit sore, but most of them are in good shape now. They can do it. I'll go with third platoon or I don't go at all." He looked at Myer defiantly.

Thatcher was talking on his personal comm unit as soon as Corporal Doyle said he'd go with third platoon. "Top, Charlie Bass says Corporal Doyle's right; most of his men are in good condition. Everybody in the platoon volunteered to be in the boarding party. He's bringing his sound men to suit up."

Myer spun and glared at Thatcher, then slowly turned back to Corporal Doyle.

"Your ass is mine, Corporal Doyle. You hear me? Your ass is mine. Stand by when this is done. Just you stand by."

"Aye aye, Top." Doyle did his best to sound firm and un-cowed, but couldn't keep his voice from cracking.

CHAPTER
TWENTY-SEVEN

Commander Spitzhaven knew at least as much of the orbital mechanics involved in the *Khe Sanh*'s overtaking the *Marquis de Rien* as Sly Henderson did. In fact, after more than twenty years working his way up the hierarchy of navy starships, he knew them better than Henderson did. Once the *Khe Sanh* closed the distance to the *Marquis de Rien*, it would take about forty-five minutes to move the hull breacher into position on the hull of the other ship. That would leave only fifteen minutes to breach the hull and to enter the ship and take possession of it before it reached slingshot. Since nobody involved with the operation was familiar with the equipment or procedure, Spitzhaven knew he had to add a fudge factor of at least fifty percent as a safety margin. That meant there were two chances in three that the smugglers' ship would slingshot before the THB was in place. In any event, it was almost certain the smugglers' ship would slingshot before the full boarding party entered her. He was certain the abrupt acceleration would throw the THB off, which meant it was necessary to have a pilot and navigator in the initial boarding party. Since the increased bulk of the armored vacuum suits shrunk the size of that party from ten men to six, that didn't seem like such a great idea. Also, he'd have to break off pursuit to rescue the sailors and Marines who'd be scattered about when the THB was thrown off. It was likely that some of those men might not survive. The *Marquis de Rien* would probably get away whether or not he stopped to pick up the cast-off men.

Commander Spitzhaven needed a way to close with the

Marquis de Rien and leave enough time to board before the slingshot. He gave the problem a few moments of thought, then angled his ship to face directly into the solar wind, hoping to reduce its drag and effectively increase its speed relative to the *Marquis*. That helped. The *Khe Sanh* closed the distance three hours and forty minutes after Henderson told it to "eat my vacuum." That gave Spitzhaven the fudge factor he needed.

Chief Petty Officer Magruder suited up to personally supervise the movement and attachment of the THB to the *Marquis de Rien*. A dozen sailors in modified vacuum suits gripped hold-ons along the edges of the THB. Engineering Mate Second Class Goldman, who knew the suit modifications better than anybody else, came along in case anyone had a problem with them. Barely visible to the naked eye from any distance, the THB looked like a pimple on the flank of the *Khe Sanh*.

At a signal from Magruder, Seaman Qim, the rating who operated the maneuver controls, threw the lever that fired the main thrusters. Flames blossomed from four points around the bottom of the breacher and flowed into a flickering blue puddle on the ship's hull. Chief Magruder watched his control panel as the thrust equaled and surpassed the mass and inertia of the THB. He released the grapples that held the massive box to the *Khe Sanh*'s hull, and it began accelerating toward the *Marquis de Rien*, which appeared to hover like a lost pyramid two and a half kilometers away. Magruder looked back and saw the twenty-four Marines in their extra-bulky armored vacuum suits trailing on their tether, which was centered below the THB where the thrusters' flames wouldn't hit them. Well, they weren't all Marines. The eleventh and twelfth men in the string were a navy pilot and a navigator.

Magruder turned back to the target ship and gave it a hard look. He wondered what he'd do if he were in command of it and saw the THB coming toward him.

"Qim," he said, jacked into the THB's comm. With radio communications impossible this close to the star, they were plugged into conduction circuits built into the body of the THB. "On my mark, shut down Thruster Two." Because their tether wasn't tied into the conduction circuit, he couldn't communicate with the Marines. Well, he'd have to rely on their much vaunted reputation for thinking fast and improvising.

"Aye, Chief," Seaman Qim replied.

"Three, two, one, mark!"

The THB slewed slightly as one thruster cut off and it began to alter its approach vector.

"Ah, Chief?" Qim said. "We aren't heading straight for the hull. Shouldn't I adjust to redirect?"

"Negative, Qim. This is what I want us to do. On my mark, cut Thruster Four."

"Aye aye, Chief." But Qim didn't sound sure.

"Three, two, one, mark!"

The THB slewed again and slowly turned so it was aimed at the edge of the *Marquis* instead of directly at its flank.

"Qim, fire Two and Four."

"Aye, Chief."

With all four thrusters again firing, the THB closed faster on the rim of the ship. It wasn't a rapid closure. As fast as it was moving in absolute terms, the THB's speed relative to the *Marquis de Rien* was little more than three kilometers per hour. In theory, allowing for braking time to match velocity when it got there, the trip to the target ship should take forty-five minutes and a few seconds. Then another fifteen minutes to position it against the hull, board the boarding party, and cut through the hull. Chief Magruder knew the skipper expected them to take longer than that because of their lack of experience with the THB. But he knew that somehow they'd have to do it faster. That was one of his reasons for changing his approach vector. The other reason was the maneuver he expected whoever was conning the *Marquis* to make.

Fifteen minutes went by with the *Marquis de Rien* growing slowly larger. The THB's relative velocity crept upward.

"Chief, isn't it time to alter thrust?" Qim asked.

"Negative," Magruder replied. "Steady as she goes."

"But, Chief—"

"Steady as she goes, Seaman Qim."

"Aye aye, Chief."

Qim was right. The book said they should have cut thrust half a minute ago and been preparing to fire forward thrusters to reduce velocity so they could match speeds with the target ship when they reached it. But Chief Magruder's twenty-five years in Engineering had taught him a few tricks.

"Give it another five minutes, Qim," he said. "I know what I'm doing."

"Aye, Chief."

Magruder heard the lack of confidence in Qim's voice and responded to it. "You ever known me to be wrong, Qim?"

Qim didn't reply. Magruder chuckled. He should have known better than to ask that question of any seaman.

When the closure rate reached five kph, Chief Magruder ordered Qim to cut the thrusters.

"Aye aye, Chief." Then a moment later, "Do you want me to fire the brakes, Chief?"

"Not until I tell you to, Qim."

Silence.

Magruder snorted. Were he in the other man's position, he'd be quaking in his suit and seriously considering firing the braking thrusters on his own. He understood the fear a sailor might have now. If they missed the target ship and failed to take proper corrective action quickly enough—and if the *Khe Sanh* dallied too long to react—they could find themselves on an inescapable spiral down into the primary. But there were three ifs in that, and Chief Magruder thought only one of them was actually possible—and he had too much confidence in his abilities to believe that one possibility would occur.

With the *Marquis de Rien* looming only five hundred meters ahead and below them, the target ship began a slow spin along its long axis. Magruder grinned tightly to himself. Whoever was commanding over there did exactly what he would have done. He snapped out orders, "Qim, fire brakes full. Fire main thrusters One and Four."

"Fire brakes full, aye," Qim immediately replied, relief clear in his voice. "Fire main thrusters One and . . . Chief, say again?"

"Fire main thrusters One and Four. Do it now."

"Fire main thrusters One and Four, aye."

The THB shuddered as the braking thrusters pushed back on it. The tether carrying the Marines began to collapse toward the box, then tautened again as Thrusters One and Four began swinging the rear of the THB away from them and the ship below. Now broadside and fully out of the shadow of the *Marquis de Rien*, the solar wind hit the THB hard, further slowing its relative motion. The slowly rotating hull of the ship was less than a hundred meters away—and the THB was circling it, staying almost directly above one spot.

"Cut main thrusters."

"Cut main thrusters, aye."

"Cut brakes."

"Cut brakes, aye."

"I am taking the con."

"You are taking the con."

Magruder took firm grip on the handles that allowed him to make the fine adjustments needed to bring the THB in contact with the hull of the *Marquis de Rien*.

The brief pulsing of the main thrusters kept the THB circling around the ship and edging closer to it. Magruder tweaked the main thrusters on and off and they closed even more. He needed to make contact before rotation took them back into the shadow of the ship. He tweaked the main thrusters back on for half a second, saw closure was too fast, tweaked the brakes. A glance at his control panel showed him the approach was a meter and a half per second. On the outer edge of safe speed, but the THB should hold up to the impact. He shifted his gaze back and forth between his control panel and the approaching hull. When they were five meters away, he slammed on the braking thrusters. The THB lurched, then touched down with a barely felt clunk.

Chief Magruder looked at the mission timer and gave a satisfied smile. They made contact thirty-eight minutes from launch.

"Reel in the boarding party."

"Reel in the boarding party, aye," Qim repeated, awe audible in his voice.

Without waiting for orders, the rest of the crew rushed to activate the magnets that would hold the THB to the hull of the *Marquis de Rien* until the sealant pumped into place and took hold, then turned their attention to the sealant. Using his suit jets and swinging from hold-on to hold-on, Chief Magruder went around to make sure everything was right. It was.

"I'm going to commend every man jack in this crew to the skipper when we get back to the *Khe Sanh*," he said into the conduction circuit when he finished his inspection. "Well done, men." Then he turned his attention to the Marines.

Magruder touched helmets with Gunnery Sergeant Bass and said, "We're ready anytime you are."

"Let's do this thing," Bass replied. They were at the entry hatch in the rear of the THB.

Magruder gestured, and Bass signaled the first man to enter. It was Corporal Doyle. Magruder gave him a guiding shove and he headed straight for the inside controls. The two senior noncommissioned officers guided six more bulky Marines into the chamber after him. Sergeant Ratliff and Corporal Pasquin, the second and third in line, carried a two and a half meter ram between them. So did PFCs Hayes and Godenov, who followed them. The Marines crowded into their assult-boarding positions. As soon as the last Marine was inside and Magruder felt the vibrations from his magnets locking onto the deck, he dogged the hatch. Magruder and Bass looked at each other, but neither had anything to say. They knew that if Doyle and the ship's engineering department were wrong, in a very few seconds they, along with the seven Marines inside the THB and the dozen sailors around it, would be dead, and the string of Marines and sailors waiting their turn in the breacher would be tumbling through space.

Corporal Doyle looked at the control panel in front of him. He deliberately didn't look directly at the button that was supposed to release atmospheric gases into the chamber. Tentatively, he moved the hatch-control lever back and forth. The hatch halves slid easily in their tracks. He froze them in position one-third closed, then turned his attention to the cutter control buttons. He held a hand over the buttons, said a quick, silent prayer to whatever god might happen to be listening, and pressed the start sequence.

Gases flowed at high pressure into the mixing chambers, then shot out of the nozzles and ignited into blue flames. The nozzles swiveled close to the hull of the *Marquis de Rien* and the tips of the flames touched metal. The Marines clearly felt the metal snapping and popping when the cutting flames bit it. The cutter frame began its slow rotation, and a rough outline of red, turning to white, traced its way onto the hull. The metal softened and pillowed out from the flatness of the hull.

Holding his breath in his anxiety, Corporal Doyle kept a close watch on his controls, waiting for the appearance of the first pinhole that would indicate the hull was about to breach. It was his job to close the hatch as soon as that pinhole began to form. That way he could quickly ensure equal pressure in the THB and the ship.

There! Corporal Doyle slapped the hatch lever, and the halves slid together.

The THB rocked as the cutout broke free of the hull and slammed into it.

Doyle hit the atmosphere release button, and air gushed into the chamber and equalized the pressure on both sides of the hatch.

Doyle turned as far as he could to look at the other Marines. All were staring at the hatch. They were ready. Doyle lifted an arm to signal them, then opened the hatch. The two rams slammed forward and punched the cutout into the ship. It clanged to the deck of the compartment they had cut into.

Schultz led the rush.

As soon as the six Marines were out of the breacher and into the ship, Corporal Doyle closed the hatch and evacuated the atmosphere. There was no time for subtlety—instead of being pumped back into tanks, the air simply gushed through cocks in the sides of the THB. Outside, Chief Magruder watched the gauge that told him the internal air pressure.

When it dropped far enough, he popped the outer hatch. Air gusted past him, but without enough force to dislodge him. He signaled to Bass and they sent in three more Marines with the pilot and navigator. Bass joined that group. Magruder dogged the hatch and Doyle cycled the six through.

Chief Magruder touched his helmet to Staff Sergeant Hyakowa's and said, "We've got time to get everybody aboard, including my sailors, if that Marine inside moves fast enough."

"He will," Hyakowa replied, and began assembling the next group to board the ship.

Corporal Doyle sped things up by not filling the breaching chamber to full pressure before opening the inner hatch. The Marines and sailors waiting to enter the ship were buffeted by the sudden gust of air from the ship, but were quickly through the inner hatch.

Gunny Bass, third platoon's first squad, and the two navy officers who would operate the *Marquis de Rien* once the Marines got control of it, filled an empty cargo hold almost to capacity. There were two entrances to the hold. One was a large cargo hatch in the inner corner of the wedge-shaped hold. The other led to a circular passageway around the cargo dropshaft and the adjacent personnel dropshaft. Given the pyramid shape of the starship, all vertical movement was restricted to its interior center line.

"Here's where we are," Bass said. He transmitted a plan of the ship's interior to his men's helmet heads-up displays. A red circle indicated their location in a hold on the fifth of eight levels, slightly aft of the ship's midpoint. The first level, just inside the bow, held the ship's sensing, guidance, and communications suites. On the second level was the bridge, operations spaces, and crew quarters. Third, fourth, and fifth levels were cargo holds. The sixth was Fuel and Engineering; the seventh, the powerplant and more fuel; the eighth, Atmosphere Landing and Launch. Each level was divided pielike into holds and smaller compartments.

"This is the layout of this class of cargo ship," Bass told his men, "but we can't rely on it for any great accuracy. We don't know how extensively the current owner changed the interior of the ship. We do know he replaced the powerplant, so he may well have made other changes." None of this was news to the men of third platoon; they'd gone over it before they suited up and left the *Khe Sanh*. Still, they'd had a very short prep time, and Bass thought it merited repetition.

"First squad, head aft. Take over Engineering. Second squad, we will go forward and take the bridge."

While he was talking, Chief Magruder entered the hold with the last of his sailors.

"Can you hear me, Chief?"

"Loud and clear, Gunny," Magruder answered.

"I want you, and as many of your men as you need, to go with first squad and take control of Engineering as soon as it's secured. Sergeant Ratliff is in command until that occurs. Understood?"

"The fighters are in command as long as there might be fighting, then the engineers take over. Got it."

"Corporal Doyle!"

"Yes, Gunny."

"You take Doc and the rest of the sailors into this hold"—another compartment on the same level lit up in the displays—"and provide security for them. Make sure you dog *this* one vacuum-tight in case the THB breaks off—we don't want anyone lost in an explosive evacuation."

"Aye aye, Gunny." Doyle was disappointed. He was proud of what he'd done with the THB and wanted to be in on the kill. Wait a minute! The kill? There might be fighting? Right, stay here and provide security for the sailors. There were going to be Marines between him and the crew of the *Marquis de Rien*. If there was any fighting, it would be somewhere else, and he'd be safe providing security for the sailors.

"Doc, you stay here to establish a med-station in case there are casualties."

"Aye aye," replied Hospitalman Third Class Hough.

"Let's do it."

*   *   *

Sly Henderson stared uncomprehendingly at the mottled, varicolored display in his viewscreen. The optical pickups on the *Marquis de Rien*'s hull displayed a visual of the space between it and the *Khe Sanh*. A box of some sort was visible in the shifting, wavering light available in the blazing flares from the primary. He muttered under his breath, wanting more data than the visual could give him. But only visual was available to him so close to the primary—all other wavelengths he had access to were too disrupted to tell him anything about the object. All he could tell was it was a box, launched from the *Khe Sanh* and closing on his ship. Damnit! He didn't even have an accurate radar reading to tell him how fast it was closing! He could only assume it would reach his ship before slingshot. So what was it?

Not a bomb, he was certain of that. The Confederation Navy had missiles capable of operating so close to a star; the navy wouldn't have to send over something like that box if they intended to blow up the *Marquis*. The only other thing he could think of was that the box was a shelter for Marines who would try to break open an airlock.

Well, let them try, he thought. As soon as he saw the box approaching, he'd sent men to the personnel airlock on level three and the cargo airlock on level six with orders to weld their inside hatches shut. When they were secured, men armed with military assault cannons would cover those airlocks just in case the Marines did breach them. No way live Marines would board *his* ship.

He glanced at the chronometer. Forty minutes to slingshot.

The box grew steadily larger in his viewscreen, and he noticed something that puzzled him. It wasn't coming straight at the *Marquis de Rien*, it was approaching at a tangent. Now why . . . ? It was a decoy! It had to be. He searched the viewscreen for the Marines who must be jetting toward him independent of the box. No joy. Well, they had to be somewhere.

"Begin spin," he ordered. The *Marquis de Rien* began a slow rotation around its long axis.

Henderson swore to himself when the box began the orbiting maneuver that held it directly above one spot on the rotating ship. He felt the *thunk* as it connected with the hull. He leaned closer to the viewscreen, amazed. The box had missed both airlocks! Maybe it was guided by some kind of malfunctioning autopilot.

"This is Sly," he said into the ship's intercom. "Those jarheads missed the airlocks. We're home free. Secure the assault cannons and prepare for acceleration, we're almost at slingshot. If it's still there after slingshot and our first jump in Beamspace, we'll have to go out and kick it off. If it slips away during slingshot, the navy scow will have to try and rescue whoever's in it. In either case, the navy has no way of knowing where we'll come back into Space 3. Out here."

Sly Henderson settled back on his command chair and gave himself a satisfied smile. *Home free!* With enough wealth in the safe right there under his eyes to set them all up as potentates for the rest of their natural lives.

He felt a clangor through his feet. "What the . . . ?" He didn't know that a hole had just been cut through the hull of the *Marquis de Rien*.

CHAPTER
TWENTY-EIGHT

The personnel dropshaft was empty for its entire length. Bass used hand signals to direct everyone into it. If the ship's crew didn't already know the Marines were aboard, he didn't want to give them any warning. As silently as they could in the armored vacuum suits, the Marines filed into the dropshaft. Power was off in the shaft, but that didn't bother them. If they were using powered lifts and power was cut off while they were using them, they would fall and suffer possibly serious injuries. It was better to use the ladder rungs mounted into the sides of the shaft. Their suits were less cumbersome in the shafts—the little bit of gravity in the ship was centrifugal force directed toward the skin of the ship, and the ladder rungs faced the skin. They had just enough "weight" to make controlling their movement along the ladder easy.

Most of first squad left the dropshaft on the engineering level, and PFC MacIlargie, on second squad's point, was just reaching the hatch to the second level when Bass felt the ship move.

"Hold on!" he commanded into his helmet comm. "Slingshot's beginning."

"Who's that?" Sly Henderson snapped when he heard Bass cry out "Hold on!" Then he exploded into the intercom, "They're on board! The Marines have boarded the ship!"

"Team leaders report," Sergeant Ratliff ordered.

"I'm all right," Hayes told Schultz. The two of them were in the lead and had firm grips that kept them on their feet.

296

"First fire team okay," Schultz reported.

"Dean, sound off," Corporal Pasquin gasped as he tried to extricate himself from the pile at the foot of the ladder.

"I'm on top of you," Dean replied as he pulled himself away from the ladder and gained his feet.

"I'm in place," MacIlargie said. He also had a firm grip.

"Second fire team's all right," Pasquin reported as he regained his feet and leaned against the skinward g-force.

"I'm all right," PFC Quick reported. "Corporal Goudanis?" he said when his fire team leader didn't respond. "Impy, is Corporal Goudanis okay?"

No reply.

"Sergeant Ratliff, I think something happened to Corporal Goudanis and Van Impe." Quick twisted around and held his face close to Goudanis's helmet. He saw that his fire team leader's eyes were closed and his jaw hung slack. "Corporal Goudanis is down!"

"What's wrong with him?" Ratliff asked.

"I don't know, he looks like he's knocked out."

"What about Van Impe?"

Quick lifted himself over Goudanis to look into Van Impe's helmet. "He's out too," he reported.

Ratliff swore. "Quick, go back up until you have communications with Doc Hough. Tell him we've got two casualties we can't move. Then rejoin the squad."

"Aye aye," Quick replied and began climbing the ladder.

Sergeant Ratliff had only himself and five men to secure the entire deck. He swore again. A full squad was barely enough to do the job. Even when Quick returned he'd be three men short of a full squad.

MacIlargie thudded forward and skidded across the deck of the passageway that circled the dropshafts. He quickly scrambled into a crouch and looked in both directions. No one was in sight and his external audio didn't pick up the sounds of anybody approaching. He looked back at the dropshaft and saw armored gloves hanging onto the lip of the opening. He lowered himself to the deck, braced his feet against the bulkhead opposite the opening, and stretched out to grasp Corporal Kerr's wrist. He pulled, and in seconds his fire team leader was in the passageway with him. Together they helped Claypoole up.

When they got Sergeant Bladon up, he told them to go five meters around the passageway in one direction and hold. Bladon helped Linsman and his men up and sent them five meters in the other direction. Then Gunny Bass joined him and they got Lance Corporal Chan's fire team up. Fortunately, when Bass gave the word, everybody in first squad had stopped climbing and grabbed tight. Nobody fell, though just about all of them had broken, bent, or missing radiator fins.

Bass hoped the damage had not had any effect on the integrity of the suits. He checked the layout of the ship in his HUD to determine where they were relative to the bridge.

"Assign two fire teams to passageway security," he ordered Bladon. "You're in command. If anyone exits any of the compartments on this level or tries to come up here from below, take them prisoner. Kill them if they resist. I'll take the other fire team onto the bridge and secure it."

Sergeant Bladon hardly had to think of which fire team to send with Bass; Corporal Kerr had been through the most with Bass, even though he'd missed Diamunde and Waygone, and probably had Bass's confidence more than Linsman or Chan. "Second fire team up. Go with Gunny Bass." Then he turned his attention to positioning the rest of his squad.

Bass drew a route on his HUD and transmitted it to Kerr and his men.

"They probably don't have any weapons, and even if they do, they probably don't have anything that'll penetrate our suits. Still, we go in ready to fight. Dial down the power on your blasters. If we do have to fight, I don't want to slag all the controls. I'll go in first and move to the left," he said. "Claypoole and Kerr follow and go right. Mac, you trail and follow me to the left. Questions?"

Nobody had any.

"Let's do it."

The traverse to the bridge was awkward. They were vertical, but had to resist an ever-shifting pull toward the skin of the ship. But it didn't take long to reach the hatch that led into the bridge.

"Ready?"

They were.

Bass drew his hand-blaster and slapped the Open button next to the hatch.

It took a couple of minutes for the pulls of the conflicting g-forces to resolve themselves. Then Sly Henderson was able to heave himself out of his command chair.

"They're coming for us," he said when he gained his feet and found balance. "Let's give them a surprise."

He made his way across the deck, which felt like it tilted precipitously toward the outer bulkhead, to a locker on one of the interior walls and broke it open. Inside were five rifles, Art Gunsel specials. They looked similar to the rifles Gunsel had made for the Cheereek, but they were modified for easy handling by human beings. The most obvious visible difference was the thirty-round magazine that protruded downward. The magazines were filled with caseless ammunition, bullets made of depleted uranium. Henderson passed a loaded rifle and two extra magazines to each of the four men with him and took the fifth for himself.

"Sam Patch didn't know about these," he said. "I had Gunsel make one for each man on the crew, sort of an extra reward to be given out when this job was done. I think we have an early use for ours." He grinned unpleasantly. The depleted uranium bullets should be able to penetrate the Marines' armored vacuum suits. "Now get behind something, don't give those Marines a clear shot when they come in."

They waited.

The gunshot reverberated loudly enough in the confines of the bridge compartment to drown out all other sound. But the bullet missed Charlie Bass, who was moving through the hatch and to the side as soon as the plate began sliding out of his way. Henderson's reactions were so fast the bullet almost miraculously made its way through the tiny time and space gap between Bass and Claypoole.

Henderson was shifting aim, looking for the first man through, and missed his chance to shoot the third man in. But Bass had instinctively dived for cover the instant he heard the report, and Henderson didn't have a target. The big man picked a place where the Marine might have gone and shot anyway. The four crew members with Henderson shot wildly—none of them was willing to risk showing himself to look for a target. Their bullets poked holes in the bulkheads and overhead. Fortunately, none of them pointed their rifles toward the ship's outer skin.

Henderson's second shot plowed through a navigation console inches above Bass, and the Marine NCO skittered forward. More shots rang out, but none came anywhere near him.

Bass toggled on his external speakers, jacked the volume high, and boomed out, "I'm Gunnery Sergeant Charles Bass, Confederation Marine Corps. We have taken control of the ship. Lay down your weapons and surrender and no one will be harmed."

Sergeant! Henderson harshly barked out a laugh. The Marines didn't even bother to send an officer to take the bridge? Who did they think they were dealing with? And they didn't control the bridge, he did, and he'd know if they took over Engineering. The *Marquis de Rien* was still his! He cranked off another shot at where he thought the amplified voice came from, his bullet plowing through an unoccupied acceleration couch and punching through the bulkhead into the next compartment. The others let off strings of undisciplined fire.

"Flame them," Bass ordered.

Kerr, from his position on the right, had damped down his external acoustics and listened carefully to the dampened sounds of gunfire. He'd barely had time when he entered the bridge to look at its layout, but he was sure he knew precisely where two of the shooters were. All he had to do was move twenty centimeters and one of them would be cleanly in his sights. He bent his knees, braced his elbows and toes against the deck, and scooted forward so the top of his head protruded beyond the console he lay behind. Right, only a few meters away, close enough that were he on his feet Kerr could take one step and jump onto him, was one of the smugglers. The man was looking directly at him. Kerr whipped his blaster into firing position and the smuggler threw his rifle away.

"I give up," the crewman said, throwing his arms into the air. "Don't shoot, I give up!" He rose awkwardly to his feet.

"Traitor!" Henderson twisted around and shot him. The depleted uranium bullet plunged through the man and slapped into the outer bulkhead. The largest fragment of the bullet penetrated to the vacuum outside the ship. The ship's atmosphere rushed the weakened hull surrounding the bullet hole. They could hear the shrill whistle of escaping gas. . . .

MacIlargie took advantage of the distraction to pop up and look for a target. He saw Henderson, but another crewman was closer. He aimed and pressed the firing lever. The reduced-power plasma bolt set fire to the man's hair and the bolt's sudden heat shattered his skull. Bone fragments plunged into his brain case and made mush of his brain. He was dead before he caught a whiff of his burning hair.

Claypoole also popped up. He fired at Henderson, but the ship's captain dropped as soon as he fired and the bolt missed, spattering against the bulkhead opposite him. The bulkhead bubbled and smoldered, but the damped-down plasma bolt wasn't enough to breach it.

Kerr swore when he saw the man who was surrendering get shot. He levered himself farther forward to a position from which he thought he could see into Henderson's hiding place.

"I count two of you down," Bass boomed. "Nobody else needs to die. Surrender now."

"After you saw me kill someone?" Henderson laughed. "That's a murder charge. I'm not getting arrested to face a capital offense charge." He fired again at where he thought Bass's voice came from, but once more Bass had moved.

Suddenly, a rifle slid across the deck. "I ain't standing up for Sly to kill, but I'm surrendering," a voice called from behind a console. "Don't shoot if you can see me."

"You're a prisoner," Bass boomed. "Lay on your back with your hands stretched out above your head so we can see you don't have a weapon in them."

"You're dead, Flinders!" Henderson screamed. "Soon as we finish with these Marines, I'm going to kill your fucking ass!"

"There're four of us and two of you," Bass boomed. "Give it up."

Another rifle slid across the deck. "I'm not dying for you, Sly," a voice called out. "Mr. Marine, I surrender. I'm on my back like you told Flinders. Don't shoot me."

"Well, to hell with all of you! That leaves just that much more for me." Henderson bolted to his feet and dashed to a side bulkhead. It seemed to Bass that he'd watched too many bad action trids if he thought he could expose himself in the middle of four armed men like that and not get shot. Four plasma bolts hit him almost simultaneously. He didn't even have time to shriek before his dead body slid up to the astrogator's couch.

"Anybody else?" Bass boomed.

"Nossir, that's everybody," someone said.

"Show yourselves. *Now!*"

Shakily, the two men stood up, their faces drawn and frightened. They held their hands high above their heads.

"Check the bridge," Bass ordered.

Kerr rose to his feet and gestured at Claypoole and MacIlargie. The three Marines quickly swept the bridge. Nobody else was alive.

"You're Flinders?" Bass asked one of them.

Flinders nodded. He tilted his head toward the other prisoner. "His name's Raj."

"Is anyone else on this level?"

"Nossir, Mr. Marine, sir. Only us on the bridge."

"Who else is on the ship, where are they, and how many are there?"

"Uh, the stone people are on level three. Four of them. I don't know where the security people are, there's four of them. And Engineering on level six."

"Secure these two," Bass ordered Kerr. "I'm going to check on first squad." He left the bridge.

That's when atmospheric pressure pushed the bullet fragment embedded in the hull into the vacuum beyond, and the edges of the tiny hole the bullet fragment had punched gave loose.

Engineering was by far the largest habitable deck on the *Marquis de Rien*. Although it had the basic pie-layout of the upper decks, it was a warren of large and small compartments.

How am I going to search and secure this place with only six of us? Ratliff wondered. Well, he was a Marine sergeant. When in doubt, act decisively.

"Second fire team, stay here. Pasquin, when Quick gets back, leave him here with Dean. Bring Godenov and join the rest of us. Got it?"

"Got it," Corporal Pasquin replied.

"Good. Hammer, lead out." He nodded in the direction he wanted Schultz to go. "Me, then Hayes."

Schultz popped a hatch and went through it in a blur. "Clear!" he shouted even as the other two were racing through the hatch.

They were in a small compartment filled with hand tools in racks.

"Keep going toward the hull," Ratliff ordered.

Schultz went through the next hatch the same way he had the first. It led into a larger compartment lined with equipment none of the Marines recognized. Ratliff pointed to a hatch on the right bulkhead. Schultz popped it open and shot through.

Two men lay in acceleration couches. They stared at the Marines and slowly lifted their arms to show their hands were empty.

"Where are the rest?" Ratliff demanded.

One of the two men pointed.

"What's there?"

"E-Engine control room," the man stammered.

"How many are there?"

"Th-Three."

"Anybody else on this level?"

"N-Nossir."

Ratliff looked back the way they'd come. He couldn't leave the two men alone, but couldn't afford to leave anybody to guard them. He saw Pasquin and Godenov headed toward them and breathed a sigh of relief.

"Corporal Pasquin, guard these prisoners. If they attempt to attack you or try to escape, flame them."

Pasquin looked at the two prisoners. His expression was grim and he swung his blaster toward them. "Roger. If they attempt to attack or try to escape, I flame them," he repeated. He shifted his grip on his blaster meaningfully.

The prisoners did their best to look immobile and unaggressive.

"Quick, come with us." Ratliff signaled Schultz to go through the hatch the prisoner had said led to the engine control room.

Aside from the fact that he and his men weren't armed, Chief Engineer Hanks was no fool. The men who burst into the control room were Confederation Marines, reputed to be the toughest fighters in all of Human Space. Nothing, not even the possibility of life imprisonment, could induce him to resist them. He threw up his hands as soon as he saw Schultz burst in.

Ratliff had told Dean to report to Bass that they'd taken the engineering level and was wondering how to properly secure his five prisoners when a Klaxon sounded and throughout the ship hatches clanged shut.

"What's going on?" Ratliff spat at Hanks, though he felt a chilling in his gut that told him what had happened.

Hanks paled. "The ship's been holed," he said. "We're open to vacuum."

CHAPTER
TWENTY-NINE

Atmosphere rushed with catastrophic force out of the
bridge through the hole in the single-skin hull. The Marines in
their armored vacuum suits were barely staggered by the
force of the air movement, but the two civilian prisoners
weren't so lucky. Raj, closer to it, was slammed back first into
it, blocking the hole. The atmosphere, much thinner by then,
stopped flowing out. Flinders grabbed a console for support
and stood gasping the thin air and gaping at Raj, whose mouth
formed the O of a terrified scream, though no sound came out.
His face was twisted from the agony of the cells bubbling and
bursting into the vacuum at his back.

Kerr began barking orders. "MacIlargie, stand by to open
that hatch—on my command, Wolfman, not before. Rock, get
Flinders to the hatch so you can get him out of here as soon as
the hatch opens." The two Marines moved quickly to obey,
and Kerr turned to the man plugging the hole.

"Raj, you're in serious trouble. I'm going to do my best to
save you. When the hatch opens, I'm going to pull you away
from the hull and move you to the hatch. But you've got to
work with me. Understand?"

Raj continued his silent scream, but he focused his haunted
eyes at Kerr and nodded.

Kerr turned on his shoe magnets to firm up his footing, and
got a firm grip on Raj's shoulder and thigh. He double-
checked his grip on Raj, shouted, "Open it!" then yanked Raj
away from the hull. Air gushed out of the hole, now several
centimeters in diameter. Cracks radiated from the hole. Kerr's
magnetic shoes held, and he gathered Raj into his arms. He

306

turned toward the hatch. It was still closed! MacIlargie was pounding on the Open button to no effect. In the rapidly thinning air, Kerr faintly heard a computer-generated voice, but couldn't make out what it was saying.

Claypoole let go of Flinders with one hand and grasped the edge of the hatch with the other. It resisted his pulling. MacIlargie reversed his blaster and slammed its butt into the panel next to the hatch to break it open, looking for an override. There was none. The two prisoners tried vainly to suck air into their lungs. Their eyes bulged and they flushed as capillaries burst beneath their skin, then Raj went limp. A moment later Flinders did too.

All of the atmosphere was gone from the bridge.

Charlie Bass needed answers fast. He scrambled down to level five as fast as he could to talk to the pilot and navigator.

"I don't think we can open the bridge with vacuum on one side and atmosphere on the other," said the pilot, Lieutenant Stolievitch.

Lieutenant Dhomhia, the navigator, wouldn't hazard a guess.

"We need to talk to the ship's engineers," Chief Magruder said. "If anybody knows, they do."

Bass knew Engineering was taken and all the engineers had been captured. "Let's go," he told Magruder. A moment later they were on the sixth level.

"This ship is designed to close all hatches in the event of a hull breach," Chief Engineer Hanks said, "to keep any hatch with vacuum on one side closed."

"There's got to be a way to get onto the bridge," Bass said. "Or is there an alternate set of controls we can get to?"

Hanks shook his head. "The only other controls on the ship are here." He swept a hand at the console bank in the engineering control room. "These only control the engines and steering. We can change speed and direction, that's it."

"What about navigation?"

"We depend totally on orders from the bridge."

"This ship was built with a single-skin hull and without re-dundant controls?" Chief Magruder asked incredulously.

Hanks slowly nodded. "It was never a popular design."

"Do you know where we're jumping to?"

Hanks shook his head. "That's Navigation. They don't tell Engineering any more than they have to."

Magruder snorted. Navigators in the navy treated Engineering the same way.

"We don't have anyone on the con. What happens when we reach jump point?"

"We go someplace." Hanks shrugged again. "Someplace" could be anywhere—in or out of Human Space.

"We need to establish comm with the *Khe Sanh*," Bass said to Magruder.

"Not from here we don't. Too much interference all across the spectrum."

The two men studied each other for a long moment, then Bass said, "Chief, if two old salts like us can't come up with a solution to this problem, we should retire."

Magruder grinned. "I'm not ready to retire yet, Gunny. So we have to find a solution, don't we?"

They didn't dare alter acceleration or direction. If they didn't maintain thrust, the star's gravity well could suck them straight in—and nobody wanted to guess what increasing thrust might do. Without access to any kind of external sensors to tell them what direction they were moving in, any change in vector might send them into the star. The first thing they had to do was find out where they were.

Even before that, though, Bass had to deal with the situation on the bridge.

"How are things in there?" Bass asked into the comm next to the bridge hatch.

"Total blowout of the hull," Kerr told him. "We're all right, but the prisoners are dead."

"How big is the hole? Can you get through it?"

"Not unless we enlarge it."

"Never mind, it was an outside chance anyway," Bass said.

"We're safe for the time being, Gunny," Kerr said after he looked over his men again, looking for a telltale wisp that would show a suit breach. If they went outside and were fully exposed to the radiation from the star, the broken and bent radiators would be much more serious than the merely cosmetic damage they appeared to have suffered thus far.

"Stand by. We'll come up with some way to get you out of there."

"Aye aye, Gunny."

Twenty minutes later they had two vid-lines running between the engine control room and the cargo hold that the Tweed Hull Breacher was attached to.

"Me? Why me?" Corporal Doyle squawked. "I'm a clerk, not a vid-tech or an engineer!"

"Because you know more about the THB's control panel than anyone else here, that's why," Gunny Bass answered. "Now move it."

"But it's just the hat . . ."

Bass shook his head slowly from side to side.

Doyle sighed and closed his helmet faceplate.

"Besides, your armored vacuum suit gives you better protection than the sailors' suits give them," Bass added.

Doyle wasn't convinced.

Sergeant Bladon leaned close and touched helmets with Doyle. "Think of it this way," he said so only Doyle could hear. "It'll look good at your court-martial."

Doyle looked at him, aghast. He'd forgotten about Top Myer claiming his ass. He'd thought maybe some extra duty; at the very worst, nonjudicial punishment and loss of a stripe. But a court-martial? That would mean serious brig time. He shuddered and went with no more complaint.

Corporal Doyle stood alone in the cargo hold. The end of the vid-line, two multispectrum pickups, and an adhesive tube dangled from his belt, and a drill was in his hand. A second vid-line cable lay on the deck. It seemed to take forever for the atmosphere to get pumped out of the hold, but entirely too soon he stood in vacuum. Awkwardly, he bent over the drill and inserted its bit into the hole a navy engineer had begun. A few zips and the hole was punched all the way through. He fed the vid-line through the hole, then cycled the hatch open and stepped through to the THB. Slowly, dragging the vid-line behind, he crossed the five-meter length of the box to its outer side. He took a moment to screw a multispectrum pickup to the end of the vid-line before drilling another, wider, hole to the outside. Moving quickly, he poked the pickup through the hole and beaded a line of adhesive around the edges of the hole. The adhesive set in seconds. Doyle tugged on the line to set the pickup against the hull, then beaded more adhesive around the line. When it set, he held an air canister next to the adhesive and gave a squirt. Assured that the seal was tight, he returned to the cargo hold and drilled another hole through the hull, just big enough for the vid-line. He fed in the line, returned to the THB, attached the pickup, back to the hold, seated the pickup, applied adhesive, and cycled the hatch closed. They had a backup in the event the THB tore loose.

Corporal Doyle clomped to the dropshaft hatch and used the plug-in on the comm box next to it to report. It seemed to him that it took longer for atmosphere to pump back into the hold than it had for it to be pumped out, though it was actually faster. In a few minutes Doyle was back in the other hold with the sailors.

"Can you slow the spin?" Lieutenant Dhomhia asked Hanks.

"How far down do you want it?" Hanks asked as his fingers played with buttons and balls on his console.

"One rpm will do."

"Give it a couple of minutes to complete spin-down," Hanks replied.

The navigator nodded. He intently watched the displays from the multispectrum pickup, then started interpreting what he read for the pilot. Gravity slowly altered as the centrifugal force lessened. Standing became easier.

Lieutenant Stolievitch silently watched the dials and flickering LEDs, which were the only instruments he had to steer by. It was going to be very tricky. "How long to jump point?"

Hanks glanced at a readout. "Ninety-seven minutes."

Stolievitch glanced at the navigation displays. Even though he couldn't read much of the data they showed, he could tell they weren't yet ready to reduce thrust or alter vector. They were cutting it very close.

Sometime later Dhomhia announced, "I see the *Khe Sanh*." He pointed at a wavery blur on one of the displays.

"Communications?" Bass asked.

"Not a chance."

"Is she gaining?"

"I'm not getting any readings to confirm it, but she has to be gaining—I didn't see her a few minutes ago."

More time passed in uncomfortable silence before Chief Magruder slapped himself on the forehead. "I've been so wrapped up with this problem, I forgot about your men on the bridge. I think I know how we can get them out of there and into someplace safe."

"Safe?" How could anyplace on this ship be safe until they had control of navigation?

"Well, you know what I mean." He turned and conferred with Hanks, then told the ship's engineer, "Let's get it done." To Bass, he said, "Get all your men off the second level. Then grab that Corporal Doyle of yours. Tell him to bring his drill."

On the second level, Hanks opened a panel next to the hatch to a different compartment and disassembled the automatic closing mechanism. Chief Magruder took Corporal Doyle through the disabled hatch, had him drill a hole through the hull and leave the bit in the hole when he was done. "There's no way to evacuate the atmosphere from the passageway," he explained, "but we can drain it this way. He molded plastic explosive around the protruding end of the bit and stuck a primer in it.

"You ever know an engineer, even an electronic engineer, to be without some kind of explosive?" he asked when Bass gave him an odd look. "Now let's get out of here and anchor ourselves to something on the opposite side of the dropshaft."

Magruder reeled out electrical wire as they went. As soon as he saw they had firm holds on the opposite side of the dropshaft, he sent a small jolt of current through the wire. The ripping wind that tore at them lasted mere seconds. In seconds the passageway and the newly holed compartment were in vacuum.

"Let's free those men," Magruder said to Hanks.

The ship's engineer happily opened a panel next to the bridge hatch and jimmied the door open. He figured that every bit of cooperation he showed the Marines and the navy was one more point in his favor when he went to trial. So far nobody had given him any reason to suspect he wouldn't have a trial.

"Welcome back," Bass said to his men when they left the bridge. He shook each man's hand.

Hanks busied himself shutting the two open hatches. "Now we can pump atmosphere back into the passageway," he said when they were closed. He used a comm next to the dropshaft to signal Engineering, and shortly their audios picked up the whistle of atmosphere reentering. When air pressure was back up, they popped open the dropshaft hatch and started down. Hanks was the last man through, and closed the hatch behind him.

"We've been waiting for you," Lieutenant Dhomhia said, grinning. "I'm ready to turn the con over to Mr. Stolievitch."

Hanks glanced at the time. "Fourteen minutes to jump."

"Engineering, cease spin," Lieutenant Stolievitch said in navy formal.

"Cease spin, aye," Hanks said, and did something on his console. He was grinning too. All was well, he thought. Let's do this the navy way.

"Give me three points, high larboard."

"Three points high larboard it is," Hanks replied, already forgetting the navy way.

"Reduce thrust to one-half."

Hanks cut the main engines and hit the forward jets to reduce thrust.

The *Marquis de Rien* shuddered as it slewed onto a new course and dropped its speed.

"Steady as she goes, Mr. Hanks."

"Steady as she goes." Hanks collapsed onto his couch. "Damn, I don't mind telling you, I was pretty scared for a while there." He caught the look Bass gave him and wondered why it looked like pity.

It took six more hours for the *Khe Sanh* to close with the *Marquis de Rien* and match velocities, but the only people the delay meant anything to were Doc Hough and Lance Corporal Van Impe. Van Impe had lost a lot of blood when his eeookk wounds broke open, and the *Marquis* had a very limited dispensary. Doc Gordon got the bleeding stopped quickly, but there was only enough plasma on hand to replace half of the lost blood. He put the still-unconscious Marine in a stasis bag to maintain his condition until he could get to surgery on the *Khe Sanh*.

"You know people are going to blame you if he doesn't recover," Bass said solemnly to Corporal Doyle.

Corporal Doyle swallowed and nodded. It seemed that once he got into trouble, the trouble just kept getting deeper.

CHAPTER
THIRTY

"Oh, my goodness!" Dr. Thelma Hoxey exclaimed. "Is that *Trimerus streptilasma* you have there, young man?" She pointed at Owen, perched happily on Dean's shoulder. The woo changed from contented pink to worried blue-green at the words.

"Excuse me, ma'am?" Dean said. He had left Owen in the care of a crewman on the *Khe Sanh* when the company deployed to Avionia. Upon return to the transport, it had surprised Dean how overjoyed he was at being reunited with Owen. And Owen, judging by the way he had clung to Dean since his return from planetside, obviously was "happy" to see him again too. Captain Conorado had permitted Dean to bring the woo along when he accompanied the officers on a final visit to Avionia Station to clear up some last minute details.

"That's *Trimerus streptilasma*, Marine," Dr. Hoxey repeated. "The *scientific*"—she emphasized the word—"name for what are commonly called 'woos,' for some reason. Very interesting alien life-form. I was just reading about them in a back issue of the *Xenobiological Journal*. Did you know there are three different species of these creatures? I recognize this one by its distinctive appendages."

"I didn't know they had a scientific name for them, ma'am," Dean replied. "Three different kinds? The ones I've seen all look alike to me." He wondered what had upset Owen. Couldn't have been this grandmotherly scientist.

"Oh, yes, yes, yes, they do. Not much is known about the creatures. May I?" She approached Owen and poked her finger at him. He shied away but his color had begun to return. "Hmmm," Hoxey mused. "Where'd you get him?"

Dean explained briefly. "He's as intelligent as any human," he added.

"Is he, now?" Hoxey looked quizzically at Dean. "Hmm," she mused.

"Some think they can actually talk," Dean volunteered, then caught himself. He couldn't tell her about the incident in the Dragon on Society 437. "Just what some people have said," he added quickly. "I haven't actually heard him myself." Dean was suddenly nervous.

They were standing in a companionway, and people were constantly passing them. Dr. Abraham came up suddenly. "Say, isn't that a woo there, Lance Corporal?"

"Yes, Omer, yes indeed," Hoxey answered before Dean could say anything.

"Thelma, we really have to get on to—" Abraham began.

"Hold on, Omer, hold on. This," she gestured at Owen, "is very intriguing. I was reading in the *Xeno Journal* that these things have a very high order of intelligence. Our young Marine thinks they're as intelligent as human beings." Hoxey laughed dismissively. "But they *are* quite intelligent creatures."

"Yes, Thelma, but—"

"Marine, your mascot there—"

"Oh, excuse me, ma'am, but Owen's not a mascot, he's not a pet either. He's a 'companion,' ma'am. He's one of us. He saved my life," Dean said proudly. Dr. Abraham gave Dean another friendly grin. It was clear to Dean that Abraham was nervous himself. He wondered why.

"Whatever. But Marine, you have a very valuable scientific specimen there. Would you, er, well, how much . . . ?"

Dean started. So that was it! "Y-You want to *buy* Owen? I'm sorry, ma'am, but he's not for sale!" From their pre-mission briefings, Dean vaguely realized who Dr. Hoxey was and that she held a protocol grade the equivalent of a general officer. But *sell* Owen?

"Well, not buy him, of course," Hoxey went on quickly,

realizing her mistake, "but maybe I could 'borrow' him for a short time? I'd pay you for the privilege, of course. That's what I meant. I'd pay you to let me study him for a while."

"Thelma!" Abraham protested. His face blanched, and Dean's nervousness turned to mild alarm. "We have our hands full with the Avionians! Besides," he rushed on, "the Marines are ready to leave. The lad doesn't have time to leave his woo with you for study."

"Okay, Marine. I'll tell you what, come with me to the lab for an hour and give me that much time to run a few tests on your, uh, woo there. I've developed a brilliant IQ exam that's designed specifically to measure nonhuman intelligence. We've tested it on the Avionians and had encouraging results. Let me administer it to your woo. Won't take long at all." Hoxey's eyes glowed with enthusiasm.

Dean could see she wanted to get her hands on Owen. He considered. Captain Conorado had dismissed him to go to the crew galley for a cup of coffee while he, General Cazombi, and Agent Nast conferred about last minute arrangements regarding the surviving prisoners. There'd be time for the IQ test. Besides, he was curious about just how smart Owen was. "I can't see any harm in it," he said.

"No!" Dr. Abraham protested. Hoxey looked at him sharply. "What I mean, Lance Corporal," Abraham continued, trying desperately to keep his voice level, "is that Dr. Hoxey and I have serious business to—"

"Oh, no, no, no, my dear Omer! We've time for this! Come along, son. You can watch. This won't take long at all." Dr. Hoxey smiled her warmest and most insincere smile. She could already see the paper she'd write for the *Xenobiological Journal*, "An Examination of the Cerebral Cortex of *Trimerus streptilasma*," by Thelma Hoxey, Ph.D., FTA, DMZ.

"I think this Herbloc is the least culpable of the bunch," General Cazombi was saying as he, Captain Conorado, and Special Agent Nast walked along a companionway toward the scientists' dining area. "Poor old sot, he was more or less forced into this caper by Patch. And this engineer, Gunsel?

Seems he went along not for profit as much as because Patch gave him a chance to build things. Those rifles of his are tiny works of art."

"I agree, sir," Nast replied, "but my great-grandma used to tell us the story of Farmer Brown when we were kids. Know that one? Farmer Brown went out into his fields to shoot some crows, and as he's knocking them down he encounters a song-bird. 'Please don't shoot me, sir!' the songbird says, 'I'm not a crow!' Well, old Farmer Brown levels his shotgun at the song-bird and says, 'You get caught with the crows, you suffer with the crows.' "

Captain Conorado laughed. "You don't give them any quarter, do you, Thom?"

"In a normal criminal proceeding, sure. But this is not normal. It's Darkside for all the survivors. Well, I'll ask the warden to put Herbloc and Gunsel together, on an island away from the hard cases, where they won't be disturbed or imposed on. And that is *all* I can or will do for them."

As they passed the companionway leading to the labs, they could hear shouting.

Captain Conorado stopped in mid-stride. "That sounds like one of my men!" he exclaimed. He pivoted and started toward the laboratory area.

A lab assistant lay curled on the deck, clutching his groin. Dean, back to the bulkhead, his fists up in a fighting stance, glowered at two other lab assistants cautiously advancing on him. Owen crouched defensively behind Dean's neck, his huge eyes peering out over his right shoulder. He had turned the dark blue of distress.

"Back off, bastards," Dean shouted, "or I'll give you what I gave your buddy there!"

"Give him over at once, young man!" Dr. Hoxey shouted. "I order you to give him up!"

"Thelma! For God's sake!" Dr. Abraham interjected.

"To hell with you, lady! Just go fuck yourself!" Dean shouted. When he had seen what was inside the lab through the one-way glass, he realized what Dr. Hoxey wanted Owen for. "One step closer and I'll bust your goddamned—"

"Belay that, Marine!" Captain Conorado said as he stepped between Dean and his adversaries. "Marine, you apologize to Dr. Hoxey," he said evenly.

Dean hesitated, surprised by his commander's sudden arrival.

"Do it now," the captain demanded softly.

"I'm sorry, ma'am," Dean said quickly, and then turning to his commander, said, "But sir, they wanted to take Owen in there—"

"At ease, Lance Corporal." General Cazombi and Special Agent Nast crowded behind Conorado. "Ma'am, I apologize for this Marine's conduct and language. I assure you that—"

"Shut up, you tin soldier!" Hoxey shrieked. "I'm in charge here and I want that—that *thing* on the boy's back!"

Seeing that the threat was now removed, the two lab assistants lifted their colleague to his feet. "Sorry," Dean told them, "but I couldn't let you have him."

"Would you mind just telling me what's going on here?" Conorado asked quietly.

"She wanted to take Owen in there and cut him up!" Dean shouted.

Conorado turned to Dean. "I told you to stand at ease, Marine," he said softly. He turned back to Dr. Hoxey. "Ma'am? The woo belongs to Lance Corporal Dean. Why do you want him?"

"This is a scientific matter, Captain! I want the creature for scientific study. I have the facilities here to do that. This is a golden opportunity to find out more about these things. I demand that you hand it over to me—now."

"Sir, *look* in there." Dean gestured toward the one-way glass window.

Conorado didn't have to look, he knew what was on the other side of that window. He remembered the laboratory was well-equipped and spotless. And he particularly remembered the Avionians crouched on perches inside cages, bedraggled and hopeless, with frayed patches on their heads and arms, looking like they had an alien form of scabies. "They don't look so healthy," Conorado remarked as though he just had looked, turning to Dr. Hoxey.

"We are *experimenting* on them, Captain," Dr. Abraham offered. Hoxey gave her deputy a withering glance.

Conorado raised an eyebrow. "What's the difference between 'studying' and 'experimenting,' Dr. Hoxey? During our in-briefing you said you were 'studying' Avionians you'd abducted from the planet's surface."

"Do you dare to interrogate me, Captain?" Hoxey hissed icily. "We have studied dozens of these creatures. It's our job."

"What happened to the others?" General Cazombi asked. He remembered too well their earlier visit to the labs.

"Most of them died. You know that," Dr. Abraham answered before Hoxey could reply.

"They don't take well to confinement," Hoxey said.

"They don't take well to being operated on, Thelma," Abraham said firmly. "They died because we did not understand their physiology that well, gentlemen."

Everyone was silent for a moment. "I want to go in there," Captain Conorado said at last.

"Impossible!" Hoxey shouted. "That space is restricted to lab personnel only."

"Dr. Abraham?" Conorado nodded toward Hoxey's deputy.

Abraham stepped to the door and punched in the code to open the cipher lock.

"Omer!" Hoxey shouted. "I order you not to open that door!" Realizing he would not obey her, she turned to the three lab assistants. "Stop him!" she ordered. They looked hesitantly at Dean and the three officers and made no move. "You're fired!" Hoxey screamed, but still no one made a move to stop Abraham.

The lab door hissed open.

"My God!" Captain Conorado exclaimed as a wave of foul air wafted out through the open door.

"We were just about to clean the lab out before this fracas got started," one of the technicians said. Captain Conorado turned to him questioningly. The man shrugged. "They have nowhere to shit so they do it in their cages. Planetside, they have special places set aside for that purpose. But up here they shit all the time in there. Near as we can figure, it's a sign of nervous disorder complicated by a form of diarrhea caused by the food we give them. But mainly, like Doctor H says," he nodded at Hoxey, "they don't take too well to being held here in captivity."

"Sir," Captain Conorado said, addressing General Cazombi, "I want to get a closer look in there." The general nodded and followed Conorado inside. The rest of the crowd filed in, but Dean remained outside with Owen.

As soon as the men stepped inside the lab, the three Avionians retreated as far back into their cages as they could. Captain Conorado looked at Dr. Abraham, who shrugged. Dr. Hoxey remained silent, a deep frown on her face. Conorado walked right up to the cages. The Avionians began to squawk loudly and flap their arms weakly, forcing themselves up against the rear bars of their cages to get as far away from the Marine officer as possible.

"They're *afraid* of me," Conorado said half to himself. "Can anyone tell me what they're trying to say?" No one spoke. "I know somebody here can speak their language. Who was it gave us that briefing? Dr. Gurselfanks? He can speak Avionian. I want to know what they're saying."

"They are saying," one of the lab techs answered, " 'No! No! No more!' Captain."

"Why?"

Everyone was silent for a moment. "Because," Dr. Abraham said at last, "they are afraid of the medical experiments."

"Silence, Omer!" Hoxey shouted. "This is *my* business! They have no right to know anything about our researches here on Avionia Station! They are not scientists! They don't understand!"

"Because of the medical experiments," Abraham continued, ignoring Hoxey. "Our protocol calls for us to 'study' the Avionians, not experiment on them. Dr. Hoxey has exceeded her authority here. I have always been against these experiments."

"Now I see what you're up to, Omer!" Hoxey said. "Now I see! You want to head this shift. If I go, you're next in line. Omer, that's—that's so—*mundane* of you, so *plebeian*."

"No, Thelma," Abraham answered tiredly, "I just want to stop you. I am through with these experiments. Our captives died because of them. It is wrong to continue."

General Cazombi turned to Nast. "What have we stepped into up here?"

"Excuse me, sir," Captain Conorado said to General Cazombi, "but I am going to remove these three from their cages and return them to the surface of their world."

A long moment of dead silence descended upon the laboratory. Everyone except Cazombi and Nast stared at Conorado in stark disbelief.

"You—You *can't* do that!" Dr. Hoxey screamed. "You have no authority!"

"Pardon me, ma'am, but I do have all the authority I need to set these people free." Again a long silence descended upon them; it was the first time anyone in the lab referred to the Avionians as "people." Finally Captain Conorado turned to the technician who had translated for him. "What's your name, sir?"

"Franny Krank," the labman answered.

"Well, Franny, I want you to tell them something for me."

Krank shrugged. "Hell, Captain, all I can do is make baby talk with them."

"Franny, I don't want you to recite the Gettysburg Address. Just tell them I am letting them go."

"No!" Hoxey screamed. "Krank, you unlock those cages for this madman and I'll see to it you never work another day in your life! I swear it!" Her face had turned beet red, and the veins in her neck stood out as she shouted. Her hair had come unbound and hung about her face Medusalike as she screamed in frustrated rage.

"Let them out, Franny," Abraham said quietly.

The man said something in a rapid series of cheeps and squeaks and then unlocked the cages. Hesitantly, the three Avionians hopped out and then gathered closely around

Conorado. They smelled heavily of excrement, but what the Marine officer noticed above all else was their shivering. He moved toward the door. The three Avionians' feet made scrabbling noises on the floor as they followed closely behind Conorado.

"You remove them from my care and they'll die!" Hoxey shouted. "You'll be responsible. Their deaths will be on you! General! Stop him!"

General Cazombi shook his head. "I'm only here to supervise planetside operations, Doctor."

"Nast! Nast!" she screamed. "Enforce the law! Stop that man!"

"Ma'am, I'm only here to take charge of the prisoners," Nast demurred.

"I'll lodge a complaint against you for this, Mr. Hotshot Marine!" Hoxey shouted after Conorado, who had begun to walk back down the companionway, the three Avionians eagerly skittering along right behind him. "I'll ruin you! You'll never get another job again! I swear."

Conorado stopped and turned slowly around until he faced Dr. Hoxey, who stood in the laboratory doorway, her fists clenched in fury.

"To hell with you, lady," he said, and then, "Dean, you come with me. And bring the woo."

Dr. Abraham had selected a remote island for the release of the captives. He explained the inhabitants were simple farmers who lived peacefully in several small villages. "Maybe they'll believe the wild stories these three will tell about being abducted by aliens and becoming the subjects of medical experiments," he'd said. "But it doesn't matter. These people never have contact with the outside world."

The Essay landed in a heavily forested area. The three captives were escorted outside. "Krank, tell them they're cut loose," Conorado said.

"You. Go. Now," Krank translated, pointing to the forest. "Nest. Over there." He pointed to the northwest. "Go."

The three hesitated. And then one by one they hopped off into the foliage.

"Well," Conorado said, "that's that, I guess."

Inarticulate with rage, delegating the running of the station to Dr. Abraham, Dr. Hoxey had confined herself to her quarters. She made it clear she was preparing a full report of the incident and would be returning to Old Earth on the next resupply ship, to personally file her complaint with the highest authorities.

"Let's get out of here," Conorado said.

"Wait! One of them's coming back," Krank exclaimed.

The creature emerged slowly from behind the fronds of a huge fernlike growth and stood staring back at the humans. He squeaked something, turned around and disappeared for good.

"What'd he say?" Bass asked Krank.

"I don't know. I couldn't catch it. It sounded like Avionian, but—"

"It sounded something like 'hank foo,' or maybe 'yank foo,' " General Cazombi observed.

"More like 'sank loo,' I think," Nast said.

Charlie Bass shook his head. "I think it was saying 'Thank you.' Skipper, our chow's getting cold."

"Well, gentlemen, thanks for coming along with me on this," Conorado said. He felt he should say something momentous, to mark the occasion—his last official action, if Hoxey had her way about it. Instead he just said, "Okay, let's go."

CHAPTER
THIRTY-ONE

The Nomads

Graakaak, High Chief of the Cheereek, was not happy as he and his warriors returned from the attack on the Aawk-vermin rookery. Angry brown scabbed most of his right side where he'd been thrown by a galumphing eeookk that stepped in a hole. The eeookk's leg was broken and it had to be destroyed, though Graakaak would have killed the beast anyway for throwing him. He'd ridden another eeookk so hard that when he had to stop to wait for his warriors to catch up, it collapsed under him dead.

Some might say the attack on the Aawk-vermin rookery was a success. All the Aawk-vermin were killed—males, fledglings, elders, females—save for some females who were taken by the warriors for their pleasure and for work in their nests. Everything of value that the Aawk-vermin rookery had held was in the possession of the returning war party. Everything else, including the excess valuables the Cheereek couldn't carry, had been destroyed in fire.

But Graakaak wouldn't call the attack a success. The Cheereek had lost eighteen warriors killed and many more wounded.

Eighteen warriors killed! In an attack on the Aawk-vermin! Graakaak, High Chief of the Cheereek, was furious at the Aawk-vermin.

All the casualties had come after the Clumsy Ones' weapons had stopped firing and the Cheereek warriors had to resort to using the weapons as clubs—a use to which they were particularly unsuited—or the short spears they had used before the Clumsy Ones came with their marvelous weapons.

The Clumsy Ones' weapons stopped working because the warriors ran out of shooting stones to feed into them. Why had they run out? Where were the Clumsy Ones? Why were the Clumsy Ones not bringing more of the shiny shooting stones, and more of the weapons?

Graakaak, High Chief of the Cheereek, was furious at the Clumsy Ones.

It was not a good enough explanation that the traitor Cheerpt had killed three of the Clumsy Ones. Graakaak had seen the greed too clearly in their eyes when they traded for the bowel stones. The Clumsy Ones did not have enough of the bowel stones; creatures such as they could never have enough of something for which they lusted so. They wanted bowel stones like a hatchling wanted regurgitation from its parents. They wanted bowel stones almost as much as Graakaak wanted to conquer the world.

Now, because the Clumsy Ones had not come with more weapons and more of the shiny shooting things, the Cheereek had lost eighteen warriors to the Aawk-vermin. The worthless Aawk-vermin!

The rookery was in sight. Reconstruction had gone well after so much of it burned in the fire started by the traitor Cheerpt. Soon, Graakaak would perch in his new High Tree and hold council with his advisers. Appointing a replacement for Cheerpt could wait for a time longer. Before then he had to send Kkaacgh and his scouts to find the Clumsy Ones. The Clumsy Ones had to bring more shooting stones. They must.

With the greatest of caution, Kkaacgh, Captain of Scouts, and seven of his scouts approached the Bower Curtain from two directions; Kkaacgh and three from one side, the other four under command of Lead Scout Cheererere from the other. They met in the place where the Clumsy Ones' High Tree had sat, the place where they first saw the Clumsy Ones' demons. It was an empty place, barren of the Clumsy Ones and their spoor.

To be sure, Kkaacgh found the dents in the ground where the Clumsy Ones' High Tree had squatted, and he found the scorch marks its leaving left behind. But the edges of the dents were crumbling, they were slowly filling in as all holes fill in, and the scorch marks were fading as weeds took root and ate them away. In another season there would be no sign remaining that the Clumsy Ones' High Tree had ever been here.

Kkaacgh sent Cheererere and three scouts a full day's galumph to the west and took the other three a full day's galumph east. They met again back at the Clumsy Ones' place two days later. Neither party had found any sign of Clumsy Ones or their demons, though both had found sign of Aawk-vermin, Koocaah-lice, and others whose identity they did not know.

It was with heavy heart and great trepidation that Kkaacgh and his scouts returned to the rookery.

"It was their demons," Chief Councilor Tschaah said firmly. "The Clumsy Ones' demons did not want them here. The demons took them away."

Graakaak shot into threat posture, his lips nearly touching the neck of the ancient councilor. "How can you say that?" he demanded.

"It is obvious," Tschaah said in a voice perilously close to condescending. "The Clumsy Ones came and went as they chose before their demons came. They have come only once since then. And that time the demons came and killed more than a hundred of our warriors to express their displeasure with us. Their demons do not want the Clumsy Ones to trade with the Cheereek."

Graakaak slowly drew back from full threat posture, but kept his neck extended and his body almost level with the floor of the High Tree. He regarded the ancient councilor with a look that should have had him dribbling uncontrollably from his cloaca, but Tschaah merely looked back, unafraid.

Graakaak turned his gaze to Kkaacgh, and the Captain of Scouts quivered in a most satisfactory manner. The High Chief withdrew completely from threat posture.

Beyond the confines of his High Tent, Graakaak heard the cackling and chittering of new fledglings. He heard the shrilling of females trying to keep their young from getting trampled by warriors unmindful of the fledglings that darted between their legs or into their eeookks' paths. The racket had been growing for days as more and more hatchlings reached age and size to leave their nests and begin exploring the world around them.

Graakaak gave thought to the words of the ancient councilor. Perhaps Tschaah was right about the Clumsy Ones' demons.

The Clumsy Ones might be gone, but there was still a world to conquer. The season's hatchlings were already fledglings big enough to leave the nests. Game animals and peckings were running low in the area of the rookery. The Cheereek could live long on the food taken from conquered enemies, but taken food was a poor substitute for the thrill of the hunt, or the joy of fresh peckings. Whether the Clumsy Ones were gone or not, it was time to seek a new roosting place.

"Scout Captain Kkaacgh, have you found our next roosting place?" Graakaak asked.

Kkaacgh pointed his face at the roof of the High Tree. He didn't want Graakaak to see in his face that he hadn't thought of sending scouts out yet to find a new roosting place. "There is a possible one to the southeast, High Chief," he replied. "But I need to see it with my own eyes to know that it is sufficiently filled with game and peckings before I can recommend it to you." He had seen that place one time when he attempted to trail the Clumsy Ones to their nest. Perhaps no other tribe had found it since then; perhaps it was as good as he remembered.

"Go and see it," Graakaak, High Chief of the Cheereek, commanded. "It is time to move our nests."

Four and a half days later Kkaacgh returned. The roosting place he'd examined was even richer than his earlier brief look had led him to suspect. He reported his findings to Graakaak, and the High Chief was pleased. When Kkaacgh

told him of seeing a herd of wild eeookks, Graakaak crowed
in ecstasy. It was many seasons since the Cheereek last had
wild eeookks to tame. Graakaak issued orders for the move.
The constant din of a Cheereek rookery doubled as warriors,
guards, and scouts exhorted their females to pack, and the females struggled to sort through what they would take and
what they would leave, all the while shrilling at their new
fledglings to keep them from getting trampled in the chaotic
movement of nomads breaking camp. They worked until after
Aaaah settled into his bed for the night, and left the old
rookery as soon as morning meals were pecked and the youn-
gest fledglings were bundled onto waiting pack-eeookks.
Aaaah was past his sky-peak by the time the last of the
Cheereek left the rookery.

"They've started their migration," a tech reported to Dr.
Hoxey.

She snorted. "They're late this year. I expected them to be
on the move days ago."

Dr. Abraham shrugged. "Not necessarily, Thelma," he said.
"They don't have calendars to move by. They stay in one place
until food becomes scarce." He nodded at the display on
which the tech showed the nomads' movement. "That's their
birthing place. They stay there until their newborns are old
enough to make the trek to their next encampment. This is
within the time range that's been established for when they
move from a birthing place to a new camp."

Dr. Hoxey curled a lip.

Abraham didn't mention it to Hoxey, but later that day he
informed General Cazombi of the move.

The next morning Captain Conorado sent first platoon to
examine the abandoned encampment. The Marines blasted
planetside in their normal "high speed on a bad road" manner,
but the Essays took them directly to the abandoned encampment instead of touching down some distance away and off-
loading the Dragons to make their own approach to the
objective. The Marines of first platoon found 682 of the 793

rifles the records on the *Marquis de Rien* said Sam Patch's crew had traded for the gizzard stones.

Without ammunition, the rifles—the weapons the Cheereek had used so proudly—would clearly now only be useful as clubs. And not very good clubs at that. As a result, it was postulated, the weapons were left behind as the useless things they were.

The Marines had no way of knowing it, but 108 of the missing rifles were in the guano pit, thrown there in disgust by departing warriors. Tschaah, thinking of a time in the future when Clumsy Ones might return, hid three away in a place only he knew.

There was one thing the Marines looked for that they didn't find. As hard and as long as they searched, they couldn't find a single spent cartridge. They didn't know that though the weapons might be worthless, the shinies they left behind when they were fired made for the best decorations any Cheereek had ever seen. They didn't leave any shinies behind.

The Philosopher

The soldiers bundled Waakakaa the Philosopher into a sedan pulled by eeookks and drew its curtains. They hauled him in this way, unseen by passersby, to the rear of the Palace of the High Priest. There, in rude manner, they made him dismount. Waakakaa found himself standing in front of a small, unmarked entrance tucked away in a sharply curved alleyway that ran around this portion of the palace wall. The facing buildings had no windows on the wall side, nor were their roofs as high as the wall. The alley was empty save for Waakakaa and the soldiers; no one saw them open the small door and hustle him through it.

Inside, they took him to a chamber crudely hacked from the stone upon which the palace perched. They roughly pushed him into the chamber, where he stumbled over something, fell onto the straw-strewn floor, and painfully banged his head against the back wall. The soldiers clanged the iron-barred door shut behind him and went away, having said not a word to him after their captain told Waakakaa he was under arrest, charged with heresy.

Still dazed by the unexpectedness of his arrest, Waakakaa lay on the thin matting of straw for a few moments before pushing himself to his feet. By the unsteady light from a torch burning in the corridor opposite the barred door of the chamber, Waakakaa took stock of this place. There was almost nothing to take stock of. The chamber was less than the length of a stretched-out person in depth, its width so narrow an adult could not drop into threat posture across it. A person could not even stretch his neck to full height. A perch, the object over which he had stumbled and fallen, stood barely above the floor in the middle of the chamber. In a corner beyond the perch he saw a ceramic pot. The fetid odor that wafted from it made clear what its purpose was.

Waakakaa the Philosopher shuffled around so he faced the door and settled himself on the poor excuse for a perch to wait. The perch was so close to the floor that he had to uncomfortably adjust his position to keep his tail-nub from resting on the floor.

In that hunched-over position, he examined the floor. The straw on it was thin, more a strewing than a matting. He saw small, sudden movements in the straw and lowered his head to better see what made them. Carapaced insects skittered through the straw, as did many-legged slitherers. Here and there, clutched triumphantly in mandibles, he saw indistinguishable bits of something that was neither straw nor a grain of sand.

Waakakaa didn't want to imagine what those somethings might be. Doing his best to ignore the crawling of his skin, he hiked his tail-nub higher above the floor and tucked his robe in close so it did not trail in the straw. Waakakaa had no desire to contribute indistinguishable bits of himself to those triumphant mandibles.

He waited. And while he waited he thought, as Philosophers are wont to do. Except he did not think of matters Philosophers normally thought about; he thought about what his heresy might be.

Never, that he could remember, had he publicly—or privately, for that matter—denied any of the gods. Indeed, he paid them no more heed than anyone else did! Nor had he ever in the slightest way challenged the primacy of the High Priest in matters of Religious Philosophy, which was not his field. He claimed no particular knowledge of it whatsoever and never had occasion to speak on it.

It was true he did not make much public obeisance to any of the gods. Few Philosophers did; as most artisans, merchants, soldiers, and high princes paid little public obeisance to the gods—unless a particular god had granted some great favor. Nor did he make public display of honoring the High Priest or his collegium. He knew of few Philosophers who did.

So what was his heresy?

That small stickle.

It had to be. Someone—he did not think the High Priest read the stickle himself—misinterpreted what he said in the stickle and reported it as heresy! Well, if that was the case, a simple explanation should suffice to clear matters with the High Priest. He had said nothing that contradicted any tenet of Religious Philosophy, he was sure of that.

Waakakaa the Philosopher waited with calm mind—and senses alert for carapaced or multilegged scavengers seeking trophies from his person—for the soldiers to come back.

After a time he got first thirsty, then hungry. After another time the torch that provided his only lumination guttered and went out. A third time passed before flickering light and clacking feet announced the approach of someone.

Waakakaa hopped off the perch and stood in front of the barred door. Momentarily, a minion of some sort—not a soldier, he had neither the garb nor the weapons of a soldier—came along the corridor. The minion bore a torch in one hand and a lamp in the other. He removed the burned-out butt of the torch across from the rough chamber in which Waakakaa was imprisoned and affixed a new one in the niche.

"I hunger, I thirst," Waakakaa told the minion. "When will the High Priest see me?" he asked.

The minion did not reply, or even look at the Philosopher, but went away and left Waakakaa alone again.

Yet more time passed, during which Waakakaa tucked his head below his arm, whispered a prayer to keep the vermin off him, and slept. Finally, soldiers came. He did not know whether they were the same ones who had arrested him, for they wore helmets and he could not see their faces. The soldiers did not speak, but ordered him with imperious gestures to exit his chamber and precede them along the corridor.

"I thirst," Waakakaa croaked, "I hunger."

A soldier, more ornately garbed than the others, assumed threat posture and pointed the way.

Waakakaa the Philosopher, hungry and more thirsty than he'd ever been in his life, shambled along the corridor. The soldiers used rough pokes and prods to guide him from one corridor to another, up a stair here, along another corridor there, each more finished than the one before, until he found himself in a vaulted hall, rich with tapestries and finely polished furniture. Narrow windows glazed with colored glass set high on the walls let in little light. At the end of the hall was a raised platform. The soldiers prodded Waakakaa to its foot and poked him into full height, neck upstretched, face pointed toward the peaked ceiling.

"Waakakaa the Philosopher," a powerful voice cawed from the platform, "you stand accused of heresy. How do you plead?"

Waakakaa started to look at who had spoken, but the soldiers struck him until he resumed proper submission posture.

"I have committed no heresy," he said, his voice cracked and weak in his dry throat.

"Are you not the author of *A Speculation on the Nature of the New Glitterer*?"

"I am the author." He wasn't sure his voice could be heard in the immensity of the hall.

"Do you deny that your 'speculation' is heresy?"

"It is but a postu . . . a postu . . . a pos . . ."

Overcome by thirst and hunger, his brain insufficiently

oxygenated in his head's uplifted position, Waakakaa the Philosopher fell unconscious in a most undignified manner.

The soldiers picked him up and took him away to a physician who treated him with drink and food. Not enough to sate his hunger and thirst, merely enough to revive him. Then the soldiers poked and prodded him back to a submission posture before the platform in the vaulted hall.

"Do you deny that your 'speculation' is heresy?" the voice again demanded.

"It is but a postulation. I am a Philosopher, and I seek to know the nature of the New Glitterer. I put forth a position seeking for others to reply with answers or questions or information that will help me gain the knowledge which I seek."

"Did you ask the Church? Did you take your 'postulation' to a priest?"

Waakakaa looked dumbly at the ceiling. The New Glitterer wasn't a matter of Religious Philosophy, something for priests to teach about. Such an approach to the question had never occurred to him. "No," was all he said.

"The gods put the New Glitterer in the sky."

"They did?"

"Indeed."

"But why?"

"You deny this truth?" the voice boomed.

The voice had the quality of a knell of doom, and Waakakaa quaked.

"I deny no truth. I merely want to know, so I ask why."

"The New Glitterer is an eye. The gods put it in the sky so we will know they watch over us even when Aaaah sleeps."

"How is this known?" And Waakakaa knew the instant he spoke those words he should not have said them.

The soldiers poked and prodded him back along steadily less finished corridors and stairways until they reached the rough-hewn chamber once more and thrust him into it. This time he knew what to expect and did not stumble and fall. He settled uncomfortably on the perch to wait again. The wait this time was longer and more painful than before. Carapaced and multilegged scavengers dined on flaking bits of his skin while he slept. When the soldiers returned for him they had to take him to the physician for revival before he could stand in submission posture.

"What is the New Glitterer?" the unseen voice demanded.

"I seek to know," Waakakaa replied.

The interview ended abruptly and the soldiers poked and prodded him back to his prison. This time they left him alone without food or drink for so long they had to carry him straightaway to the physician when they came back. The physician stripped him naked and used tweezers and sharpened probes to remove insectoid scavengers and their eggs from his flesh before reviving him with small amounts of drink and food. Someone gave Waakakaa a simple robe, the kind worn by the most menial of servants, to drape himself with. At least the simple robe was clean and vermin-free. The soldiers poked and prodded him back to submission in the vaulted hall.

"What is the New Glitterer?" the voice demanded again.

"It is the eye of the gods, telling us they watch over us even when Aaaah sleeps." Waakakaa the Philosopher had no desire to return to the rough-hewn chamber.

"Then why did you publish that stickle?"

"Because I wished to know the nature of the New Glitterer."

"And now you know?"

"And now I know."

"You repent of heresy?"

Waakakaa opened his mouth to deny heresy, but thought better of it and answered simply, "Yes."

"It is the order of this court that you shall immediately return to your home. You will not return to the University of Rhaachtown. When you reach your home you will not leave it again until such time as you die. You will never again publish a stickle on any subject or in any wise.

"Is that clear?"

Imprisoned in his own home for the rest of his life? Never again publish a postulation, a speculation, or any other work? Waakakaa the Philosopher shivered almost in despair. His voice wavered as he answered, "Yes."

"Go now."

The soldiers guided him using pointing arms and hands rather than pokes and prods. They took him to the physician, who gave him food and drink enough to return his strength. Then they took him out of the Palace of the High Priest via a different door from which he first entered. There awaited a cart laden with all his property from his quarters at the University of Rhaachtown, and a quartet of soldiers mounted on eeookks.

Thusly Waakakaa the Philosopher was returned to his home.

The High Priest's court had forbidden him to leave his home, but he was not barred from looking at the night sky. Neither was his eyestretcher taken from him, nor the tools and equipment he used to make new eyestretchers. He could not publish, but he still had writing materials with which to keep notes on what he saw. So he looked and he noted.

Waakakaa the Philosopher puzzled for the rest of his days over what he saw in the night sky during those first several days after his return to his prison-home. He took copious notes during those nights, and elaborated and speculated on them over the many years that followed.

There was the series of points of light that flashed into and out of being during all those first several days. They looked very like the random flashes of light-points that struck the heavens every night, except these always went from northwest to southeast. They came at regular intervals. They shifted slightly to the east with each reappearance. He puzzled over these flashes for a day or two until he divined the pattern of their appearance. Then he was able to predict the place and time of their comings. He could not help but notice that every third night the flashes intersected a spot near the New Glitterer. When he turned his eyestretcher on that place, he sometimes made out a dim form, almost as though a ghost-mirror near the New Glitterer was reflecting a distant light.

Once, while he was trying to bring that cloudy reflection into sharper focus with his eyestretcher, he saw a sharp point of light flash from it. He did not need the eyestretcher to watch that point of light flash across the sky and vanish over the southeastern horizon. Bemused, he watched the rest of the night for a reappearance of that light and was rewarded by seeing, before dawn, a flash streak from the southwest to the ghostly reflection where it vanished. He saw that phenomenon one more time. The night after that the patterned flashes failed to reappear after nearing the ghost-mirror. That same night the ghost-mirror briefly flashed into dazzling brilliance and grew steadily smaller as it drifted from its position near the New Glitterer. Over a period of nights it grew smaller and smaller, until Waakakaa's eyestretcher could no longer distinguish it.

EPILOGUE

"Corporal Doyle reporting as ordered, sir!" Corporal Doyle said as he snapped to attention in front of Captain Conorado's desk and fixed his eyes on a spot on the bulkhead above the company commander's head.

Captain Conorado didn't look up immediately from the paper he was reading. When he did, he picked up a stylus and tapped a slow beat on his desktop with it. The way his gaze bored into Doyle made the tapping sound ominous.

"Corporal Doyle, are you aware of the fact that the army and navy give medals for extraordinary achievement not involving combat?"

Doyle blinked. As much as he didn't want to see Top Myer, the first sergeant was clear in his peripheral vision. He thought he was called before the Skipper for whatever punishment the first sergeant had in mind for him. What did army and navy medals have to do with that? "I've heard that they give out—" He caught himself before he said "merit badges" and changed it to "such medals, sir."

Conorado dipped his head slightly in a nod. The tapping of the stylus stopped while he adjusted his position on his chair, then resumed its slow drumbeat. "Major General Cazombi, as commander of this mission, has the authority to award such medals to personnel assigned to this mission regardless of branch of service. Did you know that?"

"Nossir."

"Then you don't know that General Cazombi intends to give you the Army Special Achievement Commendation?"

"Sir?" Doyle jerked; he'd hardly expected this. He wasn't

going to get court-martialed? He was going to get a medal? Maybe that's why Top Myer was glowering so much more than usual. He resisted the urge to grin.

"You figured out how to fix the Tweed Hull Breacher, and that allowed us to successfully complete our mission. Without what you did, the mission would have been only partly successful. Major General Cazombi thinks that merits a medal."

"Thank you, sir."

"Are you also aware that First Sergeant Myer wants you to be court-martialed for refusing to operate the THB cutter with anyone other than third platoon as the boarding party? The specific charges are violation of Articles Eight and Seventy-two of the Uniform Code of Military Justice: disobedience of a lawful order, and conduct unbecoming a noncommissioned officer. Considering the circumstances under which your actions took place and what was at stake, I don't think it would be possible to convene a court-martial board that wouldn't convict you and hand down the severest possible sentence."

Corporal Doyle tried to swallow, but his mouth was too dry. He imagined the tapping of Captain Conorado's stylus was a drum tattoo, the kind that was played in ancient days when a man was humiliated by being stripped of everything in front of the entire battalion and sent out in disgrace.

"And you realize that the injuries Lance Corporal Van Impe suffered were greater than those a man who wasn't recovering from injuries would have suffered, and that's because you usurped authority?"

"Yessir," Doyle squeaked.

"You understand what you did wrong, don't you, Corporal Doyle? By the way you forced the first sergeant to change our operation plans, not only did you disobey him, but you usurped my authority. That's pretty serious, don't you agree?"

"Yessir," Doyle croaked.

The tapping abruptly stopped and Conorado leaned back in his chair. "That would be rather embarrassing, wouldn't it, Corporal Doyle?"

"Sir?" Doyle rasped. A court-martial would certainly be embarrassing for him. Especially one that resulted in him being reduced in rank to private, forfeiting all pay and allowances and spending several years in the navy prison at New Portsmouth—but he didn't think that was what Captain Conorado meant.

"Here we court-martial and convict a man at the same time that the army gives him a medal. Yes, that would be very embarrassing. Don't you agree?"

"Yessir," Corporal Doyle squeaked through a too-tight throat.

"There is a solution to the problem, though." Conorado straightened in his chair. "I have spoken with both Major General Cazombi and First Sergeant Myer. They concur. You will not be awarded a medal, you will not be court-martialed. You are confined to the troop berthing areas until the *Khe Sanh* returns to Thorsfinni's World. You will only leave the troop berthing area for assigned meals or under the direct orders of the ship's surgeon. Upon arrival at Thorsfinni's World you will report to FIST headquarters until such time as you can be reassigned to another FIST or non-Fleet unit.

"Do you understand?"

Corporal Doyle did his best to swallow, but failed again to work up a trace of saliva. "Yessir," he said in a dispirited voice. Leave Company L under disgrace? He was due for rotation anyway, but to leave like that—the humiliation almost went beyond the embarrassment of being court-martialed and convicted.

"Then get out of my sight before I change my mind and request a court-martial board be convened after all."

"Aye aye, sir," Corporal Doyle forced himself to say. He pivoted about-face, almost tottered, caught himself, and marched out of Captain Conorado's office.

Conorado continued to look at the hatch long after Doyle disappeared from sight. Finally he turned to Top Myer. "It's a damn shame," he said softly. "Doyle could be a pain in the ass at times, but he was a good clerk and a good Marine." Doyle had clearly been in the wrong, but no harm was done except to the first sergeant's pride. Van Impe was almost fully recovered. And the argument could be made that he'd acted out of conscience. Just then Captain Conorado had his own problems arising out of acts of conscience.

Captain Conorado sat in his tiny stateroom on board the *Khe Sanh*, sipping a mug of Kevorian coffee. He propped his feet up on his writing table and contemplated his future. It looked mighty grim. Hoxey was going to file a formal complaint against him with her superiors as soon as she returned to Earth, charging him with unauthorized interference in scientific matters of the utmost importance to the Confederation, blah blah blah. It would certainly result in an official inquiry, and possibly court-martial proceedings against him.

He thought of the bedraggled creatures they'd freed on the planet's surface after taking them out of Hoxey's laboratory. If only he could be sure that it had thanked him.

Someone knocked sharply on the door twice, the ancient signal among military men that a superior wished entry. "Come," Conorado said, putting his feet on the floor.

General Cazombi stepped in, the grimace that passed for a smile twisting up one side of his face. "May I join you for a few moments, Captain?"

"Yessir, but I'm afraid just now I'm not the best of company," Conorado said as he stood up and offered the general the only other chair in the compartment.

Cazombi sniffed at the coffee. "Smells good. What is it?" he asked.

"Kevorian coffee, sir. Care for a cup?"

"Don't mind if I do, thank you very much." The general took a sip. "Jesus!" he exclaimed. "Whew! What the hell did you put in there?"

Conorado smiled. "Bourbon whiskey, sir. I got it off that Herbloc guy."

"That was against the Rules of Engagement, Captain," Cazombi reminded him, taking another sip.

"I know, sir."

Cazombi just nodded. "Damned good stuff." Cazombi smacked his lips. "Isn't it against navy regulations to have alcohol aboard one of their vessels?"

"Yessir."

"Hmmm. Captain, you are becoming quite a scofflaw in your old age, aren't you?"

"I guess so, sir." Conorado sounded resigned. "Sir," he said suddenly, rushing on, "I wanted to thank you for briefing us on Society 437."

"Forget it. Have you seen Hoxey's complaint?" Conorado said he had not. "Well, I have," the general continued. "She accuses you of just about everything." Cazombi's face twitched in a grimace-grin.

"What'll happen, sir?"

Cazombi shrugged and finished his coffee. He held out the mug for a refill. "Oh, formal inquiry, for sure. Then possibly a court-martial. Well, two court-martials. The bitch named me as a corespondent, because I backed you up. We're going down together, Captain." He grimace-grinned again. "Oh, she named Nast too," he added, "but he just supported me on moral grounds. He had no decision-making authority, and besides, he was picked for his job by the Confederation President personally, so nobody like Hoxey'll ever cool his jets. But he'll make a good witness for our side, if it comes to that."

"Will the charges stick, sir?" Conorado asked, handing the general another cup of coffee.

"Well, as we say in the army, 'Not only no, but *hell* no!' You were right to do what you did. You see, Captain, there's more to being a good leader than risking your life under fire. There are other dimensions to leadership. Look at those smugglers, for instance. Some of them were very brave when you breached the hull of the *Marquis*. But you wouldn't let them command a fire team. They are neither leaders nor heroes. You are."

"All I've ever done is my duty, sir."

Cazombi nodded. "Sure." He sipped his coffee. "But you have the other dimension of true heroism, Captain, that which distinguishes a merely brave man from a heroic one, a manager of men from a leader of men. That's moral courage. Plenty of physically brave men lack that quality. When it comes to facing death, they do it without hesitation, but when it comes to risking everything on a matter of principle, they cave in. I think the morally courageous man is the superior man. You've got it both ways, Captain, and any board of inquiry, any court-martial, will see it as clearly as I do. And if they don't, I'll damned well tell them." He finished his coffee, stood up, shook Conorado's hand and left.

Conorado sat silently, thinking about what the general had said. He knew Cazombi was right, about principle being more important than physical bravery, although he'd never think of himself as any kind of hero. He was sure now that he knew what that Avionian had tried to tell him before he disappeared in the foliage: "Thank you." Charlie Bass was right. That simple expression of thanks from another intelligent being was all the justification he needed for what he had done. The future looked a whole lot brighter.

Madam Piggott Thigpen was desperately calling in favors, but nobody was responding.

As soon as it had been announced that Val Carney and Henri Morgan had both been "lost" in a suborbital flight over the Pacific Ocean, she called the Attorney General. She terminated the call as soon as she learned the AG had been relieved, replaced by a hard-nosed lawman who hated the representative from Carhart's World. The day before, when the media had been full of reports that Oncho Tweed, the prominent undersea developer, was killed in a shootout with the Philippine coast guard, Thigpen had suspected that the Ministry of Justice was on to them. The relief of the Attorney General and the "tragic disappearance" of her partners confirmed it. Both men had promised to meet with her that very evening, so she knew the report of their being "lost" on a transoceanic flight was false. The Special Investigations Bureau had snatched the men, she was certain of it.

She returned to her apartment immediately, to await the imminent arrival of the SIB goons. Evidently, that goddamned ridiculous little man, Nast, had broken the case. Well, there'd be plenty of time later on to figure out what had gone wrong.

Once home, she activated her security systems. The SIB would have to breach them in order to get to her, and that wouldn't be easy. She'd make her arrest as hard on them as she could. She sighed and slipped out of her sweat-soaked clothes. She commanded a servo to get her a cold glass of Katzenwasser '36 as she sank into the nearest orthosofa. She wondered what life would be like on Darkside. On the other hand, there was very little she didn't know about Confederation secrets. Maybe she could capitalize on that knowledge. If she went down, others would go with her. Send *her* to *Darkside*? Hah! She'd see about *that*!

The future was brightening slightly. She wondered what had happened to Patch. Dirty bastard had probably gotten away, she mused. He *always* got away.

"Uh!" she exclaimed, dropping her wineglass. It shattered wetly on the plush carpet. The orthosofa had just readjusted itself—to an *uncomfortable* position, squeezing her lower legs—most unusual. "Aiiiikkk!" she screamed shrilly as the pressure abruptly increased, snapping the bones in her legs and feet with a loud series of cracks. The pain was unbearable! She emitted a high-pitched, wailing scream for help. Where were the police when you really needed them? She pounded helplessly at the component squeezing her legs. Gasping in pain and terror, she struggled to pull herself loose from the chair's grip, but then it began to enfold her upper body, squeezing her into a ball. Chin buried deep in the flab of her midsection, she began to smother in her own fat as one by one her vertebrae cracked under the enormous pressure. One last thought flashed through her mind before blessed unconsciousness enveloped her: "Patch!"

Madam Piggott Thigpen's intestines burst with a sickening *plop*. Goo squirted through small gaps in the quickly closing mechanism, and several thin, high-powered streams of red spray reached as high as the ceiling and the farthest walls of the room.

Like a huge fist crushing an overripe tomato, the orthosofa continued squeezing her into a smaller and smaller glob of pulp. Eventually the room turned quiet except for the occasional popping of a bone here and there and the gentle drip of body fluids onto the floor.

In the relative silence following the shrieks and screams of their mistress, the automated mechanisms throughout the apartment whirred and clicked and hummed as they performed their assorted tasks. The servo sat mutely in its recess, patiently waiting for another command. In the early morning, the scrubbers and cleaners would emerge from their niches at the programmed hour and start to work on the mess surrounding the orthosofa, which stood like a huge volcanic island in the center of Lake Madam Piggott Thigpen. But that would not be for hours.

The mechanisms that had once obeyed her every command and kept Madam Thigpen's housekeeping affairs in order could not detect the horrible stench that now pervaded the apartment. The air scrubbers could only be activated by human action. There would be no one in the place to do that for some time yet.

At last the setting sun peeked in through the west windows, suffusing the luxurious apartment with a pleasant orange-red glow. Tiny motes of dust floated gently in the air, and the light reflected brightly, as if off a mirror, from the enormous pool of muck slowly coalescing about the tightly closed sofa.

Gunsel crouched expectantly beside the makeshift array of tubes, retorts, and a pressure cooker he'd devised from cast-off kitchen apparatus. "See, Spence, it's vaporized in here, cools off in these tubes, and the juice drips out here." He pointed to a beaker sitting on the floor of the tiny room that served as his living quarters in the prison complex reserved for nonviolent inmates. He'd explained the distillation process dozens of times before, but he felt he had to say something to break the tension of the moment.

Spencer Herbloc squatted silently nearby, anxiously rubbing his hands together. It had been a year since Special Agent Nast delivered the survivors of the *Marquis de Rien* to Darkside, and he hadn't had a drink since before then. He picked nervously at the scar on his right arm where the monitoring device had been implanted.

The penal colony known informally as Darkside existed to isolate a handful of incorrigibles, not to punish them. Total separation from humanity for the rest of each inmate's life was considered punishment enough—and a very good thing for society. The thousand or so inmates on Darkside were left almost entirely on their own, except they were segregated into different regions on the planet by psychological profile. All were provided with the materials for survival, but each was left to sink or swim on his own. The tiny monitor embedded under the skin of each inmate's left forearm was there strictly for accountability, not to ensure individual safety.

"Ahhhh," Herbloc sighed as the first drop of colorless fluid fell into the beaker.

"Patience, patience," Gunsel advised. "Ninety percent grain alcohol, that's what we should get, Spence."

"You are a genius, boy-o, a pure genius!" Herbloc crowed.

Gradually, slowly, the beaker filled. When it was full, Gunsel replaced it with an empty container. The still bubbled away happily.

"Now, Artie, boy-o, let us repair to the convivial couch," Herbloc cried. They sat at the table. Carefully, Gunsel poured each of them a generous dollop of the precious liquid. Cautiously they sipped the drink.

"Oh, my dear God," Herbloc whispered, his eyes filling with tears. "It is—" He coughed. "—pure nectar!" His voice rose several octaves as he spoke, but he drank again.

"Could use a mixer, don't you think?" Gunsel observed. In the past year some of Herbloc's habits had rubbed off on the engineer, especially a newfound interest in poetry. He held his glass to the light and inspected the fluid. "Well, as old Bobbie put it, 'O Whiskey! Soul o' plays an' pranks! Accept a Bardie's gratefu' thanks!' " He sipped again, smacked his lips and shook himself as the fiery liquid scorched its way down into his stomach. He coughed appreciatively.

Herbloc too addressed his glass. " 'But oil'd by thee / The wheels o' life gae downhill, scrievin / Wi' rattlin glee!' " he recited with alcoholic gravity.

They clinked their glasses in a silent toast and drank again. Life on Darkside had just turned a little bit brighter.